THE INVISIBLE
A Grotesque Romance

◆

THE FOOD OF THE GODS
and How It Came to Earth

The Invisible Man
A Grotesque Romance

◆

The Food of the Gods
and How It Came to Earth

———◆———

H. G. WELLS

with an Introduction and Notes by
LINDA DRYDEN

WORDSWORTH CLASSICS

This volume is dedicated by the publisher to
ANTONY and **ROSEMARY GRAY**,
who typeset and proofread our books
from 1994 to 2017, with affection
and gratitude.

The H. G. Wells titles were the last
project Antony worked on.

Readers who are interested in other titles from
Wordsworth Editions are invited to visit our website at
www.wordsworth-editions.com

First published in 2017 by Wordsworth Editions Limited
8B East Street, Ware, Hertfordshire SG12 9HJ

ISBN 978 1 84022 741 3

Text © Wordsworth Editions Limited, 2017
Introduction © Linda Dryden, 2017

Wordsworth® is a registered trademark of
Wordsworth Editions Limited

Wordsworth Editions
is the company founded in 1987 by
MICHAEL TRAYLER

Typeset in Great Britain by Antony Gray
Printed and bound by Clays Ltd, St Ives plc

Contents

GENERAL INTRODUCTION

Wordsworth Classics are inexpensive editions designed to appeal to the general reader and students. We commissioned teachers and specialists to write wide ranging, jargon-free Introductions intended to assist the understanding of our readers rather than interpret the stories for them. In the same spirit, because the pleasures of reading are inseparable from the surprises, secrets and revelations that all narratives contain, we strongly advise you to enjoy these two novels before turning to the Introduction.

KEITH CARABINE
General Adviser
Rutherford College, University of Kent at Canterbury

BIOGRAPHY OF THE AUTHOR

Herbert George Wells, known as 'Bertie' or 'H. G.', was born on 21 September 1866 in Atlas House, on the High Street of what was then the Kentish market town of Bromley. His father Joseph, a former gardener, kept a shop and played professional cricket; after his father broke his leg when Wells was ten, Wells's mother Sarah returned to domestic service at the country house Uppark, near Midhurst, in Sussex.

Wells's elder brothers had both been apprenticed to drapers, a trade that Sarah Wells considered to be highly respectable. Wells was apprenticed to drapers in Windsor and Southsea but was much keener to continue to be educated, and he persuaded his mother to let him become a pupil-teacher at Midhurst Grammar School. Wells's exam results at Midhurst were so strong that he won a scholarship, aimed at increasing the number of science teachers in Britain, at the Normal School (now Imperial College London), under 'Darwin's bulldog', the biologist T. H. Huxley. Wells drew extensively on his experiences as a student for his 1900 novel *Love and Mr Lewisham*. Ill-fed, poor and increasingly discontent by both the quality of the teaching he received and the social organisation of the world, Wells became more and more interested in politics and in imaginative literature, especially Plato, Blake and Carlyle. He also began writing, providing articles and a time-travel story, 'The Chronic Argonauts', for the college magazine, the *Science Schools Journal*.

Wells failed his final exams and found work as a teacher in Wales. After being fouled in a rugby game, he suffered severe kidney damage, and for much of the 1890s Wells feared he would die prematurely. Returning to London and completing his degree, he worked as a correspondence tutor and in 1893 wrote his first books, *Honours Physiography* and *Textbook of Biology*. His writing branched out into literary journalism and popular scientific writing, and in 1895 alone Wells published four further books: *Select Conversations with an Uncle*, *The Wonderful Visit*, *The Stolen Bacillus and Other Incidents* and his masterpiece *The Time Machine*. This first 'scientific romance' was swiftly followed by *The Island of Doctor Moreau* (1896), *The Invisible Man* (1897) and *The War of the Worlds* (1898). None has ever been out of print since; Wells was swiftly hailed as a man of genius by his contemporaries. Both sociable and irascible, Wells became friends, and fell out, with other writers such as George Gissing, Joseph Conrad, Stephen Crane, George Bernard Shaw, Arnold Bennett, Ford Madox Ford and Henry James, whom Wells would later cruelly lampoon in his 1915 novel *Boon*, the climax of a long disagreement between the two writers about the purpose and nature of the novel.

Wells never wanted to be limited to writing scientific romances, and during this period he also wrote realistic prose fiction set in a recognisable real world, whose disorganisation and unfairness these novels sought to diagnose: *The Wheels of Chance* (1896), *Kipps* (1905), *Tono-Bungay*, *Ann Veronica* (both 1909) and *The History of Mr Polly* (1910). Wells's early-twentieth-century science fiction, such as *The Food of the Gods* (1905) and *In the Days of the Comet* (1906), increasingly showed a vision of the world as Wells would want to order it. His political and utopian writing from *Anticipations of the Reactions of Mechanical and Scientific Progress upon Human Life and Thought* (1901) and *A Modern Utopia* (1905) also demonstrated Wells's commitment to creating a utopian government, a World State that would ensure that mankind would never go to war.

Following the First World War, Wells's passion for this project intensified, and he embarked on an ambitious collaborative project to write the first history of the world, hoping that if future generations were better educated, then rivalries between nations would be unnecessary, and world government would follow. *The Outline of History*

(1919) was Wells's best-selling book in his own lifetime, selling millions of copies internationally, and was followed by the school version *A Short History of the World* (1922) and by equivalents for biology, *The Science of Life* (1930), and social science, *The Work, Wealth and Happiness of Mankind* (1931). At its height, Wells's fame was as much as a thinker and public intellectual as a novelist. He met or corresponded with the greatest figures of the first half of the twentieth century, notably Winston Churchill, Lenin and Stalin, Theodore and Franklin Roosevelt, Albert Einstein and Sigmund Freud. His later novels from *The New Machiavelli* (1911) onward tend to be more overtly engaged with Wells's 'Open Conspiracy' to convert his readership to his own political point of view, often at a cost to these books' literary merit and subsequent afterlife.

Wells had married his cousin Isabel in 1891, but the couple proved incompatible and he left her for his pupil Amy Catherine Robbins, whom he rechristened 'Jane'. In spite of Wells's many infidelities, which Jane seemed prepared to tolerate, the couple were happily married until Jane's death from cancer in 1928; and they had two sons, Gip and Frank. An affair with the writer Amber Reeves produced a daughter, Anna Jane, and Wells's long affair with novelist Rebecca West saw the birth of a further son, Anthony West. Wells also enjoyed liaisons with, amongst others, Dorothy Richardson, Elizabeth von Arnim, Margaret Sanger and, following Jane's death, Odette Keun and Moura Budberg.

Wells's writing was prophetic in both senses of the term: as exhorting humankind to mend its ways, and in foreseeing the future. His writing imagined before they existed the aeroplane, the tank, space travel, the atomic bomb and the internet. In later life, the emphasis of his political writing turned more towards the rights of the individual, and his 1940 book *The Rights of Man: Or, What Are We Fighting For?* is a key text in the history of human rights.

Wells often despaired of his warnings ever being sufficiently heeded, declaring that his epitaph should be: 'I told you so. You *damned* fools.' None the less, the influence of his hundred and fifty books and pamphlets of science fiction, novels, politics, utopia, history, biography and autobiography has been enormous throughout the twentieth century and into the twenty-first.

SIMON J. JAMES
Professor of English Literature at Durham University
and author of *Maps of Utopia: H. G. Wells,
Modernity and the End of Culture*

INTRODUCTION

Physical invisibility in *The Invisible Man* (1897) and extreme gigantism in *The Food of the Gods* (1904) are the extraordinary premises on which Wells predicates these two stories, brought together here in one volume for the first time. They may share a common theme of bizarrely altered bodies, but there is no doubt that *The Invisible Man* is the more successful of these two romances. It begins as an exemplar in knockabout humour that anticipates the Keystone Cops, but its subtitle, *A Grotesque Romance*, signals how, in Chapter 17, Wells shifts the narrative tone from comedy to unsettling, and at times grim, scientific fantasy.[1] This pivot in the story allows for the invisible man's own account of his fantastic experiment and the revelation of his deep psychological dysfunction to dominate the second half of the book without diminishing its power and impact as a tale of the extraordinary bursting into the everyday. The book's violent denouement cuts across the earlier comedy bringing a visceral humanity to the tale, and ensuring that it remains one of Wells's most accomplished early works of science fiction.

Artistically, structurally and thematically, *The Food of the Gods* is a less satisfying read, but, none the less, it is an accomplished, entertaining and thought-provoking tale. It is evident that Wells was trying to reproduce the combination of comic social realism and scientific fantasy of *The Invisible Man* when he set his novel of phenomenal physical growth in the southern English countryside. To a large extent he succeeded; but the middle portion of the story lacks the narrative agility, economy of style and clarity of purpose of his extraordinary tale of invisibility. By the end of *The Food of the Gods* Wells's narrative trajectory is compromised by his increasingly utopian polemic, a tendency that had begun to characterise his writings from about 1901 onwards. Like *The Invisible Man*, the novel turns, about halfway through, from knockabout comedy to the humane and the tragic; but in *The Invisible Man* Wells focused his attention on the moral dimensions to his tale rather than

1   The American Hugo Gernsback coined the term 'science fiction' in the 1920s. Prior to this such tales were called 'scientific fantasies'.

the aspirational future: it is the better novel for it, and for that reason the subsequent discussion is confined largely to this most comic of tragic tales.

The Invisible Man and the Fin-de-Siècle

The *fin-de-siècle* in Britain was characterised by an excitement over the new technologies and scientific possibilities that were emerging at an unprecedented rate. Earlier in the century, developments in daguerreo-types had demonstrated that reality could be captured and frozen in time, retained and viewed repeatedly: a craze for photographic portraits as opposed to the more expensive oil-painted canvases of individuals and families ensued. By the end of the nineteenth century when Wells began his literary career electricity was poised to transform the domestic sphere, the telegraph was connecting people over huge distances, and the telephone would soon provide an even more intimate means of communication. Work and leisure were to become transformed as inventions from the bicycle to the motor car to moving pictures to the phonograph became accessible to more and more of the populace.

However, one development in particular, the X-ray, was causing wonder and speculation over the possibility of other dimensions. The Polish-born author, and sometime friend of Wells, Joseph Conrad, travelled from Kent to Glasgow in 1898 for an X-ray of his hand, and the experience caused him to ponder the scientific possibilities of multiple universes.[2] Conrad may well have been influenced in this direction by his reading of Wells's work because he was particularly taken with *The Invisible Man*.[3] While *The Time Machine* (1895) imagines an extraordinary contraption that sends a man hurtling into the future, *The Invisible Man* imagines a chemical process that makes living tissue transparent. It is part of Wells's genius as a storyteller that he can capitalise on contemporary scientific innovations and create from these developments fantastic tales of moral depth and often of

---

2 Joseph Conrad, *The Collected Letters of Joseph Conrad*, Volume 2: 1898–1902, edited by Frederick R. Karl and Laurence Davies, Cambridge University Press, Cambridge, 1986, pp. 94–5

3 For more discussion of Conrad's admiration for *The Invisible Man*, see Linda Dryden, *Joseph Conrad and H. G. Wells: The Fin-de-Siècle Literary Scene*, Palgrave, Basingstoke, 2015, pp. 20–1. It is likely that Conrad's reading of Wells's tale coupled with his experience of the X-ray caused him to agree to collaborate with Ford Madox Ford on a little-known tale *The Inheritors* (1901).

political and social significance. Such is the case with *The Invisible Man*
and the possibilities presented by late-nineteenth-century scientific
discoveries.

The capacity of the X-ray machine to strip away the flesh of the
body, thus rendering the hidden bones, cartilage and ligaments visible,
must have fired the imagination of this precociously talented young
writer and opened up all sorts of imaginative possibilities for speculative
stories. In the end, he produced a relatively short book, *The Invisible
Man*, which took the possibilities of the new X-ray technology to its
logical extremes: the rendering of the entire human body completely
invisible. Indeed, Wells signals the influence of X-ray technology on
his story when he has Griffin, the invisible man of the title, tell his
fellow ex-student, Kemp, that he is not using Röntgen vibrations.[4]
Wells's extraordinary novel examines the physical consequences of such
a seemingly miraculous experiment and its associated scientific, moral
and psychological consequences with playfully comic irony in the
opening chapters before a shift to the grotesque and tragic.

Wells believed that science had the potential to open up new, exciting
futures. As Simon James points out, he predicted 'to a greater or lesser
degree genetic engineering, the tank, aerial bombardment, the nuclear
bomb, the European Union, environmentalism, the human-rights
movement, and the internet'.[5] With his solid scientific and biological
training under Thomas Huxley, Wells was uniquely positioned as an
author to understand how the future could be moulded by science, and
he was also uniquely positioned to understand the dangers that scientific
discovery could pose, if misused or exploited, and to express those
dangers through his fictional writings. Thus Wells was fascinated by
the possibilities for science and technology to improve the situation
for humanity, but he was also concerned with the moral and ethical
dimensions to the deployment of scientific discovery. These are the
parameters that define the atmosphere of *The Invisible Man*, *The Food of
the Gods*, and many of Wells's other scientific fantasies.

The Invisible Man – 'A Grotesque Romance' indeed

---

4 Wilhelm Roentgën was the pioneer of X-ray technology in the late
   nineteenth century.
5 Simon J. James, *Maps of Utopia: H. G. Wells, Modernity and the End of Culture*,
   Oxford University Press, Oxford, 2012, p. x

For the reader coming to Wells's third work of long fiction for the first time, the title gives it away: *The Invisible Man* concerns a man, Griffin, who creates a chemical formula that renders living tissue transparent. It is indeed, as the subtitle states, '*A Grotesque Romance*', and Wells delivers on that promise by offering up a narrative that is both a comical and a fantastical tale of physical transformation. From the first line of the book, 'The stranger came in early February', we sense that something uncanny is going to transpire, and when we read that this stranger is swathed in bandages we are assured that Wells's narrative will live up to its enigmatic title.

In fact Wells reveals the mystery in the book's title partly in order to maintain the grotesque comic tone of the story. We laugh at the astonishment and bewilderment of the locals in the village of Iping, where the opening action takes place, because they are oblivious to the bizarre truth that those bandages and goggles mask. And Wells grounds the impossible occurrences in the everyday, in the stumbling attempts of the villagers to rationalise the fantastic sights they witness. One man, Fearnside, comes to the conclusion that ' "the 'marn's a piebald" ': ' "Black here and white there – in patches. And he's ashamed of it. He's a kind of half-breed, and the colour's come off patchy instead of mixing. I've heard of such things before. And it's the common way with horses, as anyone can see." ' Fearnside thinks he is seeking a rational explanation for the invisible man's outlandish appearance, but his notion that 'half-breed' humans are piebald like horses is just plain daft. It is at moments like this that Wells brilliantly exploits the Sussex vernacular to simultaneously satirise the Iping villagers and make them the vehicles for his affectionate humour.

The villagers' astonished reactions to such bizarre irruptions into their quiet community thus provide some of the best comic passages, as when Jaffers, the village constable, determines that ' " 'Ed or no 'ed [. . .] I got to 'rest en, and 'rest en I will." ' As the bumbling tramp, Thomas Marvell, puts it, ' "If this don't beat cock-fighting! Most remarkable! – And there I can see a rabbit clean through you, 'arf a mile away!" ' Wells's use of the vernacular coupled with his brilliant characterisation make the first sixteen chapters of *The Invisible Man* a comic tour de force.

Only slowly does the realisation dawn that they are dealing with something remarkable: empty coat sleeves seeming to move of their own volition, drawers opening by themselves, candles spontaneously combusting, bedclothes gathering in a heap and throwing themselves off the end of the bed, a seemingly headless man, money floating in the air, disembodied voices, ambulatory iron rods. Through all of these irrational occurrences, Wells turns the uncanny into the comic as Griffin wreaks havoc in and around the west-Sussex village of Iping and the town of Port Burdock.

Griffin's transparency is also the catalyst for a series of hilarious set pieces, such as the moment when his invisibility is revealed:

> Then he put his open palm over his face and withdrew it. The centre of his face became a black cavity. 'Here,' he said. He stepped forward and handed Mrs Hall something which she, staring at his meta-morphosed face, accepted automatically. Then, when she saw what it was, she screamed loudly, dropped it, and staggered back. The nose – it was the stranger's nose! pink and shining – rolled on to the floor.
>
> [p. 58]

There are two obvious points to make about the early comic scenes: one, that Wells was using the notion of uncanny and bizarre occurrences irrupting into familiar domestic spaces to create a sense of comic unease in his tale; and two, that the floating objects and strange ghostliness of the invisible man mock the late-Victorian fascination with spiritualism and séances. In the chapter titled 'The Furniture That Went Mad', Griffin sends his bedclothes flying and a chair hurtling through the air. Seeing no cause for these phenomena, the landlady, Mrs Hall, concludes that it must be ghosts: ' " 'Tas sperits," said Mrs Hall. "I know 'tas sperits. I've read in papers of en. Tables and chairs leaping and dancing . . . " ' As such, the Victorian fascination with spiritualism offers Wells an ideal opportunity for some splendid slapstick humour and comedic dialogue.

But it is the juxtaposition of the bizarre with the everyday that really affords Wells the opportunity for knockabout comedy. It is a common-place of the gothic that its tension and subsequent horror is in part realised by the sudden appearance of the strange and unaccountable within the calm, ordered domestic space of the home, the village, or even the city street. These gothic phenomena are part of what Sigmund Freud called the 'uncanny' or 'unheimlich', and their effect is to jolt both the characters who witness the event, and the reader, out of their sense of normal reality: we literally 'jump back' in surprise and astonishment.[6] As Wells explains in his entertaining reflection on his literary life, *Experiment in Autobiography* (1934): 'I had realised that the more impossible the story I had to tell, the more ordinary must be the setting.'[7] Wells's humorous narratives of the uncanny bursting in upon the familiar and the satirising

6   See Sigmund Freud, *The Uncanny* (1919), Penguin, London, 2003.

of irrational fads are thus deliberate comic strategies. Wells was a consummate observer of the follies of his fellow human beings and nowhere did he exercise his amusement at, and, some may say, his disdain for, common humanity more effectively than in *The Invisible Man*.

Halfway through the novel, however, the tone shifts from knockabout humour to dark psychodrama: there is a dramatic narrative shift from confused speculation to Griffin's detailed account of how he became invisible. In Chapter 17, Griffin finds someone for whom he has respect as a fellow scientist; in fact, Kemp, an old student friend and now a respectable doctor, is the only person in the novel whom Griffin does not patronise. When he describes to Kemp how his first experiment in invisibility was on his neighbour's cat, we begin to understand the perverted obsession behind this invisible man. He discovered that there were parts of a cat that could not be rendered invisible: ' "The bones and sinews and the fat were the last to go, and the tips of the coloured hairs. And, as I say, the back part of the eye, tough iridescent stuff it is, wouldn't go at all." ' He sedates the cat, but even when asleep and nearly wholly invisible, ' "there remained two little ghosts of her eyes" ', reminders of her corporeality. It is a startlingly callous moment in the story, and Griffin's subsequent cruel abandonment of the helpless creature prepares the ground for his later murderous rampage.

When he finally decides to experiment on himself, Griffin finds the pain excruciating, a 'night of racking anguish, sickness and fainting':

> 'I shall never forget that dawn, and the strange horror of seeing that my hands had become as clouded glass, and watching them grow clearer and thinner as the day went by, until at last I could see the sickly disorder of my room through them, though I closed my transparent eyelids. My limbs became glassy, the bones and arteries faded, vanished, and the little white nerves went last. I gritted my teeth and stayed there to the end. At last only the dead tips of the fingernails remained, pallid and white, and the brown stain of some acid upon my fingers.'   [p. 111]

This is a physical transformation as strange and as horrific as Dr Jekyll's mutation into his horrific doppelganger in Stevenson's *Strange Case of Dr Jekyll and Mr Hyde* (1886). Indeed, Griffin's transformation scene bears a tantalising similarity to Jekyll's explanation of how he painfully morphs into Hyde:

7 H. G. Wells, *An Experiment in Autobiography*, Volume 2, Faber & Faber, London, 2008, p. 516

The most racking pangs succeeded; a grinding in the bones, deadly
nausea, and a horror of the spirit that cannot be exceeded at the hour
of birth or death. Then these agonies began swiftly to subside, and I
came to myself as if out of a great sickness. There was something
strange in my sensations, something indescribably new, and, from its
very novelty, incredibly sweet.[8]

In both texts physical pain and nausea give way to an initial sense of
liberation followed inevitably by the protagonists' grim realisation that
their unnatural state provides not freedom, but mortal danger, per-
secution and frightening possibilities.

Thus it does not take Griffin long to understand that the invisibility
he craved is not the release he had imagined. As James points out:
'Griffin's megalomaniacal plans of world domination are compromised
by his simple needs to eat, sleep and protect himself from the British
climate; the appearance of his blood is a reminder of his body's fissibility'
(James, p. 72). Even food causes problems because it takes time to
become absorbed into the body and thus remains visible while being
digested, causing Griffin to clothe himself to disguise his transparent
state, and also to keep warm. Fleeing through the streets of London,
Griffin becomes a petty thief in order to survive and ends up burning
down his landlord's property before escaping to the countryside in his
disguise, pilfered, aptly, from a theatrical shop in Drury Lane.

Later, having escaped the increasingly curious citizens of Iping, Griffin
becomes more and more desperate as the plot becomes darker and
more bleakly comic. It is characteristic of Wells to begin a tale on a note
of comic social realism, and for it to gradually turn from the comic to a
grotesque romance. Griffin admits to Kemp that he had ' "dreamt of a
thousand advantages" ' to the condition of invisibility. However, once
invisible the practicalities of existence become apparent: ' "The more I
thought it over, Kemp, the more I realised what a helpless absurdity an
Invisible Man was – in a cold and dirty climate and a crowded civilised
city." ' Through snow, rain and all sorts of inclement weather the
necessity for physical protection becomes apparent, and, rather than
being invisible, Griffin is forced to become only too strangely visible
through bandages, goggles and false noses that paradoxically mask his
transparency and yet draw the attention of onlookers by their very
eccentricity.

8 Robert Louis Stevenson, *Strange Case of Dr Jekyll and Mr Hyde*, Longman,
   Green & Co., London, 1886, pp. 111–12.

It is thus one of the ironies of Wells's story that while Griffin sought invisibility and detachment from his fellow human beings, his actual transparent state forces him into a theatrical disguise that makes him all the more fascinating for the very people from whom he sought to isolate himself. Hence, while the unwitting locals are the subject and the vehicles of much of the comedy of the novel, in the end it is Griffin himself who suffers the cruelest of ironies. As his scheme backfires and he becomes a hunted fugitive, it is clear to Griffin that his transparency has turned into a curse. Like Jekyll before him, Griffin had sought anonymity and freedom through an altered physical state. Jekyll prefigures Griffin when he states that he was ' "the first that could thus plod in the public eye with a load of genial respectability, and in a moment [. . .] strip off these lendings and spring headlong into the sea of liberty. But for me, in my impenetrable mantle, the safety was complete. Think of it – I did not even exist!' (*Jekyll and Hyde*, p. 117).

In fact, Wells's story has many of the hallmarks of Victorian tales of the weird and supernatural. As with *Jekyll and Hyde*, the protagonist's version of events is kept back until much of the action of the story has transpired. And, like Stevenson, Wells is dealing with a man who seeks liberation, who experiments upon himself, and then cannot reverse the catastrophic effects of that experimentation. Wells's story even features an apparently motiveless murder, much like the bludgeoning of Sir Danvers Carew in Stevenson's tale. The narrative shifts from a knockabout comedy to a black satire from Chapter 17 onwards, but in Chapter 26, 'The Wicksteed Murder', it becomes darker still as the hapless, innocent Mr Wicksteed is beaten to death with the iron rod that he has seen moving about the countryside, apparently of its own accord. The unnamed narrator speculates that Griffin tried to escape Wicksteed's attention, but became trapped ' "between a drift of stinging nettles and a gravel pit" '. Such is Griffin's ' "extraordinary irascibility" ' that the narrator leaves it up to the reader to speculate as to what ensued.

With the murder of Wicksteed the tale's true horror starts to unfold. His lack of remorse over stealing from his father is heinous enough, but Griffin's callous selfishness is never more apparent than in his response to his father's suicide following the theft: ' "I did not feel a bit sorry for my father. He seemed to me to be the victim of his own foolish sentimentality. The current cant required my attendance at his funeral, but it was really not my affair." ' Griffin is an egomaniac with little respect for his fellow human beings, and this brutal appraisal of his own father confirms that he is an inhuman monster.

Which leaves us with the question of what this book is really trying to do. At one level it is another of Wells's meditations on the need for ethical considerations when dealing with the power of science to change the conditions of life. At another, we are dealing with a text whose protagonist is a misanthrope – his desire for invisibility is an arrogant manifestation of his lack of connection with, and disdain for, his fellow human beings. He imagines ' "all that invisibility might mean to a man – the mystery, the power, the freedom" ', but sees no drawbacks. By becoming invisible Griffin imagines he would severely limit his contact with his fellow human beings, and for such a sociopath this situation is highly desirable; but he fails to take into account the practicalities of maintaining his invisible state.

Having attended his father's funeral, apparently under duress from social expectations, Griffin walks back through the village that was once his home and feels a 'strange sense of detachment' from the 'squalid respectability, the sordid commercialism of the place': his attitude displays a familiar contempt for the bourgeoisie. Even the girl he recognises and is moved to stop and speak to is dismissed: ' "She was a very ordinary person." ' These incidents, and the casual treatment of his own father, reveal Griffin to be a sociopath striving to prove his superiority to his fellow human beings.

His apparent disdain for others and his overarching arrogance make Griffin repellent. He describes his job to Kemp with scorn: ' "And I, a shabby, poverty-struck, hemmed-in demonstrator, teaching fools in a provincial college, might suddenly become – this." ' So, Griffin emulates the typical 'mad scientists' Jekyll and Frankenstein before him, and creates a monstrous incarnation of a human being that cannot be controlled. Like its gothic forebears, *The Invisible Man* offers us a scientific genius whose researches unveil a process that fundamentally transforms human bodies into something strange and uncanny. The result of such experimentation is inevitable: murder and mayhem.

Through his encounter with Kemp, Wells provides Griffin with a major motive for revealing his backstory and describing the experiments: he is thus able to set up the scientific basis of the story. Griffin has shunned his fellow humanity, but in Kemp he thinks he has found 'a confederate' who will help him to achieve his aim of world domination. Essentially, by this point Griffin appears to have gone completely insane, proposing that invisibility is ' "only good in two cases: it's useful in getting away, it's useful in approaching" '. Griffin concludes that invisibility is ' "particularly useful, therefore, in killing" '. He proposes that, ' "It is killing we must do, Kemp," '

'Not wanton killing, but a judicious slaying. The point is, they know there is an Invisible Man – as well as we know there is an Invisible Man. And that Invisible Man, Kemp, must now establish a Reign of Terror. Yes; no doubt it's startling. But I mean it. A Reign of Terror. He must take some town like your Burdock and terrify and dominate it. He must issue his orders. [. . .] And all who disobey his orders he must kill, and kill all who would defend them.'   [p. 132]

This is unnerving stuff, and 'judicious slaying' implies cold, calculated murder: at this point Wells shifts the psychology of Griffin from that of contempt for the lives of ordinary people to that of a callous megalo-maniac. When Colonel Adye, Burdock's Chief of Police, arrives at Kemp's house Griffin is in full flight and Kemp sums up the readers' assumptions about the trajectory of the invisible man's psychology: ' "He is mad," said Kemp; "inhuman. He is pure selfishness. He thinks of nothing but his own advantage, his own safety. I have listened to such a story this morning of brutal self-seeking . . . He has wounded men. He will kill them unless we can prevent him." ' And indeed Griffin goes on to do just that.

The climax of the story sees Griffin cornered in the town of Port Burdock and hunted down by an enraged, uncontrollable mob bent on his capture. Despite his earlier rampage, this is the most disturbing portion of the book, and in some ways it unexpectedly challenges and undermines our initial assessments of Griffin, ushering in a note of human frailty. Having murdered Wicksteed and badly wounded Adye, Griffin runs amuck in Port Burdock pursued by a crowd of navvies and various townsfolk. The denouement is swift and brutal. When he tries to throttle Kemp, Griffin is overwhelmed by a bloodthirsty mob: ' "There was, I am afraid, some savage kicking. Then suddenly a wild scream of 'Mercy! Mercy!' that died down swiftly to a sound like choking." ' The violence of the scene is chillingly understated.

The fact that the navvy is holding a 'bloodstained spade' is a sinister suggestion of the actual violence meted out to Griffin in his final moments. But it is his appearance in death that gives pathos and humanity to Griffin's plight. As the body slowly assumes its corporeality, Griffin is seen for the first time, his 'bruised and broken body [that] of a young man about thirty' lying 'naked and pitiful on the ground'. Most disturbing of all is the discvery that: 'His hair and beard were white – not grey with age, but white with the whiteness of albinism, and his eyes were like garnets.' It is a description of Griffin's appearance that tallies with the account that he gave to Kemp to identify himself:

' "almost an albino, six feet high and broad, with a pink and white face and red eyes" '.

The bleaching effect of the invisibility process is thus thematically linked to Griffin's actual physical appearance, and with this proof of his 'otherness' we can begin to unravel some of the motivation behind Griffin's rampant psychosis: he had always been an albino, strangely lacking in definition, and his rage against his fellow human beings was the rage of an outcast who has been ridiculed and vilified throughout his life. His desire for invisibility relates to his determination to evade the gaze of those fascinated and repelled by his albino condition. The pathos of the death scene is emphasised by an anonymous voice in the crowd: ' "Cover his face!" said a man. "For Gawd's sake, cover that face!" ' In death, naked and broken, Griffin compels a humane response to appalling physical abuse, and Wells ends his remarkable life on a note of humanity and compassion. It is this kind of human dimension to his tales of scientific fantasy that makes Wells's works so compelling. Conrad recognises this when he writes that he is impressed by Wells's ability in *The Invisible Man* to 'contrive to give over humanity into the clutches of the impossible and yet manage to keep it down (or up) to its humanity, to its flesh, blood, sorrow, folly.'[9]

In the Epilogue we find that the Invisible Man's story has been reduced to an anecdote told by Marvell at the Empire Music Hall, and emblematised in the name of his pub: 'The sign of the inn is an empty board save for a hat and boots, and the name is the title of this story.' All of Griffin's plans for 'A Reign of Terror' and world domination, and the unique, extraordinary circumstances of his life, have become the stuff of popular entertainment and bar-room chatter. That the illiterate tramp Marvell should become the custodian of Griffin's notebooks and the narrator of his incredible story is another of the tale's cruel ironies. It is a wry end to a black comedy that touches on some serious issues concerning the ethics of scientific experimentation, the ingenuity of human endurance in the face of adversity, and the corrupting effects of the prospects of absolute power. In the end, humanity and compassion prevail, but not before the human potential for brutality has been graphically laid bare, both through Griffin's monomaniacal rampage and the mindless violence of the mob who murder him.

The Food of the Gods, and How It Came to Earth

Unlike *The Invisible Man*, *The Food of the Gods and How It Came to*

Frederick R. Karl and Laurence Davies (eds), *The Collected Letters of Joseph Conrad*, op. cit., p. 126

Earth (1904) is a little-known Wells story, but it contains many thematic and stylistic parallels with his more famous tale of invisibility. It is a fitting companion piece to this edition of *The Invisible Man* because it uses the same tone of comic irony and social observation within a tale of fantastic physical transformation through the agency of science practised without due ethical consideration. *The Food of the Gods* is a moral fable, designed to prove, as John Batchelor argues, that 'far-sighted scientists – not Faustian over-reachers, but Nietzschean overmen – will sweep away petty, dirty and disorganised mankind, and replace it with a new race of giants.'[10] However, it is philosophically problematic, as we shall see.

The opening chapters of *The Food of the Gods* are the most successful and the most gripping. The main action, as with most of *The Invisible Man*, takes place in the rural southern English towns and countryside that Wells knew well: in this case it is Kent, where he was resident at the time of writing. And he uses this setting to reveal how the misuse of science, coupled with human folly, could effect irreversible damage, not only to humanity, but to the entire natural world. As the narrator says very early in the novel: 'The reef of science that these little "scientists" built and are yet building is so wonderful, so portentous, so full of mysterious half-shapen promises for the mighty future of man! They do not seem to realise the things that they are doing!' This is an early warning that the utopian dreams of the scientists at the heart of the novel, Mr Bensington and Professor Redwood, will end in disaster; or, as Batchelor puts it: 'Great inventions are made by little men and mishandled by the incompetence of the pure intellectual' (Batchelor, p. 66). However, despite the disastrous consequences of the scientists' neglectful practice, Wells uses this cautionary tale to gesture towards a potentially utopian future for humankind.

Wells's focus in the early chapters of *The Food of the Gods* is on the ethical implications of genetic engineering. He explores what happens when scientists tamper with nature: the answer is catastrophe. Wells casts his satirical eye upon scientists whose single-minded pursuit of their vocation blinds them to the ramifications of their actions. This is signalled early on in the novel when Bensington engages the Skinners to run the Experimental Farm on which he and Redwood will trial their growth-enhancing serum on chickens. The Skinners, however,

10 John Batchelor, *H. G. Wells*, Cambridge University Press, Cambridge, 1985, p. 63

are extremely old, uneducated and dirty, unfit custodians for an experimental scientific unit; but this fact is lost on Bensington because 'nothing destroys the powers of general observation quite so much as a life of experimental science'. It is one of many instances in the novel where Wells's irony exposes the shortcomings of scientific inquiry conducted in a vacuum.

The serum created by Bensington and Redwood, Herakleophorbia, is the 'nutrition of a possible Hercules': it is the titular 'Food of the Gods', later to be dubbed 'Boomfood'. Their intention is utopian, their practice slipshod: through the naïve agency of Mrs Skinner, this miracle food escapes the confines of their Experimental Farm and contaminates the countryside, resulting in giant plants, animals, insects and, ultimately, children. Like many of Wells's stories, the tale is grimly prophetic, prefiguring as it does the oil spillages, nuclear meltdowns and man-made disasters of our own time, and the consequent environmental damage. Wells spells out the dangers of unnatural substances leaking into the natural world with portentous vividness when he describes the giant wasps that terrorise the local population. Lieutenant-Colonel Rupert Hick manages to kill one with a shotgun, and the description of the beast is spine-chillingly detailed:

When he came to measure the thing, he found it was twenty-seven and a half inches across its open wings, and its sting was three inches long. The abdomen was blown clean off from its body, but he estimated the length of the creature from head to sting as eighteen inches – which is very nearly correct. Its compound eyes were the size of penny pieces.   [p. 182]

When one realises that the size of a penny in Wells's time was about the size of a current fifty-pence piece, the full scale of the horrific possibilities becomes apparent. It is hardly surprising that the monstrous insects go on to kill two people and tear a puppy to pieces. The wasps, and subsequently the giant rats that run amuck around the farm and the village, coupled with the rampant vegetation, presage nature out of control; but it is the administering of the growth serum to human children that presents the biggest moral and philosophical dilemma of the story.

The Food of the Gods was written in the context of the explosion in quack medicines and nostrums sold by tricksters and charlatans in the early years of the twentieth century, capitalising on the public desire for health cures. It was a cultural development that Wells would later explore fully in *Tono-Bungay* (1909), but it is included here as a warning against the encroaching commercialisation of health products, the most pernicious of which, of course, is the fictional Herakleophorbia. In *The Food of the Gods*, unthinking parents, wanting to make their children stronger, feed this growth-enhancing substance to their babies believing it to be another modern miracle potion such as those for which advertisements light up the London night sky:

TUPPER'S TONIC WINE FOR VIGOUR

and

YANKER'S YELLOW PILLS

And indeed it is a miraculous formula, but one with disastrous consequences, not only for the children themselves, but for the entire planet and its population. The children develop into giants, each reminiscent of Gulliver in Lilliput, and Wells has much fun describing the increasingly bizarre efforts and constructions created to contain these monstrously outsized children.

The poor, uneducated child, Caddles, grandson of the thoughtless Mrs Skinner, grows into a forty-foot adult, but, without the benefit of being able to read and write, is unable to make sense of a world in which he is exploited for his strength, yet given no guidance or human sympathy. Wells clearly enjoys himself describing the antics of the giant children, but his underlying message is grim. As they emerge into adulthood their desire for autonomy and normal human relationships inevitably leads to frustration and conflict. Thus, when the grown-up Caddles, neglected, confused and confined to working in a chalk pit as a virtual slave, strikes out for London, the story turns, like *The Invisible Man*, from a tale of wry comedy to one of the blackest humour. Caddles is illiterate and emotionally deprived: 'It was the whole gigantic social side of this lonely dumb monster crying out for his race, for the things akin to him, for something he might love and something he might serve, for a purpose he might comprehend and a command he could obey.' It is at times like this that Wells reveals a consummate ability to draw upon our human empathy.

Grimly anticipating King Kong, disoriented and rampaging through New York, Caddles's bewilderment turns to fury at the efforts of the London police to return him to his chalk pit, and he strikes out, killing at least one constable and wounding many more. In the end, like Griffin, he is mown down, and his death evokes the same humanity that Conrad so admired in *The Invisible Man*:

He seems to have made three stumbling strides, to have raised and dropped his huge mace, and to have clutched his chest. He was stung and wrenched by pain.

What was this, warm and wet, on his hand?

One man peering from a bedroom window saw his face, saw him staring, with a grimace of weeping dismay, at the blood upon his hand, and then his knees bent under him and ...   [p. 323]

Unlike Griffin, Caddles is a poor, dumb creature, but his giant form excites the same terror and brutality as Griffin's invisibility, and Wells deals with his demise by invoking our compassion.

Back in Kent, the other children, now grown to adulthood, but afforded the education and articulate voices denied to Caddles, create a fortress from which to launch their ambition to 'grow out of these cracks and crannies, out of these shadows and darknesses, into greatness and the light!' The book ends with their leader, Cossar, striking a heroic and defiant pose, 'standing out gigantic with hand upraised against the sky':

For one instant he shone, looking up fearlessly into the starry deeps, mail-clad, young and strong, resolute and still. Then the light had passed, and he was no more than a great black outline against the starry sky – a great black outline that threatened with one mighty gesture the firmament of heaven and all its multitude of stars.

[p. 349]

This is a familiar image for Wells, one that he had used in his political and scientifically visionary works, *Anticipations* (1901) and *The Discovery of the Future* (1902), to suggest that humankind could transcend its physical and earthly boundaries and become super beings. Wells claimed that he wanted to foster a 'world-wide "Open Conspiracy" to rescue human society from the net of tradition in which it is entangled and to reconstruct it along planetary lines'.[11] Many of his fictions and other writings played with this notion of overturning the old order and establishing a radical new one, often through revolutionary thinking or the agency of unexpected events or scientific discoveries.

For all of its optimism about a potential future race of physical and intellectual giants, *The Food of the Gods and How It Came to Earth* is sometimes a problematic novel: Wells never quite seems to have a coherent purpose, and the problem is compounded by the fact that the story lacks a unifying central character. As Batchelor says, we are left

11   H. G. Wells, *An Experiment in Autobiography*, Volume 2, Faber & Faber, London, 2008, p. 643

with the feeling that Wells 'scrambles thus from one narrative centre to another because he is not happy with any of them' (Batchelor, pp. 67–8). In effect, it lacks the narrative control and clear pivotal tonal shift of *The Invisible Man*: a ruthless editor would have been required to knock the book into shape, endowing it with more artistic structure and a unifying argument. None the less, what Wells has achieved here is, as ever, a strikingly imaginative, comic, and philosophically challenging story.

*   *   *

In both *The Invisible Man* and *The Food of the Gods* Wells's imagination is preoccupied with fantastical physical states. In the case of Griffin it is the very insubstantiality of the body that drives the narrative; conversely, in *The Food of the Gods* it is the grossly exaggerated physical presence of giant children, frighteningly oversized wasps and rats, and rampant, invasive nature on which the narrative initially turns, before it rather loses its way. But, what is most striking about reading these two books together is just how fertile and imaginatively agile was the mind of the young H. G. Wells. He had a unique capacity to combine comic realism and grotesque romance with science fiction and turn this generic hybrid into narratives that are startling, visceral, intellectually challenging and enduringly readable and entertaining.

LINDA DRYDEN
Edinburgh Napier University

FURTHER READING

Biographies

Batchelor, John, *H. G. Wells*, Cambridge University Press, Cambridge, 1985

Brome, Vincent, *H. G. Wells: A Biography*, Longmans, Green & Co., London, New York and Toronto, 1951

Foot, Michael, *H. G.: History of Mr Wells*, Black Swan, London, 1996

Sherborne, Michael, *H. G. Wells: Another Kind of Life*, Peter Owen, London, 2010

Smith, David C., *H. G. Wells: Desperately Mortal: A Biography*, Yale University Press, New Haven and London, 1986

West, Anthony, *H. G. Wells: Aspects of a Life*, Hutchinson, London, 1984

H. G. Wells

Wells, H. G., *An Experiment in Autobiography: Discoveries and Conclusions of a Very Ordinary Brain (Since 1866)*, 2 volumes (1934), Faber & Faber, London, 2008

Wells, H. G., *H. G. Wells: Literary Criticism*, edited by Patrick Parrinder and Robert Philmus, Harvester, Sussex, 1980

Critical Works

Beaumont, Matthew, *The Spectre of Utopia: Utopian and Science Fiction at the Fin-de-Siècle*, Peter Lang, Bern, 2012

Bergonzi, Bernard, *The Early H. G. Wells: A Study of the Scientific Romances*, Manchester University Press, Manchester, 1961

Dryden, Linda, *The Modern Gothic and Literary Doubles: Stevenson, Wilde and Wells*, Palgrave, Basingstoke, 2003

Dryden, Linda, *Joseph Conrad and H. G. Wells: The Fin-de-Siècle Literary Scene*, Palgrave, Basingstoke, 2015

Haynes, Roslynn D., *H. G. Wells, Discoverer of the Future: The Influence of Science on His Thought*, New York University Press, New York, 1980

Huntington, John, *The Logic of Fantasy: H. G. Wells and Science Fiction*, Columbia University Press, New York, 1982

James, Simon J., *Maps of Utopia: H. G. Wells, Modernity and the End of Culture*, Oxford University Press, Oxford, 2012

McLean, Steven, *The Early Fiction of H. G. Wells: Fantasies of Science*, Palgrave, Basingstoke, 2009

Parrinder, Patrick, *H. G. Wells: The Critical Heritage*, Routledge & Kegan Paul, London, 1972

Parrinder, Patrick, *Shadows of the Future: H. G. Wells, Science Fiction, and Prophesy*, Syracuse University Press, Syracuse, 1995

Wagar, W. Warren, *H. G. Wells: Traversing Time*, Wesleyan University Press, Middletown, Conn., 2004

The Invisible Man: A Grotesque Romance

The Invisible Man
A Grotesque Romance

———— ◆ ————

H. G. WELLS

The Invisible Man was published in Great Britain in 1897
first in serial form in *Pearson's Weekly* and
later in the same year in hardback
by Arthur Pearson Limited, London
and in the United States by Harper Brothers, New York

Contents

CHAPTER 1

The Strange Man's Arrival

THE STRANGER CAME EARLY in February, one wintry day, through a biting wind and a driving snow, the last snowfall of the year, over the down, walking from Bramblehurst[1] railway station, and carrying a little black portmanteau in his thickly gloved hand. He was wrapped up from head to foot, and the brim of his soft felt hat hid every inch of his face but the shiny tip of his nose; the snow had piled itself against his shoulders and chest, and added a white crest to the burden he carried. He staggered into the Coach and Horses more dead than alive, and flung his portmanteau down. 'A fire,' he cried, 'in the name of human charity! A room and a fire!' He stamped and shook the snow from off himself in the bar, and followed Mrs Hall into her guest parlour to strike his bargain. And with that much introduction, that and a couple of sovereigns flung upon the table, he took up his quarters in the inn.

Mrs Hall lit the fire and left him there while she went to prepare him a meal with her own hands. A guest to stop at Iping[2] in the wintertime was an unheard-of piece of luck, let alone a guest who was no 'haggler', and she was resolved to show herself worthy of her good fortune. As soon as the bacon was well under way, and Millie, her lymphatic maid, had been brisked up a bit by a few deftly chosen expressions of contempt, she carried the cloth, plates and glasses into the parlour and began to lay them with the utmost *éclat*. Although the fire was burning up briskly, she was surprised to see that her visitor still wore his hat and coat, standing with his back to her and staring out of the window at the falling snow in the yard. His gloved hands were clasped behind him, and he seemed to be lost in thought. She noticed that the melting snow that still sprinkled his shoulders dripped upon her carpet. 'Can I take your hat and coat, sir?' she said, 'and give them a good dry in the kitchen?'

'No,' he said without turning.

She was not sure she had heard him, and was about to repeat her question.

He turned his head and looked at her over his shoulder. 'I prefer to keep them on,' he said with emphasis, and she noticed that he wore big blue spectacles with side-lights, and had bushy side-whiskers over his coat-collar that completely hid his cheeks and face.

'Very well, sir,' she said. '*As* you like. In a bit the room will be warmer.'

He made no answer, and had turned his face away from her again, and Mrs Hall, feeling that her conversational advances were ill-timed, laid the rest of the table things in a quick staccato and whisked out of the room. When she returned he was still standing there, like a man of stone, his back hunched, his collar turned up, his dripping hat-brim turned down, hiding his face and ears completely. She put down the eggs and bacon with considerable emphasis, and called rather than said to him, 'Your lunch is served, sir.'

'Thank you,' he said at the same time, and did not stir until she was closing the door. Then he swung round and approached the table with a certain eager quickness.

As she went behind the bar to the kitchen she heard a sound repeated at regular intervals. Chirk, chirk, chirk, it went, the sound of a spoon being rapidly whisked round a basin. 'That girl!' she said. 'There! I clean forgot it. It's her being so long!' And while she herself finished mixing the mustard, she gave Millie a few verbal stabs for her excessive slowness. She had cooked the ham and eggs, laid the table, and done everything, while Millie (help indeed!) had only succeeded in delaying the mustard. And him a new guest and wanting to stay! Then she filled the mustard pot, and, putting it with a certain stateliness upon a gold and black tea-tray, carried it into the parlour.

She rapped and entered promptly. As she did so her visitor moved quickly, so that she got but a glimpse of a white object disappearing behind the table. It would seem he was picking something from the floor. She rapped down the mustard pot on the table, and then she noticed the overcoat and hat had been taken off and put over a chair in front of the fire, and a pair of wet boots threatened rust to her steel fender. She went to these things resolutely. 'I suppose I may have them to dry now,' she said in a voice that brooked no denial.

'Leave the hat,' said her visitor, in a muffled voice, and turning she saw he had raised his head and was sitting and looking at her.

For a moment she stood gaping at him, too surprised to speak.

He held a white cloth – it was a serviette he had brought with him – over the lower part of his face, so that his mouth and jaws were completely hidden, and that was the reason of his muffled voice. But it was not that which startled Mrs Hall. It was the fact that all his forehead above his blue glasses was covered by a white bandage, and that another covered his ears, leaving not a scrap of his face exposed excepting only his pink, peaked nose. It was bright, pink, and shiny just as it had been at first. He wore a dark-brown velvet jacket with a high, black, linen-lined collar turned up about his neck. The thick black hair, escaping as it could below and between the cross bandages, projected in curious tails and horns, giving him the strangest appearance conceivable. This muffled and bandaged head was so unlike what she had anticipated, that for a moment she was rigid.

He did not remove the serviette, but remained holding it, as she saw now, with a brown-gloved hand, and regarding her with his inscrutable blue glasses. 'Leave the hat,' he said, speaking very distinctly through the white cloth.

Her nerves began to recover from the shock they had received. She placed the hat on the chair again by the fire. 'I didn't know, sir,' she began, 'that – ' and she stopped embarrassed.

'Thank you,' he said drily, glancing from her to the door and then at her again.

'I'll have them nicely dried, sir, at once,' she said, and carried his clothes out of the room. She glanced at his white-swathed head and blue goggles again as she was going out of the door; but his napkin was still in front of his face. She shivered a little as she closed the door behind her, and her face was eloquent of her surprise and perplexity. 'I *never*,' she whispered. 'There!' She went quite softly to the kitchen, and was too preoccupied to ask Millie what she was messing about with *now*, when she got there.

The visitor sat and listened to her retreating feet. He glanced enquiringly at the window before he removed his serviette and resumed his meal. He took a mouthful, glanced suspiciously at the window, took another mouthful, then rose and, taking the serviette in his hand, walked across the room and pulled the blind down to the top of the white muslin that obscured the lower panes. This left the room in a twilight. This done, he returned with an easier air to the table and his meal.

'The poor soul's had an accident or an op'ration or somethin',' said Mrs Hall. 'What a turn them bandages did give me, to be sure!'

She put on some more coal, unfolded the clothes-horse, and extended the traveller's coat upon this. 'And they goggles! Why, he looked more like somethin' in a divin' helmet than a human man!' She hung his muffler on a corner of the horse. 'And holdin' that handkerchief over his mouth all the time. Talkin' through it! . . . Perhaps his mouth was hurt too – maybe.' She turned round, as one who suddenly remembers. 'Bless my soul alive!' she said, going off at a tangent; 'ain't you done them taters *yet*, Millie?'

When Mrs Hall went to clear away the stranger's lunch, her idea that his mouth must also have been cut or disfigured, in the accident she supposed him to have suffered, was confirmed, for he was smoking a pipe, and all the time that she was in the room he never loosened the silk muffler he had wrapped round the lower part of his face to put the mouthpiece to his lips. Yet it was not forgetfulness, for she saw he glanced at it as it smouldered out. He sat in the corner with his back to the window-blind and spoke now, having eaten and drunk and being comfortably warmed through, with less aggressive brevity than before. The reflection of the fire lent a kind of red animation to his big spectacles they had lacked hitherto.

'I have some luggage,' he said, 'at Bramblehurst station,' and he asked her how he could have it sent. He bowed his bandaged head quite politely in acknowledgement of her explanation. 'Tomorrow?' he said. 'There is no speedier delivery?' and seemed quite disappointed when she answered, 'No.' Was she quite sure? No man with a trap who would go over?

Mrs Hall, nothing loath, answered his questions and developed a conversation. 'It's a steep road by the down, sir,' she said in answer to the question about a trap; and then, snatching at an opening, said, 'It was there a carriage was upsettled, a year ago and more. A gentleman killed, besides his coachman. Accidents, sir, happen in a moment, don't they?'

But the visitor was not to be drawn so easily. 'They do,' he said through his muffler, eyeing her quietly through his impenetrable glasses.

'But they take long enough to get well, don't they? . . . There was my sister's son, Tom, jest cut his arm with a scythe, tumbled on it in the 'ayfield, and, bless me! he was three months tied up sir. You'd hardly believe it. It's regular given me a dread of a scythe, sir.'

'I can quite understand that,' said the visitor.

'He was afraid, one time, that he'd have to have an op'ration – he was that bad, sir.'

The visitor laughed abruptly, a bark of a laugh that he seemed to bite and kill in his mouth. '*Was* he?' he said.

'He was, sir. And no laughing matter to them as had the doing for him, as I had – my sister being took up with her little ones so much. There was bandages to do, sir, and bandages to undo. So that if I may make so bold as to say it, sir – '

'Will you get me some matches?' said the visitor, quite abruptly. 'My pipe is out.'

Mrs Hall was pulled up suddenly. It was certainly rude of him, after telling him all she had done. She gasped at him for a moment, and then remembered the two sovereigns. She went for the matches.

'Thanks,' he said concisely, as she put them down, and turned his shoulder upon her and stared out of the window again. It was altogether too discouraging. Evidently he was sensitive on the topic of operations and bandages. She did not 'make so bold as to say', however, after all. But his snubbing way had irritated her, and Millie had a hot time of it that afternoon.

The visitor remained in the parlour until four o'clock, without giving the ghost of an excuse for an intrusion. For the most part he was quite still during that time; it would seem he sat in the growing darkness smoking in the firelight – perhaps dozing.

Once or twice a curious listener might have heard him at the coals, and for the space of five minutes he was audible pacing the room. He seemed to be talking to himself. Then the armchair creaked as he sat down again.

CHAPTER 2

Mr Teddy Henfrey's First Impression

At four o'clock, when it was fairly dark and Mrs Hall was screwing up her courage to go in and ask her visitor if he would take some tea, Teddy Henfrey, the clock-jobber, came into the bar. 'My sakes! Mrs Hall,' said he, 'but this is terrible weather for thin boots!' The snow outside was falling faster.

Mrs Hall agreed, and then noticed he had his bag with him. 'Now you're here, Mr Teddy,' said she, 'I'd be glad if you'd give th' old clock in the parlour a bit of a look. 'Tis going, and it strikes well and hearty; but the hour-hand won't do nuthin' but point at six.'

And leading the way, she went across to the parlour door and rapped and entered.

Her visitor, she saw as she opened the door, was seated in the armchair before the fire, dozing it would seem, with his bandaged head drooping on one side. The only light in the room was the red glow from the fire – which lit his eyes like adverse railway signals, but left his downcast face in darkness – and the scanty vestiges of the day that came in through the open door. Everything was ruddy, shadowy and indistinct to her, the more so since she had just been lighting the bar lamp, and her eyes were dazzled. But for a second it seemed to her that the man she looked at had an enormous mouth wide open – a vast and incredible mouth that swallowed the whole of the lower portion of his face. It was the sensation of a moment: the white-bound head, the monstrous goggle eyes and this huge yawn below it. Then he stirred, started up in his chair, put up his hand. She opened the door wide, so that the room was lighter, and she saw him more clearly, with the muffler held up to his face just as she had seen him hold the serviette before. The shadows, she fancied, had tricked her.

'Would you mind, sir, this man a-coming to look at the clock, sir?' she said, recovering from the momentary shock.

'Look at the clock?' he said, staring round in a drowsy manner, and speaking over his hand, and then, getting more fully awake, 'certainly.'

Mrs Hall went away to get a lamp, and he rose and stretched himself. Then came the light, and Mr Teddy Henfrey, entering, was confronted by this bandaged person. He was, he says, 'taken aback'.

'Good-afternoon,' said the stranger, regarding him – as Mr Henfrey says, with a vivid sense of the dark spectacles – 'like a lobster.'

'I hope,' said Mr Henfrey, 'that it's no intrusion.'

'None whatever,' said the stranger. 'Though, I understand,' he said turning to Mrs Hall, 'that this room is really to be mine for my own private use.'

'I thought, sir,' said Mrs Hall, 'you'd prefer the clock – ' She was going to say 'mended'.

'Certainly,' said the stranger, 'certainly – but, as a rule, I like to be alone and undisturbed. But I'm really glad to have the clock seen to,' he said, seeing a certain hesitation in Mr Henfrey's manner. 'Very glad.'

Mr Henfrey had intended to apologise and withdraw, but this anticipation reassured him. The stranger turned round with his back to the fireplace and put his hands behind his back. 'And presently,' he said, 'when the clock-mending is over, I think I should like to have some tea. But not till the clock-mending is over.'

Mrs Hall was about to leave the room – she made no conversational advances this time, because she did not want to be snubbed in front of Mr Henfrey – when her visitor asked her if she had made any arrangements about his boxes at Bramblehurst. She told him she had mentioned the matter to the postman, and that the carrier could bring them over on the morrow. 'You are certain that is the earliest?' he said.

She was certain, with a marked coldness.

'I should explain,' he added, 'what I was really too cold and fatigued to do before, that I am an experimental investigator.'

'Indeed, sir,' said Mrs Hall, much impressed.

'And my baggage contains apparatus and appliances.'

'Very useful things indeed they are, sir,' said Mrs Hall.

'And I'm very naturally anxious to get on with my enquiries.'

'Of course, sir.'

'My reason for coming to Iping,' he proceeded, with a certain deliberation of manner, 'was . . . a desire for solitude. I do not wish to be disturbed in my work. In addition to my work, an accident – '

'I thought as much,' said Mrs Hall to herself.

' – necessitates a certain retirement. My eyes – are sometimes so weak and painful that I have to shut myself up in the dark for hours together. Lock myself up. Sometimes – now and then. Not at present, certainly. At such times the slightest disturbance, the entry of a stranger into the room, is a source of excruciating annoyance to me – it is well these things should be understood.'

'Certainly, sir,' said Mrs Hall. 'And if I might make so bold as to ask – '

'That I think, is all,' said the stranger, with that quietly irresistible air of finality he could assume at will. Mrs Hall reserved her question and sympathy for a better occasion.

After Mrs Hall had left the room, he remained standing in front of the fire, glaring, so Mr Henfrey puts it, at the clock-mending. Mr Henfrey not only took off the hands of the clock, and the face, but extracted the works; and he tried to work in as slow and quiet and unassuming a manner as possible. He worked with the lamp close to him, and the green shade threw a brilliant light upon his hands, and upon the frame and wheels, and left the rest of the room shadowy. When he looked up, coloured patches swam in his eyes. Being con- stitutionally of a curious nature, he had removed the works – a quite unnecessary proceeding – with the idea of delaying his departure and perhaps falling into conversation with the stranger. But the stranger stood there, perfectly silent and still. So still, it got on Henfrey's nerves. He felt alone in the room and looked up, and there, grey and dim, was the bandaged head and huge blue lenses staring fixedly, with a mist of green spots drifting in front of them. It was so uncanny to Henfrey that for a minute they remained staring blankly at one another. Then Henfrey looked down again. Very uncomfortable position! One would like to say something. Should he remark that the weather was very cold for the time of year?

He looked up as if to take aim with that introductory shot. 'The weather – ' he began.

'Why don't you finish and go?' said the rigid figure, evidently in a state of painfully suppressed rage. 'All you've got to do is to fix the hour-hand on its axle. You're simply humbugging – '

'Certainly, sir – one minute more. I overlooked – ' and Mr Henfrey finished and went.

But he went feeling excessively annoyed. 'Damn it!' said Mr Henfrey to himself, trudging down the village through the thawing snow; 'a man must do a clock at times, sure-lie.'

And again, 'Can't a man look at you? – Ugly!'

And yet again, 'Seemingly not. If the police was wanting you, you couldn't be more wropped and bandaged.'

At Gleeson's corner he saw Hall, who had recently married the stranger's hostess at the Coach and Horses, and who now drove the Iping conveyance, when occasional people required it, to Sidderbridge Junction, coming towards him on his return from that place. Hall had evidently been 'stopping a bit' at Sidderbridge, to judge by his driving.

' 'Ow do, Teddy?' he said, passing.

'You got a rum un up home!' said Teddy.

Hall very sociably pulled up. 'What's that?' he asked.

'Rum-looking customer stopping at the Coach and Horses,' said Teddy. 'My sakes!'

And he proceeded to give Hall a vivid description of his grotesque guest. 'Looks a bit like a disguise, don't it? I'd like to see a man's face if I had him stopping in *my* place,' said Henfrey. 'But women are that trustful – where strangers are concerned. He's took your rooms and he ain't even given a name, Hall.'

'You don't say so!' said Hall, who was a man of sluggish apprehension.

'Yes,' said Teddy. 'By the week. Whatever he is, you can't get rid of him under the week. And he's got a lot of luggage coming tomorrow, so he says. Let's hope it won't be stones in boxes, Hall.'

He told Hall how his aunt at Hastings had been swindled by a stranger with empty portmanteaux.[3] Altogether he left Hall vaguely suspicious. 'Get up, old girl,' said Hall. 'I s'pose I must see 'bout this.'

Teddy trudged on his way with his mind considerably relieved.

Instead of 'seeing 'bout it', however, Hall on his return was severely rated by his wife on the length of time he had spent in Sidderbridge, and his mild enquiries were answered snappishly and in a manner not to the point. But the seed of suspicion Teddy had sown germinated in the mind of Mr Hall in spite of these discouragements. 'You wim' don't know everything,' said Mr Hall, resolved to ascertain more about the personality of his guest at the earliest possible opportunity. And after the stranger had gone to bed, which he did about half-past nine, Mr Hall went very aggressively into the parlour and looked very hard at his wife's furniture, just to show that the stranger wasn't master there, and scrutinised closely and a little contemptuously a sheet of mathematical computations the stranger had left. When retiring for the night he instructed Mrs Hall to look very closely at the stranger's luggage when it came next day.

'You mind your own business, Hall,' said Mrs Hall, 'and I'll mind mine.'

She was all the more inclined to snap at Hall because the stranger was undoubtedly an unusually strange sort of stranger, and she was by no means assured about him in her own mind. In the middle of the night she woke up dreaming of huge white heads like turnips, that came trailing after her, at the end of interminable necks, and with vast black eyes. But being a sensible woman, she subdued her terrors and turned over and went to sleep again.

CHAPTER 3

The Thousand and One Bottles

So it was that on the twenty-ninth day of February, at the beginning of the thaw, this singular person fell out of infinity into Iping village. Next day his luggage arrived through the slush – and very remarkable luggage it was. There were a couple of trunks indeed, such as a rational man might need, but in addition there were a box of books – big, fat books, of which some were just in an incomprehensible handwriting – and a dozen or more crates, boxes and cases, containing objects packed in straw, as it seemed to Hall, tugging with a casual curiosity at the straw – glass bottles. The stranger, muffled in hat, coat, gloves and wrapper, came out impatiently to meet Fearenside's cart, while Hall was having a word or so of gossip preparatory to helping bring them in. Out he came, not noticing Fearenside's dog, who was sniffing in a dilettante spirit at Hall's legs. 'Come along with those boxes,' he said. 'I've been waiting long enough.'

And he came down the steps towards the tail of the cart as if to lay hands on the smaller crate. No sooner had Fearenside's dog caught sight of him, however, than it began to bristle and growl savagely, and when he rushed down the steps it gave an undecided hop and then sprang straight at his hand. 'Whup!' cried Hall, jumping back, for he was no hero with dogs, and Fearenside howled, 'Lie down!' and snatched his whip.

They saw the dog's teeth had slipped the hand, heard a kick, saw the dog execute a flanking jump and get home on the stranger's leg, and heard the rip of his trousering. Then the finer end of Fearenside's whip reached his property, and the dog, yelping with dismay, retreated under the wheels of the waggon. It was all the business of a swift half-minute. No one spoke, everyone shouted. The stranger glanced swiftly at his torn glove and at his leg, made as if he would stoop to the latter, then turned and rushed swiftly up the steps into the inn. They heard him go headlong across the passage and up the uncarpeted stairs to his bedroom.

'You brute, you!' said Fearenside, climbing off the waggon with his whip in his hand, while the dog watched him through the wheel. 'Come here,' said Fearenside – 'You'd better.'

Hall had stood gaping. 'He wuz bit,' said Hall. 'I'd better go and see to en,' and he trotted after the stranger. He met Mrs Hall in the passage. 'Carrier's darg,' he said 'bit en.'

He went straight upstairs, and the stranger's door being ajar, he pushed it open and was entering without any ceremony, being of a naturally sympathetic turn of mind.

The blind was down and the room dim. He caught a glimpse of a most singular thing, what seemed a handless arm waving towards him, and a face of three huge indeterminate spots on white, very like the face of a pale pansy. Then he was struck violently in the chest, hurled back, and the door slammed in his face and locked. It was so rapid that it gave him no time to observe. A waving of indecipherable shapes, a blow and a concussion. There he stood on the dark little landing, wondering what it might be that he had seen.

A couple of minutes after, he rejoined the little group that had formed outside the Coach and Horses. There was Fearenside telling about it all over again for the second time; there was Mrs Hall saying his dog didn't have no business to bite her guests; there was Huxter, the general dealer from over the road, interrogative; and Sandy Wadgers from the forge, judicial; besides women and children, all of them saying fatuities: 'Wouldn't let en bite *me*, I knows'; ' 'Tasn't right *have* such dargs'; 'Whad 'e bite 'n for, then?' and so forth.

Mr Hall, staring at them from the steps and listening, found it incredible that he had seen anything so very remarkable happen upstairs. Besides, his vocabulary was altogether too limited to express his impressions.

'He don't want no help, he says,' he said in answer to his wife's enquiry. 'We'd better be a-takin' of his luggage in.'

'He ought to have it cauterised at once,' said Mr Huxter; 'especially if it's at all inflamed.'

'I'd shoot en, that's what I'd do,' said a lady in the group.

Suddenly the dog began growling again.

'Come along,' cried an angry voice in the doorway, and there stood the muffled stranger with his collar turned up, and his hat-brim bent down. 'The sooner you get those things in the better I'll be pleased.' It is stated by an anonymous bystander that his trousers and gloves had been changed.

'Was you hurt, sir?' said Fearenside. 'I'm rare sorry the darg – '

'Not a bit,' said the stranger. 'Never broke the skin. Hurry up with those things.'

He then swore to himself, so Mr Hall asserts.

Directly the first crate was, in accordance with his directions, carried into the parlour, the stranger flung himself upon it with extraordinary eagerness, and began to unpack it, scattering the straw with an utter disregard of Mrs Hall's carpet. And from it he began to produce bottles – little fat bottles containing powders, small and slender bottles containing coloured and white fluids, fluted blue bottles labelled 'Poison', bottles with round bodies and slender necks, large green-glass bottles, large white-glass bottles, bottles with glass stoppers and frosted labels, bottles with fine corks, bottles with bungs, bottles with wooden caps, wine bottles, salad-oil bottles – putting them in rows on the chiffonnier, on the mantel, on the table under the window, round the floor, on the bookshelf – everywhere. The chemist's shop in Bramblehurst could not boast half so many. Quite a sight it was. Crate after crate yielded bottles, until all six were empty and the table high with straw; the only things that came out of these crates besides the bottles were a number of test-tubes and a carefully packed balance.

And directly the crates were unpacked, the stranger went to the window and set to work, not troubling in the least about the litter of straw, the fire which had gone out, the box of books outside, nor for the trunks and other luggage that had gone upstairs.

When Mrs Hall took his dinner in to him, he was already so absorbed in his work, pouring little drops out of the bottles into test-tubes, that he did not hear her until she had swept away the bulk of the straw and put the tray on the table, with some little emphasis perhaps, seeing the state that the floor was in. Then he half turned his head and immediately turned it away again. But she saw he had removed his glasses; they were beside him on the table, and it seemed to her that his eye sockets were extraordinarily hollow. He put on his spectacles again, and then turned and faced her. She was about to complain of the straw on the floor when he anticipated her.

'I wish you wouldn't come in without knocking,' he said in the tone of abnormal exasperation that seemed so characteristic of him.

'I knocked, but seemingly – '

'Perhaps you did. But in my investigations – my really very urgent and necessary investigations – the slightest disturbance, the jar of a door – I must ask you – '

'Certainly, sir. You can turn the lock if you're like that, you know. Any time.'

'A very good idea,' said the stranger.

'This stror, sir, if I might make so bold as to remark – '

'Don't. If the straw makes trouble put it down in the bill.' And he mumbled at her – words suspiciously like curses.

He was so odd, standing there, so aggressive and explosive, bottle in one hand and test-tube in the other, that Mrs Hall was quite alarmed.

But she was a resolute woman. 'In which case, I should like to know, sir, what you consider – '

'A shilling – put down a shilling. Surely a shilling's enough?'

'So be it,' said Mrs Hall, taking up the tablecloth and beginning to spread it over the table. 'If you're satisfied, of course – '

He turned and sat down, with his coat-collar towards her.

All the afternoon he worked with the door locked and, as Mrs Hall testifies, for the most part in silence. But once there was a concussion and a sound of bottles ringing together as though the table had been hit, and the smash of a bottle flung violently down, and then a rapid pacing athwart the room. Fearing 'something was the matter', she went to the door and listened, not caring to knock.

'I can't go on,' he was raving. 'I *can't* go on. Three hundred thousand, four hundred thousand! The huge multitude! Cheated! All my life it may take me! . . . Patience! Patience indeed! . . . Fool and liar!'

There was a noise of hobnails on the bricks in the bar, and Mrs Hall had very reluctantly to leave the rest of his soliloquy. When she returned the room was silent again, save for the faint crepitation[4] of his chair and the occasional clink of a bottle. It was all over; the stranger had resumed work.

When she took in his tea she saw broken glass in the corner of the room under the concave mirror, and a golden stain that had been carelessly wiped. She called attention to it.

'Put it down in the bill,' snapped her visitor. 'For God's sake don't worry me. If there's damage done, put it down in the bill,' and he went on ticking a list in the exercise book before him.

'I'll tell you something,' said Fearenside, mysteriously. It was late in the afternoon, and they were in the little beer-shop of Iping Hanger.

'Well?' said Teddy Henfrey.

'This chap you're speaking of, what my dog bit. Well – he's black. Leastways, his legs are. I seed through the tear of his trousers and the tear of his glove. You'd have expected a sort of pinky to show, wouldn't you? Well – there wasn't none. Just blackness. I tell you, he's as black as my hat.'

'My sakes!' said Henfrey. 'It's a rummy case altogether. Why, his nose is as pink as paint!'

'That's true,' said Fearenside. 'I knows that. And I tell 'ee what I'm thinking. That marn's a piebald, Teddy. Black here and white there – in patches. And he's ashamed of it. He's a kind of half-breed, and the colour's come off patchy instead of mixing. I've heard of such things before. And it's the common way with horses, as anyone can see.'

CHAPTER 4

Mr Cuss Interviews the Stranger

I have told the circumstances of the stranger's arrival in Iping with a certain fullness of detail, in order that the curious impression he created may be understood by the reader. But excepting two odd incidents, the circumstances of his stay until the extraordinary day of the club festival may be passed over very cursorily. There were a number of skirmishes with Mrs Hall on matters of domestic discipline, but in every case until late April, when the first signs of penury began, he over-rode her by the easy expedient of an extra payment. Hall did not like him, and whenever he dared he talked of the advisability of getting rid of him; but he showed his dislike chiefly by concealing it ostentatiously, and avoiding his visitor as much as possible. 'Wait till the summer,' said Mrs Hall sagely, 'when the artisks are beginning to come. Then we'll see. He may be a bit overbearing, but bills settled punctual is bills settled punctual, whatever you'd like to say.'

The stranger did not go to church, and indeed made no difference between Sunday and the irreligious days, even in costume. He worked, as Mrs Hall thought, very fitfully. Some days he would come down early and be continuously busy. On others he would rise late, pace his room, fretting audibly for hours together, smoke, sleep in the armchair by the fire. Communication with the world beyond the village he had none. His temper continued very uncertain; for the most part his manner was that of a man suffering under almost unendurable provocation, and once or twice things were snapped, torn, crushed or broken in spasmodic gusts of violence. He seemed under a chronic irritation of the greatest intensity. His habit of talking to himself in a low voice grew steadily upon him, but though Mrs Hall listened conscientiously she could make neither head nor tail of what she heard.

He rarely went abroad by daylight, but at twilight he would go out muffled up invisibly, whether the weather were cold or not, and he chose the loneliest paths and those most overshadowed by trees and banks. His goggling spectacles and ghastly bandaged face, under the penthouse of his hat, came with a disagreeable suddenness out of the darkness upon one or two home-going labourers, and Teddy Henfrey, tumbling out of the Scarlet Coat one night, at half-past nine, was scared shamefully by the stranger's skull-like head (he was walking hat in hand) lit by the sudden light of the opened inn door. Such children as saw him at nightfall dreamt of bogies, and it seemed doubtful whether he disliked boys more than they disliked him, or the reverse; but there was certainly a vivid enough dislike on either side.

It was inevitable that a person of so remarkable an appearance and bearing should form a frequent topic in such a village as Iping. Opinion was greatly divided about his occupation. Mrs Hall was sensitive on the point. When questioned, she explained very carefully that he was an 'experimental investigator', going gingerly over the syllables as one who dreads pitfalls. When asked what an experimental investigator was, she would say with a touch of superiority that most educated people knew such things as that, and would thus explain that he 'discovered things'. Her visitor had had an accident, she said, which temporarily discoloured his face and hands, and being of a sensitive disposition, he was averse to any public notice of the fact.

Out of her hearing there was a view largely entertained that he was a criminal trying to escape from justice by wrapping himself up so as to conceal himself altogether from the eye of the police. This idea sprang from the brain of Mr Teddy Henfrey. No crime of any magnitude dating from the middle or end of February was known to have occurred. Elaborated in the imagination of Mr Gould, the probationary assistant in the National School,[5] this theory took the form that the stranger was an Anarchist in disguise, preparing explosives, and he resolved to undertake such detective operations as his time permitted. These consisted for the most part in looking very hard at the stranger whenever they met, or in asking people who had never seen the stranger leading questions about him. But he detected nothing.

Another school of opinion followed Mr Fearenside, and either accepted the piebald view or some modification of it; as, for instance, Silas Durgan, who was heard to assert that 'if he chooses to show enself at fairs he'd make his fortune in no time', and being a bit of a theologian, compared the stranger to the man with the one talent. Yet another view explained the entire matter by regarding the stranger as a harmless lunatic. That had the advantage of accounting for everything straight away.

Between these main groups there were waverers and compromisers. Sussex folk have few superstitions, and it was only after the events of early April that the thought of the supernatural was first whispered in the village. Even then it was only credited among the womenfolk.

But whatever they thought of him, people in Iping, on the whole, agreed in disliking him. His irritability, though it might have been comprehensible to an urban brain-worker, was an amazing thing to these quiet Sussex villagers. The frantic gesticulations they surprised now and then, the headlong pace after nightfall that swept him upon them round quiet corners, the inhuman bludgeoning of all tentative advances of curiosity, the taste for twilight that led to the closing of doors, the pulling down of blinds, the extinction of candles and lamps – who could agree with such goings on? They drew aside as he passed down the village, and when he had gone by, young humourists would up with coat-collars and down with hat-brims, and go pacing nervously after him in imitation of his occult bearing. There was a song popular at that time called 'The Bogey Man'. Miss Statchell sang it at the school-room concert (in aid of the church lamps), and thereafter whenever one or two of the villagers were gathered together and the stranger appeared, a bar or so of this tune, more or less sharp or flat, was whistled in the midst of them. Also belated little children would call 'Bogey Man!' after him, and make off tremulously elated.

Cuss, the general practitioner, was devoured by curiosity. The bandages excited his professional interest, the report of the thousand and one bottles aroused his jealous regard. All through April and May he coveted an opportunity of talking to the stranger, and at last, towards Whitsuntide, he could stand it no longer, but hit upon the subscription-list for a village nurse as an excuse. He was surprised to find that Mr Hall did not know his guest's name. 'He give a name,' said Mrs Hall – an assertion which was quite unfounded – 'but I didn't rightly hear it.' She thought it seemed so silly not to know the man's name.

Cuss rapped at the parlour door and entered. There was a fairly audible imprecation from within. 'Pardon my intrusion,' said Cuss, and then the door closed and cut Mrs Hall off from the rest of the conversation.

She could hear the murmur of voices for the next ten minutes, then a cry of surprise, a stirring of feet, a chair flung aside, a bark of laughter, quick steps to the door, and Cuss appeared, his face white, his eyes staring over his shoulder. He left the door open behind him, and without looking at her strode across the hall and went down the steps, and she heard his feet hurrying along the road. He carried his hat in his hand. She stood behind the door, looking at the open door of the parlour. Then she heard the stranger laughing quietly, and then his footsteps came across the room. She could not see his face where she stood. The parlour door slammed, and the place was silent again.

Cuss went straight up the village to Bunting the vicar. 'Am I mad?'

Cuss began abruptly, as he entered the shabby little study. 'Do I look like an insane person?'

'What's happened?' said the vicar, putting the ammonite on the loose sheets of his forthcoming sermon.

'That chap at the inn – '

'Well?'

'Give me something to drink,' said Cuss, and he sat down.

When his nerves had been steadied by a glass of cheap sherry – the only drink the good vicar had available – he told him of the interview he had just had. 'Went in,' he gasped, 'and began to demand a subscription for that Nurse Fund. He'd stuck his hands in his pockets as I came in, and he sat down lumpily in his chair. Sniffed. I told him I'd heard he took an interest in scientific things. He said yes. Sniffed again. Kept on sniffing all the time; evidently recently caught an infernal cold. No wonder, wrapped up like that! I developed the nurse idea, and all the while kept my eyes open. Bottles – chemicals – everywhere. Balance, test-tubes in stands, and a smell of – evening primrose. Would he subscribe? Said he'd consider it. Asked him, point-blank, was he researching. Said he was. A long research? Got quite cross. "A damnable long research," said he, blowing the cork out, so to speak. "Oh," said I. And out came the grievance. The man was just on the boil, and my question boiled him over. He had been given a prescription, most valuable prescription – what for he wouldn't say. Was it medical? "Damn you! What are you fishing after?" I apologised. Dignified sniff and cough. He resumed. He'd read it. Five ingredients. Put it down; turned his head. Draught of air from window lifted the paper. Swish, rustle. He was working in a room with an open fireplace, he said. Saw a flicker, and there was the prescription burning and lifting chimneyward. Rushed towards it just as it whisked up the chimney. So! Just at that point, to illustrate his story, out came his arm.'

'Well?'

'No hand – just an empty sleeve. Lord! I thought, *that's* a deformity! Got a cork arm, I suppose, and has taken it off. Then, I thought, there's something odd in that. What the devil keeps that sleeve up and open, if there's nothing in it? There was nothing in it, I tell you. Nothing down it, right down to the joint. I could see right down it to the elbow, and there was a glimmer of light shining through a tear of the cloth. "Good God!" I said. Then he stopped. Stared at me with those black goggles of his, and then at his sleeve.'

'Well?'

'That's all. He never said a word; just glared, and put his sleeve back in his pocket quickly. "I was saying," said he, "that there was the prescription burning, wasn't I?" Interrogative cough. "How the devil," said I, "can you move an empty sleeve like that?" "Empty sleeve?" "Yes," said I, "an empty sleeve."

' "It's an empty sleeve, is it? You saw it was an empty sleeve?" He stood up right away. I stood up too. He came towards me in three very slow steps, and stood quite close. Sniffed venomously. I didn't flinch, though I'm hanged if that bandaged knob of his, and those blinkers, aren't enough to unnerve anyone, coming quietly up to you.

' "You said it was an empty sleeve?" he said.

' "Certainly," I said.

Then very quietly he pulled his sleeve out of his pocket again, and raised his arm towards me as though he would show it to me again. He did it very, very slowly. I looked at it. Seemed an age. "Well?" said I, clearing my throat, "there's nothing in it."

'Had to say something. I was beginning to feel frightened. I could see right down it. He extended it straight towards me, slowly, slowly – just like that – until the cuff was six inches from my face. Queer thing to see an empty sleeve come at you like that! And then – '

'Well?'

'Something – exactly like a finger and thumb it felt – nipped my nose.'

Bunting began to laugh.

'There wasn't anything *there*!' said Cuss, his voice running up into a shriek at the 'there'. 'It's all very well for you to laugh, but I tell you I was so startled, I hit his cuff hard, and turned around, and cut out of the room. I left him – '

Cuss stopped. There was no mistaking the sincerity of his panic. He turned round in a helpless way and took a second glass of the excellent vicar's very inferior sherry. 'When I hit his cuff,' said Cuss, 'I tell you, it felt exactly like hitting an arm. And there wasn't an arm! There wasn't the ghost of an arm!'

Mr Bunting thought it over. He looked suspiciously at Cuss. 'It's a most remarkable story,' he said. He looked very wise and grave indeed. 'It's really,' said Mr Bunting with judicial emphasis, 'a most remarkable story.'

CHAPTER 5

The Burglary at the Vicarage

The facts of the burglary at the vicarage came to us chiefly through the medium of the vicar and his wife. It occurred in the small hours of Whit Monday, the day devoted in Iping to the Club festivities. Mrs Bunting, it seems, woke up suddenly in the stillness that comes before the dawn, with the strong impression that the door of their bedroom had opened and closed. She did not arouse her husband at first, but sat up in bed listening. She then distinctly heard the pad, pad, pad of bare feet coming out of the adjoining dressing-room and walking along the passage towards the staircase. As soon as she felt assured of this, she aroused the Rev. Mr Bunting as quietly as possible. He did not strike a light, but putting on his spectacles, her dressing-gown and his bath slippers, he went out on the landing to listen. He heard quite distinctly a fumbling going on at his study desk downstairs, and then a violent sneeze.

At that he returned to his bedroom, armed himself with the most obvious weapon, the poker, and descended the staircase as noiselessly as possible. Mrs Bunting came out on the landing.

The hour was about four, and the ultimate darkness of the night was past. There was a faint shimmer of light in the hall, but the study doorway yawned impenetrably black. Everything was still except for the faint creaking of the stairs under Mr Bunting's tread and the slight movements in the study. Then something snapped, the drawer was opened, and there was a rustle of papers. Then came an imprecation, and a match was struck and the study was flooded with yellow light. Mr Bunting was now in the hall, and through the crack of the door he could see the desk and the open drawer and a candle burning on the desk. But the robber he could not see. He stood there in the hall undecided what to do, and Mrs Bunting, her face white and intent, crept slowly downstairs after him. One thing kept up Mr Bunting's courage; the persuasion that this burglar was a resident in the village.

They heard the chink of money, and realised that the robber had found the housekeeping reserve of gold – two pounds ten in half-sovereigns altogether. At that sound Mr Bunting was nerved to abrupt action. Gripping the poker firmly, he rushed into the room, closely followed by Mrs Bunting. 'Surrender!' cried Mr Bunting, fiercely, and then stopped amazed. Apparently the room was perfectly empty.

Yet their conviction that they had, that very moment, heard somebody moving in the room had amounted to a certainty. For half a minute, perhaps, they stood gaping, then Mrs Bunting went across the room and looked behind the screen, while Mr Bunting, by a kindred impulse, peered under the desk. Then Mrs Bunting turned back the window-curtains, and Mr Bunting looked up the chimney and probed it with the poker. Then Mrs Bunting scrutinised the wastepaper basket and Mr Bunting opened the lid of the coal-scuttle. Then they came to a stop and stood with eyes interrogating each other.

'I could have sworn – ' said Mr Bunting.

'The candle!' said Mr Bunting. 'Who lit the candle?'

'The drawer!' said Mrs Bunting. 'And the money's gone!'

She went hastily to the doorway.

'Of all the strange occurrences – '

There was a violent sneeze in the passage. They rushed out, and as they did so the kitchen door slammed. 'Bring the candle,' said Mr Bunting, and led the way. They both heard a sound of bolts being hastily shot back.

As he opened the kitchen door he saw through the scullery that the back door was just opening, and the faint light of early dawn displayed the dark masses of the garden beyond. He is certain that nothing went out of the door. It opened, stood open for a moment, and then closed with a slam. As it did so, the candle Mrs Bunting was carrying from the study flickered and flared. It was a minute or more before they entered the kitchen.

The place was empty. They refastened the back door, examined the kitchen, pantry and scullery thoroughly, and at last went down into the cellar. There was not a soul to be found in the house, search as they would.

Daylight found the vicar and his wife, a quaintly-costumed little couple, still marvelling about on their own ground floor by the unnecessary light of a guttering candle.

CHAPTER 6

The Furniture that Went Mad

Now it happened that in the early hours of Whit Monday, before Millie was hunted out for the day, Mr Hall and Mrs Hall both rose and went noiselessly down into the cellar. Their business there was of a private nature, and had something to do with the specific gravity of their beer. They had hardly entered the cellar when Mrs Hall found she had forgotten to bring down a bottle of sarsaparilla[6] from their joint-room. As she was the expert and principal operator in this affair, Hall very properly went upstairs for it.

On the landing he was surprised to see that the stranger's door was ajar. He went on into his own room and found the bottle as he had been directed.

But returning with the bottle, he noticed that the bolts of the front door had been shot back, that the door was in fact simply on the latch. And with a flash of inspiration he connected this with the stranger's room upstairs and the suggestions of Mr Teddy Henfrey. He distinctly remembered holding the candle while Mrs Hall shot these bolts overnight. At the sight he stopped, gaping, then with the bottle still in his hand went upstairs again. He rapped at the stranger's door. There was no answer. He rapped again; then pushed the door wide open and entered. It was as he expected. The bed, the room also, was empty. And what was stranger, even to his heavy intelligence, on the bedroom chair and along the rail of the bed were scattered the garments, the only garments so far as he knew, and the bandages of their guest. His big slouch hat even was cocked jauntily over the bedpost.

As Hall stood there he heard his wife's voice coming out of the depth of the cellar, with that rapid telescoping of the syllables and interrogative cocking up of the final words to a high note, by which the West Sussex villager is wont to indicate a brisk impatience. 'George! You gart whad a wand?'

At that he turned and hurried down to her. 'Janny,' he said, over the rail of the cellar steps, ' 'tas the truth what Henfrey sez. 'E's not in uz room, 'e en't. And the front door's onbolted.'

At first Mrs Hall did not understand, and as soon as she did she resolved to see the empty room for herself. Hall, still holding the bottle, went first. 'If 'e en't there,' he said, ' 'is close are. And what's 'e doin' 'ithout 'is close, then? 'Tas a most curious business.'

As they came up the cellar steps they both, it was afterwards ascertained, fancied they heard the front door open and shut, but seeing it closed and nothing there, neither said a word to the other about it at the time. Mrs Hall passed her husband in the passage and ran on first upstairs. Someone sneezed on the staircase. Hall, following six steps behind, thought that he heard her sneeze. She, going on first, was under the impression that Hall was sneezing. She flung open the door and stood regarding the room. 'Of all the curious!' she said.

She heard a sniff close behind her head as it seemed, and turning, was surprised to see Hall a dozen feet off on the topmost stair. But in another moment he was beside her. She bent forward and put her hand on the pillow and then under the clothes.

'Cold,' she said. 'He's been up this hour or more.'

As she did so, a most extraordinary thing happened. The bedclothes gathered themselves together, leapt up suddenly into a sort of peak, and then jumped headlong over the bottom rail. It was exactly as if a hand had clutched them in the centre and flung them aside. Immediately after, the stranger's hat hopped off the bedpost, described a whirling flight in the air through the better part of a circle, and then dashed straight at Mrs Hall's face. Then as swiftly came the sponge from the washstand; and then the chair, flinging the stranger's coat and trousers carelessly aside, and laughing drily in a voice singularly like the stranger's, turned itself up with its four legs at Mrs Hall, seemed to take aim at her for a moment, and charged at her. She screamed and turned, and then the chair legs came gently but firmly against her back and impelled her and Hall out of the room. The door slammed violently and was locked. The chair and bed seemed to be executing a dance of triumph for a moment, and then abruptly everything was still.

Mrs Hall was left almost in a fainting condition in Mr Hall's arms on the landing. It was with the greatest difficulty that Mr Hall and Millie, who had been roused by her scream of alarm, succeeded in getting her downstairs, and applying the restoratives customary in such cases.

' 'Tas sperits,' said Mrs Hall. 'I know 'tas sperits. I've read in papers of en. Tables and chairs leaping and dancing . . . '

'Take a drop more, Janny,' said Hall. ' 'Twill steady ye.'

'Lock him out,' said Mrs Hall. 'Don't let him come in again. I half guessed – I might ha' known. With them goggling eyes and bandaged head, and never going to church of a Sunday. And all they bottles – more'n it's right for anyone to have. He's put the sperits into the furniture . . . My good old furniture! 'Twas in that very chair my poor dear mother used to sit when I was a little girl. To think it should rise up against me now!'

'Just a drop more, Janny,' said Hall. 'Your nerves is all upset.'

They sent Millie across the street through the golden five o'clock sunshine to rouse up Mr Sandy Wadgers, the blacksmith. Mr Hall's compliments and the furniture upstairs was behaving most extra-ordinary. Would Mr Wadgers come round? He was a knowing man, was Mr Wadgers, and very resourceful. He took quite a grave view of the case. 'Arm darmed if thet ent witchcraft,' was the view of Mr Sandy Wadgers. 'You warnt horseshoes for such gentry as he.'

He came round greatly concerned. They wanted him to lead the way upstairs to the room, but he didn't seem to be in any hurry. He preferred to talk in the passage. Over the way Huxter's apprentice came out and began taking down the shutters of the tobacco window. He was called over to join the discussion. Mr Huxter naturally followed over in the course of a few minutes. The Anglo-Saxon genius for parliamentary government asserted itself; there was a great deal of talk and no decisive action. 'Let's have the facts first,' insisted Mr Sandy Wadgers. 'Let's be sure we'd be acting perfectly right in bustin' that there door open. A door onbust is always open to bustin', but ye can't onbust a door once you've busted en.'

And suddenly and most wonderfully the door of the room upstairs opened of its own accord, and as they looked up in amazement, they saw descending the stairs the muffled figure of the stranger staring more blackly and blankly than ever with those unreasonably large blue glass eyes of his. He came down stiffly and slowly, staring all the time; he walked across the passage staring, then stopped.

'Look there!' he said, and their eyes followed the direction of his gloved finger and saw a bottle of sarsaparilla hard by the cellar door. Then he entered the parlour, and suddenly, swiftly, viciously, slammed the door in their faces.

Not a word was spoken until the last echoes of the slam had died away. They stared at one another. 'Well, if that don't lick everything!' said Mr Wadgers, and left the alternative unsaid.

'I'd go in and ask'n 'bout it,' said Wadgers, to Mr Hall. 'I'd d'mand an explanation.'

It took some time to bring the landlady's husband up to that pitch. At last he rapped, opened the door, and got as far as, 'Excuse me – '

'Go to the devil!' said the stranger in a tremendous voice, and, 'Shut that door after you.' So that brief interview terminated.

CHAPTER 7

The Unveiling of the Stranger

The stranger went into the little parlour of the Coach and Horses about half-past five in the morning, and there he remained until near midday, the blinds down, the door shut, and none, after Hall's repulse, venturing near him.

All that time he must have fasted. Thrice he rang his bell, the third time furiously and continuously, but no one answered him. 'Him and his "go to the devil" indeed!' said Mrs Hall. Presently came an imperfect rumour of the burglary at the vicarage, and two and two were put together. Hall, assisted by Wadgers, went off to find Mr Shuckleforth, the magistrate, and take his advice. No one ventured upstairs. How the stranger occupied himself is unknown. Now and then he would stride violently up and down, and twice came an outburst of curses, a tearing of paper and a violent smashing of bottles.

The little group of scared but curious people increased. Mrs Huxter came over; some gay young fellows resplendent in black ready-made jackets and *piqué* paper ties – for it was Whit Monday – joined the group with confused interrogations. Young Archie Harker distinguished himself by going up the yard and trying to peep under the window-blinds. He could see nothing, but gave reason for supposing that he did, and others of the Iping youth presently joined him.

It was the finest of all possible Whit Mondays, and down the village street stood a row of nearly a dozen booths, a shooting gallery, and on the grass by the forge were three yellow and chocolate waggons and some picturesque strangers of both sexes putting up a coconut shy. The gentlemen wore blue jerseys, the ladies white aprons and quite fashionable hats with heavy plumes. Wodger, of the Purple Fawn, and Mr Jaggers, the cobbler, who also sold second-hand ordinary bicycles, were stretching a string of union-jacks and royal ensigns (which had originally celebrated the first Victorian jubilee) across the road.

And inside, in the artificial darkness of the parlour, into which only one thin jet of sunlight penetrated, the stranger, hungry, we must suppose, and fearful, hidden in his uncomfortable hot wrappings, pored through his dark glasses upon his paper or chinked his dirty little bottles, and occasionally swore savagely at the boys, audible if invisible, outside the windows. In the corner by the fireplace lay the fragments of half a dozen smashed bottles, and a pungent twang of chlorine tainted the air. So much we know from what was heard at the time and from what was subsequently seen in the room.

About noon he suddenly opened his parlour door and stood glaring fixedly at the three or four people in the bar. 'Mrs Hall,' he said. Somebody went sheepishly and called for Mrs Hall.

Mrs Hall appeared after an interval, a little short of breath, but all the fiercer for that. Hall was still out. She had deliberated over this scene, and she came holding a little tray with an unsettled bill upon it. 'Is it your bill you're wanting, sir?' she said.

'Why wasn't my breakfast laid? Why haven't you prepared my meals and answered my bell? Do you think I live without eating?'

'Why isn't my bill paid?' said Mrs Hall. 'That's what I want to know.'

'I told you three days ago I was awaiting a remittance – '

'I told you two days ago I wasn't going to await no remittances. You can't grumble if your breakfast waits a bit, if my bill's been waiting these five days, can you?'

The stranger swore briefly but vividly.

'Nar, nar!' from the bar.

'And I'd thank you kindly, sir, if you'd keep your swearing to yourself, sir,' said Mrs Hall.

The stranger stood looking more like an angry diving-helmet than ever. It was universally felt in the bar that Mrs Hall had the better of him. His next words showed as much.

'Look here, my good woman – ' he began.

'Don't "good woman" *me*,' said Mrs Hall.

'I've told you my remittance hasn't come.'

'Remittance indeed!' said Mrs Hall.

'Still, I dare say in my pocket – '

'You told me three days ago that you hadn't anything but a sovereign's worth of silver upon you.'

'Well, I've found some more – '

' 'Ul–*lo*!' from the bar.

'I wonder where you found it,' said Mrs Hall.

That seemed to annoy the stranger very much. He stamped his foot. 'What do you mean?' he said.

'That I wonder where you found it,' said Mrs Hall. 'And before I take any bills or get any breakfasts, or do any such things whatsoever, you got to tell me one or two things I don't understand, and what nobody don't understand, and what everybody is very anxious to understand. I want to know what you been doing t'my chair upstairs, and I want to know how 'tis your room was empty, and how you got in again. Them as stops in this house comes in by the doors – that's the rule of the house, and that you *didn't* do, and what I want to know is how you *did* come in. And I want to know – '

Suddenly the stranger raised his gloved hands clenched, stamped his foot, and said, 'Stop!' with such extraordinary violence that he silenced her instantly.

'You don't understand,' he said, 'who I am or what I am. I'll show you. By heaven! I'll show you.' Then he put his open palm over his face and withdrew it. The centre of his face became a black cavity. 'Here,' he said. He stepped forward and handed Mrs Hall something which she, staring at his metamorphosed face, accepted automatically. Then, when she saw what it was, she screamed loudly, dropped it, and staggered back. The nose – it was the stranger's nose! pink and shining – rolled on to the floor.

Then he removed his spectacles, and everyone in the bar gasped. He took off his hat, and with a violent gesture tore at his whiskers and bandages. For a moment they resisted him. A flash of horrible antici-pation passed through the bar. 'Oh, my Gard!' said someone. Then off they came.

It was worse than anything. Mrs Hall, standing open-mouthed and horror-struck, shrieked at what she saw, and made for the door of the house. Everyone began to move. They were prepared for scars, disfigurements, tangible horrors, but *nothing*! The bandages and false hair flew across the passage into the bar, making a hobbledehoy jump to avoid them. Everyone tumbled on everyone else down the steps. For the man who stood there, shouting some incoherent explanation, was a solid gesticulating figure up to the coat-collar of him, and then – nothingness, no visible thing at all!

People down the village heard shouts and shrieks, and looking up the street saw the Coach and Horses violently firing out its humanity. They saw Mrs Hall fall down and Mr Teddy Henfrey jump to avoid tumbling over her, and then they heard the frightful screams of Millie, who, emerging suddenly from the kitchen at the noise of the tumult, had come upon the headless stranger from behind.

Forthwith everyone all down the street, the sweetstuff seller, coconut-shy proprietor and his assistant, the swing man, little boys and girls, rustic dandies, smart wenches, smocked elders and aproned gypsies – began running towards the inn, and in a miraculously short space of time a crowd of perhaps forty people, and rapidly increasing, swayed and hooted and enquired and exclaimed and suggested, in front of Mrs Hall's establishment. Everyone seemed eager to talk at once, and the result was Babel. A small group supported Mrs Hall, who was picked up in a state of collapse. There was a conference, and the incredible evidence of a vociferous eye-witness. 'O Bogey!' 'What's he been doin', then?' 'Ain't hurt the girl, 'as 'e?' 'Run at en with a knife, I believe.' 'No 'ed, I tell ye. I don't mean no manner of speaking. I mean *marn 'ithout a 'ed*!' 'Narnsense! 'tis some conjuring trick.' 'Fetched off 'is wrapping, 'e did – '

In its struggles to see in through the open door, the crowd formed itself into a straggling wedge, with the more adventurous apex nearest the inn. 'He stood for a moment, I heerd the gal scream, and he turned. I saw her skirts whisk, and he went after her. Didn't take ten seconds. Back he comes with a knife in uz hand and a loaf; stood just as if he was staring. Not a moment ago. Went in that there door. I tell 'e, 'e ain't gart no 'ed at all. You just missed en – '

There was a disturbance behind, and the speaker stopped to step aside for a little procession that was marching very resolutely towards the house: first Mr Hall, very red and determined, then Mr Bobby Jaffers, the village constable, and then the wary Mr Wadgers. They had come now armed with a warrant.

People shouted conflicting information of the recent circumstances. ' 'Ed or no 'ed,' said Jaffers, 'I got to 'rest en, and 'rest en I *will*.'

Mr Hall marched up the steps, marched straight to the door of the parlour and flung it open. 'Constable,' he said, 'do your duty.'

Jaffers marched in. Hall next, Wadgers last. They saw in the dim light the headless figure facing them, with a gnawed crust of bread in one gloved hand and a chunk of cheese in the other.

'That's him!' said Hall.

'What the devil's this?' came in a tone of angry expostulation from above the collar of the figure.

'You're a damned rum customer, mister,' said Mr Jaffers. 'But 'ed or no 'ed, the warrant says "body", and duty's duty – '

'Keep off!' said the figure, starting back.

Abruptly he whipped down the bread and cheese, and Mr Hall just grasped the knife on the table in time to save it. Off came the stranger's left glove and was slapped in Jaffers's face. In another moment Jaffers, cutting short some statement concerning a warrant, had gripped him by the handless wrist and caught his invisible throat. He got a sounding kick on the shin that made him shout, but he kept his grip. Hall sent the knife sliding along the table to Wadgers, who acted as goalkeeper for the offensive, so to speak, and then stepped forward as Jaffers and the stranger swayed and staggered towards him, clutching and hitting in. A chair stood in the way, and went aside with a crash as they came down together.

'Get the feet,' said Jaffers between his teeth.

Mr Hall, endeavouring to act on instructions, received a sounding kick in the ribs that disposed of him for a moment, and Mr Wadgers, seeing the decapitated stranger had rolled over and got the upper side of Jaffers, retreated towards the door, knife in hand, and so collided with Mr Huxter and the Sidderbridge carter coming to the rescue of law and order. At the same moment down came three or four bottles from the chiffonnier and shot a web of pungency into the air of the room.

'I'll surrender,' cried the stranger, though he had Jaffers down, and in another moment he stood up panting, a strange figure, headless and handless – for he had pulled off his right glove now as well as his left. 'It's no good,' he said, as if sobbing for breath.

It was the strangest thing in the world to hear that voice coming as if out of empty space, but the Sussex peasants are perhaps the most matter-of-fact people under the sun. Jaffers got up also and produced a pair of handcuffs. Then he stared.

'I say!' said Jaffers, brought up short by a dim realisation of the incongruity of the whole business, 'Darn it! Can't use 'em as I can see.'

The stranger ran his arm down his waistcoat, and as if by a miracle the buttons to which his empty sleeve pointed became undone. Then he said something about his shin, and stooped down. He seemed to be fumbling with his shoes and socks.

'Why!' said Huxter, suddenly, 'that's not a man at all. It's just empty clothes. Look! You can see down his collar and the linings of his clothes. I could put my arm – '

He extended his hand; it seemed to meet something in midair, and he drew it back with a sharp exclamation. 'I wish you'd keep your fingers out of my eye,' said the aerial voice, in a tone of savage expostulation. 'The fact is, I'm all here – head, hands, legs, and all the rest of it, but it happens I'm invisible. It's a confounded nuisance, but I am. That's no reason why I should be poked to pieces by every stupid bumpkin in Iping, is it?'

The suit of clothes, now all unbuttoned and hanging loosely upon its unseen supports, stood up, arms akimbo.

Several other of the men folks had now entered the room, so that it was closely crowded. 'Invisible, eh?' said Huxter, ignoring the stranger's abuse. 'Who ever heard the likes of that?'

'It's strange, perhaps, but it's not a crime. Why am I assaulted by a policeman in this fashion?'

'Ah! that's a different matter,' said Jaffers. 'No doubt you are a bit difficult to see in this light, but I got a warrant and it's all correct. What I'm after ain't no invisibility – it's burglary. There's a house been broke into and money took.'

'Well?'

'And circumstances certainly point – '

'Stuff and nonsense!' said the Invisible Man.

'I hope so, sir; but I've got my instructions.'

'Well,' said the stranger, 'I'll come. I'll *come*. But no handcuffs.'

'It's the regular thing,' said Jaffers.

'No handcuffs,' stipulated the stranger.

'Pardon me,' said Jaffers.

Abruptly the figure sat down, and before anyone could realise was was being done, the slippers, socks and trousers had been kicked off under the table. Then he sprang up again and flung off his coat.

'Here, stop that,' said Jaffers, suddenly realising what was happening. He gripped at the waistcoat; it struggled, and the shirt slipped out of it and left it limp and empty in his hand. 'Hold him!' said Jaffers, loudly. 'Once he gets the things off – '

'Hold him!' cried everyone, and there was a rush at the fluttering white shirt which was now all that was visible of the stranger.

The shirt-sleeve planted a shrewd blow in Hall's face that stopped his open-armed advance, and sent him backwards into old Toothsome the sexton, and in another moment the garment was lifted up and became convulsed and vacantly flapping about the arms, even as a shirt that is being thrust over a man's head. Jaffers clutched at it, and only helped to pull it off; he was struck in the mouth out of the air, and incontinently threw his truncheon and smote Teddy Henfrey savagely upon the crown of his head.

'Look out!' said everybody, fencing at random and hitting at nothing. 'Hold him! Shut the door! Don't let him loose! I got something! Here he is!' A perfect Babel of noises they made. Everybody, it seemed, was being hit all at once, and Sandy Wadgers, knowing as ever and his wits sharpened by a frightful blow in the nose, reopened the door and led the rout. The others, following incontinently, were jammed for a moment in the corner by the doorway. The hitting continued. Phipps, the Unitarian,[7] had a front tooth broken, and Henfrey was injured in the cartilage of his ear. Jaffers was struck under the jaw, and, turning, caught at something that intervened between him and Huxter in the mêlée, and prevented their coming together. He felt a muscular chest, and in another moment the whole mass of struggling, excited men shot out into the crowded hall.

'I got him!' shouted Jaffers, choking and reeling through them all, and wrestling with purple face and swelling veins against his unseen enemy.

Men staggered right and left as the extraordinary conflict swayed swiftly towards the house door, and went spinning down the half-dozen steps of the inn. Jaffers cried in a strangled voice – holding tight, nevertheless, and making play with his knee – spun around, and fell heavily undermost with his head on the gravel. Only then did his fingers relax.

There were excited cries of 'Hold him!' 'Invisible!' and so forth, and a young fellow, a stranger in the place whose name did not come to light, rushed in at once, caught something, missed his hold, and fell over the constable's prostrate body. Halfway across the road a woman screamed as something pushed by her; a dog, kicked apparently, yelped and ran howling into Huxter's yard, and with that the transit of the Invisible Man was accomplished. For a space people stood amazed and gesticulating, and then came Panic, and scattered them abroad through the village as a gust scatters dead leaves.

But Jaffers lay quite still, face upward and knees bent, at the foot of the steps of the inn.

CHAPTER 8

In Transit

The eighth chapter is exceedingly brief, and relates that Gibbons, the amateur naturalist of the district, while lying out on the spacious open downs without a soul within a couple of miles of him, as he thought, and almost dozing, heard close to him the sound as of a man coughing, sneezing, and then swearing savagely to himself; and looking, beheld nothing. Yet the voice was indisputable. It continued to swear with that breadth and variety that distinguishes the swearing of a cultivated man. It grew to a climax, diminished again, and died away in the distance, going as it seemed to him in the direction of Adderdean.[8] It lifted to a spasmodic sneeze and ended. Gibbons had heard nothing of the morning's occurrences, but the phenomenon was so striking and disturbing that his philosophical tranquillity vanished; he got up hastily, and hurried down the steepness of the hill towards the village, as fast as he could go.

CHAPTER 9

Mr Thomas Marvel

You must picture Mr Thomas Marvel as a person of copious, flexible visage, a nose of cylindrical protrusion, a liquorish, ample, fluctuating mouth, and a beard of bristling eccentricity. His figure inclined to embonpoint; his short limbs accentuated this inclination. He wore a furry silk hat, and the frequent substitution of twine and shoelaces for buttons, apparent at critical points of his costume, marked a man essentially bachelor.

Mr Thomas Marvel was sitting with his feet in a ditch by the roadside over the down towards Adderdean, about a mile and a half out of Iping. His feet, save for socks of irregular open-work, were bare, his big toes were broad, and pricked like the ears of a watchful dog. In a leisurely manner – he did everything in a leisurely manner – he was contemplating trying on a pair of boots. They were the soundest boots he had come across for a long time, but too large for him; whereas the ones he had were, in dry weather, a very comfortable fit, but too thin-soled for damp. Mr Thomas Marvel hated roomy shoes, but then he hated damp. He had never properly thought out which he hated most, and it was a pleasant day, and there was nothing better to do. So he put the four shoes in a graceful group on the turf and looked at them. And seeing them there among the grass and springing agrimony, it suddenly occurred to him that both pairs were exceedingly ugly to see. He was not at all startled by a voice behind him.

'They're boots, anyhow,' said the Voice.

'They are – charity boots,' said Mr Thomas Marvel, with his head on one side regarding them distastefully; 'and which is the ugliest pair in the whole blessed universe, I'm darned if I know!'

'H'm,' said the Voice.

'I've worn worse – in fact, I've worn none. But none so owdacious ugly – if you'll allow the expression. I've been cadging boots – in particular – for days. Because I was sick of *them*. They're sound enough, of course. But a gentleman on tramp sees such a thundering lot of his boots. And if you'll believe me, I've raised nothing in the whole blessed country, try as I would, but *them*. Look at 'em! And a good country for boots, too, in a general way. But it's just my promiscuous luck. I've got my boots in this country ten years or more. And then they treat you like this.'

'It's a beast of a country,' said the Voice. 'And pigs for people.'

'Ain't it?' said Mr Thomas Marvel. 'Lord! But them boots! It beats it.'

He turned his head over his shoulder to the right, to look at the boots of his interlocutor with a view to comparisons, and lo! where the boots of his interlocutor should have been were neither legs nor boots. He was irradiated by the dawn of a great amazement. 'Where *are* yer?' said Mr Thomas Marvel over his shoulder and coming on all fours. He saw a stretch of empty downs with the wind swaying the remote green-pointed furze bushes.

'Am I drunk?' said Mr Marvel. 'Have I had visions? Was I talking to myself? What the – '

'Don't be alarmed,' said the Voice.

'None of your ventriloquising *me*,' said Mr Thomas Marvel, rising sharply to his feet. 'Where *are* yer? Alarmed, indeed!'

'Don't be alarmed,' repeated the Voice.

'*You'll* be alarmed in a minute, you silly fool,' said Mr Thomas Marvel. 'Where *are* yer? Lemme get my mark on yer . . .

'Are yer *buried*?' said Mr Thomas Marvel, after an interval.

There was no answer. Mr Thomas Marvel stood bootless and amazed, his jacket nearly thrown off.

'Peewit,' said a peewit, very remote.

'Peewit, indeed!' said Mr Thomas Marvel. 'This ain't no time for foolery.' The down was desolate, east and west, north and south; the road with its shallow ditches and white bordering stakes, ran smooth and empty north and south, and, save for that peewit, the blue sky was empty too. 'So help me,' said Mr Thomas Marvel, shuffling his coat on to his shoulders again. 'It's the drink! I might ha' known.'

'It's not the drink,' said the Voice. 'You keep your nerves steady.'

'Ow!' said Mr Marvel, and his face grew white amidst its patches. 'It's the drink!' his lips repeated noiselessly. He remained staring about him, rotating slowly backwards. 'I could have *swore* I heard a voice,' he whispered.

'Of course you did.'

'It's there again,' said Mr Marvel, closing his eyes and clasping his hand on his brow with a tragic gesture. He was suddenly taken by the collar and shaken violently, and left more dazed than ever. 'Don't be a fool,' said the Voice.

'I'm – off – my – blooming – chump,' said Mr Marvel. 'It's no good.

It's fretting about them blarsted boots. I'm off my blessed blooming chump. Or it's spirits.'

'Neither one thing nor the other,' said the Voice. 'Listen!'

'Chump,' said Mr Marvel.

'One minute,' said the Voice, penetratingly, tremulous with self-control.

'Well?' said Mr Thomas Marvel, with a strange feeling of having been dug in the chest by a finger.

'You think I'm just imagination? Just imagination?'

'What else *can* you be?' said Mr Thomas Marvel, rubbing the back of his neck.

'Very well,' said the Voice, in a tone of relief. 'Then I'm going to throw flints at you till you think differently.'

'But where *are* yer?'

The Voice made no answer. Whizz came a flint, apparently out of the air, and missed Mr Marvel's shoulder by a hair's breadth. Mr Marvel, turning, saw a flint jerk up into the air, trace a complicated path, hang for a moment, and then fling at his feet with almost invisible rapidity. He was too amazed to dodge. Whizz it came, and ricocheted from a bare toe into the ditch. Mr Thomas Marvel jumped a foot and howled aloud. Then he started to run, tripped over an unseen obstacle, and came head over heels into a sitting position.

'*Now*,' said the Voice, as a third stone curved upward and hung in the air above the tramp. 'Am I imagination?'

Mr Marvel by way of reply struggled to his feet, and was immediately rolled over again. He lay quiet for a moment. 'If you struggle any more,' said the Voice, 'I shall throw the flint at your head.'

'It's a fair do,' said Mr Thomas Marvel, sitting up, taking his wounded toe in hand and fixing his eye on the third missile. 'I don't understand it. Stones flinging themselves. Stones talking. Put yourself down. Rot away. I'm done.'

The third flint fell.

'It's very simple,' said the Voice. 'I'm an invisible man.'

'Tell us something I don't know,' said Mr Marvel, gasping with pain. 'Where you've hid – how you do it – I *don't* know. I'm beat.'

'That's all,' said the Voice. 'I'm invisible. That's what I want you to understand.'

'Anyone could see that. There is no need for you to be so confounded impatient, mister. *Now* then. Give us a notion. How are you hid?'

'I'm invisible. That's the great point. And what I want you to understand is this – '

'But whereabouts?' interrupted Mr Marvel.

'Here! Six yards in front of you.'

'Oh, *come*! I ain't blind. You'll be telling me next you're just thin air. I'm not one of your ignorant tramps – '

'Yes, I am – thin air. You're looking through me.'

'What! Ain't there any stuff to you. *Vox et* – what is it? – jabber. Is it that?'

'I am just a human being – solid, needing food and drink, needing covering too – But I'm invisible. You see? Invisible. Simple idea. Invisible.'

'What, real like?'

'Yes, real.'

'Let's have a hand of you,' said Marvel, 'if you *are* real. It won't be so darn out-of-the-way like, then – *Lord!*' he said, 'how you made me jump! – gripping me like that!'

He felt the hand that had closed round his wrist with his disengaged fingers, and his fingers went timorously up the arm, patted a muscular chest, and explored a bearded face. Marvel's face was astonishment.

'I'm dashed!' he said. 'If this don't beat cockfighting! Most remarkable! – And there I can see a rabbit clean through you, 'arf a mile away! Not a bit of you visible – except – '

He scrutinised the apparently empty space keenly. 'You 'aven't been eatin' bread and cheese?' he asked, holding the invisible arm.

'You're quite right, and it's not quite assimilated into the system.'

'Ah!' said Mr Marvel. 'Sort of ghostly, though.'

'Of course, all this isn't half so wonderful as you think.'

'It's quite wonderful enough for *my* modest wants,' said Mr Thomas Marvel. 'Howjer manage it! How the dooce is it done?'

'It's too long a story. And besides – '

'I tell you, the whole business fairly beats me,' said Mr Marvel.

'What I want to say at present is this: I need help. I have come to that – I came upon you suddenly. I was wandering, mad with rage, naked, impotent. I could have murdered. And I saw you – '

'*Lord!*' said Mr Marvel.

'I came up behind you – hesitated – went on – '

Mr Marvel's expression was eloquent.

' – then stopped. "Here," I said, "is an outcast like myself. This is the man for me." So I turned back and came to you – you. And – '

'*Lord!*' said Mr Marvel. 'But I'm all in a tizzy. May I ask – How is it? And what you may be requiring in the way of help? – Invisible!'

'I want you to help me get clothes – and shelter – and then, with

other things. I've left them long enough. If you won't – well! But you
will – must.'

'Look here,' said Mr Marvel. 'I'm too flabbergasted. Don't knock me
about any more. And leave me go. I must get steady a bit. And you've
pretty near broken my toe. It's all so unreasonable. Empty downs, empty
sky. Nothing visible for miles except the bosom of nature. And then
comes a voice. A voice out of heaven! And stones! And a fist – Lord!'

'Pull yourself together,' said the Voice, 'for you have to do the job
I've chosen for you.'

Mr Marvel blew out his cheeks, and his eyes were round.

'I've chosen you,' said the Voice. 'You are the only man, except for
some of those fools down there, who knows there is such a thing as an
invisible man. You have to be my helper. Help me – and I will do great
things for you. An invisible man is a man of power.' He stopped for a
moment to sneeze violently.

'But if you betray me,' he said, 'if you fail to do as I direct you – ' He
paused and tapped Mr Marvel's shoulder smartly.

Mr Marvel gave a yelp of terror at the touch. '*I* don't want to betray
you,' said Mr Marvel, edging away from the direction of the fingers.
'Don't you go a-thinking that, whatever you do. All I want to do is to
help you – just tell me what I got to do. (Lord!) Whatever you want
done, that I'm most willing to do.'

CHAPTER 10

Mr Marvel's Visit to Iping

After the first gusty panic had spent itself Iping became argumentative. Scepticism suddenly reared its head – rather nervous scepticism, not at all assured of its back, but scepticism nevertheless. It is so much easier not to believe in an invisible man; and those who had actually seen him dissolve into air, or felt the strength of his arm, could be counted on the fingers of two hands. And of these witnesses Mr Wadgers was presently missing, having retired impregnably behind the bolts and bars of his own house, and Jaffers was lying stunned in the parlour of the Coach and Horses. Great and strange ideas transcending experience often have less effect upon men and women than smaller, more tangible considerations. Iping was gay with bunting, and everybody was in gala dress. Whit Monday had been looked forward to for a month or more. By the afternoon even those who believed in the Unseen were beginning to resume their little amusements in a tentative fashion, on the supposition that he had quite gone away, and with the sceptics he was already a jest. But people, sceptics and believers alike, were remarkably sociable all that day.

Haysman's meadow was gay with a tent, in which Mrs Bunting and other ladies were preparing tea, while, without, the Sunday-school children ran races and played games under the noisy guidance of the curate and the Misses Cuss and Sackbut. No doubt there was a slight uneasiness in the air, but people for the most part had the sense to conceal whatever imaginative qualms they experienced. On the village green an inclined strong rope, down which, clinging the while to a pulley-swung handle, one could be hurled violently against a sack at the other end, came in for considerable favour among the adolescents, as also did the swings and the coconut shies. There was also promenading, and the steam organ attached to a small roundabout filled the air with a pungent flavour of oil and with equally pungent music. Members of the club, who had attended church in the morning, were splendid in badges of pink and green, and some of the gayer-minded had also adorned their bowler hats with brilliant-coloured favours of ribbon. Old Fletcher, whose conceptions of holiday-making were severe, was visible through the jasmine about his window or through the open door (whichever way you chose to look), poised delicately on a plank supported on two chairs, and whitewashing the ceiling of his front room.

About four o'clock a stranger entered the village from the direction of the downs. He was a short, stout person in an extraordinarily shabby top hat, and he appeared to be very much out of breath. His cheeks were alternately limp and tightly puffed. His mottled face was apprehensive, and he moved with a sort of reluctant alacrity. He turned the corner of the church, and directed his way to the Coach and Horses. Among others old Fletcher remembers seeing him, and indeed the old gentleman was so struck by his peculiar agitation that he inadvertently allowed a quantity of whitewash to run down the brush into the sleeve of his coat while regarding him.

This stranger, to the perceptions of the proprietor of the coconut shy, appeared to be talking to himself, and Mr Huxter remarked the same thing. He stopped at the foot of the Coach and Horses steps, and, according to Mr Huxter, appeared to undergo a severe internal struggle before he could induce himself to enter the house. Finally he marched up the steps, and was seen by Mr Huxter to turn to the left and open the door of the parlour. Mr Huxter heard voices from within the room and from the bar apprising the man of his error. 'That room's private!' said Hall, and the stranger shut the door clumsily and went into the bar.

In the course of a few minutes he reappeared, wiping his lips with the back of his hand with an air of quiet satisfaction that somehow impressed Mr Huxter as assumed. He stood looking about him for some moments, and then Mr Huxter saw him walk in an oddly furtive manner towards the gates of the yard, upon which the parlour window opened. The stranger, after some hesitation, leant against one of the gateposts, produced a short clay pipe, and prepared to fill it. His fingers trembled while doing so. He lit it clumsily, and folding his arms began to smoke in a languid attitude, an attitude which his occasional glances up the yard altogether belied.

All this Mr Huxter saw over the canisters of the tobacco window, and the singularity of the man's behaviour prompted him to maintain his observation.

Presently the stranger stood up abruptly and put his pipe in his pocket. Then he vanished into the yard. Forthwith Mr Huxter, conceiving he was witness of some petty larceny, leapt round his counter and ran out into the road to intercept the thief. As he did so, Mr Marvel reappeared, his hat askew, a big bundle in a blue tablecloth in one hand, and three books tied together – as it proved afterwards with the vicar's braces – in the other. Directly he saw Huxter he gave a sort of gasp, and turning sharply to the left, began to run. 'Stop, thief!' cried Huxter, and set off after him. Mr Huxter's sensations were vivid but brief. He saw the man just before him and spurting briskly for the church corner and the hill road. He saw the village flags and festivities beyond, and a face or so turned towards him. He bawled, 'Stop!' again. He had hardly gone ten strides before his shin was caught in some mysterious fashion, and he was no longer running but flying with inconceivable rapidity through the air. He saw the ground suddenly close to his face. The world seemed to splash into a million whirling specks of light and subsequent proceedings interested him no more.

CHAPTER 11

In the Coach and Horses

Now, in order clearly to understand what had happened in the inn, it is necessary to go back to the moment when Mr Marvel first came into view of Mr Huxter's window.

At that precise moment Mr Cuss and Mr Bunting were in the parlour. They were seriously investigating the strange occurrences of the morning, and were, with Mr Hall's permission, making a thorough examination of the Invisible Man's belongings. Jaffers had partially recovered from his fall and had gone home in the charge of his sympathetic friends. The stranger's scattered garments had been removed by Mrs Hall and the room tidied up. And on the table under the window where the stranger had been wont to work, Cuss had hit almost at once on three big books in manuscript labelled 'Diary'.

'Diary!' said Cuss, putting the three books on the table. 'Now, at any rate, we shall learn something.' The vicar stood with his hands on the table.

'Diary,' repeated Cuss, sitting down, putting two volumes to support the third, and opening it. 'H'm – no name on the flyleaf. Bother! – cypher. And figures.'

The vicar came round to look over his shoulder.

Cuss turned the pages over with a face suddenly disappointed. 'I'm – dear me! It's all cypher, Bunting.'

'There are no diagrams?' asked Mr Bunting. 'No illustrations throwing light – '

'See for yourself,' said Mr Cuss. 'Some of it's mathematical and some of it's Russian or some such language (to judge by the letters), and some of it's Greek. Now the Greek I thought *you* – '

'Of course,' said Mr Bunting, taking out and wiping his spectacles and feeling suddenly very uncomfortable – for he had no Greek left in his mind worth talking about; 'yes – the Greek, of course, may furnish a clue.'

'I'll find you a place.'

'I'd rather glance through the volumes first,' said Mr Bunting, still wiping. 'A general impression first, Cuss, and *then*, you know, we can go looking for clues.'

He coughed, put on his glasses, arranged them fastidiously, coughed again, and wished something would happen to avert the seemingly inevitable exposure. Then he took the volume Cuss handed him in a leisurely manner. And then something did happen.

The door opened suddenly.

Both gentlemen started violently, looked round, and were relieved to see a sporadically rosy face beneath a furry silk hat. 'Tap?' asked the face, and stood staring.

'No,' said both gentlemen at once.

'Over the other side, my man,' said Mr Bunting. And, 'Please shut that door,' said Mr Cuss, irritably.

'All right,' said the intruder, as it seemed in a low voice curiously different from the huskiness of its first enquiry. 'Right you are,' said the intruder in the former voice. 'Stand clear!' and he vanished and closed the door.

'A sailor, I should judge,' said Mr Bunting. 'Amusing fellows, they are. Stand clear! indeed. A nautical term, referring to his getting back out of the room, I suppose.'

'I dare say so,' said Cuss. 'My nerves are all loose today. It quite made me jump – the door opening like that.'

Mr Bunting smiled as if he had not jumped. 'And now,' he said with a sigh, 'these books.'

Someone sniffed as he did so.

'One thing is indisputable,' said Bunting, drawing up a chair next to that of Cuss. 'There certainly have been very strange things happen in Iping during the last few days – very strange. I cannot of course believe in this absurd invisibility story – '

'It's incredible,' said Cuss – 'incredible. But the fact remains that I saw – I certainly saw right down his sleeve – '

'But did you – are you sure? Suppose a mirror, for instance – hallucinations are so easily produced. I don't know if you have ever seen a really good conjuror – '

'I won't argue again,' said Cuss. 'We've thrashed that out, Bunting. And just now there's these books – Ah! here's some of what I take to be Greek! Greek letters certainly.'

He pointed to the middle of the page. Mr Bunting flushed slightly and brought his face nearer, apparently finding some difficulty with his glasses. Suddenly he became aware of a strange feeling at the nape of his neck. He tried to raise his head, and encountered an immovable resistance. The feeling was a curious pressure, the grip of a heavy, firm hand, and it bore his chin irresistibly to the table. *'Don't move, little men,*' whispered a voice, '*or I'll brain you both!*' He looked into the face of Cuss, close to his own, and each saw a horrified reflection of his own sickly astonishment.

'I'm sorry to handle you so roughly,' said the Voice, 'but it's unavoidable.

'Since when did you learn to pry into an investigator's private memoranda,' said the Voice; and two chins struck the table simultaneously, and two sets of teeth rattled.

'Since when did you learn to invade the private rooms of a man in misfortune?' and the concussion was repeated.

'Where have they put my clothes?

'Listen,' said the Voice. 'The windows are fastened and I've taken the key out of the door. I am a fairly strong man, and I have the poker handy – besides being invisible. There's not the slightest doubt that I could kill you both and get away quite easily if I wanted to – do you understand? Very well. If I let you go will you promise not to try any nonsense and do what I tell you?'

The vicar and the doctor looked at one another, and the doctor pulled a face. 'Yes,' said Mr Bunting, and the doctor repeated it. Then the pressure on the necks relaxed, and the doctor and the vicar sat up, both very red in the face and wriggling their heads.

'Please keep sitting where you are,' said the Invisible Man. 'Here's the poker, you see.

'When I came into this room,' continued the Invisible Man, after presenting the poker to the tip of the nose of each of his visitors, 'I did not expect to find it occupied, and I expected to find, in addition to my books of memoranda, an outfit of clothing. Where is it? No – don't rise. I can see it's gone. Now, just at present, though the days are quite warm enough for an invisible man to run about stark, the evenings are quite chilly. I want clothing – and other accommodation; and I must also have those three books.'

CHAPTER 12

The Invisible Man Loses his Temper

It is unavoidable that at this point the narrative should break off again, for a certain very painful reason that will presently be apparent. While these things were going on in the parlour, and while Mr Huxter was watching Mr Marvel smoking his pipe against the gate, not a dozen yards away were Mr Hall and Teddy Henfrey discussing in a state of cloudy puzzlement the one Iping topic.

Suddenly there came a violent thud against the door of the parlour, a sharp cry, and then – silence.

'*He*l–lo!' said Teddy Henfrey.

'Hel–*lo*!' from the Tap.

Mr Hall took things in slowly but surely. 'That ain't right,' he said, and came round from behind the bar towards the parlour door.

He and Teddy approached the door together, with intent faces. Their eyes considered. 'Summat wrong,' said Hall, and Henfrey nodded agreement. Whiffs of an unpleasant chemical odour met them, and there was a muffled sound of conversation, very rapid and subdued.

'You all right thur?' asked Hall, rapping.

The muttered conversation ceased abruptly, for a moment silence, then the conversation was resumed, in hissing whispers, then a sharp cry of, 'No! no, you don't!' There came a sudden motion and the over-setting of a chair, a brief struggle. Silence again.

'What the dooce?' exclaimed Henfrey, *sotto voce*.

'You – all – right thur?' asked Mr Hall, sharply, again.

The vicar's voice answered with a curious jerking intonation: 'Quite ri-right. Please don't – interrupt.'

'Odd!' said Mr Henfrey.

'Odd!' said Mr Hall.

'Says, "Don't interrupt," ' said Henfrey.

'I heerd'n,' said Hall.

'And a sniff,' said Henfrey.

They remained listening. The conversation was rapid and subdued. 'I *can't*,' said Mr Bunting, his voice rising; 'I tell you, sir, I *will* not.'

'What was that?' asked Henfrey.

'Says he wi' nart,' said Hall. 'Warn't speaking to us, wuz he?'

'Disgraceful!' said Mr Bunting, within.

' "Disgraceful," ' said Mr Henfrey. 'I heard it – distinct.'

'Who's that speaking now?' asked Henfrey.

'Mr Cuss, I s'pose,' said Hall. 'Can you hear – anything?'

Silence. The sounds within indistinct and perplexing.

'Sounds like throwing the tablecloth about,' said Hall.

Mrs Hall appeared behind the bar. Hall made gestures of silence and invitation. This aroused Mrs Hall's wifely opposition. 'What yer listenin' there for, Hall?' she asked. 'Ain't you nothin' better to do – busy day like this?'

Hall tried to convey everything by grimaces and dumb show, but Mrs Hall was obdurate. She raised her voice. So Hall and Henfrey, rather crestfallen, tiptoed back to the bar, gesticulating to explain to her.

At first she refused to see anything in what they had heard at all. Then she insisted on Hall keeping silence, while Henfrey told her his story. She was inclined to think the whole business nonsense – perhaps they were just moving the furniture about.

'I heerd'n say "disgraceful"; *that* I did,' said Hall.

'*I* heerd that, Mrs Hall,' said Henfrey.

'Like as not – ' began Mrs Hall.

'Hsh!' said Mr Teddy Henfrey. 'Didn't I hear the window?'

'What window?' asked Mrs Hall.

'Parlour window,' said Henfrey.

Everyone stood listening intently. Mrs Hall's eyes, directed straight before her, saw without seeing the brilliant oblong of the inn door, the road white and vivid, and Huxter's shop-front blistering in the June sun. Abruptly Huxter's door opened and Huxter appeared, eyes staring with excitement, arms gesticulating. '*Yap!*' cried Huxter. 'Stop thief!' and he ran obliquely across the oblong towards the yard gates, and vanished.

Simultaneously came a tumult from the parlour, and a sound of windows being closed.

Hall, Henfrey, and the human contents of the tap rushed out at once pell-mell into the street. They saw someone whisk round the corner towards the road, and Mr Huxter executing a complicated leap in the air that ended on his face and shoulder. Down the street people were standing astonished or running towards them.

Mr Huxter was stunned. Henfrey stopped to discover this, but Hall and the two labourers from the tap rushed at once to the corner, shouting incoherent things, and saw Mr Marvel vanishing by the corner of the church wall. They appear to have jumped to the impossible conclusion that this was the Invisible Man suddenly become visible, and set off at once along the lane in pursuit. But Hall had hardly run a dozen yards before he gave a loud shout of astonishment and went flying headlong sideways, clutching one of the labourers and bringing him to the ground. He had been charged just as one charges a man at football. The second labourer came round in a circle, stared, and conceiving that Hall had tumbled over of his own accord, turned to resume the pursuit, only to be tripped by the ankle just as Huxter had been. Then, as the first labourer struggled to his feet, he was kicked sideways by a blow that might have felled an ox.

As he went down, the rush from the direction of the village green came round the corner. The first to appear was the proprietor of the coconut shy, a burly man in a blue jersey. He was astonished to see the lane empty save for three men sprawling absurdly on the ground. And then something happened to his rearmost foot, and he went headlong and rolled sideways just in time to graze the feet of his brother and partner, following headlong. The two were then kicked, knelt on, fallen over and cursed by quite a number of over-hasty people.

Now when Hall and Henfrey and the labourers ran out of the house, Mrs Hall, who had been disciplined by years of experience, remained in the bar next the till. And suddenly the parlour door was opened, and Mr Cuss appeared, and without glancing at her rushed at once down the steps towards the corner. 'Hold him!' he cried. 'Don't let him drop that parcel.'

He knew nothing of the existence of Marvel. For the Invisible Man had handed over the books and bundle in the yard. The face of Mr Cuss was angry and resolute, but his costume was defective, a sort of limp white kilt that could only have passed muster in Greece. 'Hold him!' he bawled. 'He's got my trousers! And every stitch of the vicar's clothes!'

' 'Tend to him in a minute!' he cried to Henfrey as he passed the prostrate Huxter, and, coming round the corner to join the tumult, was promptly knocked off his feet into an indecorous sprawl. Somebody in full flight trod heavily on his finger. He yelled, struggled to regain his feet, was knocked against and thrown on all fours again, and became aware that he was involved not in a capture, but a rout. Everyone was running back to the village. He rose again and was hit severely behind the ear. He staggered and set off back to the Coach and Horses forthwith, leaping over the deserted Huxter, who was now sitting up, on his way.

Behind him as he was halfway up the inn steps he heard a sudden yell of rage, rising sharply out of the confusion of cries, and a sounding smack in someone's face. He recognised the voice as that of the Invisible Man, and the note was that of a man suddenly infuriated by a painful blow.

In another moment Mr Cuss was back in the parlour. 'He's coming back, Bunting!' he said, rushing in. 'Save yourself!'

Mr Bunting was standing in the window engaged in an attempt to clothe himself in the hearthrug and a *West Surrey Gazette*.[9] 'Who's coming?' he said, so startled that his costume narrowly escaped disintegration.

'Invisible Man,' said Cuss, and rushed on to the window. 'We'd better clear out from here! He's fighting mad! Mad!'

In another moment he was out in the yard.

'Good heavens!' said Mr Bunting, hesitating between two horrible alternatives. He heard a frightful struggle in the passage of the inn, and his decision was made. He clambered out of the window, adjusted his costume hastily, and fled up the village as fast as his fat little legs would carry him.

From the moment when the Invisible Man screamed with rage and Mr Bunting made his memorable flight up the village, it became impossible to give a consecutive account of affairs in Iping. Possibly the Invisible Man's original intention was simply to cover Marvel's retreat with the clothes and books. But his temper, at no time very good, seems to have gone completely at some chance blow, and forthwith he set to smiting and overthrowing, for the mere satisfaction of hurting.

You must figure the street full of running figures, of doors slamming and fights for hiding-places. You must figure the tumult suddenly striking on the unstable equilibrium of old Fletcher's planks and two chairs – with cataclysmic results. You must figure an appalled couple caught dismally in a swing. And then the whole tumultuous rush has passed and the Iping street with its gauds and flags is deserted save for the still raging unseen, and littered with coconuts, overthrown canvas screens, and the scattered stock in trade of a sweetstuff stall. Everywhere there is a sound of closing shutters and shoving bolts, and the only visible humanity is an occasional flitting eye under a raised eyebrow in the corner of a window pane.

The Invisible Man amused himself for a little while by breaking all the windows in the Coach and Horses, and then he thrust a street lamp through the parlour window of Mrs Gribble. He it must have been who cut the telegraph wire to Adderdean just beyond Higgins's cottage on the Adderdean road. And after that, as his peculiar qualities allowed, he passed out of human perceptions altogether, and he was neither heard, seen, nor felt in Iping any more. He vanished absolutely.

But it was the best part of two hours before any human being ventured out again into the desolation of Iping Street.

CHAPTER 13

Mr Marvel Discusses his Resignation

When the dusk was gathering and Iping was just beginning to peep timorously forth again upon the shattered wreckage of its Bank Holiday, a short, thickset man in a shabby silk hat was marching painfully through the twilight behind the beechwoods on the road to Bramblehurst. He carried three books bound together by some sort of ornamental elastic ligature, and a bundle wrapped in a blue tablecloth. His rubicund face expressed consternation and fatigue; he appeared to be in a spasmodic sort of hurry. He was accompanied by a voice other than his own, and ever and again he winced under the touch of unseen hands.

'If you give me the slip again,' said the Voice, 'if you attempt to give me the slip again – '

'Lord!' said Mr Marvel. 'That shoulder's a mass of bruises as it is.'

'On my honour,' said the Voice, 'I will kill you.'

'I didn't try to give you the slip,' said Marvel, in a voice that was not far remote from tears. 'I swear I didn't. I didn't know the blessed turning, that was all! How the devil was I to know the blessed turning? As it is, I've been knocked about – '

'You'll get knocked about a great deal more if you don't mind,' said the Voice, and Mr Marvel abruptly became silent. He blew out his cheeks, and his eyes were eloquent of despair.

'It's bad enough to let these floundering yokels explode my little secret, without *your* cutting off with my books. It's lucky for some of them they cut and ran when they did! Here am I . . . No one knew I was invisible! And now what am I to do?'

'What am *I* to do?' asked Marvel, *sotto voce*.

'It's all about. It will be in the papers! Everybody will be looking for me; everyone on their guard – ' The Voice broke off into vivid curses and ceased.

The despair of Mr Marvel's face deepened, and his pace slackened.

'Go on!' said the Voice.

Mr Marvel's face assumed a greyish tint between the ruddier patches.

'Don't drop those books, stupid,' said the Voice, sharply – overtaking him.

'The fact is,' said the Voice, 'I shall have to make use of you . . . You're a poor tool, but I must.'

'I'm a *miserable* tool,' said Marvel.

'You are,' said the Voice.

'I'm the worst possible tool you could have,' said Marvel. 'I'm not strong,' he said after a discouraging silence. 'I'm not over strong,' he repeated.

'No?'

'And my heart's weak. That little business – I pulled it through, of course – but bless you! I could have dropped.'

'Well?'

'I haven't the nerve and strength for the sort of thing you want.'

'*I'll* stimulate you.'

'I wish you wouldn't. I wouldn't like to mess up your plans, you know. But I might – out of sheer funk and misery.'

'You'd better not,' said the Voice, with quiet emphasis.

'I wish I was dead,' said Marvel. 'It ain't justice,' he said; 'you must admit . . . It seems to me I've a perfect right – '

'*Get* on!' said the Voice.

Mr Marvel mended his pace, and for a time they went in silence again.

'It's devilish hard,' said Mr Marvel.

This was quite ineffectual. He tried another tack.

'What do I make by it?' he began again in a tone of unendurable wrong.

'Oh! *shut up!*' said the Voice, with sudden amazing vigour. 'I'll see to you all right. You do what you're told. You'll do it all right. You're a fool and all that, but you'll do – '

'I tell you, sir, I'm not the man for it. Respectfully – but it *is* so – '

'If you don't shut up I shall twist your wrist again,' said the Invisible Man. 'I want to think.'

Presently two oblongs of yellow light appeared through the trees, and the square tower of a church loomed through the gloaming. 'I shall keep my hand on your shoulder,' said the Voice, 'all through the village. Go straight through and try no foolery. It will be the worse for you if you do.'

'I know that,' sighed Mr Marvel. 'I know all that.'

The unhappy-looking figure in the obsolete silk hat passed up the street of the little village with his burdens, and vanished into the gathering darkness beyond the lights of the windows.

CHAPTER 14

At Port Stowe[10]

Ten o'clock the next morning found Mr Marvel, unshaven, dirty and travel-stained, sitting with the books beside him and his hands deep in his pockets, looking very weary, nervous and uncomfortable, and inflating his cheeks at infrequent intervals, on the bench outside a little inn on the outskirts of Port Stowe. Beside him were the books, but now they were tied with string. The bundle had been abandoned in the pinewoods beyond Bramblehurst, in accordance with a change in the plans of the Invisible Man. Mr Marvel sat on the bench, and although no one took the slightest notice of him, his agitation remained at fever heat. His hands would go ever and again to his various pockets with a curious nervous fumbling.

When he had been sitting for the best part of an hour, however, an elderly mariner, carrying a newspaper, came out of the inn and sat down beside him. 'Pleasant day,' said the mariner.

Mr Marvel glanced about him with something very like terror. 'Very,' he said.

'Just seasonable weather for the time of year,' said the mariner, taking no denial.

'Quite,' said Mr Marvel.

The mariner produced a toothpick, and (saving his regard) was engrossed thereby for some minutes. His eyes meanwhile were at liberty to examine Mr Marvel's dusty figure, and the books beside him. As he had approached Mr Marvel he had heard a sound like the dropping of coins into a pocket. He was struck by the contrast of Mr Marvel's appearance with this suggestion of opulence. Thence his mind wandered back again to a topic that had taken a curiously firm hold of his imagination.

'Books?' he said suddenly, noisily finishing with the toothpick.

Mr Marvel started and looked at them. 'Oh, yes,' he said. 'Yes, they're books.'

'There's some extra-ordinary things in books,' said the mariner.

'I believe you,' said Mr Marvel.

'And some extra-ordinary things out of 'em,' said the mariner.

'True likewise,' said Mr Marvel. He eyed his interlocutor, and then glanced about him.

'There's some extra-ordinary things in newspapers, for example,' said the mariner.

'There are.'

'In *this* newspaper,' said the mariner.

'Ah!' said Mr Marvel.

'There's a story,' said the mariner, fixing Mr Marvel with an eye that was firm and deliberate; 'there's a story about an Invisible Man, for instance.'

Mr Marvel pulled his mouth askew and scratched his cheek and felt his ears glowing.

'What will they be writing next?' he asked faintly. 'Ostria, or America?'

'Neither,' said the mariner. '*Here!*'

'Lord!' said Mr Marvel, starting.

'When I say *here*,' said the mariner, to Mr Marvel's intense relief, 'I don't of course mean here in this place, I mean hereabouts.'

'An Invisible Man!' said Mr Marvel. 'And what's *he* been up to?'

'Everything,' said the mariner, controlling Marvel with his eye, and then amplifying, 'every – blessed – thing.'

'I ain't seen a paper these four days,' said Marvel.

'Iping's the place he started at,' said the mariner.

'In-*deed*!' said Mr Marvel.

'He started there. And where he came from, nobody don't seem to know. Here it is: "Pe-culiar Story from Iping". And it says in this paper that the evidence is extra-ordinary strong – extra-ordinary.'

'Lord!' said Mr Marvel.

'But then, it's an extra-ordinary story. There is a clergyman and a medical gent witnesses – saw 'im all right and proper – or leastways didn't see 'im. He was staying, it says, at the Coach an' Horses, and no one don't seem to have been aware of his misfortune, it says, aware of his misfortune, until in an Altercation in the inn, it says, his bandages on his head was torn off. It was then ob-served that his head was invisible. Attempts were At Once made to secure him, but casting off his garments, it says, he succeeded in escaping, but not until after a desperate struggle, in which he had inflicted serious injuries, it says, on our worthy and able constable, Mr J. A. Jaffers. Pretty straight story, eh? Names and everything.'

'Lord!' said Mr Marvel, looking nervously about him, trying to count the money in his pockets by his unaided sense of touch, and full of a strange and novel idea. 'It sounds most astonishing.'

'Don't it? Extra-ordinary, *I* call it. Never heard tell of Invisible Men before, I haven't, but nowadays one hears such a lot of extra-ordinary things – that – '

'That all he did?' asked Marvel, trying to seem at his ease.

'It's enough, ain't it?' said the mariner.

'Didn't go back by any chance?' asked Marvel. 'Just escaped and that's all, eh?'

'All!' said the mariner. 'Why! – ain't it enough?'

'Quite enough,' said Marvel.

'I should think it was enough,' said the mariner. 'I should think it was enough.'

'He didn't have any pals – it don't say he had any pals, does it?' asked Mr Marvel, anxious.

'Ain't one of a sort enough for you?' asked the mariner. 'No, thank heaven, as one might say, he didn't.'

He nodded his head slowly. 'It makes me regular uncomfortable, the bare thought of that chap running about the country! He is at present At Large, and from certain evidence it is supposed that he has taken – *took*, I suppose they mean – the road to Port Stowe. You see we're right *in* it! None of your American wonders, this time. And just think of the things he might do! Where'd you be, if he took a drop over and above, and had a fancy to go for you? Suppose he wants to rob – who can prevent him? He can trespass, he can burgle, he could walk through a cordon of policemen as easy as me or you could give the slip to a blind man! Easier! For these here blind chaps hear uncommon sharp, I'm told. And wherever there was liquor he fancied – '

'He's got a tremenjous advantage, certainly,' said Mr Marvel. 'And – well . . .'

'You're right,' said the mariner. 'He *has*.'

All this time Mr Marvel had been glancing about him intently, listening for faint footfalls, trying to detect imperceptible movements. He seemed on the point of some great resolution. He coughed behind his hand.

He looked about him again, listened, bent towards the mariner, and lowered his voice: 'The fact of it is – I happen – to know just a thing or two about this Invisible Man. From private sources.'

'Oh!' said the mariner, interested. '*You?*'

'Yes,' said Mr Marvel. 'Me.'

'Indeed!' said the mariner. 'And may I ask – '

'You'll be astonished,' said Mr Marvel behind his hand. 'It's tremenjous.'

'Indeed!' said the mariner.

'The fact is,' began Mr Marvel eagerly in a confidential undertone. Suddenly his expression changed marvellously. 'Ow!' he said. He rose stiffly in his seat. His face was eloquent of physical suffering. 'Wow!' he said.

'What's up?' said the mariner, concerned.

'Toothache,' said Mr Marvel, and put his hand to his ear. He caught hold of his books. 'I must be getting on, I think,' he said. He edged in a curious way along the seat away from his interlocutor.

'But you was just a-going to tell me about this here Invisible Man!' protested the mariner.

Mr Marvel seemed to consult with himself. 'Hoax,' said a Voice. 'It's a hoax,' said Mr Marvel.

'But it's in the paper,' said the mariner.

'Hoax all the same,' said Marvel. 'I know the chap that started the lie. There ain't no Invisible Man whatsoever – Blimey.'

'But how 'bout this paper? D'you mean to say – ?'

'Not a word of it,' said Marvel, stoutly.

The mariner stared, paper in hand. Mr Marvel jerkily faced about. 'Wait a bit,' said the mariner, rising and speaking slowly, 'D'you mean to say – ?'

'I do,' said Mr Marvel.

'Then why did you let me go on and tell you all this blarsted stuff, then? What d'yer mean by letting a man make a fool of himself like that for? Eh?'

Mr Marvel blew out his cheeks.

The mariner was suddenly very red indeed; he clenched his hands. 'I been talking here this ten minutes,' he said; 'and you, you little pot-bellied, leathery-faced son of an old boot, couldn't have the elementary manners – '

'Don't you come bandying words with *me*,' said Mr Marvel.

'Bandying words! I'm a jolly good mind – '

'Come up,' said a Voice, and Mr Marvel was suddenly whirled about and started marching off in a curious spasmodic manner.

'You'd better move on,' said the mariner.

'*Who's* moving on?' said Mr Marvel. He was receding obliquely with a curious hurrying gait, with occasional violent jerks forward. Some way along the road he began a muttered monologue, protests and recriminations.

'Silly devil!' said the mariner, legs wide apart, elbows akimbo, watching the receding figure. 'I'll show you, you silly ass – hoaxing *me*! It's here – in the paper!'

Mr Marvel retorted incoherently and, receding, was hidden by a bend in the road, but the mariner still stood magnificent in the midst of the way, until the approach of a butcher's cart dislodged him. Then he turned himself towards Port Stowe. 'Full of extra-ordinary asses,' he said softly to himself. 'Just to take me down a bit – that was his silly game – It's in the paper!'

And there was another extraordinary thing he was presently to hear, that had happened quite close to him. And that was a vision of a 'fist full of money' (no less) travelling without visible agency, along by the wall at the corner of St Michael's Lane. A brother mariner had seen this wonderful sight that very morning. He had snatched at the money forthwith and had been knocked headlong, and when he had got to his feet the butterfly money had vanished. Our mariner was in the mood to believe anything, he declared, but that was a bit *too* stiff. Afterwards, however, he began to think things over.

The story of the flying money was true. And all about that neighbourhood, even from the august London and Country Banking Company, from the tills of shops and inns – doors standing that sunny weather entirely open – money had been quietly and dexterously making off that day in handfuls and rouleaux, floating quietly along by walls and shady places, dodging quickly from the approaching eyes of men. And it had, though no man had traced it, invariably ended its mysterious flight in the pocket of that agitated gentleman in the obsolete silk hat, sitting outside the little inn on the outskirts of Port Stowe.

It was ten days after – and indeed only when the Burdock[11] story was already old – that the mariner collated these facts and began to understand how near he had been to the wonderful Invisible Man.

CHAPTER 15

The Man Who was Running

In the early evening time, Dr Kemp was sitting in his study in the belvedere on the hill overlooking Burdock. It was a pleasant little room, with three windows – north, west and south – and bookshelves covered with books and scientific publications, and a broad writing-table, and, under the north window, a microscope, glass slips, minute instruments, some cultures and scattered bottles of reagents. Dr Kemp's solar lamp was lit, albeit the sky was still bright with the sunset light, and his blinds were up because there was no offence of peering outsiders to require them pulled down. Dr Kemp was a tall and slender young man, with flaxen hair and a moustache almost white, and the work he was upon would earn him, he hoped, the fellowship of the Royal Society, so highly did he think of it.

And his eye, presently wandering from his work, caught the sunset blazing at the back of the hill that is over against his own. For a minute perhaps he sat, pen in mouth, admiring the rich golden colour above the crest, and then his attention was attracted by the little figure of a man, inky black, running over the hill-brow towards him. He was a shortish little man, and he wore a high hat, and he was running so fast that his legs verily twinkled.

'Another of those fools,' said Dr Kemp. 'Like that ass who ran into me this morning round a corner, with the " 'Visible Man a-coming, sir!" I can't imagine what possesses people. One might think we were in the thirteenth century.'

He got up, went to the window, and stared at the dusky hillside, and the dark little figure tearing down it. 'He seems in a confounded hurry,' said Dr Kemp, 'but he doesn't seem to be getting on. If his pockets were full of lead, he couldn't run heavier.

'Spurted, sir,' said Dr Kemp.

In another moment the higher of the villas that had clambered up the hill from Burdock had occulted the running figure. He was visible again for a moment, and again, and then again, three times between the three detached houses that came next, and then the terrace hid him.

'Asses!' said Dr Kemp, swinging round on his heel and walking back to his writing-table.

But those who saw the fugitive nearer, and perceived the abject terror on his perspiring face, being themselves in the open roadway, did not share in the doctor's contempt. By the man pounded, and as he ran he chinked like a well-filled purse that is tossed to and fro. He looked neither to the right nor the left, but his dilated eyes stared straight downhill to where the lamps were being lit, and the people were crowded in the street. And his ill-shaped mouth fell apart, and a glairy foam lay on his lips, and his breath came hoarse and noisy. All he passed stopped and began staring up the road and down, and interrogating one another with an inkling of discomfort for the reason of his haste.

And then presently, far up the hill, a dog playing in the road yelped and ran under a gate, and as they still wondered, something – a wind – a pad, pad, pad – a sound like a panting breathing, rushed by.

People screamed. People sprang off the pavement. It passed in shouts, it passed by instinct down the hill. They were shouting in the street before Marvel was halfway there. They were bolting into houses and slamming the doors behind them, with the news. He heard it and made one last desperate spurt. Fear came striding by, rushed ahead of him, and in a moment had seized the town.

'The Invisible Man is coming! *The Invisible Man!*'

CHAPTER 16

In the Jolly Cricketers

The Jolly Cricketers is just at the bottom of the hill, where the tram-lines begin. The barman leant his fat red arms on the counter and talked of horses with an anaemic cabman, while a black-bearded man in grey snapped up biscuit and cheese, drank Burton, and conversed in American with a policeman off duty.

'What's the shouting about!' said the cabman, going off at a tangent, trying to see up the hill over the dirty yellow blind in the low window of the inn. Somebody ran by outside. 'Fire, perhaps,' said the barman.

Footsteps approached, running heavily, the door was pushed open violently, and Marvel, weeping and dishevelled, his hat gone, the neck of his coat torn open, rushed in, made a convulsive turn, and attempted to shut the door. It was held half open by a strap.

'Coming!' he bawled, his voice shrieking with terror. 'He's coming. The 'Visible Man! After me! For Gawd's sake! 'Elp! 'Elp! 'Elp!'

'Shut the doors,' said the policeman. 'Who's coming? What's the row?' He went to the door, released the strap, and it slammed. The American closed the other door.

'Lemme go inside,' said Marvel, staggering and weeping, but still clutching the books. 'Lemme go inside. Lock me in – somewhere. I tell you he's after me. I give him the slip. He said he'd kill me and he will.'

'*You're* safe,' said the man with the black beard. 'The door's shut. What's it all about?'

'Lemme go inside,' said Marvel, and shrieked aloud as a blow suddenly made the fastened door shiver and was followed by a hurried rapping and a shouting outside. 'Hello,' cried the policeman, 'who's there?' Mr Marvel began to make frantic dives at panels that looked like doors. 'He'll kill me – he's got a knife or something. For Gawd's sake – !'

'Here you are,' said the barman. 'Come in here.' And he held up the flap of the bar.

Mr Marvel rushed behind the bar as the summons outside was repeated. 'Don't open the door,' he screamed. '*Please* don't open the door. *Where* shall I hide?'

'This, this Invisible Man, then?' asked the man with the black beard, with one hand behind him. 'I guess it's about time we saw him.'

The window of the inn was suddenly smashed in, and there was a screaming and running to and fro in the street. The policeman had been standing on the settee staring out, craning to see who was at the door. He got down with raised eyebrows. 'It's that,' he said. The barman stood in front of the bar-parlour door which was now locked on Mr Marvel, stared at the smashed window, and came round to the two other men.

Everything was suddenly quiet. 'I wish I had my truncheon,' said the policeman, going irresolutely to the door. 'Once we open, in he comes. There's no stopping him.'

'Don't you be in too much hurry about that door,' said the anaemic cabman, anxiously.

'Draw the bolts,' said the man with the black beard, 'and if he comes – ' He showed a revolver in his hand.

'That won't do,' said the policeman; 'that's murder.'

'I know what country I'm in,' said the man with the beard. 'I'm going to let off at his legs. Draw the bolts.'

'Not with that blinking thing going off behind me,' said the barman, craning over the blind.

'Very well,' said the man with the black beard, and stooping down, revolver ready, drew them himself. Barman, cabman and policeman faced about.

'Come in,' said the bearded man in an undertone, standing back and facing the unbolted door with his pistol behind him. No one came in, the door remained closed. Five minutes afterwards when a second cabman pushed his head in cautiously, they were still waiting, and an anxious face peered out of the bar-parlour and supplied information. 'Are all the doors of the house shut?' asked Marvel. 'He's going round – prowling round. He's as artful as the devil.'

'Good Lord!' said the burly barman. 'There's the back! Just watch them doors! I say – !' He looked about him helplessly. The bar-parlour door slammed and they heard the key turn. 'There's the yard door and the private door. The yard door – '

He rushed out of the bar.

In a minute he reappeared with a carving-knife in his hand. 'The yard door was open!' he said, and his fat underlip dropped.

'He may be in the house now!' said the first cabman.

'He's not in the kitchen,' said the barman. 'There's two women there, and I've stabbed every inch of it with this little beef slicer. And they don't think he's come in. They haven't noticed – '

'Have you fastened it?' asked the first cabman.

'I'm out of frocks,' said the barman.

The man with the beard replaced his revolver. And even as he did so the flap of the bar was shut down and the bolt clicked, and then with a tremendous thud the catch of the door snapped and the bar-parlour door burst open. They heard Marvel squeal like a caught leveret, and forthwith they were clambering over the bar to his rescue. The bearded man's revolver cracked and the looking-glass at the back of the parlour starred and came smashing and tinkling down.

As the barman entered the room he saw Marvel, curiously crumpled up and struggling against the door that led to the yard and kitchen. The door flew open while the barman hesitated, and Marvel was dragged into the kitchen. There was a scream and a clatter of pans. Marvel, head down, and lugging back obstinately, was forced to the kitchen door, and the bolts were drawn.

Then the policeman, who had been trying to pass the barman, rushed in, followed by one of the cabmen, gripped the wrist of the invisible hand that collared Marvel, was hit in the face and went reeling back. The door opened, and Marvel made a frantic effort to obtain a lodgment behind it. Then the cabman collared something. 'I got him,' said the cabman. The barman's red hands came clawing at the unseen. 'Here he is!' said the barman.

Mr Marvel, released, suddenly dropped to the ground and made an attempt to crawl behind the legs of the fighting men. The struggle blundered round the edge of the door. The voice of the Invisible Man was heard for the first time, yelling out sharply as the policeman trod on his foot. Then he cried out passionately and his fists flew round like flails. The cabman suddenly whooped and doubled up, kicked under the diaphragm. The door into the bar-parlour from the kitchen slammed and covered Mr Marvel's retreat. The men in the kitchen found themselves clutching at and struggling with empty air.

'Where's he gone?' cried the man with the beard. 'Out?'

'This way,' said the policeman, stepping into the yard and stopping.

A piece of tile whizzed by his head and smashed among the crockery on the kitchen table.

'I'll show him,' shouted the man with the black beard, and suddenly a steel barrel shone over the policeman's shoulder, and five bullets had followed one another into the twilight whence the missile had come. As he fired, the man with the beard moved his hand in a horizontal curve, so that his shots radiated out into the narrow yard like spokes from a wheel.

A silence followed. 'Five cartridges,' said the man with the black beard. 'That's the best of all. Four aces and a joker. Get a lantern, someone, and come and feel about for his body.'

CHAPTER 17

Dr Kemp's Visitor

Dr Kemp had continued writing in his study until the shots aroused him. Crack, crack, crack, they came one after the other.

'Hello!' said Dr Kemp, putting his pen into his mouth again and listening. 'Who's letting off revolvers in Burdock? What are the asses at now?'

He went to the south window, threw it up, and leaning out stared down on the network of windows, beaded gas-lamps and shops, with its black interstices of roof and yard that made up the town at night. 'Looks like a crowd down the hill,' he said, 'by the Cricketers,' and remained watching. Thence his eyes wandered over the town to far away where the ships' lights shone, and the pier glowed – a little illuminated, faceted pavilion like a gem of yellow light. The moon in its first quarter hung over the westward hill, and the stars were clear and almost tropically bright.

After five minutes, during which his mind had travelled into a remote speculation on social conditions of the future and lost itself at last over the time dimension, Dr Kemp roused himself with a sigh, pulled down the window again, and returned to his writing desk.

It must have been about an hour after this that the front-door bell rang. He had been writing slackly, and with intervals of abstraction, since the shots. He sat listening. He heard the servant answer the door, and waited for her feet on the staircase, but she did not come. 'Wonder what that was,' said Dr Kemp.

He tried to resume his work, failed, got up, went downstairs from his study to the landing, rang, and called over the balustrade to the house-maid as she appeared in the hall below. 'Was that a letter?' he asked.

'Only a runaway ring, sir,' she answered.

'I'm restless tonight,' he said to himself. He went back to his study, and this time attacked his work resolutely. In a little while he was hard at work again, and the only sounds in the room were the ticking of the clock and the subdued shrillness of his quill, hurrying in the very centre of the circle of light his lampshade threw on his table.

It was two o'clock before Dr Kemp had finished his work for the night. He rose, yawned, and went downstairs to bed. He had already removed his coat and waistcoat, when he noticed that he was thirsty. He took a candle and went down to the dining-room in search of a syphon and whisky.

Dr Kemp's scientific pursuits had made him a very observant man, and as he recrossed the hall, he noticed a dark spot on the linoleum near the mat at the foot of the stairs. He went on upstairs, and then it suddenly occurred to him to ask himself what the spot on the linoleum might be. Apparently some subconscious element was at work. At any rate, he turned with his burden, went back to the hall, put down the syphon and whisky, and bending down, touched the spot. Without any great surprise he found it had the stickiness and colour of drying blood.

He took up his burden again, and returned upstairs, looking about him and trying to account for the blood-spot. On the landing he saw something and stopped astonished. The door-handle of his own room was blood-stained.

He looked at his own hand. It was quite clean, and then he remembered that the door of his room had been open when he came down from his study, and that consequently he had not touched the handle at all. He went straight into his room, his face quite calm – perhaps a trifle more resolute than usual. His glance, wandering inquisitively, fell on the bed. On the counterpane was a mess of blood, and the sheet had been torn. He had not noticed this before because he had walked straight to the dressing-table. On the farther side the bedclothes were depressed as if someone had been recently sitting there.

Then he had an odd impression that he had heard a low voice say, 'Good heavens! – Kemp!' But Dr Kemp was no believer in voices.

He stood staring at the tumbled sheets. Was that really a voice? He looked about again, but noticed nothing further than the disordered and blood-stained bed. Then he distinctly heard a movement across the room, near the wash-hand stand. All men, however highly educated, retain some superstitious inklings. The feeling that is called 'eerie' came upon him. He closed the door of the room, came forward to the dressing-table and put down his burdens. Suddenly, with a start, he perceived a coiled and blood-stained bandage of linen rag hanging in mid-air, between him and the wash-hand stand.

He stared at this in amazement. It was an empty bandage, a bandage properly tied but quite empty. He would have advanced to grasp it, but a touch arrested him, and a voice speaking quite close to him.

'Kemp!' said the Voice.

'Eh?' said Kemp, with his mouth open.

'Keep your nerve,' said the Voice. 'I'm an Invisible Man.'

Kemp made no answer for a space, simply stared at the bandage. 'Invisible Man,' he said.

'I am an Invisible Man,' repeated the Voice.

The story he had been active to ridicule only that morning rushed through Kemp's brain. He does not appear to have been either very much frightened or very greatly surprised at the moment. Realisation came later.

'I thought it was all a lie,' he said. The thought uppermost in his mind was the reiterated arguments of the morning. 'Have you a bandage on?' he asked.

'Yes,' said the Invisible Man.

'Oh!' said Kemp, and then roused himself. 'I say!' he said. 'But this is nonsense. It's some trick.' He stepped forward suddenly, and his hand, extended towards the bandage, met invisible fingers.

He recoiled at the touch and his colour changed.

'Keep steady, Kemp, for God's sake! I want help badly. Stop!'

The hand gripped his arm. He struck at it.

'Kemp!' cried the Voice. 'Kemp! Keep steady!' and the grip tightened.

A frantic desire to free himself took possession of Kemp. The hand of the bandaged arm gripped his shoulder, and he was suddenly tripped and flung backwards upon the bed. He opened his mouth to shout, and the corner of the sheet was thrust between his teeth. The Invisible Man had him down grimly, but his arms were free and he struck and tried to kick savagely.

'Listen to reason, will you?' said the Invisible Man, sticking to him in spite of a pounding in the ribs. 'By heaven! you'll madden me in a minute! Lie still, you fool!' he bawled in Kemp's ear.

Kemp struggled for another moment and then lay still.

'If you shout, I'll smash your face,' said the Invisible Man, relieving his mouth. 'I'm an Invisible Man. It's no foolishness, and no magic. I really am an Invisible Man. And I want your help. I don't want to hurt you, but if you behave like a frantic rustic, I must. Don't you remember me, Kemp? Griffin, of University College?'

'Let me get up,' said Kemp. 'I'll stop where I am. And let me sit quiet for a minute.'

He sat up and felt his neck.

'I am Griffin, of University College, and I have made myself invisible. I am just an ordinary man – a man you have known – made invisible.'

'Griffin?' said Kemp.

'Griffin,' answered the Voice. A younger student than you were, almost an albino, six feet high, and broad, with a pink and white face and red eyes, who won the medal for chemistry.'

'I am confused,' said Kemp. 'My brain is rioting. What has this to do with Griffin?'

'I *am* Griffin.'

Kemp thought. 'It's horrible,' he said. 'But what devilry must happen to make a man invisible?'

'It's no devilry. It's a process, sane and intelligible enough – '

'It's horrible!' said Kemp. 'How on earth – ?'

'It's horrible enough. But I'm wounded and in pain, and tired . . . Great God! Kemp, you are a man. Take it steady. Give me some food and drink, and let me sit down here.'

Kemp stared at the bandage as it moved across the room, then saw a basket chair dragged across the floor and come to rest near the bed. It creaked, and the seat was depressed a quarter of an inch or so. He rubbed his eyes and felt his neck again. 'This beats ghosts,' he said, and laughed stupidly.

'That's better. Thank heaven, you're getting sensible!'

'Or silly,' said Kemp, and knuckled his eyes.

'Give me some whisky. I'm near dead.'

'It didn't feel so. Where are you? If I get up shall I run into you? *There!* All right. Whisky? Here. Where shall I give it to you?'

The chair creaked and Kemp felt the glass drawn away from him. He let go by an effort; his instinct was all against it. It came to rest poised twenty inches above the front edge of the seat of the chair. He stared at it in infinite perplexity. 'This is – this *must* be – hypnotism. You have suggested you are invisible.'

'Nonsense,' said the Voice.

'It's frantic.'

'Listen to me.'

'I demonstrated conclusively this morning,' began Kemp, 'that invisibility – '

'Never mind what you've demonstrated! – I'm starving,' said the Voice, 'and the night is chilly to a man without clothes.'

'Food?' said Kemp.

The tumbler of whisky tilted itself. 'Yes,' said the Invisible Man rapping it down. 'Have you a dressing-gown?'

Kemp made some exclamation in an undertone. He walked to a wardrobe and produced a robe of dingy scarlet. 'This do?' he asked. It was taken from him. It hung limp for a moment in midair, fluttered weirdly, stood full and decorous buttoning itself, and sat down in his chair. 'Drawers, socks, slippers would be a comfort,' said the Unseen, curtly. 'And food.'

'Anything. But this is the insanest thing I ever was in, in my life!'

He turned out his drawers for the articles, and then went downstairs to ransack his larder. He came back with some cold cutlets and bread, pulled up a light table, and placed them before his guest. 'Never mind knives,' said his visitor, and a cutlet hung in mid-air, with a sound of gnawing.

'Invisible!' said Kemp, and sat down on a bedroom chair.

'I always like to get something about me before I eat,' said the Invisible Man, with a full mouth, eating greedily. 'Queer fancy!'

'I suppose that wrist is all right,' said Kemp.

'Trust me,' said the Invisible Man.

'Of *all* the strange and wonderful – '

'Exactly. But it's odd I should blunder into *your* house to get my bandaging. My first stroke of luck! Anyhow I meant to sleep in this house tonight. You must stand that! It's a filthy nuisance, my blood showing, isn't it? Quite a clot over there. Gets visible as it coagulates, I see. It's only the living tissue I've changed, and only for as long as I'm alive . . . I've been in the house three hours.'

'But how's it done?' began Kemp, in a tone of exasperation. 'Confound it! The whole business – it's unreasonable from beginning to end.'

'Quite reasonable,' said the Invisible Man. 'Perfectly reasonable.' He reached over and secured the whisky bottle.

Kemp stared at the devouring dressing-gown. A ray of candlelight, penetrating a torn patch in the right shoulder, made a triangle of light under the left ribs. 'What were the shots?' he asked. 'How did the shooting begin?'

'There was a real fool of a man – a sort of confederate of mine – curse him! – who tried to steal my money. *Has* done so.'

'Is *he* invisible too?'

'No.'

'Well?'

'Can't I have some more to eat before I tell you all that? I'm hungry – in pain. And you want me to tell stories!'

Kemp got up. '*You* didn't do any shooting?' he asked.

'Not me,' said his visitor. 'Some fool I'd never seen fired at random. A lot of them got scared. They all got scared at me. Curse them! – I say – I want more to eat than this, Kemp.'

'I'll see what more there is to eat downstairs,' said Kemp. 'Not much, I'm afraid.'

After he had done eating, and he made a heavy meal, the Invisible Man demanded a cigar. He bit the end savagely before Kemp could find a knife, and cursed when the outer leaf loosened. It was strange to see him smoking; his mouth and throat, pharynx and nares, became visible as a sort of whirling smoke cast.

'This blessed gift of smoking!' he said, and puffed vigorously. 'I'm lucky to have fallen upon you, Kemp. You must help me. Fancy tumbling on you just now! I'm in a devilish scrape – I've been mad, I think. The things I have been through! But we will do things yet. Let me tell you – '

He helped himself to more whisky and soda. Kemp got up, looked about him, and fetched a glass from his spare room. 'It's wild – but I suppose I may drink.'

'You haven't changed much, Kemp, these dozen years. You fair men don't. Cool and methodical – after the first collapse. I must tell you. We will work together!'

'But how was it all done?' said Kemp, 'and how did you get like this?'

'For God's sake, let me smoke in peace for a little while! And then I will begin to tell you.'

But the story was not told that night. The Invisible Man's wrist was growing painful; he was feverish, exhausted, and his mind came round to brood upon his chase down the hill and the struggle about the inn. He spoke in fragments of Marvel, he smoked faster, his voice grew angry. Kemp tried to gather what he could.

'He was afraid of me, I could see that he was afraid of me,' said the Invisible Man many times over. 'He meant to give me the slip – he was always casting about! What a fool I was!

'The cur!

'I should have killed him!'

'Where did you get the money?' asked Kemp, abruptly.

The Invisible Man was silent for a space. 'I can't tell you tonight,' he said.

He groaned suddenly and leant forward, supporting his invisible head on invisible hands. 'Kemp,' he said, 'I've had no sleep for near three days, except a couple of dozes of an hour or so. I must sleep soon.'

'Well, have my room – have this room.'

'But how can I sleep? If I sleep – he will get away. Ugh! What does it matter?'

'What's the shot wound?' asked Kemp, abruptly.

'Nothing – scratch and blood. Oh, God! How I want sleep!'

'Why not?'

The Invisible Man appeared to be regarding Kemp. 'Because I've a particular objection to being caught by my fellow men,' he said slowly.

Kemp started.

'Fool that I am!' said the Invisible Man, striking the table smartly. 'I've put the idea into your head.'

CHAPTER 18

The Invisible Man Sleeps

Exhausted and wounded as the Invisible Man was, he refused to accept Kemp's word that his freedom should be respected. He examined the two windows of the bedroom, drew up the blinds and opened the sashes, to confirm Kemp's statement that a retreat by them would be possible. Outside the night was very quiet and still, and the new moon was setting over the down. Then he examined the keys of the bedroom and the two dressing-room doors, to satisfy himself that these also could be made an assurance of freedom. Finally he expressed himself satisfied. He stood on the hearth rug and Kemp heard the sound of a yawn.

'I'm sorry,' said the Invisible Man, 'if I cannot tell you all that I have done tonight. But I am worn out. It's grotesque, no doubt. It's horrible! But believe me, Kemp, in spite of your arguments of this morning, it is quite a possible thing. I have made a discovery. I meant to keep it to myself. I can't. I must have a partner. And you . . . We can do such things . . . But tomorrow. Now, Kemp, I feel as though I must sleep or perish.'

Kemp stood in the middle of the room staring at the headless garment. 'I suppose I must leave you,' he said. 'It's – incredible. Three things happening like this, overturning all my preconceptions – would make me insane. But it's real! Is there anything more that I can get you?'

'Only bid me good-night,' said Griffin.

'Good-night,' said Kemp, and shook an invisible hand. He walked sideways to the door. Suddenly the dressing-gown walked quickly towards him. 'Understand me!' said the dressing-gown. 'No attempts to hamper me, or capture me! Or – '

Kemp's face changed a little. 'I thought I gave you my word,' he said.

Kemp closed the door softly behind him, and the key was turned upon him forthwith. Then, as he stood with an expression of passive amazement on his face, the rapid feet came to the door of the dressing-room and that too was locked. Kemp slapped his brow with his hand. 'Am I dreaming? Has the world gone mad – or have I?'

He laughed, and put his hand to the locked door. 'Barred out of my own bedroom, by a flagrant absurdity!' he said.

He walked to the head of the staircase, turned, and stared at the locked doors. 'It's fact,' he said. He put his fingers to his slightly bruised neck. 'Undeniable fact!

'But –'

He shook his head hopelessly, turned, and went downstairs.

He lit the dining-room lamp, got out a cigar, and began pacing the room, ejaculating. Now and then he would argue with himself.

'Invisible!' he said.

'Is there such a thing as an invisible animal? . . . In the sea, yes. Thousands – millions. All the larvae, all the little nauplii and tornarias, all the microscopic things, the jellyfish. In the sea there are more things invisible than visible! I never thought of that before. And in the ponds too! All those little pond-life things – specks of colourless translucent jelly! But in air? No!

'It can't be.

'But after all – why not?

'If a man was made of glass he would still be visible.'

His meditation became profound. The bulk of three cigars had passed into the invisible or diffused as a white ash over the carpet before he spoke again. Then it was merely an exclamation. He turned aside, walked out of the room, and went into his little consulting-room and lit the gas there. It was a little room, because Dr Kemp did not live by practice, and in it were the day's newspapers. The morning's paper lay carelessly opened and thrown aside. He caught it up, turned it over, and read the account of a 'Strange Story from Iping' that the mariner at Port Stowe had spelt over so painfully to Mr Marvel. Kemp read it swiftly.

'Wrapped up!' said Kemp. 'Disguised! Hiding it! "No one seems to have been aware of his misfortune." What the devil *is* his game?'

He dropped the paper, and his eye went seeking. 'Ah!' he said, and caught up the *St James's Gazette*,[12] lying folded up as it arrived. 'Now we shall get at the truth,' said Dr Kemp. He rent the paper open; a couple of columns confronted him. 'An Entire Village in Sussex goes Mad' was the heading.

'Good heavens!' said Kemp, reading eagerly an incredulous account of the events in Iping of the previous afternoon that have already been described. Over the leaf the report in the morning paper had been reprinted.

He re-read it. 'Ran through the streets striking right and left. Jaffers insensible. Mr Huxter in great pain – still unable to describe what he saw. Painful humiliation – vicar. Woman ill with terror! Windows smashed. This extraordinary story probably a fabrication. Too good not to print – *cum grano*!'[13]

He dropped the paper and stared blankly in front of him. 'Probably a fabrication!'

He caught up the paper again, and re-read the whole business. 'But when does the tramp come in? Why the deuce was he chasing a tramp?'

He sat down abruptly on the surgical bench. 'He's not only invisible,' he said, 'but he's mad! Homicidal!'

When dawn came to mingle its pallor with the lamplight and cigar smoke of the dining-room, Kemp was still pacing up and down, trying to grasp the incredible.

He was altogether too excited to sleep. His servants, descending sleepily, discovered him, and were inclined to think that over-study had worked this ill on him. He gave them extraordinary but quite explicit instructions to lay breakfast for two in the belvedere study – and then to confine themselves to the basement and ground-floor. Then he continued to pace the dining-room until the morning's paper came. That had much to say and little to tell, beyond the confirmation of the evening before, and a very badly written account of another remarkable tale from Port Burdock. This gave Kemp the essence of the happenings at the Jolly Cricketers, and the name of Marvel. 'He has made me keep with him twenty-four hours,' Marvel testified. Certain minor facts were added to the Iping story, notably the cutting of the village telegraph-wire. But there was nothing to throw light on the connection between the Invisible Man and the tramp; for Mr Marvel had supplied no information about the three books, or the money with which he was lined. The incredulous tone had vanished and a shoal of reporters and enquirers were already at work elaborating the matter.

Kemp read every scrap of the report and sent his housemaid out to get every one of the morning papers she could. These also he devoured.

'He is invisible!' he said. 'And it reads like rage growing to mania! The things he may do! The things he may do! And he's upstairs free as the air. What on earth ought I to do?

'For instance, would it be a breach of faith if – ? No.'

He went to a little untidy desk in the corner, and began a note. He tore this up half written, and wrote another. He read it over and considered it. Then he took an envelope and addressed it to 'Colonel Adye, Port Burdock'.

The Invisible Man awoke even as Kemp was doing this. He awoke in an evil temper, and Kemp, alert for every sound, heard his pattering feet rush suddenly across the bedroom overhead. Then a chair was flung over and the wash-hand-stand tumbler smashed. Kemp hurried upstairs and rapped eagerly.

CHAPTER 19

Certain First Principles

'What's the matter?' asked Kemp, when the Invisible Man admitted him.

'Nothing,' was the answer.

'But, confound it! The smash?'

'Fit of temper,' said the Invisible Man. 'Forgot this arm; and it's sore.'

'You're rather liable to that sort of thing.'

'I am.'

Kemp walked across the room and picked up the fragments of broken glass. 'All the facts are out about you,' said Kemp, standing up with the glass in his hand; 'all that happened in Iping, and down the hill. The world has become aware of its invisible citizen. But no one knows you are here.'

The Invisible Man swore.

'The secret's out. I gather it was a secret. I don't know what your plans are, but of course I'm anxious to help you.'

The Invisible Man sat down on the bed.

'There's breakfast upstairs,' said Kemp, speaking as easily as possible, and he was delighted to find his strange guest rose willingly. Kemp led the way up the narrow staircase to the belvedere.

'Before we can do anything else,' said Kemp, 'I must understand a little more about this invisibility of yours.' He had sat down, after one nervous glance out of the window, with the air of a man who has talking to do. His doubts of the sanity of the entire business flashed and vanished again as he looked across to where Griffin sat at the breakfast-table – a headless, handless dressing-gown, wiping unseen lips on a miraculously held serviette.

'It's simple enough – and credible enough,' said Griffin, putting the serviette aside and leaning the invisible head on an invisible hand.

'No doubt, to you, but – ' Kemp laughed.

'Well, yes; to me it seemed wonderful at first, no doubt. But now, great God! . . . But we will do great things yet! I came on the stuff first at Chesilstowe.'[14]

'Chesilstowe?'

'I went there after I left London. You know I dropped medicine and took up physics? No; well, I did. *Light* fascinated me.'

'Ah!'

'Optical density! The whole subject is a network of riddles – a network with solutions glimmering elusively through. And being but two-and-twenty and full of enthusiasm, I said, "I will devote my life to this. This is worth while." You know what fools we are at two-and-twenty?'

'Fools then or fools now,' said Kemp.

'As though knowing could be any satisfaction to a man!

'But I went to work – like a slave. And I had hardly worked and thought about the matter six months before light came through one of the meshes suddenly – blindingly! I found a general principle of pigments and refraction – a formula, a geometrical expression involving four dimensions. Fools, common men, even common mathematicians, do not know anything of what some general expression may mean to the student of molecular physics. In the books – the books that tramp has hidden – there are marvels, miracles! But this was not a method, it was an idea, that might lead to a method by which it would be possible, without changing any other property of matter – except, in some instances colours – to lower the refractive index of a substance, solid or liquid, to that of air – so far as all practical purposes are concerned.'

'Phew!' said Kemp. 'That's odd! But still I don't see quite . . . I can understand that thereby you could spoil a valuable stone, but personal invisibility is a far cry.'

'Precisely,' said Griffin. 'But consider, visibility depends on the action of the visible bodies on light. Either a body absorbs light, or it reflects or refracts it, or does all these things. If it neither reflects nor refracts nor absorbs light, it cannot of itself be visible. You see an opaque red box, for instance, because the colour absorbs some of the light and reflects the rest, all the red part of the light, to you. If it did not absorb any particular part of the light, but reflected it all, then it would be a shining white box. Silver! A diamond box would neither absorb much of the light nor reflect much from the general surface, but just here and there where the surfaces were favourable the light would be reflected and refracted, so that you would get a brilliant appearance of flashing reflections and translucencies – a sort of skeleton of light. A glass box would not be so brilliant, nor so clearly visible, as a diamond box, because there would be less refraction and reflection. See that? From certain points of view you would see quite clearly through it. Some kinds of glass would be more visible than others, a box of flint glass would be brighter than a box of ordinary window glass. A box of very thin common glass would be hard to see in a bad light, because it would absorb hardly any light and refract and reflect very little. And if you put a sheet of common white glass in water, still more if you put it in some denser liquid than water, it would vanish almost altogether, because light passing from water to glass is only slightly refracted or reflected or indeed affected in any way. It is almost as invisible as a jet of coal gas or hydrogen is in air. And for precisely the same reason!'

'Yes,' said Kemp, 'that is pretty plain sailing.'

'And here is another fact you will know to be true. If a sheet of glass is smashed, Kemp, and beaten into a powder, it becomes much more visible while it is in the air; it becomes at last an opaque white powder. This is because the powdering multiplies the surfaces of the glass at which refraction and reflection occur. In the sheet of glass there are only two surfaces; in the powder the light is reflected or refracted by each grain it passes through, and very little gets right through the powder. But if the white powdered glass is put into water, it forthwith vanishes. The powdered glass and water have much the same refractive index; that is, the light undergoes very little refraction or reflection in passing from one to the other.

'You make the glass invisible by putting it into a liquid of nearly the same refractive index; a transparent thing becomes invisible if it is put in any medium of almost the same refractive index. And if you will consider only a second, you will see also that the powder of glass might be made to vanish in air, if its refractive index could be made the same as that of air; for then there would be no refraction or reflection as the light passed from glass to air.'

'Yes, yes,' said Kemp. 'But a man's not powdered glass!'

'No,' said Griffin. 'He's more transparent!'

'Nonsense!'

'That from a doctor! How one forgets! Have you already forgotten your physics, in ten years? Just think of all the things that are transparent and seem not to be so. Paper, for instance, is made up of transparent fibres, and it is white and opaque only for the same reason that a powder of glass is white and opaque. Oil white paper, fill up the interstices between the particles with oil so that there is no longer refraction or reflection except at the surfaces, and it becomes as transparent as glass. And not only paper, but cotton fibre, linen fibre, wool fibre, woody fibre, and *bone*, Kemp, *flesh*, Kemp, *hair*, Kemp, *nails* and *nerves*, Kemp, in fact the whole fabric of a man except the red of his blood and the black pigment of hair, are all made up of transparent, colourless tissue. So little suffices to make us visible one to the other. For the most part the fibres of a living creature are no more opaque than water.'

'Great heavens!' cried Kemp. 'Of course, of course! I was thinking only last night of the sea larvae and all jellyfish!'

'*Now* you have me! And all that I knew and had in mind a year after I left London – six years ago. But I kept it to myself. I had to do my work under frightful disadvantages. Oliver, my professor, was a scientific bounder, a journalist by instinct, a thief of ideas – he was always prying! And you know the knavish system of the scientific world. I simply would not publish and let him share my credit. I went on working; I got nearer and nearer making my formula into an experiment, a reality. I told no living soul, because I meant to flash my work upon the world with crushing effect and become famous at a blow. I took up the question of pigments to fill up certain gaps. And suddenly, not by design but by accident, I made a discovery in physiology.'

'Yes?'

'You know the red colouring matter of blood; it can be made white – colourless – and remain with all the functions it has now!'

Kemp gave a cry of incredulous amazement.

The Invisible Man rose and began pacing the little study. 'You may well exclaim. I remember that night. It was late at night – in the daytime one was bothered with the gaping, silly students – and I worked then sometimes till dawn. It came suddenly, splendid and complete into my mind. I was alone; the laboratory was still, with the tall lights burning brightly and silently. In all my great moments I have been alone. "One could make an animal – a tissue – transparent! One could make it invisible! All except the pigments. I could be invisible!" I said, suddenly realising what it meant to be an albino with such knowledge. It was overwhelming. I left the filtering I was doing, and went and stared out of the great window at the stars. "I could be invisible!" I repeated.

'To do such a thing would be to transcend magic. And I beheld, unclouded by doubt, a magnificent vision of all that invisibility might mean to a man – the mystery, the power, the freedom. Drawbacks I saw none. You have only to think! And I, a shabby, poverty-struck, hemmed-in demonstrator, teaching fools in a provincial college, might suddenly become – this. I ask you, Kemp, if *you* . . . Anyone, I tell you, would have flung himself upon that research. And I worked three years, and every mountain of difficulty I toiled over showed another from its summit. The infinite details! And the exasperation! A professor, a provincial professor, always prying. "When are you going to publish this work of yours?" was his everlasting question. And the students, the cramped means! Three years I had of it –

'And after three years of secrecy and exasperation, I found that to complete it was impossible – impossible.'

'How?' asked Kemp.

'Money,' said the Invisible Man, and went again to stare out of the window.

He turned around abruptly. 'I robbed the old man – robbed my father.

'The money was not his, and he shot himself.'

CHAPTER 20

At the House in Great Portland Street

For a moment Kemp sat in silence, staring at the back of the headless figure at the window. Then he started, struck by a thought, rose, took the Invisible Man's arm, and turned him away from the outlook.

'You are tired,' he said, 'and while I sit, you walk about. Have my chair.'

He placed himself between Griffin and the nearest window.

For a space Griffin sat silent, and then he resumed abruptly: 'I had left the Chesilstowe cottage already,' he said, 'when that happened. It was last December. I had taken a room in London, a large unfurnished room in a big ill-managed lodging-house in a slum near Great Portland Street. The room was soon full of the appliances I had bought with his money; the work was going on steadily, successfully, drawing near an end. I was like a man emerging from a thicket, and suddenly coming on some unmeaning tragedy. I went to bury him. My mind was still on this research, and I did not lift a finger to save his character. I remember the funeral, the cheap hearse, the scant ceremony, the windy frost-bitten hillside, and the old college friend of his who read the service over him – a shabby, black, bent old man with a snivelling cold.

'I remember walking back to the empty house, through the place that had once been a village and was now patched and tinkered by the jerry builders into the ugly likeness of a town. Every way the roads ran out at last into the desecrated fields and ended in rubble heaps and rank wet weeds. I remember myself as a gaunt black figure, going along the slippery, shiny pavement, and the strange sense of detachment I felt from the squalid respectability, the sordid commercialism of the place.

'I did not feel a bit sorry for my father. He seemed to me to be the victim of his own foolish sentimentality. The current cant required my attendance at his funeral, but it was really not my affair.

'But going along the High Street, my old life came back to me for a space, for I met the girl I had known ten years since. Our eyes met.

'Something moved me to turn back and talk to her. She was a very ordinary person.

'It was all like a dream, that visit to the old places. I did not feel then that I was lonely, that I had come out from the world into a desolate place. I appreciated my loss of sympathy, but I put it down to the general inanity of things. Re-entering my room seemed like the recovery of reality. There were the things I knew and loved. There stood the apparatus, the experiments arranged and waiting. And now there was scarcely a difficulty left, beyond the planning of details.

'I will tell you, Kemp, sooner or later, all the complicated processes. We need not go into that now. For the most part, saving certain gaps I chose to remember, they are written in cypher in those books that tramp has hidden. We must hunt him down. We must get those books again. But the essential phase was to place the transparent object whose refractive index was to be lowered between two radiating centres of a sort of ethereal vibration, of which I will tell you more fully later. No, not those Roentgën vibrations[15] – I don't know that these others of mine have been described. Yet they are obvious enough. I needed two little dynamos, and these I worked with a cheap gas engine. My first experiment was with a bit of white wool fabric. It was the strangest thing in the world to see it in the flicker of the flashes soft and white, and then to watch it fade like a wreath of smoke and vanish.

'I could scarcely believe I had done it. I put my hand into the emptiness, and there was the thing as solid as ever. I felt it awkwardly, and threw it on the floor. I had a little trouble finding it again.

'And then came a curious experience. I heard a miaow behind me, and turning, saw a lean white cat, very dirty, on the cistern cover outside the window. A thought came into my head. "Everything ready for you," I said, and went to the window, opened it, and called softly. She came in, purring – the poor beast was starving, and I gave her some milk. All my food was in a cupboard in the corner of the room. After that she went smelling round the room, evidently with the idea of making herself at home. The invisible rag upset her a bit; you should have seen her spit at it! But I made her comfortable on the pillow of my truckle-bed. And I gave her butter to get her to wash.'

'And you processed her?'

'I processed her. But giving drugs to a cat is no joke, Kemp! And the process failed.'

'Failed!'

'In two particulars. These were the claws and the pigment stuff, what is it? – at the back of the eye in a cat. You know?'

'*Tapetum*.'[16]

'Yes, the *tapetum*. It didn't go. After I'd given the stuff to bleach the blood and done certain other things to her, I gave the beast opium, and put her and the pillow she was sleeping on, on the apparatus. And after all the rest had faded and vanished, there remained two little ghosts of her eyes.'

'Odd!'

'I can't explain it. She was bandaged and clamped, of course – so I had her safe; but she woke while she was still misty, and miaowed dismally, and someone came knocking. It was an old woman from downstairs, who suspected me of vivisecting – a drink-sodden old creature, with only a white cat to care for in all the world. I whipped out some chloroform, applied it, and answered the door. "Did I hear a cat?" she asked. "My cat?" "Not here," said I, very politely. She was a little doubtful and tried to peer past me into the room; strange enough to her no doubt – bare walls, uncurtained windows, truckle-bed, with the gas engine vibrating, and the seethe of the radiant points, and that faint ghastly stinging of chloroform in the air. She had to be satisfied at last and went away again.'

'How long did it take?' asked Kemp.

'Three or four hours – the cat. The bones and sinews and the fat were the last to go, and the tips of the coloured hairs. And, as I say, the back part of the eye, tough, iridescent stuff it is, wouldn't go at all.

'It was night outside long before the business was over, and nothing was to be seen but the dim eyes and the claws. I stopped the gas engine, felt for and stroked the beast, which was still insensible, and then, being tired, left it sleeping on the invisible pillow and went to bed. I found it hard to sleep. I lay awake thinking weak aimless stuff, going over the experiment over and over again, or dreaming feverishly of things growing misty and vanishing about me, until everything, the ground I stood on, vanished, and so I came to that sickly falling nightmare one gets. About two, the cat began miaowing about the room. I tried to hush it by talking to it, and then I decided to turn it out. I remember the shock I had when striking a light – there were just the round eyes shining green – and nothing round them. I would have given it milk, but I hadn't any. It wouldn't be quiet, it just sat down and miaowed at the door. I tried to catch it, with an idea of putting it out of the window, but it wouldn't be caught, it vanished. Then it began miaowing in different parts of the room. At last I opened the window and made a bustle. I suppose it went out at last. I never saw any more of it.

'Then – heaven knows why – I fell to thinking of my father's funeral again, and the dismal windy hillside, until the day had come. I found sleeping was hopeless, and, locking my door after me, wandered out into the morning streets.'

'You don't mean to say there's an invisible cat at large!' said Kemp.

'If it hasn't been killed,' said the Invisible Man. 'Why not?'

'Why not?' said Kemp. 'I didn't mean to interrupt.'

'It's very probably been killed,' said the Invisible Man. 'It was alive four days after, I know, and down a grating in Great Titchfield Street; because I saw a crowd round the place, trying to see whence the miaowing came.'

He was silent for the best part of a minute. Then he resumed abruptly: 'I remember that morning before the change very vividly. I must have gone up Great Portland Street. I remember the barracks in Albany Street, and the horse soldiers coming out, and at last I found the summit of Primrose Hill. It was a sunny day in January – one of those sunny, frosty days that came before the snow this year. My weary brain tried to formulate the position, to plot out a plan of action.

'I was surprised to find, now that my prize was within my grasp, how inconclusive its attainment seemed. As a matter of fact I was worked out; the intense stress of nearly four years' continuous work left me incapable of any strength of feeling. I was apathetic, and I tried in vain to recover the enthusiasm of my first enquiries, the passion of discovery that had enabled me to compass even the downfall of my father's grey hairs. Nothing seemed to matter. I saw pretty clearly this was a transient mood, due to overwork and want of sleep, and that either by drugs or rest it would be possible to recover my energies.

'All I could think clearly was that the thing had to be carried through; the fixed idea still ruled me. And soon, for the money I had was almost exhausted. I looked about me at the hillside, with children playing and girls watching them, and tried to think of all the fantastic advantages an invisible man would have in the world. After a time I crawled home, took some food and a strong dose of strychnine, and went to sleep in my clothes on my unmade bed. Strychnine is a grand tonic, Kemp, to take the flabbiness out of a man.'

'It's the devil,' said Kemp. 'It's the palaeolithic in a bottle.'

'I awoke vastly invigorated and rather irritable. You know?'

'I know the stuff.'

'And there was someone rapping at the door. It was my landlord with threats and enquiries, an old Polish Jew in a long grey coat and greasy slippers. I had been tormenting a cat in the night, he was sure – the old woman's tongue had been busy. He insisted on knowing all about it. The laws in this country against vivisection were very severe – he might be liable. I denied the cat. Then the vibration of the little gas engine could be felt all over the house, he said. That was true, certainly. He edged round me into the room, peering about over his German-silver spectacles, and a sudden dread came into my mind that he might carry away something of my secret. I tried to keep between him and the concentrating apparatus I had arranged, and that only made him more curious. What was I doing? Why was I always alone and secretive? Was it legal? Was it dangerous? I paid nothing but the usual rent. His had always been a most respectable house – in a disreputable neighbourhood. Suddenly my temper gave way. I told him to get out. He began to protest, to jabber of his right of entry. In a moment I had him by the collar; something ripped and he went spinning out into his own passage. I slammed and locked the door and sat down quivering.

'He made a fuss outside, which I disregarded, and after a time he went away.

'But this brought matters to a crisis. I did not know what he would do, nor even what he had the power to do. To move to fresh apartments would have meant delay; altogether I had barely twenty pounds left in the world, for the most part in a bank – and I could not afford that. Vanish! It was irresistible. Then there would be an inquiry, the sacking of my room.

'At the thought of the possibility of my work being exposed or interrupted at its very climax, I became very angry and active. I hurried out with my three books of notes, my chequebook – the tramp has them now – and directed them from the nearest Post Office to a house of call for letters and parcels in Great Portland Street. I tried to go out noiselessly. Coming in, I found my landlord going quietly upstairs; he had heard the door close, I suppose. You would have laughed to see him jump aside on the landing as I came tearing after him. He glared at me as I went by him, and I made the house quiver with the slamming of my door. I heard him come shuffling up to my floor, hesitate, and go down. I set to work upon my preparations forthwith.

'It was all done that evening and night. While I was still sitting under the sickly, drowsy influence of the drugs that decolourise blood, there came a repeated knocking at the door. It ceased, footsteps went away and returned, and the knocking was resumed. There was an attempt to push something under the door – a blue paper. Then in a fit of irritation I rose and went and flung the door wide open. "Now then?" said I.

'It was my landlord, with a notice of ejectment or something. He held it out to me, saw something odd about my hands, I expect, and lifted his eyes to my face.

'For a moment he gaped. Then he gave a sort of inarticulate cry, dropped candle and writ together, and went blundering down the dark passage to the stairs. I shut the door, locked it, and went to

the looking-glass. Then I understood his terror . . . My face was white –
like white stone.

'But it was all horrible. I had not expected the suffering. A night of
racking anguish, sickness and fainting. I set my teeth, though my skin
was presently afire, all my body afire; but I lay there like grim death. I
understood now how it was the cat had howled until I chloroformed it.
Lucky it was I lived alone and untended in my room. There were times
when I sobbed and groaned and talked. But I stuck to it . . . I became
insensible and woke languid in the darkness.

'The pain had passed. I thought I was killing myself and I did not
care. I shall never forget that dawn, and the strange horror of seeing
that my hands had become as clouded glass, and watching them grow
clearer and thinner as the day went by, until at last I could see the sickly
disorder of my room through them, though I closed my transparent
eyelids. My limbs became glassy, the bones and arteries faded, vanished,
and the little white nerves went last. I gritted my teeth and stayed there
to the end. At last only the dead tips of the fingernails remained, pallid
and white, and the brown stain of some acid upon my fingers.

'I struggled up. At first I was as incapable as a swathed infant –
stepping with limbs I could not see. I was weak and very hungry. I went
and stared at nothing in my shaving-glass, at nothing save where an
attenuated pigment still remained behind the retina of my eyes, fainter
than mist. I had to hang on to the table and press my forehead against
the glass.

'It was only by a frantic effort of will that I dragged myself back to the
apparatus and completed the process.

'I slept during the forenoon, pulling the sheet over my eyes to shut
out the light, and about midday I was awakened again by a knocking.
My strength had returned. I sat up and listened and heard a whispering.
I sprang to my feet and as noiselessly as possible began to detach the
connections of my apparatus, and to distribute it about the room, so as
to destroy the suggestions of its arrangement. Presently the knocking
was renewed and voices called, first my landlord's, and then two others.
To gain time I answered them. The invisible rag and pillow came to
hand and I opened the window and pitched them out on to the cistern
cover. As the window opened, a heavy crash came at the door. Someone
had charged it with the idea of smashing the lock. But the stout bolts I
had screwed up some days before stopped him. That startled me, made
me angry. I began to tremble and do things hurriedly.

'I tossed together some loose paper, straw, packing paper and so
forth, in the middle of the room, and turned on the gas. Heavy blows

began to rain upon the door. I could not find the matches. I beat my hands on the wall with rage. I turned down the gas again, stepped out of the window on to the cistern cover, very softly lowered the sash, and sat down, secure and invisible, but quivering with anger, to watch events. They split a panel, I saw, and in another moment they had broken away the staples of the bolts and stood in the open doorway. It was the landlord and his two stepsons, sturdy young men of three or four and twenty. Behind them fluttered the old hag of a woman from downstairs.

'You may imagine their astonishment to find the room empty. One of the younger men rushed to the window at once, flung it up and stared out. His staring eyes and thick-lipped bearded face came a foot from my face. I was half minded to hit his silly countenance, but I arrested my doubled fist. He stared right through me. So did the others as they joined him. The old man went and peered under the bed, and then they all made a rush for the cupboard. They had to argue about it at length in Yiddish and cockney English. They concluded I had not answered them, that their imagination had deceived them. A feeling of extraordinary elation took the place of my anger as I sat outside the window and watched these four people – for the old lady came in, glancing suspiciously about her like a cat, trying to understand the riddle of my behaviour.

'The old man, so far as I could understand his *patois*, agreed with the old lady that I was a vivisectionist. The sons protested in garbled English that I was an electrician, and appealed to the dynamos and radiators. They were all nervous about my arrival, although I found subsequently that they had bolted the front door. The old lady peered into the cupboard and under the bed, and one of the young men pushed up the register and stared up the chimney. One of my fellow lodgers, a costermonger who shared the opposite room with a butcher, appeared on the landing, and he was called in and told incoherent things.

'It occurred to me that the radiators, if they fell into the hands of some acute well-educated person, would give me away too much, and watching my opportunity, I came into the room and tilted one of the little dynamos off its fellow on which it was standing, and smashed both apparatus. Then, while they were trying to explain the smash, I dodged out of the room and went softly downstairs.

'I went into one of the sitting-rooms and waited until they came down, still speculating and argumentative, all a little disappointed at finding no "horrors", and all a little puzzled how they stood legally towards me. Then I slipped up again with a box of matches, fired my heap of paper and rubbish, put the chairs and bedding thereby, led the gas to the affair, by means of an india-rubber tube, and waving a farewell to the room left it for the last time.'

'You fired the house!' exclaimed Kemp.

'Fired the house. It was the only way to cover my trail – and no doubt it was insured. I slipped the bolts of the front door quietly and went out into the street. I was invisible, and I was only just beginning to realise the extraordinary advantage my invisibility gave me. My head was already teeming with plans of all the wild and wonderful things I had now impunity to do.'

CHAPTER 21

In Oxford Street

'In going downstairs the first time I found an unexpected difficulty because I could not see my feet; indeed I stumbled twice, and there was an unaccustomed clumsiness in gripping the bolt. By not looking down, however, I managed to walk on the level passably well.

'My mood, I say, was one of exaltation. I felt as a seeing man might do, with padded feet and noiseless clothes, in a city of the blind. I experienced a wild impulse to jest, to startle people, to clap men on the back, fling people's hats astray, and generally revel in my extraordinary advantage.

'But hardly had I emerged upon Great Portland Street, however (my lodging was close to the big draper's shop there), when I heard a clashing concussion and was hit violently behind, and turning saw a man carrying a basket of soda-water syphons, and looking in amazement at his burden. Although the blow had really hurt me, I found something so irresistible in his astonishment that I laughed aloud. "The devil's in the basket," I said, and suddenly twisted it out of his hand. He let go incontinently, and I swung the whole weight into the air.

'But a fool of a cabman, standing outside a public house, made a sudden rush for this, and his extending fingers took me with excruciating violence under the ear. I let the whole down with a smash on the cabman, and then, with shouts and the clatter of feet about me, people coming out of shops, vehicles pulling up, I realised what I had done for myself, and cursing my folly, backed against a shop window and prepared to dodge out of the confusion. In a moment I should be wedged into a crowd and inevitably discovered. I pushed by a butcher boy, who luckily did not turn to see the nothingness that shoved him aside, and dodged behind the cabman's four-wheeler. I do not know how they settled the business. I hurried straight across the road, which was happily clear, and hardly heeding which way I went, in the fright of detection the incident had given me, plunged into the afternoon throng of Oxford Street.

'I tried to get into the stream of people, but they were too thick for me, and in a moment my heels were being trodden upon. I took to the gutter, the roughness of which I found painful to my feet, and forthwith the shaft of a crawling hansom dug me forcibly under the shoulder blade, reminding me that I was already bruised severely. I staggered out of the way of the cab, avoided a perambulator by a convulsive movement, and found myself behind the hansom. A happy thought saved me, and as this drove slowly along I followed in its immediate wake, trembling and astonished at the turn of my adventure. And not only trembling, but shivering. It was a bright day in January and I was stark naked and the thin slime of mud that covered the road was freezing. Foolish as it seems to me now, I had not reckoned that, transparent or not, I was still amenable to the weather and all its consequences.

'Then suddenly a bright idea came into my head. I ran round and got into the cab. And so, shivering, scared, and sniffing with the first intimations of a cold, and with the bruises in the small of my back growing upon my attention, I drove slowly along Oxford Street and past Tottenham Court Road. My mood was as different from that in which I had sallied forth ten minutes ago as it is possible to imagine. This invisibility indeed! The one thought that possessed me was – how was I to get out of the scrape I was in.

'We crawled past Mudie's,[17] and there a tall woman with five or six yellow-labelled books hailed my cab, and I sprang out just in time to escape her, shaving a railway van narrowly in my flight. I made off up the roadway to Bloomsbury Square, intending to strike north past the Museum and so get into the quiet district. I was now cruelly chilled, and the strangeness of my situation so unnerved me that I whimpered as I ran. At the northward corner of the square a little white dog ran out of the Pharmaceutical Society's offices, and incontinently made for me, nose down.

'I had never realised it before, but the nose is to the mind of a dog what the eye is to the mind of a seeing man. Dogs perceive the scent of a man moving as men perceive his vision. This brute began barking and leaping, showing, as it seemed to me, only too plainly that he was aware of me. I crossed Great Russell Street, glancing over my shoulder as I did so, and went some way along Montague Street before I realised what I was running towards.

'Then I became aware of a blare of music, and looking along the street saw a number of people advancing out of Russell Square, red shirts, and the banner of the Salvation Army to the fore. Such a crowd, chanting in the roadway and scoffing on the pavement, I could not hope to penetrate, and dreading to go back and farther from home again, and deciding on the spur of the moment, I ran up the white steps of a house facing the museum railings, and stood there until the crowd should have passed. Happily the dog stopped at the noise of the band too, hesitated, and turned tail, running back to Bloomsbury Square again.

'On came the band, bawling with unconscious irony some hymn about "When shall we see His face?" and it seemed an interminable time to me before the tide of the crowd had washed along the pavement by me. Thud, thud, thud, came the drum with a vibrating resonance, and for the moment I did not notice two urchins stopping at the railings by me. "See 'em," said one. "See what?" said the other. "Why – them footmarks – *bare*. Like what you makes in mud."

'I looked down and saw the youngsters had stopped and were gaping at the muddy footmarks I had left behind me up the newly whitened steps. The passing people elbowed and jostled them, but their confounded intelligence was arrested. "Thud, thud, thud, When, thud, shall we see, thud, His face, thud, thud." "There's a barefoot man gone up them steps, or I don't know nothing," said one. "And he ain't never come down again. And his foot was a-bleeding."

'The thick of the crowd had already passed. "Looky there, Ted," quoth the younger of the detectives, with the sharpness of surprise in his voice, and pointed straight to my feet. I looked down and saw at once the dim suggestion of their outline sketched in splashes of mud. For a moment I was paralysed.

' "Why, that's rum," said the elder. "Dashed rum! It's just like the ghost of a foot, ain't it?" He hesitated and advanced with outstretched hand. A man pulled up short to see what he was catching, and then a girl. In another moment he would have touched me. Then I saw what to do. I made a step, the boy started back with an exclamation, and with a rapid movement I swung myself over into the portico of the next house. But the smaller boy was sharp-eyed enough to follow the movement, and before I was well down the steps and upon the pavement, he had recovered from his momentary astonishment and was shouting out that the feet had gone over the wall.

'They rushed round and saw my new footmarks flash into being on the lower step and upon the pavement. "What's up?" asked someone. "Feet! Look! Feet running!"

'Everybody in the road, except my three pursuers, was pouring along after the Salvation Army, and this blow not only impeded me but them. There was an eddy of surprise and interrogation. At the cost of bowling over one young fellow I got through, and in another moment I was rushing headlong round the circuit of Russell Square, with six or seven astonished people following my footmarks. There was no time for explanation, or else the whole host would have been after me.

'Twice I doubled round corners, thrice I crossed the road and came back upon my tracks, and then, as my feet grew hot and dry, the damp impressions began to fade. At last I had a breathing space and rubbed my feet clean with my hands, and so got away altogether. The last I saw of the chase was a little group of a dozen people perhaps, studying with infinite perplexity a slowly drying footprint that had resulted from a puddle in Tavistock Square, a footprint as isolated and incomprehensible to them as Crusoe's solitary discovery.

'This running warmed me to a certain extent, and I went on with a better courage through the maze of less frequented roads that runs hereabouts. My back had now become very stiff and sore, my tonsils were painful from the cabman's fingers, and the skin of my neck had been scratched by his nails; my feet hurt exceedingly and I was lame from a little cut on one foot. I saw in time a blind man approaching me, and fled limping, for I feared his subtle intuitions. Once or twice accidental collisions occurred and I left people amazed, with un-accountable curses ringing in their ears. Then came something silent and quiet against my face, and across the square fell a thin veil of slowly falling flakes of snow. I had caught a cold, and do as I would I could not avoid an occasional sneeze. And every dog that came in sight, with its pointing nose and curious sniffing, was a terror to me.

'Then came men and boys running, first one and then others, and shouting as they ran. It was a fire. They ran in the direction of my lodging, and looking back down a street I saw a mass of black smoke streaming up above the roofs and telephone wires. It was my lodging burning; my clothes, my apparatus, all my resources indeed, except my chequebook and the three volumes of memoranda that awaited me in Great Portland Street, were there. Burning! I had burnt my boats – if ever a man did! The place was blazing.'

The Invisible Man paused and thought. Kemp glanced nervously out of the window. 'Yes?' he said. 'Go on.'

CHAPTER 22

In the Emporium

'So last January, with the beginning of a snowstorm in the air about me – and if it settled on me it would betray me! – weary, cold, painful, inexpressibly wretched, and still but half convinced of my invisible quality, I began this new life to which I am committed. I had no refuge, no appliances, no human being in the world in whom I could confide. To have told my secret would have given me away – made a mere show and rarity of me. Nevertheless, I was half-minded to accost some passer-by and throw myself upon his mercy. But I knew too clearly the terror and brutal cruelty my advances would evoke. I made no plans in the street. My sole object was to get shelter from the snow, to get myself covered and warm; then I might hope to plan. But even to me, an Invisible Man, the rows of London houses stood latched, barred, and bolted impregnably.

'Only one thing could I see clearly before me – the cold exposure and misery of the snowstorm and the night.

'And then I had a brilliant idea. I turned down one of the roads leading from Gower Street to Tottenham Court Road, and found my-self outside Omniums, the big establishment where everything is to be bought – you know the place: meat, grocery, linen, furniture, clothing, oil paintings even – a huge meandering collection of shops rather than a shop. I had thought I should find the doors open, but they were closed; and as I stood in the wide entrance a carriage stopped outside, and a man in uniform – you know the kind of personage with OMNIUM on his cap – flung open the door. I contrived to enter, and walking down the shop – it was a department where they were selling ribbons and gloves and stockings and that kind of thing – came to a more spacious region devoted to picnic baskets and wicker furniture.

'I did not feel safe there, however; people were going to and fro, and I prowled restlessly about until I came upon a huge section in an upper floor containing multitudes of bedsteads, and over these I clambered, and found a resting-place at last among a huge pile of folded flock mattresses. The place was already lit up and agreeably warm, and I decided to remain where I was, keeping a cautious eye on the two or three sets of shopmen and customers who were meandering through the place, until closing time came. Then I should be able, I thought, to rob the place for food and clothing, and disguised, prowl through it and examine its resources, perhaps sleep on some of the bedding. That seemed an acceptable plan. My idea was to procure clothing to make myself a muffled but acceptable figure, to get money, and then to recover my books and parcels where they awaited me, take a lodging somewhere and elaborate plans for the complete realisation of the advantages my invisibility gave me (as I still imagined) over my fellow men.

'Closing time arrived quickly enough. It could not have been more than an hour after I took up my position on the mattresses before I noticed the blinds of the windows being drawn, and customers being marched doorwards. And then a number of brisk young men began with remarkable alacrity to tidy up the goods that remained disturbed. I left my lair as the crowds diminished, and prowled cautiously out into the less desolate parts of the shop. I was really surprised to observe how rapidly the young men and women whipped away the goods displayed for sale during the day. All the boxes of goods, the hanging fabrics, the festoons of lace, the boxes of sweets in the grocery section, the displays of this and that, were being whipped down, folded up, slapped into tidy receptacles, and everything that could not be taken down and put away had sheets of some coarse stuff like sacking flung over them. Finally all the chairs were turned up on to the counters, leaving the floor clear. Directly each of these young people had done, he or she made promptly for the door with such expression of animation as I have rarely observed in a shop assistant before. Then came a lot of youngsters scattering sawdust and carrying pails and brooms. I had to dodge to get out of the way, and as it was, my ankle got stung with the sawdust. For some time, wandering through the swathed and darkened departments, I could hear the brooms at work. And at last a good hour or more after the shop had been closed, came a noise of locking doors. Silence came upon the place, and I found myself wandering through the vast and intricate shops, galleries, showrooms of the place, alone. It was very still; in one place I remember passing near one of the Tottenham Court Road entrances and listening to the tapping of the boot-heels of the passers-by.

'My first visit was to the place where I had seen stockings and gloves for sale. It was dark, and I had the devil of a hunt after matches, which I found at last in the drawer of the little cash desk. Then I had to get a candle. I had to tear down wrappings and ransack a number of boxes and drawers, but at last I managed to turn out what I sought; the box label called them lambswool pants, and lambswool vests. Then socks, a thick comforter, and then I went to the clothing place and got trousers, a lounge jacket, an overcoat and a slouch hat – a clerical sort of hat with the brim turned down. I began to feel a human being again, and my next thought was food.

'Upstairs was a refreshment department, and there I got cold meat. There was coffee still in the urn, and I lit the gas and warmed it up again, and altogether I did not do badly. Afterwards, prowling through the place in search of blankets – I had to put up at last with a heap of down quilts – I came upon a grocery section with a lot of chocolate and candied fruits, more than was good for me indeed – and some white burgundy. And near that was a toy department, and I had a brilliant idea. I found some artificial noses – dummy noses, you know, and I thought of dark spectacles. But Omniums had no optical department. My nose had been a difficulty indeed – I had thought of paint. But the discovery set my mind running on wigs and masks and the like. Finally I went to sleep in a heap of down quilts, very warm and comfortable.

'My last thoughts before sleeping were the most agreeable I had had since the change. I was in a state of physical serenity, and that was reflected in my mind. I thought that I should be able to slip out unobserved in the morning with my clothes upon me, muffling my face with a white wrapper I had taken, purchase, with the money I had taken, spectacles and so forth, and so complete my disguise. I lapsed into disorderly dreams of all the fantastic things that had happened during the last few days. I saw the ugly little Jew of a landlord vociferating in his rooms; I saw his two sons marvelling, and the wrinkled old woman's gnarled face as she asked for her cat. I experienced again the strange sensation of seeing the cloth disappear, and so I came round to the windy hillside and the sniffing old clergyman mumbling, "Earth to earth, ashes to ashes, dust to dust," at my father's open grave.

' "You also," said a voice, and suddenly I was being forced towards the grave. I struggled, shouted, appealed to the mourners, but they continued stonily following the service; the old clergyman, too, never faltered, droning and sniffing through the ritual. I realised I was invisible and inaudible, that overwhelming forces had their grip on me. I struggled in vain, I was forced over the brink, the coffin rang hollow as I fell upon it, and the gravel came flying after me in spadefuls. Nobody heeded me, nobody was aware of me. I made convulsive struggles and awoke.

'The pale London dawn had come, the place was full of a chilly grey light that filtered round the edges of the window blinds. I sat up, and for a time I could not think where this ample apartment, with its counters, its piles of rolled stuff, its heap of quilts and cushions, its iron pillars, might be. Then, as recollection came back to me, I heard voices in conversation.

'Then far down the place, in the brighter light of some department which had already raised its blinds, I saw two men approaching. I scrambled to my feet, looking about me for some way of escape, and even as I did so the sound of my movement made them aware of me. I suppose they saw merely a figure moving quietly and quickly away. "Who's that?" cried one, and "Stop there!" shouted the other. I dashed around a corner and came full tilt – a faceless figure, mind you! – on a lanky lad of fifteen. He yelled and I bowled him over, rushed past him, turned another corner, and by a happy inspiration threw myself behind a counter. In another moment feet went running past and I heard voices shouting, "All hands to the doors!" asking what was "up", and giving one another advice how to catch me.

'Lying on the ground, I felt scared out of my wits. But – odd as it may seem – it did not occur to me at the moment to take off my clothes as I should have done. I had made up my mind, I suppose, to get away in them, and that ruled me. And then down the vista of the counters came a bawling of, "Here he is!"

'I sprang to my feet, whipped a chair off the counter, and sent it whirling at the fool who had shouted, turned, came into another round a corner, sent him spinning, and rushed up the stairs. He kept his footing, gave a view halloo! and came up the staircase hot after me. Up the staircase were piled a multitude of those bright-coloured pot things – what are they?'

'Art pots,' suggested Kemp.

'That's it! Art pots. Well, I turned at the top step and swung round, plucked one out of a pile and smashed it on his silly head as he came at me. The whole pile of pots went headlong, and I heard shouting and footsteps running from all parts. I made a mad rush for the refreshment place, and there was a man in white like a man cook, who took up the chase. I made one last desperate turn and found myself among lamps and ironmongery. I went behind the counter of this, and waited for my cook, and as he bolted in at the head of the chase, I doubled him up with a lamp. Down he went, and I crouched down behind the counter and began whipping off my clothes as fast as I could. Coat, jacket, trousers, shoes were all right, but a lambswool vest fits a man like a skin. I heard more men coming, my cook was lying quiet on the other side of the counter, stunned or scared speechless, and I had to make another dash for it, like a rabbit hunted out of a woodpile.

' "This way, policeman!" I heard someone shouting. I found myself in my bedstead storeroom again, and at the end of a wilderness of wardrobes. I rushed among them, went flat, got rid of my vest after infinite wriggling, and stood a free man again, panting and scared, as the policeman and three of the shopmen came round the corner. They made a rush for the vest and pants, and collared the trousers. "He's dropping his plunder," said one of the young men. "He *must* be somewhere here."

'But they did not find me all the same.

'I stood watching them hunt for me for a time, and cursing my ill-luck in losing the clothes. Then I went into the refreshment-room, drank a little milk I found there, and sat down by the fire to consider my position.

'In a little while two assistants came in and began to talk over the business very excitedly and like the fools they were. I heard a magnified account of my depredations, and other speculations as to my where-abouts. Then I fell to scheming again. The insurmountable difficulty of the place, especially now it was alarmed, was to get any plunder out of it. I went down into the warehouse to see if there was any chance of packing and addressing a parcel, but I could not understand the system of checking. About eleven o'clock, the snow having thawed as it fell, and the day being finer and a little warmer than the previous one, I decided that the Emporium was hopeless, and went out again, exasperated at my want of success, with only the vaguest plans of action in my mind.'

CHAPTER 23

In Drury Lane

'But you begin now to realise,' said the Invisible Man, 'the full disadvantage of my condition. I had no shelter – no covering – to get clothing was to forgo all my advantage, to make myself a strange and terrible thing. I was fasting; for to eat, to fill myself with unassimilated matter, would be to become grotesquely visible again.'

'I never thought of that,' said Kemp.

'Nor had I. And the snow had warned me of other dangers. I could not go abroad in snow – it would settle on me and expose me. Rain, too, would make me a watery outline, a glistening surface of a man – a bubble. And fog – I should be like a fainter bubble in a fog, a surface, a greasy glimmer of humanity. Moreover, as I went abroad – in the London air – I gathered dirt about my ankles, floating smuts and dust upon my skin. I did not know how long it would be before I should become visible from that cause also. But I saw clearly it could not be for long.

'Not in London at any rate.

'I went into the slums towards Great Portland Street, and found myself at the end of the street in which I had lodged. I did not go that way, because of the crowd halfway down it opposite to the still smoking ruins of the house I had fired. My most immediate problem was to get clothing. What to do with my face puzzled me. Then I saw in one of those little miscellaneous shops – news, sweets, toys, stationery, belated Christmas tomfoolery, and so forth – an array of masks and noses. I realised that problem was solved. In a flash I saw my course. I turned about, no longer aimless, and went – circuitously in order to avoid the busy ways, towards the back streets north of the Strand; for I remembered, though not very distinctly where, that some theatrical costumiers had shops in that district.

'The day was cold, with a nipping wind down the northward running streets. I walked fast to avoid being overtaken. Every crossing was a danger, every passenger a thing to watch alertly. One man as I was about to pass him at the top of Bedford Street, turned upon me abruptly and came into me, sending me into the road and almost under the wheel of a passing hansom. The verdict of the cab-rank was that he had

had some sort of stroke. I was so unnerved by this encounter that I went into Covent Garden Market and sat down for some time in a quiet corner by a stall of violets, panting and trembling. I found I had caught a fresh cold, and had to turn out after a time lest my sneezes should attract attention.

'At last I reached the object of my quest, a dirty, flyblown little shop in a byway near Drury Lane, with a window full of tinsel robes, sham jewels, wigs, slippers, dominoes and theatrical photographs. The shop was old-fashioned and low and dark, and the house rose above it for four storeys, dark and dismal. I peered through the window and, seeing no one within, entered. The opening of the door set a clanking bell ringing. I left it open, and walked round a bare costume stand, into a corner behind a cheval glass. For a minute or so no one came. Then I heard heavy feet striding across a room, and a man appeared down the shop.

'My plans were now perfectly definite. I proposed to make my way into the house, secrete myself upstairs, watch my opportunity, and when everything was quiet, rummage out a wig, mask, spectacles, and costume, and go into the world, perhaps a grotesque but still a credible figure. And incidentally of course I could rob the house of any available money.

'The man who had just entered the shop was a short, slight, hunched, beetle-browed man, with long arms and very short bandy legs. Apparently I had interrupted a meal. He stared about the shop with an expression of expectation. This gave way to surprise, and then to anger, as he saw the shop empty. "Damn the boys!" he said. He went to stare up and down the street. He came in again in a minute, kicked the door to with his foot spitefully, and went muttering back to the house door.

'I came forward to follow him, and at the noise of my movement he stopped dead. I did so too, startled by his quickness of ear. He slammed the house door in my face.

'I stood hesitating. Suddenly I heard his quick footsteps returning, and the door reopened. He stood looking about the shop like one who was still not satisfied. Then, murmuring to himself, he examined the back of the counter and peered behind some fixtures. Then he stood doubtful. He had left the house door open and I slipped into the inner room.

'It was a queer little room, poorly furnished and with a number of big masks in the corner. On the table was his belated breakfast, and it was a confoundedly exasperating thing for me, Kemp, to have to sniff his coffee and stand watching while he came in and resumed his meal. And his table manners were irritating. Three doors opened into the little room, one going upstairs and one down, but they were all shut. I could not get out of the room while he was there; I could scarcely move because of his alertness, and there was a draught down my back. Twice I strangled a sneeze just in time.

'The spectacular quality of my sensations was curious and novel, but for all that I was heartily tired and angry long before he had done his eating. But at last he made an end and putting his beggarly crockery on the black tin tray upon which he had had his teapot, and gathering all the crumbs up on the mustard-stained cloth, he took the whole lot of things after him. His burden prevented his shutting the door behind him – as he would have done; I never saw such a man for shutting doors – and I followed him into a very dirty underground kitchen and scullery. I had the pleasure of seeing him begin to wash up, and then, finding no good in keeping down there, and the brick floor being cold on my feet, I returned upstairs and sat in his chair by the fire. It was burning low, and scarcely thinking, I put on a little coal. The noise of this brought him up at once, and he stood aglare. He peered about the room and was within an ace of touching me. Even after that examination, he scarcely seemed satisfied. He stopped in the doorway and took a final inspection before he went down.

'I waited in the little parlour for an age, and at last he came up and opened the upstairs door. I just managed to get by him.

'On the staircase he stopped suddenly, so that I very nearly blundered into him. He stood looking back right into my face and listening. "I could have sworn," he said. His long hairy hand pulled at his lower lip. His eye went up and down the staircase. Then he grunted and went on up again.

'His hand was on the handle of a door, and then he stopped again with the same puzzled anger on his face. He was becoming aware of the faint sounds of my movements about him. The man must have had diabolically acute hearing. He suddenly flashed into rage. "If there's anyone in this house – " he cried with an oath, and left the threat unfinished. He put his hand in his pocket, failed to find what he wanted, and rushing past me went blundering noisily and pugnaciously downstairs. But I did not follow him. I sat on the head of the staircase until his return.

'Presently he came up again, still muttering. He opened the door of the room, and before I could enter, slammed it in my face.

'I resolved to explore the house, and spent some time in doing so as noiselessly as possible. The house was very old and tumbledown, damp so that the paper in the attics was peeling from the walls, and rat infested. Some of the door handles were stiff and I was afraid to turn them.

Several rooms I did inspect were unfurnished, and others were littered with theatrical lumber, bought second-hand, I judged, from its appearance. In one room next to his I found a lot of old clothes. I began routing among these, and in my eagerness forgot again the evident sharpness of his ears. I heard a stealthy footstep and, looking up just in time, saw him peering in at the tumbled heap and holding an old-fashioned revolver in his hand. I stood perfectly still while he stared about open-mouthed and suspicious. "It must have been her," he said slowly. "Damn her!"

'He shut the door quietly, and immediately I heard the key turn in the lock. Then his footsteps retreated. I realised abruptly that I was locked in. For a minute I did not know what to do. I walked from door to window and back, and stood perplexed. A gust of anger came upon me. But I decided to inspect the clothes before I did anything further, and my first attempt brought down a pile from an upper shelf. This brought him back, more sinister than ever. That time he actually touched me, jumped back with amazement and stood astonished in the middle of the room.

'Presently he calmed a little. "Rats," he said in an undertone, fingers on lips. He was evidently a little scared. I edged quietly out of the room, but a plank creaked. Then the infernal little brute started going all over the house, revolver in hand and locking door after door and pocketing the keys. When I realised what he was up to I had a fit of rage – I could hardly control myself sufficiently to watch my opportunity. By this time I knew he was alone in the house, and so I made no more ado, but knocked him on the head.'

'Knocked him on the head?' exclaimed Kemp.

'Yes – stunned him – as he was going downstairs. Hit him from behind with a stool that stood on the landing. He went downstairs like a bag of old boots.'

'But – I say! The common conventions of humanity – '

'Are all very well for common people. But the point was, Kemp, that I had to get out of that house in a disguise without his seeing me. I couldn't think of any other way of doing it. And then I gagged him with a Louis Quatorze vest and tied him up in a sheet.'

'Tied him up in a sheet!'

'Made a sort of bag of it. It was rather a good idea to keep the idiot scared and quiet, and a devilish hard thing to get out of – head away from the string. My dear Kemp, it's no good your sitting glaring as though I was a murderer. It had to be done. He had his revolver. If once he saw me he would be able to describe me – '

'But still,' said Kemp, 'in England – today. And the man was in his own house, and you were – well, robbing.'

'Robbing! Confound it! You'll call me a thief next! Surely, Kemp, you're not fool enough to dance on the old strings. Can't you see my position?'

'And his too,' said Kemp.

The Invisible Man stood up sharply. 'What do you mean to say?'

Kemp's face grew a trifle hard. He was about to speak and checked himself. 'I suppose, after all,' he said with a sudden change of manner, 'the thing had to be done. You were in a fix. But still – '

'Of course I was in a fix – an infernal fix. And he made me wild too – hunting me about the house, fooling about with his revolver, locking and unlocking doors. He was simply exasperating. You don't blame me, do you? You don't blame me?'

'I never blame anyone,' said Kemp. 'It's quite out of fashion. What did you do next?'

'I was hungry. Downstairs I found a loaf and some rank cheese – more than sufficient to satisfy my hunger. I took some brandy and water, and then went up past my impromptu bag – he was lying quite still – to the room containing the old clothes. This looked out upon the street, two lace curtains brown with dirt guarding the window. I went and peered out through their interstices. Outside the day was bright – by contrast with the brown shadows of the dismal house in which I found myself, dazzlingly bright. A brisk traffic was going by, fruit carts, a hansom, a four-wheeler with a pile of boxes, a fish-monger's cart. I turned with spots of colour swimming before my eyes to the shadowy fixtures behind me. My excitement was giving place to a clear apprehension of my position again. The room was full of a faint scent of benzoline, used, I suppose, in cleaning the garments.

'I began a systematic search of the place. I should judge the hunchback had been alone in the house for some time. He was a curious person. Everything that could possibly be of service to me I collected in the clothes storeroom, and then I made a deliberate selection. I found a handbag I thought a suitable possession, and some powder, rouge and sticking-plaster.

'I had thought of painting and powdering my face and all that there was to show of me, in order to render myself visible, but the disadvantage of this lay in the fact that I should require turpentine and other appliances and a considerable amount of time before I could vanish again. Finally I chose a mask of the better type, slightly grotesque but not more so than many human beings, dark glasses, greyish whiskers and a wig. I could find no underclothing, but that I could buy subsequently, and for the time I swathed myself in calico dominoes and some white cashmere scarfs. I could find no socks, but the hunchback's boots were rather a loose fit and sufficed. In a desk in the shop were three sovereigns and about thirty shillings' worth of silver, and in a locked cupboard I burst in the inner room were eight pounds in gold. I could go forth into the world again, equipped.

'Then came a curious hesitation. Was my appearance really credible? I tried myself with a little bedroom looking-glass, inspecting myself from every point of view to discover any forgotten chink, but it all seemed sound. I was grotesque to the theatrical pitch, a stage miser, but I was certainly not a physical impossibility. Gathering confidence, I took my looking-glass down into the shop, pulled down the shop blinds, and surveyed myself from every point of view with the help of the cheval glass in the corner.

'I spent some minutes screwing up my courage and then unlocked the shop door and marched out into the street, leaving the little man to get out of his sheet again when he liked. In five minutes a dozen turnings intervened between me and the costumier's shop. No one appeared to notice me very pointedly. My last difficulty seemed overcome.'

He stopped again.

'And you troubled no more about the hunchback?' said Kemp.

'No,' said the Invisible Man. 'Nor have I heard what became of him. I suppose he untied himself or kicked himself out. The knots were pretty tight.'

He became silent and went to the window and stared out.

'What happened when you went out into the Strand?'

'Oh! – disillusionment again. I thought my troubles were over. Practically I thought I had impunity to do whatever I chose, everything – save to give away my secret. So I thought. Whatever I did, whatever the consequences might be, was nothing to me. I had merely to fling aside my garments and vanish. No person could hold me. I could take my money where I found it. I decided to treat myself to a sumptuous feast, and then put up at a good hotel, and accumulate a new outfit of property. I felt amazingly confident; it's not particularly pleasant recalling that I was an ass. I went into a place and was already ordering lunch, when it occurred to me that I could not eat unless I exposed my invisible face. I finished ordering the lunch, told the man I should be back in ten minutes, and went out exasperated. I don't know if you have ever been disappointed in your appetite.'

'Not quite so badly,' said Kemp, 'but I can imagine it.'

'I could have smashed the silly devils. At last, faint with the desire for tasteful food, I went into another place and demanded a private room. "I am disfigured," I said. "Badly." They looked at me curiously, but of course it was not their affair – and so at last I got my lunch. It was not particularly well served, but it sufficed; and when I had had it, I sat over a cigar, trying to plan my line of action. And outside a snowstorm was beginning.

'The more I thought it over, Kemp, the more I realised what a helpless absurdity an Invisible Man was – in a cold and dirty climate and a crowded civilised city. Before I made this mad experiment I had dreamt of a thousand advantages. That afternoon it seemed all disappointment. I went over the heads of the things a man reckons desirable. No doubt invisibility made it possible to get them, but it made it impossible to enjoy them when they are got. Ambition – what is the good of pride of place when you cannot appear there? What is the good of the love of a woman when her name must needs be Delilah? I have no taste for politics, for the blackguardisms of fame, for philanthropy, for sport. What was I to do? And for this I had become a wrapped-up mystery, a swathed and bandaged caricature of a man!'

He paused, and his attitude suggested a roving glance at the window.

'But how did you get to Iping?' said Kemp, anxious to keep his guest busy talking.

'I went there to work. I had one hope. It was a half idea! I have it still. It is a full-blown idea now. A way of getting back! Of restoring what I have done. When I choose. When I have done all I mean to do invisibly. And that is what I chiefly want to talk to you about now.'

'You went straight to Iping?'

'Yes. I had simply to get my three volumes of memoranda and my chequebook, my luggage and underclothing, order a quantity of chemicals to work out this idea of mine – I will show you the calculations as soon as I get my books – and then I started. Jove! I remember the snowstorm now, and the accursed bother it was to keep the snow from damping my pasteboard nose.'

'At the end,' said Kemp, 'the day before yesterday, when they found you out, you rather – to judge by the papers – '

'I did. Rather. Did I kill that fool of a constable?'

'No,' said Kemp. 'He's expected to recover.'

'That's his luck, then. I clean lost my temper, the fools! Why couldn't they leave me alone? And that grocer lout?'

'There are no deaths expected,' said Kemp.

'I don't know about that tramp of mine,' said the Invisible Man, with an unpleasant laugh. 'By heaven, Kemp, you don't know what rage *is*! . . . To have worked for years, to have planned and plotted, and then to get some fumbling purblind idiot messing across your course! . . . Every conceivable sort of silly creature that has ever been created has been sent to cross me.

'If I have much more of it, I shall go wild – I shall start mowing 'em. As it is, they've made things a thousand times more difficult.'

'No doubt it's exasperating,' said Kemp, drily.

CHAPTER 24

The Plan that Failed

'But now,' said Kemp, with a side glance out of the window, 'what are we to do?'

He moved nearer his guest as he spoke in such a manner as to prevent the possibility of a sudden glimpse of the three men who were advancing up the hill road – with an intolerable slowness, as it seemed to Kemp.

'What were you planning to do when you were heading for Port Burdock? *Had* you any plan?'

'I was going to clear out of the country. But I have altered that plan rather since seeing you. I thought it would be wise, now the weather is hot and invisibility possible, to make for the south. Especially as my secret was known, and everyone would be on the lookout for a masked and muffled man. You have a line of steamers from here to France. My idea was to get aboard one and run the risks of the passage. Thence I could go by train into Spain, or else get to Algiers. It would not be difficult. There a man might always be invisible – and yet live. And do things. I was using that tramp as a money box and luggage carrier, until I decided how to get my books and things sent over to meet me.'

'That's clear.'

'And then the filthy brute must needs try and rob me! He *has* hidden my books, Kemp. Hidden my books! If I can lay my hands on him!'

'Best plan to get the books out of him first.'

'But where is he? Do you know?'

'He's in the town police station, locked up, by his own request, in the strongest cell in the place.'

'Cur!' said the Invisible Man.

'But that hangs up your plans a little.'

'We must get those books; those books are vital.'

'Certainly,' said Kemp, a little nervously, wondering if he heard foot-steps outside. 'Certainly we must get those books. But that won't be difficult, if he doesn't know they're for you.'

'No,' said the Invisible Man, and thought.

Kemp tried to think of something to keep the talk going, but the Invisible Man resumed of his own accord.

'Blundering into your house, Kemp,' he said, 'changes all my plans.

For you are a man that can understand. In spite of all that has happened, in spite of this publicity, of the loss of my books, of what I have suffered, there still remain great possibilities, huge possibilities –

'You have told no one I am here?' he asked abruptly.

Kemp hesitated. 'That was implied,' he said.

'No one?' insisted Griffin.

'Not a soul.'

'Ah! Now – ' The Invisible Man stood up, and sticking his arms akimbo began to pace the study.

'I made a mistake, Kemp, a huge mistake, in carrying this thing through alone. I have wasted strength, time, opportunities. Alone – it is wonderful how little a man can do alone! To rob a little, to hurt a little, and there is the end.

'What I want, Kemp, is a goalkeeper, a helper and a hiding-place, an arrangement whereby I can sleep and eat and rest in peace, and unsuspected. I must have a confederate. With a confederate, with food and rest – a thousand things are possible.

'Hitherto I have gone on vague lines. We have to consider all that invisibility means, all that it does not mean. It means little advantage for eavesdropping and so forth – one makes sounds. It's of little help – a little help perhaps – in housebreaking and so forth. Once you've caught me you could easily imprison me. But on the other hand I am hard to catch. This invisibility, in fact, is only good in two cases. It's useful in getting away, it's useful in approaching. It's particularly useful, therefore, in killing. I can walk round a man, whatever weapon he has, choose my point, strike as I like. Dodge as I like. Escape as I like.'

Kemp's hand went to his moustache. Was that a movement downstairs?

'And it is killing we must do, Kemp.'

'It is killing we must do,' repeated Kemp. 'I'm listening to your plan, Griffin, but I'm not agreeing, mind. *Why* killing?'

'Not wanton killing, but a judicious slaying. The point is, they know there is an Invisible Man – as well as we know there is an Invisible Man. And that Invisible Man, Kemp, must now establish a Reign of Terror. Yes; no doubt it's startling. But I mean it. A Reign of Terror. He must take some town like your Burdock and terrify and dominate it. He must issue his orders. He can do that in a thousand ways – scraps of paper thrust under doors would suffice. And all who disobey his orders he must kill, and kill all who would defend them.'

'Humph!' said Kemp, no longer listening to Griffin but to the sound of his front door opening and closing.

'It seems to me, Griffin,' he said, to cover his wandering attention, 'that your confederate would be in a difficult position.'

'No one would know he was a confederate,' said the Invisible Man, eagerly. And then suddenly, '*Hush!* What's that downstairs?'

'Nothing,' said Kemp, and suddenly began to speak loud and fast. 'I don't agree to this, Griffin,' he said. 'Understand me, I don't agree to this. Why dream of playing a game against the race? How can you hope to gain happiness? Don't be a lone wolf. Publish your results; take the world – take the nation at least – into your confidence. Think what you might do with a million helpers – '

The Invisible Man interrupted – arm extended. 'There are footsteps coming upstairs,' he said in a low voice.

'Nonsense,' said Kemp.

'Let me see,' said the Invisible Man, and advanced, arm extended, to the door.

And then things happened very swiftly. Kemp hesitated for a second and then moved to intercept him. The Invisible Man started and stood still. 'Traitor!' cried the Voice, and suddenly the dressing-gown opened, and sitting down the Unseen began to disrobe. Kemp made three swift steps to the door, and forthwith the Invisible Man – his legs had vanished – sprang to his feet with a shout. Kemp flung the door open.

As it opened, there came a sound of hurrying feet downstairs and voices.

With a quick movement Kemp thrust the Invisible Man back, sprang aside, and slammed the door. The key was outside and ready. In another moment Griffin would have been alone in the belvedere study, a prisoner. Save for one little thing. The key had been slipped in hastily that morning. As Kemp slammed the door it fell noisily upon the carpet.

Kemp's face became white. He tried to grip the door handle with both hands. For a moment he stood lugging. Then the door gave six inches. But he got it closed again. The second time it was jerked a foot wide, and the dressing-gown came wedging itself into the opening. His throat was gripped by invisible fingers, and he left his hold on the handle to defend himself. He was forced back, tripped and pitched heavily into the corner of the landing. The empty dressing-gown was flung on top of him.

Halfway up the staircase was Colonel Adye, the recipient of Kemp's letter, the chief of the Burdock police. He was staring aghast at the sudden appearance of Kemp, followed by the extraordinary sight of clothing tossing empty in the air. He saw Kemp felled, and struggling to his feet. He saw him rush forward, and go down again, felled like an ox.

Then suddenly he was struck violently. By nothing! A vast weight, it seemed, leapt upon him, and he was hurled headlong down the staircase, with a grip on his throat and a knee in his groin. An invisible foot trod on his back, a ghostly patter passed downstairs, he heard the two police officers in the hall shout and run, and the front door of the house slammed violently.

He rolled over and sat up staring. He saw, staggering down the staircase, Kemp, dusty and dishevelled, one side of his face white from a blow, his lip bleeding, and a pink dressing-gown and some underclothing held in his arms.

'My God!' cried Kemp, 'the game's up! He's gone!'

CHAPTER 25

The Hunting of the Invisible Man

For a space Kemp was too inarticulate to make Adye understand the swift things that had just happened. They stood on the landing, Kemp speaking swiftly, the grotesque swathings of Griffin still on his arm. But presently Adye began to grasp something of the situation.

'He is mad,' said Kemp; 'inhuman. He is pure selfishness. He thinks of nothing but his own advantage, his own safety. I have listened to such a story this morning of brutal self-seeking . . . He has wounded men. He will kill them unless we can prevent him. He will create a panic. Nothing can stop him. He is going out now – furious!'

'He must be caught,' said Adye. 'That is certain.'

'But how?' cried Kemp, and suddenly became full of ideas. 'You must begin at once. You must set every available man to work; you must prevent his leaving this district. Once he gets away, he may go through the countryside as he wills, killing and maiming. He dreams of a reign of terror! A reign of terror, I tell you. You must set a watch on trains and roads and shipping. The garrison must help. You must wire for help. The only thing that may keep him here is the thought of recovering some books of notes he counts of value. I will tell you of that! There is a man in your police station – Marvel.'

'I know,' said Adye, 'I know. Those books – yes. But the tramp – '

'Says he hasn't them. But he *thinks* the tramp has. And you must prevent him from eating or sleeping; day and night the country must be astir for him. Food must be locked up and secured, all food, so that he will have to break his way to it. The houses everywhere must be barred against him. Heaven send us cold nights and rain! The whole country-side must begin hunting and keep hunting. I tell you, Adye, he is a danger, a disaster; unless he is pinned and secured, it is frightful to think of the things that may happen.'

'What else can we do?' said Adye. 'I must go down at once and begin organising. But why not come? Yes – you come too! Come, and we must hold a sort of council of war – get Hopps to help – and the railway managers. By Jove! it's urgent. Come along – tell me as we go. What else is there we can do? Put that stuff down.'

In another moment Adye was leading the way downstairs. They found the front door open and the policemen standing outside staring at empty air. 'He's got away, sir,' said one.

'We must go to the central station at once,' said Adye. 'One of you go on down and get a cab to come up and meet us – quickly. And now, Kemp, what else?'

'Dogs,' said Kemp. 'Get dogs. They don't see him, but they wind him. Get dogs.'

'Good,' said Adye. 'It's not generally known, but the prison officials over at Halstead know a man with bloodhounds. Dogs. What else?'

'Bear in mind,' said Kemp, 'his food shows. After eating, his food shows until it is assimilated. So that he has to hide after eating. You must keep on beating. Every thicket, every quiet corner. And put all weapons – all implements that might be weapons, away. He can't carry such things for long. And what he can snatch up and strike men with must be hidden away.'

'Good again,' said Adye. 'We shall have him yet!'

'And on the roads – ' said Kemp, and hesitated.

'Yes?' said Adye.

'Powdered glass,' said Kemp. 'It's cruel, I know. But think of what he may do!'

Adye drew the air in sharply between his teeth. 'It's unsportsman–like. I don't know. But I'll have powdered glass got ready. If he goes too far . . .'

'The man's become inhuman, I tell you,' said Kemp. 'I am as sure he will establish a reign of terror – so soon as he has got over the emotions of this escape – as I am sure I am talking to you. Our only chance is to be ahead. He has cut himself off from his kind. His blood be upon his own head.'

CHAPTER 26

The Wicksteed Murder

The Invisible Man seems to have rushed out of Kemp's house in a state of blind fury. A little child playing near Kemp's gateway was violently caught up and thrown aside, so that its ankle was broken, and thereafter for some hours the Invisible Man passed out of human perceptions. No one knows where he went nor what he did. But one can imagine him hurrying through the hot June forenoon, up the hill and on to the open downland behind Port Burdock, raging and despairing at his intolerable fate, and sheltering at last, heated and weary, amid the thickets of Hintondean,[18] to piece together again his shattered schemes against his species. That seems the most probable refuge for him, for there it was he reasserted himself in a grimly tragical manner about two in the afternoon.

One wonders what his state of mind may have been during that time, and what plans he devised. No doubt he was almost ecstatically exasperated by Kemp's treachery, and though we may be able to understand the motives that led to that deceit, we may still imagine and even sympathise a little with the fury the attempted surprise must have occasioned. Perhaps something of the stunned astonishment of his Oxford Street experiences may have returned to him, for he had evidently counted on Kemp's co-operation in his brutal dream of a terrorised world. At any rate he vanished from human ken about midday, and no living witness can tell what he did until about half-past two. It was a fortunate thing, perhaps, for humanity, but for him it was a fatal inaction.

During that time a growing multitude of men scattered over the countryside was busy. In the morning he had still been simply a legend, a terror; in the afternoon, by virtue chiefly of Kemp's drily worded proclamation, he was presented as a tangible antagonist, to be wounded, captured or overcome, and the countryside began organising itself with inconceivable rapidity. By two o'clock even he might still have removed himself out of the district by getting aboard a train, but after two that became impossible. Every passenger train along the lines on a great parallelogram between Southampton, Manchester, Brighton and Horsham, travelled with locked doors, and the goods traffic was almost entirely suspended. And in a great circle of twenty miles round Port Burdock, men armed with guns and bludgeons were presently setting out in groups of three and four, with dogs, to beat the roads and fields.

Mounted policemen rode along the country lanes, stopping at every cottage and warning the people to lock up their houses, and keep indoors unless they were armed, and all the elementary schools had broken up by three o'clock, and the children, scared and keeping together in groups, were hurrying home. Kemp's proclamation – signed indeed by Adye – was posted over almost the whole district by four or five o'clock in the afternoon. It gave briefly but clearly all the conditions of the struggle, the necessity of keeping the Invisible Man from food and sleep, the necessity for incessant watchfulness and for a prompt attention to any evidence of his movements. And so swift and decided was the action of the authorities, so prompt and universal was the belief in this strange being, that before nightfall an area of several hundred square miles was in a stringent state of siege. And before nightfall, too, a thrill of horror went through the whole watching nervous countryside. Going from whispering mouth to mouth, swift and certain over the length and breadth of the country, passed the story of the murder of Mr Wicksteed.

If our supposition that the Invisible Man's refuge was the Hintondean thickets, then we must suppose that in the early afternoon he sallied out again bent upon some project that involved the use of a weapon. We cannot know what the project was, but the evidence that he had the iron rod in hand before he met Wicksteed is to me at least overwhelming.

Of course we can know nothing of the details of that encounter. It occurred on the edge of a gravel pit, not two hundred yards from Lord Burdock's lodge gate. Everything points to a desperate struggle – the trampled ground, the numerous wounds Mr Wicksteed received, his splintered walking-stick; but why the attack was made, save in a murderous frenzy, it is impossible to imagine. Indeed the theory of madness is almost unavoidable. Mr Wicksteed was a man of forty-five or forty-six, steward to Lord Burdock, of inoffensive habits and appearance, the very last person in the world to provoke such a terrible antagonist. Against him it would seem the Invisible Man used an iron rod dragged from a broken piece of fence. He stopped this quiet man, going quietly home to his midday meal, attacked him, beat down his feeble defences, broke his arm, felled him and smashed his head to a jelly.

Of course, he must have dragged this rod out of the fencing before he met his victim – he must have been carrying it ready in his hand. Only two details beyond what has already been stated seem to bear on the matter. One is the circumstance that the gravel pit was not in Mr Wicksteed's direct path home, but nearly a couple of hundred yards out of his way. The other is the assertion of a little girl to the effect that, going to her afternoon school, she saw the murdered man '*trotting*' in a peculiar manner across a field towards the gravel pit. Her pantomime of his action suggests a man pursuing something on the ground before him and striking at it ever and again with his walking-stick. She was the last person to see him alive. He passed out of her sight to his death, the struggle being hidden from her only by a clump of beech trees and a slight depression in the ground.

Now this, to the present writer's mind at least, lifts the murder out of the realm of the absolutely wanton. We may imagine that Griffin had taken the rod as a weapon indeed, but without any deliberate intention of using it in murder. Wicksteed may then have come by and noticed this rod inexplicably moving through the air. Without any thought of the Invisible Man – for Port Burdock is miles away – he may have pursued it. It is quite conceivable that he may not even have heard of the Invisible Man. One can then imagine the Invisible Man making off – quietly in order to avoid discovering his presence in the neighbourhood, and Wicksteed, excited and curious, pursuing this unaccountably locomotive object – finally striking at it.

No doubt the Invisible Man could easily have out-distanced his middle-aged pursuer under ordinary circumstances, but the position in which Wicksteed's body was found suggests that he had the ill luck to drive his quarry into a corner between a drift of stinging nettles and the gravel pit. To those who appreciate the extraordinary irascibility of the Invisible Man, the rest of the encounter will be easy to imagine.

But this is pure hypothesis. The only undeniable facts – for stories of children are often unreliable – are the discovery of Wicksteed's body, done to death, and of the blood-stained iron rod flung among the nettles. The abandonment of the rod by Griffin suggests that in the emotional excitement of the affair the purpose for which he took it – if he had a purpose – was abandoned. He was certainly an intensely egotistical and unfeeling man, but the sight of his victim, his first victim, bloody and pitiful at his feet, may have released some long pent fountain of remorse which for a time may have flooded whatever scheme of action he had contrived.

After the murder of Mr Wicksteed, he would seem to have struck across the country towards the downland. There is a story of a voice heard about sunset by a couple of men in a field near Fern Bottom. It was wailing and laughing, sobbing and groaning, and ever and again it shouted. It must have been queer hearing. It drove up across the middle of a clover field and died away towards the hills.

That afternoon the Invisible Man must have learnt something of the rapid use Kemp had made of his confidences. He must have found houses locked and secured; he may have loitered about railway stations and prowled about inns, and no doubt he read the proclamations and realised something of the nature of the campaign against him. And as the evening advanced, the fields became dotted here and there with groups of three or four men and noisy with the yelping of dogs. These men-hunters had particular instructions in the case of an encounter as to the way they should support one another. But he avoided them all. We may understand something of his exasperation, and it could have been none the less because he himself had supplied the information that was being used so remorselessly against him. For that day at least he lost heart; for nearly twenty-four hours, save when he turned on Wicksteed, he was a hunted man. In the night, he must have eaten and slept, for in the morning he was himself again, active, powerful, angry and malignant, prepared for his last great struggle against the world.

CHAPTER 27

The Siege at Kemp's House

Kemp read a strange missive, written in pencil on a greasy sheet of paper.

> You have been amazingly energetic and clever [this letter ran], though what you stand to gain by it I cannot imagine. You are against me. For a whole day you have chased me; you have tried to rob me of a night's rest. But I have had food in spite of you, I have slept in spite of you, and the game is only beginning. The game is only beginning. There is nothing for it, but to start the Terror. This announces the first day of the Terror. Port Burdock is no longer under the Queen, tell your colonel of police, and the rest of them; it is under me – the Terror! This is day one of year one of the new epoch – the Epoch of the Invisible Man. I am Invisible Man the First. To begin with the rule will be easy. The first day there will be one execution for the sake of example – a man named Kemp. Death starts for him today. He may lock himself away, hide himself away, get guards about him, put on armour if he likes – Death, the unseen Death, is coming. Let him take precautions; it will impress my people. Death starts from the pillar box by midday. The letter will fall in as the postman comes along, then off! The game begins. Death starts. Help him not, my people, lest Death fall upon you also. Today Kemp is to die.

Kemp read this letter twice. 'It's no hoax,' he said. 'That's his voice! And he means it.'

He turned the folded sheet over and saw on the addressed side of it the postmark Hintondean, and the prosaic detail '2*d*. to pay'.

He got up slowly, leaving his lunch unfinished – the letter had come by the one o'clock post – and went into his study. He rang for his housekeeper, and told her to go round the house at once, examine all the fastenings of the windows, and close all the shutters. He closed the shutters of his study himself. From a locked drawer in his bedroom he took a little revolver, examined it carefully, and put it into the pocket of his lounge jacket. He wrote a number of brief notes, one to Colonel Adye, and gave them to his servant to take, with explicit instructions as to her way of leaving the house. 'There is no danger,' he said, and added a mental reservation, 'to you'. He remained meditative for a space after doing this, and then returned to his cooling lunch.

He ate with gaps of thought. Finally he struck the table sharply. 'We will have him!' he said; 'and I am the bait. He will come too far.'

He went up to the belvedere, carefully shutting every door after him. 'It's a game,' he said, 'an odd game – but the chances are all for me, Mr Griffin, in spite of your invisibility. Griffin *contra mundum*[19] . . . with a vengeance.'

He stood at the window staring at the hot hillside. 'He must get food every day – and I don't envy him. Did he really sleep last night? Out in the open somewhere – secure from collisions. I wish we could get some good cold wet weather instead of the heat.

'He may be watching me now.'

He went close to the window. Something rapped smartly against the brickwork over the frame, and made him start violently back.

'I'm getting nervous,' said Kemp. But it was five minutes before he went to the window again. 'It must have been a sparrow,' he said.

Presently he heard the front-door bell ringing, and hurried downstairs. He unbolted and unlocked the door, examined the chain, put it up, and opened cautiously without showing himself. A familiar voice hailed him. It was Adye.

'Your servant's been assaulted, Kemp,' he said round the door.

'What!' exclaimed Kemp.

'Had that note of yours taken away from her. He's close about here. Let me in.'

Kemp released the chain, and Adye entered through as narrow an opening as possible. He stood in the hall, looking with infinite relief at Kemp refastening the door. 'Note was snatched out of her hand. Scared her horribly. She's down at the station. Hysterics. He's close here. What was it about?'

Kemp swore.

'What a fool I was,' said Kemp. 'I might have known. It's not an hour's walk from Hintondean. Already?'

'What's up?' said Adye.

'Look here!' said Kemp, and led the way into his study. He handed Adye the Invisible Man's letter. Adye read it and whistled softly. 'And you – ?' said Adye.

'Proposed a trap – like a fool,' said Kemp, 'and sent my proposal out by a maidservant. To him.'

Adye followed Kemp's profanity.

'He'll clear out,' said Adye.

'Not he,' said Kemp.

A resounding smash of glass came from upstairs. Adye had a silvery glimpse of a little revolver half out of Kemp's pocket. 'It's a window, upstairs!' said Kemp, and led the way up. There came a second smash while they were still on the staircase. When they reached the study they found two of the three windows smashed, half the room littered with splintered glass, and one big flint lying on the writing table. The two men stopped in the doorway, contemplating the wreckage. Kemp swore again, and as he did so the third window went with a snap like a pistol, hung starred for a moment, and collapsed in jagged, shivering triangles into the room.

'What's this for?' said Adye.

'It's a beginning,' said Kemp.

'There's no way of climbing up here?'

'Not for a cat,' said Kemp.

'No shutters?'

'Not here. All the downstairs rooms – Hello!'

Smash, and then the whack of boards hit hard came from downstairs. 'Confound him!' said Kemp. 'That must be – yes – it's one of the bedrooms. He's going to do all the house. But he's a fool. The shutters are up, and the glass will fall outside. He'll cut his feet.'

Another window proclaimed its destruction. The two men stood on the landing perplexed. 'I have it!' said Adye. 'Let me have a stick or something, and I'll go down to the station and get the bloodhounds put on. That ought to settle him! They're hard by – not ten minutes – '

Another window went the way of its fellows.

'You haven't a revolver?' asked Adye.

Kemp's hand went to his pocket. Then he hesitated. 'I haven't one – at least to spare.'

'I'll bring it back,' said Adye, 'you'll be safe here.'

Kemp, ashamed of his momentary lapse from truthfulness, handed him the weapon.

'Now for the door,' said Adye.

As they stood hesitating in the hall, they heard one of the first-floor bedroom windows crack and crash. Kemp went to the door and began to slip the bolts as silently as possible. His face was a little paler than usual. 'You must step straight out,' said Kemp. In another moment Adye was on the doorstep and the bolts were dropping back into the staples. He hesitated for a moment, feeling more comfortable with his back against the door. Then he marched, upright and square, down the steps. He crossed the lawn and approached the gate. A little breeze seemed to ripple over the grass. Something moved near him. 'Stop a bit,' said a Voice, and Adye stopped dead and his hand tightened on the revolver.

'Well?' said Adye, white and grim, and every nerve tense.

'Oblige me by going back to the house,' said the Voice, as tense and grim as Adye.

'Sorry,' said Adye a little hoarsely, and moistened his lips with his tongue. The Voice was on his left front, he thought. Suppose he were to take his luck with a shot?

'What are you going for?' said the Voice, and there was a quick movement of the two, and a flash of sunlight from the open lip of Adye's pocket.

Adye desisted and thought. 'Where I go,' he said slowly, 'is my own business.' The words were still on his lips, when an arm came round his neck, his back felt a knee, and he was sprawling backward. He drew clumsily and fired absurdly, and in another moment he was struck in the mouth and the revolver wrested from his grip. He made a vain clutch at a slippery limb, tried to struggle up and fell back. 'Damn!' said Adye. The Voice laughed. 'I'd kill you now if it wasn't the waste of a bullet,' it said. He saw the revolver in midair, six feet off, covering him.

'Well?' said Adye, sitting up.

'Get up,' said the Voice.

Adye stood up.

'Attention!' said the Voice, and then fiercely, 'Don't try any games. Remember I can see your face if you can't see mine. You've got to go back to the house.'

'He won't let me in,' said Adye.

'That's a pity,' said the Invisible Man. 'I've got no quarrel with you.'

Adye moistened his lips again. He glanced away from the barrel of the revolver and saw the sea far off very blue and dark under the midday sun, the smooth green down, the white cliff of the Head, and the multitudinous town, and suddenly he knew that life was very sweet. His eyes came back to this little metal thing hanging between heaven and earth, six yards away. 'What am I to do?' he said sullenly.

'What am *I* to do?' asked the Invisible Man. 'You will get help. The only thing is for you to go back.'

'I will try. If he lets me in will you promise not to rush the door?'

'I've got no quarrel with you,' said the Voice.

Kemp had hurried upstairs after letting Adye out, and now, crouching among the broken glass and peering cautiously over the edge of the study window sill, he saw Adye stand parleying with the Unseen. 'Why doesn't he fire?' whispered Kemp to himself. Then the revolver moved a little and the glint of the sunlight flashed in Kemp's eyes. He shaded his eyes and tried to see the source of the blinding beam.

'Surely,' he said, 'Adye hasn't given up the revolver?'

'Promise not to rush the door,' Adye was saying. 'Don't push a winning game too far. Give a man a chance.'

'You go back to the house. I tell you flatly I will not promise anything.'

Adye's decision seemed suddenly made. He turned towards the house, walking slowly with his hands behind him. Kemp watched him – puzzled. The revolver vanished, flashed again into sight, vanished again, and became evident on a closer scrutiny as a little dark object following Adye. Then things happened very quickly. Adye leapt backwards, swung around, clutched at this little object, missed it, threw up his hands and fell forward on his face, leaving a little puff of blue in the air. Kemp did not hear the sound of the shot. Adye writhed, raised himself on one arm, fell forward and lay still.

For a space Kemp remained staring at the quiet carelessness of Adye's attitude. The afternoon was very hot and still, nothing seemed stirring in all the world save a couple of yellow butterflies chasing each other through the shrubbery between the house and the road gate. Adye lay on the lawn near the gate. The blinds of all the villas down the hill-road were drawn, but in one little green summerhouse was a white figure, apparently an old man asleep. Kemp scrutinised the surroundings of the house for a glimpse of the revolver, but it had vanished. His eyes came back to Adye. The game was opening well.

Then came a ringing and knocking at the front door that grew at last tumultuous, but pursuant to Kemp's instructions the servants had locked themselves into their rooms. This was followed by a silence. Kemp sat listening and then began peering cautiously out of the three windows, one after another. He went to the staircase head and stood listening uneasily. He armed himself with his bedroom poker, and went to examine the interior fastenings of the ground-floor windows again. Everything was safe and quiet. He returned to the belvedere. Adye lay motionless over the edge of the gravel just as he had fallen. Coming along the road by the villas were the housemaid and two policemen.

Everything was deadly still. The three people seemed very slow in approaching. He wondered what his antagonist was doing.

He started. There was a smash from below. He hesitated and went downstairs again. Suddenly the house resounded with heavy blows and the splintering of wood. He heard a smash and the destructive clang of the iron fastenings of the shutters. He turned the key and opened the kitchen door. As he did so, the shutters, split and splintering, came flying inward. He stood aghast. The window frame, save for one cross-bar, was still intact, but only little teeth of glass remained in the frame. The shutters had been driven in with an axe, and now the axe was descending in sweeping blows upon the window frame and the iron bars defending it. Then suddenly it leapt aside and vanished. He saw the revolver lying on the path outside, and then the little weapon sprang into the air. He dodged back. The revolver cracked just too late, and a splinter from the edge of the closing door flashed over his head. He slammed and locked the door, and as he stood outside he heard Griffin shouting and laughing. Then the blows of the axe with its splitting and smashing consequences, were resumed.

Kemp stood in the passage trying to think. In a moment the Invisible Man would be in the kitchen. This door would not keep him a moment, and then –

A ringing came at the front door again. It would be the policemen. He ran into the hall, put up the chain and drew the bolts. He made the girl speak before he dropped the chain, and the three people blundered into the house in a heap, and Kemp slammed the door again.

'The Invisible Man!' said Kemp. 'He has a revolver, with two shots – left. He's killed Adye. Shot him anyhow. Didn't you see him on the lawn? He's lying there.'

'Who?' said one of the policemen.

'Adye,' said Kemp.

'We came in the back way,' said the girl.

'What's that smashing?' asked one of the policemen.

'He's in the kitchen – or will be. He has found an axe – '

Suddenly the house was full of the Invisible Man's resounding blows on the kitchen door. The girl stared towards the kitchen, shuddered, and retreated into the dining-room. Kemp tried to explain in broken sentences. They heard the kitchen door give.

'This way,' said Kemp, starting into activity, and bundled the police-men into the dining-room doorway.

'Poker,' said Kemp, and rushed to the fender. He handed the poker he had carried to the policeman and the dining-room one to the other. He suddenly flung himself backwards.

'Whup!' said one policeman, ducked, and caught the axe on his poker. The pistol snapped its penultimate shot and ripped a valuable Sidney Cooper.[20] The second policeman brought his poker down on the little weapon, as one might knock down a wasp, and sent it rattling to the floor.

At the first clash the girl screamed, stood screaming for a moment by the fireplace, and then ran to open the shutters – possibly with an idea of escaping by the shattered window.

The axe receded into the passage, and fell to a position about two feet from the ground. They could hear the Invisible Man breathing. 'Stand away, you two,' he said. 'I want that man Kemp.'

'We want you,' said the first policeman, making a quick step forward and swiping with his poker at the Voice. The Invisible Man must have started back, and he blundered into the umbrella stand.

Then, as the policeman staggered with the swing of the blow he had aimed, the Invisible Man countered with the axe, the helmet crumpled like paper, and the blow sent the man spinning to the floor at the head of the kitchen stairs. But the second policeman, aiming behind the axe with his poker, hit something soft that snapped. There was a sharp exclamation of pain and then the axe fell to the ground. The policeman swiped again at vacancy and hit nothing; he put his foot on the axe, and struck again. Then he stood, poker clubbed, listening intently for the slightest movement.

He heard the dining-room window open, and a quick rush of feet within. His companion rolled over and sat up, with the blood running down between his eye and ear. 'Where is he?' asked the man on the floor.

'Don't know. I've hit him. He's standing somewhere in the hall. Unless he's slipped past you. Dr Kemp – sir.'

Pause.

'Dr Kemp,' cried the policeman again.

The second policeman began struggling to his feet. He stood up. Suddenly the faint pad of bare feet on the kitchen stairs could be heard. 'Yap!' cried the first policeman, and incontinently flung his poker. It smashed a little gas bracket.

He made as if he would pursue the Invisible Man downstairs. Then he thought better of it and stepped into the dining-room.

'Dr Kemp – ' he began, and stopped short.

'Dr Kemp isn't here,' he said, as his companion looked over his shoulder.

The dining-room window was wide open, and neither housemaid nor Kemp was to be seen.

The second policeman's opinion of Kemp was terse and vivid.

CHAPTER 28

The Hunter Hunted

Mr Heelas, Mr Kemp's nearest neighbour among the villa holders, was asleep in his summer house when the siege of Kemp's house began. Mr Heelas was one of the sturdy minority who refused to believe 'in all this nonsense' about an Invisible Man. His wife, however, as he was subsequently to be reminded, did. He insisted upon walking about his garden just as if nothing was the matter, and he went to sleep in the afternoon in accordance with the custom of years. He slept through the smashing of the windows, and then woke up suddenly with a curious persuasion of something wrong. He looked across at Kemp's house, rubbed his eyes and looked again. Then he put his feet to the ground, and sat listening. He said he was damned, but still the strange thing was visible. The house looked as though it had been deserted for weeks – after a violent riot. Every window was broken, and every window, save those of the belvedere study, was blinded by the internal shutters.

'I could have sworn it was all right' – he looked at his watch – 'twenty minutes ago.'

He became aware of a measured concussion and the clash of glass, far away in the distance. And then, as he sat open-mouthed, came a still more wonderful thing. The shutters of the drawing-room window were flung open violently, and the housemaid in her outdoor hat and garments, appeared struggling in a frantic manner to throw up the sash. Suddenly a man appeared beside her, helping her – Dr Kemp! In another moment the window was open, and the housemaid was struggling out; she pitched forward and vanished among the shrubs. Mr Heelas stood up, exclaiming vaguely and vehemently at all these wonderful things. He saw Kemp stand on the sill, spring from the window, and reappear almost instantaneously running along a path in the shrubbery and stooping as he ran, like a man who evades observation. He vanished behind a laburnum, and appeared again clambering over a fence that abutted on the open down. In a second he had tumbled over and was running at a tremendous pace down the slope towards Mr Heelas.

'Lord!' cried Mr Heelas, struck with an idea; 'it's that Invisible Man brute! It's right, after all!'

With Mr Heelas to think things like that was to act, and his cook watching him from the top window was amazed to see him come pelting towards the house at a good nine miles an hour. There was a slamming of doors, a ringing of bells, and the voice of Mr Heelas bellowing like a bull. 'Shut the doors, shut the windows, shut everything! – the Invisible Man is coming!' Instantly the house was full of screams and directions, and scurrying feet. He ran himself to shut the French windows that opened on the veranda; as he did so Kemp's head and shoulders and knee appeared over the edge of the garden fence. In another moment Kemp had ploughed through the asparagus, and was running across the tennis lawn to the house.

'You can't come in,' said Mr Heelas, shutting the bolts. 'I'm very sorry if he's after you, but you can't come in!'

Kemp appeared with a face of terror close to the glass, rapping and then shaking frantically at the French windows. Then, seeing his efforts were useless, he ran along the veranda, vaulted the end, and went to hammer at the side door. Then he ran round by the side gate to the front of the house, and so into the hill-road. And Mr Heelas staring from his window – a face of horror – had scarcely witnessed Kemp vanish, ere the asparagus was being trampled this way and that by feet unseen. At that Mr Heelas fled precipitately upstairs, and the rest of the chase was beyond his purview. But as he passed the staircase window, he heard the side gate slam.

Emerging into the hill-road, Kemp naturally took the downward direction, and so it was he came to run in his own person the very race he had watched with such a critical eye from the belvedere study only four days ago. He ran it well, for a man out of training, and though his face was white and wet, his wits were cool to the last. He ran with wide strides, and wherever a patch of rough ground intervened, wherever there came a patch of raw flints, or a bit of broken glass shone dazzling, he crossed it and left the bare invisible feet that followed to take what line they would.

For the first time in his life Kemp discovered that the hill-road was indescribably vast and desolate, and that the beginnings of the town far below at the hill foot were strangely remote. Never had there been a slower or more painful method of progression than running. All the gaunt villas, sleeping in the afternoon sun, looked locked and barred; no doubt they were locked and barred – by his own orders. But at any rate they might have kept a lookout for an eventuality like this! The town was rising up now, the sea had dropped out of sight behind it, and people down below were stirring. A tram was just arriving at the hill foot. Beyond that was the police station. Was that footsteps he heard behind him? Spurt.

The people below were staring at him, one or two were running, and his breath was beginning to saw in his throat. The tram was quite near now, and the Jolly Cricketers was noisily barring its doors. Beyond the tram were posts and heaps of gravel – the drainage works. He had a transitory idea of jumping into the tram and slamming the doors, and then he resolved to go for the police station. In another moment he had passed the door of the Jolly Cricketers, and was in the blistering fag end of the street, with human beings about him. The tram driver and his helper – arrested by the sight of his furious haste – stood staring with the tram horses unhitched. Farther on the astonished features of navvies appeared above the mounds of gravel.

His pace broke a little, and then he heard the swift pad of his pursuer, and leapt forward again. 'The Invisible Man!' he cried to the navvies, with a vague indicative gesture, and by an inspiration leapt the excavation and placed a burly group between him and the chase. Then, abandoning the idea of the police station, he turned into a little side street, rushed by a greengrocer's cart, hesitated for the tenth of a second at the door of a sweetstuff shop, and then made for the mouth of an alley that ran back into the main Hill Street again. Two or three little children were playing here, and shrieked and scattered at his apparition, and forthwith doors and windows opened and excited mothers revealed their hearts. Out he shot into Hill Street again, three hundred yards from the tramline end, and immediately he became aware of a tumultuous vociferation and running people.

He glanced up the street towards the hill. Hardly a dozen yards off ran a huge navvy, cursing in fragments and slashing viciously with a spade, and hard behind him came the tram conductor with his fists clenched. Up the street others followed these two, striking and shouting. Down towards the town, men and women were running, and he noticed clearly one man coming out of a shop-door with a stick in his hand. 'Spread out! Spread out!' cried someone. Kemp suddenly grasped the altered condition of the chase. He stopped, and looked round, panting. 'He's close here!' he cried. 'Form a line across – '

He was hit hard under the ear, and went reeling, trying to face round towards his unseen antagonist. He just managed to keep his feet, and he struck a vain counter swipe in the air. Then he was hit again under the jaw, and sprawled headlong on the ground. In another moment a knee compressed his diaphragm, and a couple of eager hands gripped his throat, but the grip of one was weaker than the other; he grasped the wrists, heard a cry of pain from his assailant, and then the spade of the navvy came whirling through the air above him, and struck something with a dull thud. He felt a drop of moisture on his face. The grip at his throat suddenly relaxed, and with a convulsive effort, Kemp loosed himself, grasped a limp shoulder and rolled uppermost. He gripped the unseen elbows near the ground. 'I've got him!' screamed Kemp. 'Help! Help – hold! He's down! Hold his feet!'

In another second there was a simultaneous rush upon the struggle, and a stranger coming into the road suddenly might have thought an exceptionally savage game of Rugby football was in progress. And there was no shouting after Kemp's cry – only a sound of blows and feet and heavy breathing.

Then came a mighty effort, and the Invisible Man threw off a couple of his antagonists and rose to his knees. Kemp clung to him in front like a hound to a stag, and a dozen hands gripped, clutched and tore at the Unseen. The tram conductor suddenly got the neck and shoulders and lugged him back.

Down went the heap of struggling men again and rolled over. There was, I am afraid, some savage kicking. Then suddenly a wild scream of, 'Mercy! Mercy!' that died down swiftly to a sound like choking.

'Get back, you fools!' cried the muffled voice of Kemp, and there was a vigorous shoving back of stalwart forms. 'He's hurt, I tell you. Stand back!'

There was a brief struggle to clear a space, and then the circle of eager faces saw the doctor kneeling, as it seemed, fifteen inches in the air, and holding invisible arms to the ground. Behind him a constable gripped invisible ankles.

'Don't you leave go of en,' cried the big navvy, holding a blood-stained spade; 'he's shamming.'

'He's not shamming,' said the doctor, cautiously raising his knee; 'and I'll hold him.' His face was bruised and already going red; he spoke thickly because of a bleeding lip. He released one hand and seemed to be feeling at the face. 'The mouth's all wet,' he said. And then, 'Good God!'

He stood up abruptly and then knelt down on the ground by the side of the thing unseen. There was a pushing and shuffling, a sound of heavy feet as fresh people turned up to increase the pressure of the crowd. People now were coming out of the houses. The doors of the Jolly Cricketers stood suddenly wide open. Very little was said.

Kemp felt about, his hand seeming to pass through empty air. 'He's not breathing,' he said, and then, 'I can't feel his heart. His side – ugh!'

Suddenly an old woman, peering under the arm of the big navvy, screamed sharply. 'Looky there!' she said, and thrust out a wrinkled finger.

And looking where she pointed, everyone saw, faint and transparent as though it was made of glass, so that veins and arteries and bones and nerves could be distinguished, the outline of a hand, a hand limp and prone. It grew clouded and opaque even as they stared.

'Hello!' cried the constable. 'Here's his feet a-showing!'

And so, slowly, beginning at his hands and feet and creeping along his limbs to the vital centres of his body, that strange change continued. It was like the slow spreading of a poison. First came the little white nerves, a hazy grey sketch of a limb, then the glassy bones and intricate arteries, then the flesh and skin, first a faint fogginess, and then growing rapidly dense and opaque. Presently they could see his crushed chest and his shoulders, and the dim outline of his drawn and battered features.

When at last the crowd made way for Kemp to stand erect, there lay, naked and pitiful on the ground, the bruised and broken body of a young man about thirty. His hair and brow were white – not grey with age, but white with the whiteness of albinism – and his eyes were like garnets. His hands were clenched, his eyes wide open, and his expression was one of anger and dismay.

'Cover his face!' said a man. 'For Gawd's sake, cover that face!' and three little children, pushing forward through the crowd, were suddenly twisted round and sent packing off again.

Someone brought a sheet from the Jolly Cricketers, and having covered him, they carried him into that house. And there it was, on a shabby bed in a tawdry, ill-lighted bedroom, surrounded by a crowd of ignorant and excited people, broken and wounded, betrayed and unpitied, that Griffin, the first of all men to make himself invisible, Griffin, the most gifted physicist the world has ever seen, ended in infinite disaster his strange and terrible career.

The Epilogue

So ends the story of the strange and evil experiments of the Invisible Man. And if you would learn more of him you must go to a little inn near Port Stowe and talk to the landlord. The sign of the inn is an empty board save for a hat and boots, and the name is the title of this story. The landlord is a short and corpulent little man with a nose of cylindrical proportions, wiry hair and a sporadic rosiness of visage. Drink generously, and he will tell you generously of all the things that happened to him after that time, and of how the lawyers tried to do him out of the treasure found upon him.

'When they found they couldn't prove whose money was which, I'm blessed,' he says, 'if they didn't try to make me out a blooming treasure trove! Do I *look* like a Treasure Trove? And then a gentleman gave me a guinea a night to tell the story at the Empire Music 'All – just to tell 'em in my own words – barring one.'

And if you want to cut off the flow of his reminiscences abruptly, you can always do so by asking if there weren't three manuscript books in the story. He admits there were and proceeds to explain, with asseverations that everybody thinks *he* has 'em! But bless you! he hasn't. 'The Invisible Man it was took 'em off to hide 'em when I cut and ran for Port Stowe. It's that Mr Kemp put people on with the idea of *my* having 'em.'

And then he subsides into a pensive state, watches you furtively, bustles nervously with glasses, and presently leaves the bar.

He is a bachelor man – his tastes were ever bachelor, and there are no women folk in the house. Outwardly he buttons – it is expected of him – but in his more vital privacies, in the matter of braces for example, he still turns to string. He conducts his house without enterprise, but with eminent decorum. His movements are slow, and he is a great thinker. But he has a reputation for wisdom and for a respectable parsimony in the village, and his knowledge of the roads of the South of England would beat Cobbett.[21]

And on Sunday mornings, every Sunday morning, all the year round, while he is closed to the outer world, and every night after ten, he goes into his bar parlour, bearing a glass of gin faintly tinged with water, and having placed this down, he locks the door and examines the blinds, and even looks under the table. And then, being satisfied of his solitude, he unlocks the cupboard and a box in the cupboard and a drawer in that box, and produces three volumes bound in brown leather, and places them solemnly in the middle of the table. The covers are weather-worn and tinged with an algal green – for once they sojourned in a ditch and some of the pages have been washed blank by dirty water. The landlord sits down in an armchair, fills a long clay pipe slowly – gloating over the books the while. Then he pulls one towards him and opens it, and begins to study it – turning over the leaves backwards and forwards.

His brows are knit and his lips move painfully. 'Hex, little two up in the air, cross and a fiddle-de-dee. Lord! what a one he was for intellect!'

Presently he relaxes and leans back, and blinks through his smoke across the room at things invisible to other eyes. 'Full of secrets,' he says. 'Wonderful secrets!

'Once I get the haul of them – *Lord!* I wouldn't do what *he* did; I'd just – well!'

He pulls at his pipe.

So he lapses into a dream, the undying wonderful dream of his life. And though Kemp has fished unceasingly, no human being save the landlord knows those books are there, with the subtle secret of invisibility and a dozen other strange secrets written therein. And none other will know of them until he dies.

The Food of the Gods
and How It Came to Earth

The Food of the Gods
and How It Came to Earth

———— ◆ ————

H. G. WELLS

The Food of the Gods was first published in 1903
by *Pearson's* magazine in London and
by *Cosmopolitan* magazine in New York.
In 1904 it was published in book form
by Macmillan & Co. in London

Contents

BOOK ONE
The Dawn of the Food

BOOK TWO
The Food in the Village

BOOK THREE
The Harvest of the Food

The Dawn of the Food

CHAPTER 1

The Discovery of the Food

IN THE MIDDLE YEARS of the nineteenth century there first became abundant in this strange world of ours a class of men, men tending for the most part to become elderly, who are called, and who are very properly called, but who dislike extremely to be called – 'Scientists'. They dislike that word so much that from the columns of *Nature*, which was from the first their distinctive and characteristic paper, it is as carefully excluded as if it were – that other word which is the basis of all really bad language in this country. But the Great Public and its Press know better, and 'Scientists' they are, and when they emerge to any sort of publicity, 'distinguished scientists' and 'eminent scientists' and 'well-known scientists' is the very least we call them.

Certainly both Mr Bensington and Professor Redwood quite merited any of these terms long before they came upon the marvellous discovery of which this story tells. Mr Bensington was a Fellow of the Royal Society and a former president of the Chemical Society, and Professor Redwood was Professor of Physiology in the Bond Street College of the London University, and he had been grossly libelled by the anti-vivisectionists time after time. And they had led lives of academic distinction from their very earliest youth.

They were of course quite undistinguished-looking men, as indeed all true scientists are. There is more personal distinction about the mildest-mannered actor alive than there is about the entire Royal Society. Mr Bensington was short and very, very bald, and he stooped slightly; he wore gold-rimmed spectacles and cloth boots that were abundantly cut open because of his numerous corns, and Professor Redwood was entirely ordinary in his appearance. Until they happened upon the Food of the Gods (as I must insist upon calling it) they led lives of such eminent and studious obscurity that it is hard to find anything whatever to tell the reader about them.

Mr Bensington won his spurs (if one may use such an expression of a gentleman in boots of slashed cloth) by his splendid researches upon the More Toxic Alkaloids, and Professor Redwood rose to eminence – I do not clearly remember how he rose to eminence! I know he was

very eminent, and that's all. Things of this sort grow. I fancy it
was a voluminous work on Reaction Times with numerous plates
of sphygmograph[22] tracings (I write subject to correction) and an
admirable new terminology that did the thing for him.

The general public saw little or nothing of either of these gentlemen.
Sometimes at places like the Royal Institution and the Society of Arts it
did in a sort of way see Mr Bensington, or at least his blushing baldness
and something of his collar and coat, and hear fragments of a lecture or
paper that he imagined himself to be reading audibly; and once I
remember – one midday in the vanished past – when the British
Association was at Dover, coming on Section C or D, or some such
letter, which had taken up its quarters in a public-house, and following
two, serious-looking ladies with paper parcels, out of mere curiosity,
through a door labelled 'Billiards' and 'Pool' into a scandalous darkness,
broken only by a magic-lantern circle of Redwood's tracings.

I watched the lantern slides come and go, and listened to a voice (I
forget what it was saying) which I believe was the voice of Professor
Redwood, and there was a sizzling from the lantern and another sound
that kept me there, still out of curiosity, until the lights were unexpectedly turned up. And then I perceived that this sound was the
sound of the munching of buns and sandwiches and things that the
assembled British Associates had come there to eat under cover of the
magic-lantern darkness.

And Redwood I remember went on talking all the time the lights were
up and dabbing at the place where his diagram ought to have been visible
on the screen – and so it was again so soon as the darkness was restored.
I remember him then as a most ordinary, slightly nervous-looking dark
man, with an air of being preoccupied with something else, and doing
what he was doing just then under an unaccountable sense of duty.

I heard Bensington also once – in the old days – at an educational
conference in Bloomsbury. Like most eminent chemists and botanists,
Mr Bensington was very authoritative upon teaching – though I am
certain he would have been scared out of his wits by an average Board
School class in half an hour – and so far as I can remember now, he
was propounding an improvement of Professor Armstrong's Heuristic
method, whereby at the cost of three or four hundred pounds' worth
of apparatus, a total neglect of all other studies and the undivided
attention of a teacher of exceptional gifts, an average child might with
a peculiar sort of thumby thoroughness learn in the course of ten or
twelve years almost as much chemistry as one could get in one of
those objectionable shilling textbooks that were then so common . . .

Quite ordinary persons you perceive, both of them, outside their science. Or, if anything, on the unpractical side of ordinary. And that you will find is the case with 'scientists' as a class all the world over. What there is great of them is an annoyance to their fellow scientists and a mystery to the general public, and what is not is evident.

There is no doubt about what is not great, no race of men have such obvious littlenesses. They live in a narrow world so far as their human intercourse goes; their researches involve infinite attention and an almost monastic seclusion; and what is left over is not very much. To witness some queer, shy, misshapen, grey-headed, self-important, little discoverer of great discoveries, ridiculously adorned with the wide ribbon of some order of chivalry and holding a reception of his fellow men, or to read the anguish of *Nature* at the 'neglect of science' when the angel of the birthday honours passes the Royal Society by, or to listen to one indefatigable lichenologist commenting on the work of another indefatigable lichenologist, such things force one to realise the unfaltering littleness of men.

And withal the reef of science that these little 'scientists' built and are yet building is so wonderful, so portentous, so full of mysterious half-shapen promises for the mighty future of man! They do not seem to realise the things that they are doing! No doubt long ago even Mr Bensington, when he chose this calling, when he consecrated his life to the alkaloids and their kindred compounds, had some inkling of the vision – more than an inkling. Without some such inspiration, for such glories and positions only as a 'scientist' may expect, what young man would have given his life to such work, as young men do? No, they *must* have seen the glory, they must have had the vision, but so near that it has blinded them. The splendour has blinded them, mercifully, so that for the rest of their lives they can hold the lights of knowledge in comfort – that we may see!

And perhaps it accounts for Redwood's touch of preoccupation, that – there can be no doubt of it now – he among his fellows was different, he was different inasmuch as something of the vision still lingered in his eyes.

The Food of the Gods I call it, this substance that Mr Bensington and Professor Redwood made between them; and having regard now to what it has already done and all that it is certainly going to do, there is surely no exaggeration in the name. So I shall continue to call it therefore throughout my story. But Mr Bensington would no more have called it that in cold blood than he would have gone out from his flat in Sloane Street clad in regal scarlet and a wreath of laurel. The phrase was a mere first cry of astonishment from him. He called it the Food of the Gods in his enthusiasm and for an hour or so at the most altogether. After that he decided he was being absurd. When he first thought of the thing he saw, as it were, a vista of enormous possibilities – literally enormous possibilities; but upon this dazzling vista, after one stare of amazement, he resolutely shut his eyes, even as a conscientious 'scientist' should. After that, the Food of the Gods sounded blatant to the pitch of indecency. He was surprised he had used the expression. Yet for all that something of that clear-eyed moment hung about him and broke out ever and again . . .

'Really, you know,' he said, rubbing his hands together and laughing nervously, 'it has more than a theoretical interest.

'For example,' he confided, bringing his face close to the professor's and dropping to an undertone, 'it would perhaps, if suitably handled, *sell* . . .

'Precisely,' he said, walking away – 'as a food. Or at least a food ingredient.

'Assuming of course that it is palatable. A thing we cannot know till we have prepared it.'

He turned upon the hearthrug, and studied the carefully designed slits upon his cloth shoes.

'Name?' he said, looking up in response to an enquiry. 'For my part I incline to the good old classical allusion. It – it makes Science res – Gives it a touch of old-fashioned dignity. I have been thinking . . . I don't know if you will think it absurd of me . . . A little fancy is surely occasionally permissible . . . Herakleophorbia. Eh? The nutrition of a possible Hercules? You know it *might* . . .

'Of course if you think *not* – '

Redwood reflected with his eyes on the fire and made no objection.

'You think it would do?'

Redwood moved his head gravely.

'It might be Titanophorbia, you know. Food of Titans ... You prefer the former?

'You're quite sure you don't think it a little *too* – '

'No.'

'Ah! I'm glad.'

And so they called it Herakleophorbia throughout their investigations, and in their report – the report that was never published, because of the unexpected developments that upset all their arrangements – it is invariably written in that way. There were three kindred substances prepared before they hit on the one their speculations had foretold and these they spoke of as Herakleophorbia I, Herakleophorbia II, and Herakleophorbia III. It is Herakleophorbia IV which I – insisting upon Bensington's original name – call here the Food of the Gods.

3

The idea was Mr Bensington's. But as it was suggested to him by one of Professor Redwood's contributions to the *Philosophical Transactions*,[23] he very properly consulted that gentleman before he carried it further. Besides which it was, as a research, a physiological quite as much as a chemical inquiry.

Professor Redwood was one of those scientific men who are addicted to tracings and curves. You are familiar – if you are at all the sort of reader I like – with the sort of scientific paper I mean. It is a paper you cannot make head nor tail of, and at the end come five or six long folded diagrams that open out and show peculiar zigzag tracings, flashes of lightning overdone or sinuous inexplicable things called 'smoothed curves' set up on ordinates and rooting in abscissae – and things like that. You puzzle over the thing for a long time and end with the suspicion that not only do you not understand it but that the author does not understand it either. But really you know many of these scientific people understand the meaning of their own papers quite well, it is simply a defect of expression that raises the obstacle between us.

I am inclined to think that Redwood thought in tracings and curves. And after his monumental work upon Reaction Times (the unscientific reader is exhorted to stick to it for a little bit longer and everything will be as clear as daylight) Redwood began to turn out smoothed curves and sphygmographeries upon Growth, and it was one of his papers upon Growth that really gave Mr Bensington his idea.

Redwood, you know, had been measuring growing things of all sorts, kittens, puppies, sunflowers, mushrooms, bean plants and (until his wife put a stop to it) his baby, and he showed that growth went out not at a regular pace, or, as he put it, so,

but with bursts and intermissions of this sort,

and that apparently nothing grew regularly and steadily, and so far as he could make out nothing could grow regularly and steadily; it was as if every living thing had just to accumulate force to grow, grew with vigour only for a time, and then had to wait for a space before it could go on growing again. And in the muffled and highly technical language of the really careful 'scientist', Redwood suggested that the process of growth probably demanded the presence of a considerable quantity of some necessary substance in the blood that was only formed very slowly, and that when this substance was used up by growth, it was only very slowly replaced, and that meanwhile the organism had to mark time. He compared his unknown substance to oil in machinery. A growing animal was rather like an engine, he suggested, that can move a certain distance and must then be oiled before it can run again. ('But why shouldn't one oil the engine from without?' said Mr Bensington, when he read the paper.) And all this, said Redwood, with the delightful nervous inconsecutiveness of his class, might very probably be found to throw a light upon the mystery of certain of the ductless glands. As though they had anything to do with it at all!

In a subsequent communication Redwood went further. He gave a perfect Brock's benefit of diagrams – exactly like rocket trajectories they were; and the gist of it – so far as it had any gist – was that the blood of puppies and kittens and the sap of sunflowers and the juice of mushrooms in what he called the 'growing phase' differed in the proportion of certain elements from their blood and sap on the days when they were not particularly growing.

And when Mr Bensington, after holding the diagrams sideways and upside down, began to see what this difference was, a great amazement came upon him. Because, you see, the difference might probably be due to the presence of just the very substance he had recently been trying to isolate in his researches upon such alkaloids as are most stimulating to the nervous system. He put down Redwood's paper on the patent reading-desk that swung inconveniently from his armchair, took off his gold-rimmed spectacles, breathed on them and wiped them very carefully.

'By Jove!' said Mr Bensington.

Then replacing his spectacles again he turned to the patent reading-desk, which immediately, as his elbow came against its arm, gave a coquettish squeak and deposited the paper, with all its diagrams in a dispersed and crumpled state, on the floor. 'By Jove!' said Mr Bensington, straining his stomach over the armchair with a patient disregard of the habits of this convenience, and then, finding the pamphlet still out of reach, he went down on all fours in pursuit. It was on the floor that the idea of calling it the Food of the Gods came to him . . .

For you see, if he was right and Redwood was right, then by injecting or administering this new substance of his in food, he would do away with the 'resting phase', and instead of growth going on in this fashion

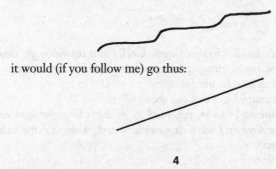

it would (if you follow me) go thus:

4

The night after his conversation with Redwood Mr Bensington could scarcely sleep a wink. He did seem once to get into a sort of doze, but it was only for a moment, and then he dreamt he had dug a deep hole into the earth and poured in tons and tons of the Food of the Gods, and the earth was swelling and swelling, and all the boundaries of the countries were bursting, and the Royal Geographical Society was at work like one great guild of tailors letting out the equator . . .

That of course was a ridiculous dream, but it shows the state of mental excitement into which Mr Bensington got and the real value he attached to his idea much better than any of the things he said or did when he was awake and on his guard. Or I should not have mentioned it, because as a general rule I do not think it is at all interesting for people to tell each other about their dreams.

By a singular coincidence Redwood also had a dream that night, and his dream was this:

It was a diagram done in fire upon a long scroll of the abyss. And he (Redwood) was standing on a planet before a sort of black platform lecturing about the new sort of growth that was now possible, to the More than Royal Institution of Primordial Forces – forces which had always previously, even in the growth of races, empires, planetary systems and worlds, gone so:

And even in some cases so:

And he was explaining to them quite lucidly and convincingly that these slow, these even retrogressive methods would be very speedily quite put out of fashion by his discovery.

Ridiculous of course! But that too shows –

That either dream is to be regarded as in any way significant or prophetic beyond what I have categorically said, I do not for one moment suggest.

CHAPTER 2

The Experimental Farm

Mr Bensington proposed originally to try this stuff, so soon as he was really able to prepare it, upon tadpoles. One always does try this sort of thing upon tadpoles to begin with; this being what tadpoles are for. And it was agreed that he should conduct the experiments and not Redwood, because Redwood's laboratory was occupied with the ballistic apparatus and animals necessary for an investigation into the Diurnal Variation in the Butting Frequency of the Young Bull Calf, an investigation that was yielding curves of an abnormal and very perplexing sort, and the presence of glass globes of tadpoles was extremely undesirable while this particular research was in progress.

But when Mr Bensington conveyed to his cousin Jane something of what he had in mind, she put a prompt veto upon the importation of any considerable number of tadpoles, or any such experimental creatures, into their flat. She had no objection whatever to his use of one of the rooms of the flat for the purposes of a non-explosive chemistry that, so far as she was concerned, came to nothing; she let him have a gas furnace and a sink and a dust-tight cupboard of refuge from the weekly storm of cleaning she would not forgo. And having known people addicted to drink, she regarded his solicitude for distinction in learned societies as an excellent substitute for the coarser form of depravity. But any sort of living things in quantity, 'wriggly' as they were bound to be alive and 'smelly' dead, she could not and would not abide. She said these things were certain to be unhealthy, and Bensington was notoriously a delicate man – it was nonsense to say he wasn't. And when Bensington tried to make the enormous importance of this possible discovery clear, she said that it was all very well, but if she consented to his making everything nasty and unwholesome in the place (and that was what it all came to) then she was certain he would be the first to complain.

And Mr Bensington went up and down the room, regardless of his corns, and spoke to her quite firmly and angrily without the slightest effect. He said that nothing ought to stand in the way of the Advancement of Science, and she said that the Advancement of Science was one thing and having a lot of tadpoles in a flat was another; he said that in Germany it was an ascertained fact that a man with an idea like his would at once have twenty thousand properly-fitted cubic feet of laboratory placed at his disposal, and she said she was glad and always had been glad that she was not a German; he said that it would make him famous for ever, and she said it was much more likely to make him ill to have a lot of tadpoles in a flat like theirs; he said he was master in his own house, and she said that rather than wait on a lot of tadpoles she'd go as matron to a school; and then he asked her to be reasonable, and she asked *him* to be reasonable then and give up all this about tadpoles; and he said she might respect his ideas, and she said not if they were smelly she wouldn't, and then he gave way completely and said – in spite of the classical remarks of Huxley[24] upon the subject – a bad word. Not a very bad word it was, but bad enough.

And after that she was greatly offended and had to be apologised to, and the prospect of ever trying the Food of the Gods upon tadpoles in their flat at any rate vanished completely in the apology.

So Bensington had to consider some other way of carrying out these experiments in feeding that would be necessary to demonstrate his discovery, so soon as he had his substance isolated and prepared. For some days he meditated upon the possibility of boarding out his tadpoles with some trustworthy person, and then the chance sight of the phrase in a newspaper turned his thoughts to an Experimental Farm.

And chicks. Directly he thought of it, he thought of it as a poultry farm. He was suddenly taken with a vision of wildly growing chicks. He conceived a picture of coops and runs, outsize and still more outsize coops, and runs progressively larger. Chicks are so accessible, so easily fed and observed, so much drier to handle and measure, that for his purpose tadpoles seemed to him now, in comparison with them, quite wild and uncontrollable beasts. He was quite puzzled to understand why he had not thought of chicks instead of tadpoles from the beginning. Among other things it would have saved all this trouble with his cousin Jane. And when he suggested this to Redwood, Redwood quite agreed with him.

Redwood said that in working so much upon needlessly small animals he was convinced experimental physiologists made a great mistake. It is exactly like making experiments in chemistry with an insufficient quantity of material; errors of observation and manipulation become disproportionately large. It was of extreme importance just at present that scientific men should assert their right to have their material *big*. That was why he was doing his present series of experiments at the Bond Street College upon bull calves, in spite of a certain amount of inconvenience to the students and professors of other subjects caused by their incidental levity in the corridors. But the curves he was getting were quite exceptionally interesting, and would, when published, amply justify his choice. For his own part, were it not for the inadequate endowment of science in this country, he would never, if he could avoid it, work on anything smaller than a whale. But a Public Vivarium[25] on a sufficient scale to render this possible was, he feared, at present, in this country at any rate, a Utopian demand. In Germany – etc.

As Redwood's bull calves needed his daily attention, the selection and equipment of the Experimental Farm fell largely on Bensington. The entire cost also, was, it was understood, to be defrayed by Bensington, at least until a grant could be obtained. Accordingly he alternated his work in the laboratory of his flat with farm hunting up and down the lines that run southward out of London, and his peering spectacles, his simple baldness and his lacerated cloth shoes filled the owners of numerous undesirable properties with vain hopes. And he advertised in several daily papers and *Nature* for a responsible couple (married), punctual, active and used to poultry, to take entire charge of an Experimental Farm of three acres.

He found the place he seemed in need of at Hickleybrow, near Urshot,[26] in Kent. It was a queer little isolated place, in a dell surrounded by old pinewoods that were black and forbidding at night. A humped shoulder of down cut it off from the sunset, and a gaunt well with a shattered penthouse dwarfed the dwelling. The little house was creeperless, several windows were broken, and the cart shed had a black shadow at midday. It was a mile and a half from the end house of the village, and its loneliness was very doubtfully relieved by an ambiguous family of echoes.

The place impressed Bensington as being eminently adapted to the requirements of scientific research. He walked over the premises sketching out coops and runs with a sweeping arm, and he found the kitchen capable of accommodating a series of incubators and foster mothers with the very minimum of alteration. He took the place there and then; on his way back to London he stopped at Dunton Green[27] and closed with an eligible couple that had answered his advertisements, and that same evening he succeeded in isolating a sufficient quantity of Herakleophorbia I to more than justify these engagements.

The eligible couple who were destined under Mr Bensington to be the first almoners on earth of the Food of the Gods were not only very perceptibly aged but also extremely dirty. This latter point Mr Bensington did not observe, because nothing destroys the powers of general observation quite so much as a life of experimental science.

They were named Skinner, Mr and Mrs Skinner, and Mr Bensington interviewed them in a small room with hermetically sealed windows, a spotted overmantel looking-glass, and some ailing calceolarias.

Mrs Skinner was a very little old woman, capless, with dirty white hair drawn back very very tightly from a face that had begun by being chiefly, and was now, through the loss of teeth and chin, and the wrinkling up of everything else, ending by being almost exclusively – nose. She was dressed in slate colour (so far as her dress had any colour) slashed in one place with red flannel. She let him in and talked to him guardedly and peered at him round and over her nose, while Mr Skinner she alleged made some alteration in his toilette. She had one tooth that got into her articulations and she held her two long wrinkled hands nervously together. She told Mr Bensington that she had managed fowls for years and knew all about incubators; in fact, they themselves had run a poultry farm at one time, and it had only failed at last through the want of pupils. 'It's the pupils as pay,' said Mrs Skinner.

Mr Skinner, when he appeared, was a large-faced man, with a lisp and a squint that made him look over the top of your head, slashed slippers that appealed to Mr Bensington's sympathies, and a manifest shortness of buttons. He held his coat and shirt together with one hand and traced patterns on the black-and-gold tablecloth with the index finger of the other, while his disengaged eye watched Mr Bensington's sword of Damocles, so to speak, with an expression of sad detachment. 'You don't want to run thith farm for profit. No, thir. Ith all the thame, thir. Ekthperimenth! Prethithely.'

He said they could go to the farm at once. He was doing nothing at Dunton Green except a little tailoring. 'It ithn't the thmart plathe I thought it wath, and what I get ithent thkarthely worth having,' he said, 'tho that if it ith any convenienth to you for uth to come . . .'

And in a week Mr and Mrs Skinner were installed in the farm, and the jobbing carpenter from Hickleybrow was diversifying the task of erecting runs and henhouses with a systematic discussion of Mr Bensington.

'I haven't theen much of 'im yet,' said Mr Skinner. 'But as far as I can make 'im out 'e theems to be a thtewpid o' fool.'

'*I* thought 'e seemed a bit dotty,' said the carpenter from Hickleybrow.

' 'E fanthieth 'imself about poultry,' said Mr Skinner. 'Oh my goodneth! You'd think nobody knew nothin' about poultry thept 'im.'

' 'E *looks* like a 'en,' said the carpenter from Hickleybrow; 'what with them spectacles of 'is.'

Mr Skinner came closer to the carpenter from Hickleybrow, and spoke in a confidential manner, and one sad eye regarded the distant village and one was bright and wicked. 'Got to be meathured every blethed day – every blethed 'en, 'e thays. Tho as to thee they grow properly. What oh . . . eh? Every blethed 'en – every blethed day.'

And Mr Skinner put up his hand to laugh behind it in a refined and contagious manner, and humped his shoulders very much – and only the other eye of him failed to participate in his laughter. Then doubting if the carpenter had quite got the point of it, he repeated in a penetrating whisper: '*Meathured!*'

' 'E's worse than our old guvnor; I'm dratted if 'e ain't,' said the carpenter from Hickleybrow.

2

Experimental work is the most tedious thing in the world (unless it be the reports of it in the *Philosophical Transactions*), and it seemed a long time to Mr Bensington before his first dream of enormous possibilities was replaced by a crumb of realisation. He had taken the Experimental Farm in October, and it was May before the first inklings of success began. Herakleophorbia I and II and III had to be tried, and failed; there was trouble with the rats of the Experimental Farm, and there was trouble with the Skinners. The only way to get Skinner to do anything he was told to do was to dismiss him. Then he would rub his unshaven chin – he was always unshaven most miraculously and yet never bearded – with a flattened hand, and look at Mr Bensington with one eye, and over him with the other, and say, 'Oo, of courthe, thir – if you're *theriouth!*'

But at last success dawned. And its herald was a letter in the long slender handwriting of Mr Skinner.

The new Brood are out [wrote Mr Skinner] and don't quite like the look of them. Growing very rank – quite unlike what the similar lot was before your last directions was given. The last, before the cat got them, was a very nice, stocky chick, but these are Growing like thistles. I never saw. They peck so hard, striking above boot top, that am unable to give exact Measures as requested. They are regular Giants, and eating as such. We shall want more corn very soon, for you never saw such chicks to eat. Bigger than Bantams. Going on at this rate, they ought to be a bird for show, rank as they are. Plymouth

Rocks won't be in it. Had a scare last night thinking that cat was at them, and when I looked out at the window could have sworn I see her getting in under the wire. The chicks was all awake and pecking about hungry when I went out, but could not see anything of the cat. So gave them a peck of corn, and fastened up safe. Shall be glad to know if the Feeding to be continued as directed. Food you mixed is pretty near all gone, and do not like to mix any more myself on account of the accident with the pudding. With best wishes from us both, and soliciting continuance of esteemed favours,

Respectfully yours,

ALFRED NEWTON SKINNER

The allusion towards the end referred to a milk pudding with which some Herakleophorbia II had got itself mixed with painful and very nearly fatal results to the Skinners.

But Mr Bensington, reading between the lines, saw in this rankness of growth the attainment of his long sought goal. The next morning he alighted at Urshot station, and in the bag in his hand he carried, sealed in three tins, a supply of the Food of the Gods sufficient for all the chicks in Kent.

It was a bright and beautiful morning late in May, and his corns were so much better that he resolved to walk through Hickleybrow to his farm. It was three miles and a half altogether, through the park and villages and then along the green glades of the Hickleybrow preserves. The trees were all dusted with the green spangles of high spring, the hedges were full of stitchwort and campion and the woods of blue hyacinths and purple orchid; and everywhere there was a great noise of birds – thrushes, blackbirds, robins, finches, and many more – and in one warm corner of the park some bracken was unrolling, and there was a leaping and rushing of fallow deer.

These things brought back to Mr Bensington his early and forgotten delight in life; before him the promise of his discovery grew bright and joyful, and it seemed to him that indeed he must have come upon the happiest day in his life. And when in the sunlit run by the sandy bank under the shadow of the pine trees he saw the chicks that had eaten the food he had mixed for them, gigantic and gawky, bigger already than many a hen that is married and settled, and still growing, still in their first soft yellow plumage (just faintly marked with brown along the back), he knew indeed that his happiest day had come.

At Mr Skinner's urgency he went into the runs but after he had been pecked through the cracks in his shoes once or twice he got out again, and watched these monsters through the wire netting. He peered close to the netting, and followed their movements as though he had never seen a chick before in his life.

'Whath they'll be when they're grown up ith impothible to think,' said Mr Skinner.

'Big as a horse,' said Mr Bensington.

'Pretty near,' said Mr Skinner.

'Several people could dine off a wing!' said Mr Bensington. 'They'd cut up into joints like butcher's meat.'

'They won't go on growing at thith pathe though,' said Mr Skinner.

'No?' said Mr Bensington.

'No,' said Mr Skinner. 'I know thith thort. They begin rank, but they don't go on, bleth you! No.'

There was a pause.

'It'th management,' said Mr Skinner modestly.

Mr Bensington turned his glasses on him suddenly.

'We got 'em almoth ath big at the other plathe,' said Mr Skinner, with his better eye piously uplifted and letting himself go a little; 'me and the mithith.'

Mr Bensington made his usual general inspection of the premises, but he speedily returned to the new run. It was, you know, in truth ever so much more than he had dared to expect. The course of science is so tortuous and so slow; after the clear promises and before the practical realisation arrives there comes almost always year after year of intricate contrivance, and here – here was the Food of the Gods arriving after less than a year of testing! It seemed too good – too good. That Hope Deferred which is the daily food of the scientific imagination was to be his no more! So at least it seemed to him then. He came back and stared at these stupendous chicks of his, time after time.

'Let me see,' he said. 'They're ten days old. And by the side of an ordinary chick I should fancy – about six or seven times as big . . . '

'Itth about time we artht for a rithe in thkrew,' said Mr Skinner to his wife. 'He'th ath pleathed ath Punth about the way we got thothe chickth on in the further run – pleathed ath Punth he ith.'

He bent confidentially towards her. 'Thinkth it'th that old food of hith,' he said behind his hands and made a noise of suppressed laughter in his pharyngeal cavity . . .

Mr Bensington was indeed a happy man that day. He was in no mood to find fault with details of management. The bright day certainly brought out the accumulating slovenliness of the Skinner couple more vividly than he had ever seen it before. But his comments were of the gentlest. The fencing of many of the runs was out of order, but he seemed to consider it quite satisfactory when Mr Skinner explained that it was a 'fokth or a dog or thomething' did it. He pointed out that the incubator had not been cleaned.

'That it *asn't*, sir,' said Mrs Skinner with her arms folded, smiling coyly behind her nose. 'We don't seem to have had time to clean it not since we been 'ere . . .'

He went upstairs to see some rat-holes that Skinner said would justify a trap – they certainly were enormous – and discovered that the room in which the Food of the Gods was mixed with meal and bran was in a quite disgraceful order. The Skinners were the sort of people who find a use for cracked saucers and old cans and pickle jars and mustard boxes, and the place was littered with these. In one corner a great pile of apples that Skinner had saved was decaying, and from a nail in the sloping part of the ceiling hung several rabbit skins, upon which he proposed to test his gift as a furrier. ('There ithn't mutth about furth and thingth that *I* don't know,' said Skinner.)

Mr Bensington certainly sniffed critically at this disorder, but he made no unnecessary fuss, and even when he found a wasp regaling itself in a gallipot[28] half full of Herakleophorbia IV, he simply remarked mildly that his substance was better sealed from the damp than exposed to the air in that manner.

And he turned from these things at once to remark – what had been for some time in his mind – 'I *think*, Skinner – you know, I shall kill one of these chicks – as a specimen. I think we will kill it this afternoon, and I will take it back with me to London.'

He pretended to peer into another gallipot and then took off his spectacles to wipe them.

'I should like,' he said, 'I should like very much, to have some relic – some memento – of this particular brood at this particular day.'

'By the by,' he said, 'you don't give those little chicks meat?'

'Oh! *no*, thir,' said Skinner, 'I can athure you, thir, we know far too much about the management of fowlth of all dethcriptionth to do anything of that thort.'

'Quite sure you don't throw your dinner refuse – I thought I noticed the bones of a rabbit scattered about the far corner of the run –'

But when they came to look at them they found they were the larger bones of a cat picked very clean and dry.

'*That's* no chick,' said Mr Bensington's cousin Jane.

'Well, I should *think* I knew a chick when I saw it,' said Mr Bensington's cousin Jane hotly.

'It's too big for a chick, for one thing, and besides you can *see* perfectly well it isn't a chick.

'It's more like a bustard than a chick.'

'For my part,' said Redwood, reluctantly allowing Bensington to drag him into the argument, 'I must confess that, considering all the evidence – '

'Oh! if you do *that*,' said Mr Bensington's cousin Jane, 'instead of using your eyes like a sensible person – '

'Well, but really, Miss Bensington – !'

'Oh! Go *on*!' said Cousin Jane. 'You men are all alike.'

'Considering all the evidence, this certainly falls within the definition – no doubt it's abnormal and hypertrophied, but still – especially since it was hatched from the egg of a normal hen – Yes, I think, Miss Bensington, I must admit – this, so far as one can call it anything, is a sort of chick.'

'You mean it's a chick?' said Cousin Jane.

'I *think* it's a chick,' said Redwood.

'What *nonsense*!' said Mr Bensington's cousin Jane, and 'Oh!' directed at Redwood's head, 'I haven't patience with you,' and then suddenly she turned about and went out of the room with a slam.

'And it's a very great relief for me to see it too, Bensington,' said Redwood, when the reverberation of the slam had died away. 'In spite of its being so big.'

Without any urgency from Mr Bensington he sat down in the low armchair by the fire and confessed to proceedings that even in an unscientific man would have been indiscreet. 'You will think it very rash of me, Bensington, I know,' he said, 'but the fact is I put a little – not very much of it – but some – into Baby's bottle, very nearly a week ago!'

'But suppose – !' cried Mr Bensington.

'I know,' said Redwood, and glanced at the giant chick upon the plate on the table. 'It's turned out all right, thank goodness,' and he felt in his pocket for his cigarettes.

He gave fragmentary details. 'Poor little chap wasn't putting on weight . . . desperately anxious. Winkles, a frightful duffer . . . former pupil of mine . . . no good . . . Mrs Redwood – unmitigated confidence in Winkles . . . *You* know, man with a manner like a cliff – towering . . . No confidence in *me*, of course . . . Taught Winkles . . . Scarcely allowed in the nursery . . . Something had to be done . . . Slipped in while the nurse was at breakfast . . . got at the bottle.'

'But he'll grow,' said Mr Bensington.

'He's growing. Twenty-seven ounces last week . . . You should hear Winkles. It's management, he said.'

'Dear me! That's what Skinner says!'

Redwood looked at the chick again. 'The bother is to keep it up,' he said. 'They won't trust me in the nursery alone, because I tried to get a growth curve out of Georgina Phyllis – you know – and how I'm to give him a second dose – '

'Need you?'

'He's been crying two days – can't get on with his ordinary food again, anyhow. He wants some more now.'

'Tell Winkles.'

'Hang Winkles!' said Redwood.

'You might get at Winkles and give him powders to give the child – '

'That's about what I shall have to do,' said Redwood, resting his chin on his fist and staring into the fire.

Bensington stood for a space smoothing the down on the breast of the giant chick. 'They will be monstrous fowls,' he said.

'They will,' said Redwood, still with his eyes on the glow.

'Big as horses,' said Bensington.

'Bigger,' said Redwood. 'That's just it!'

Bensington turned away from the specimen. 'Redwood,' he said, 'these fowls are going to create a sensation.'

Redwood nodded his head at the fire.

'And by Jove!' said Bensington, coming round suddenly with a flash in his spectacles, 'so will your little boy!'

'That's just what I'm thinking of,' said Redwood.

He sat back, sighed, threw his unconsumed cigarette into the fire and thrust his hands deep into his trouser pockets. 'That's precisely what I'm thinking of. This Herakleophorbia is going to be queer stuff to handle. The pace that chick must have grown at – !'

'A little boy growing at that pace,' said Mr Bensington slowly, and stared at the chick as he spoke.

'I *say*!' said Bensington, 'he'll be Big.'

'I shall give him diminishing doses,' said Redwood. 'Or at any rate Winkles will.'

'It's rather too much of an experiment.'

'Much.'

'Yet still, you know, I must confess – . . . Some baby will sooner or later have to try it.'

'Oh, we'll try it on *some* baby – certainly.'

'Exactly so,' said Bensington, and came and stood on the hearthrug and took off his spectacles to wipe them.

'Until I saw these chicks, Redwood, I don't think I *began* to realise – anything – of the possibilities of what we were making. It's only beginning to dawn upon me . . . the possible consequences . . . '

And even then, you know, Mr Bensington was far from any conception of the mine that little train would fire.

4

That happened early in June. For some weeks Bensington was kept from revisiting the Experimental Farm by a severe imaginary catarrh, and one necessary flying visit was made by Redwood. He returned an even more anxious-looking parent than he had gone. Altogether there were seven weeks of steady, uninterrupted growth . . .

And then the wasps began their career.

It was late in July and nearly a week before the hens escaped from Hickleybrow that the first of the big wasps was killed. The report of it appeared in several papers, but I do not know whether the news reached Mr Bensington, much less whether he connected it with the general laxity of method that prevailed at the Experimental Farm.

There can be but little doubt now, that while Mr Skinner was plying Mr Bensington's chicks with Herakleophorbia IV, a number of wasps were just as industriously – perhaps more industriously – carrying quantities of the same paste to their early summer broods in the sandbanks beyond the adjacent pinewoods. And there can be no dispute whatever that these early broods found just as much growth and benefit in the substance as Mr Bensington's hens. It is in the nature of the wasp to attain to effective maturity before the domestic fowl – and in fact of all the creatures that were – through the generous carelessness of the Skinners – partaking of the benefits Mr Bensington heaped upon his hens, the wasps were the first to make any sort of figure in the world.

It was a keeper named Godfrey, on the estate of Lieutenant-Colonel Rupert Hick, near Maidstone, who encountered and had the luck to kill the first of these monsters of whom history has any record. He was walking knee high in bracken across an open space in the beechwoods that diversify Lieutenant-Colonel Hick's park, and he was carrying his gun – very fortunately for him a double-barrelled gun – over his shoulder, when he first caught sight of the thing. It was, he says, coming down against the light, so that he could not see it very distinctly, and as it came it made a drone 'like a motor car'. He admits he was frightened. It was evidently as big or bigger than a barn owl, and, to his practised eye, its flight and particularly the misty whirl of its wings must have seemed weirdly unbirdlike. The instinct of self-defence, I fancy, mingled with long habit, when, as he says, he 'let fly, right away'.

The queerness of the experience probably affected his aim; at any rate most of his shot missed, and the thing merely dropped for a moment with an angry 'Wuzzzz' that revealed the wasp at once, and then rose again, with all its stripes shining against the light. He says it turned on him. At any rate, he fired his second barrel at less than twenty yards and threw down his gun, ran a pace or so, and ducked to avoid it.

It flew, he is convinced, within a yard of him, struck the ground, rose again, came down again perhaps thirty yards away, and rolled over with its body wriggling and its sting stabbing out and back in its last agony. He emptied both barrels into it again before he ventured to go near.

When he came to measure the thing, he found it was twenty-seven and a half inches across its open wings, and its sting was three inches long. The abdomen was blown clean off from its body, but he estimated the length of the creature from head to sting as eighteen inches – which is very nearly correct. Its compound eyes were the size of penny pieces.

That is the first authenticated appearance of these giant wasps. The day after, a cyclist riding, feet up, down the hill between Sevenoaks and Tonbridge, very narrowly missed running over a second of these giants that was crawling across the roadway. His passage seemed to alarm it, and it rose with a noise like a sawmill. His bicycle jumped the footpath in the drama of the moment, and when he could look back, the wasp was soaring away above the woods towards Westerham.[29]

After riding unsteadily for a little time, he put on his brake, dismounted – he was trembling so violently that he fell over his machine in doing so – and sat down by the roadside to recover. He had intended to ride to Ashford, but he did not get beyond Tonbridge that day . . .

After that, curiously enough, there is no record of any big wasps being seen for three days. I find on consulting the meteorological record of those days that they were overcast and chilly with local showers, which may perhaps account for this intermission. Then on the fourth day came blue sky and brilliant sunshine and such an outburst of wasps as the world had surely never seen before.

How many big wasps came out that day it is impossible to guess. There are at least fifty accounts of their apparition. There was one victim, a grocer, who discovered one of these monsters in a sugar-cask and very rashly attacked it with a spade as it rose. He struck it to the ground for a moment, and it stung him through the boot as he struck at it again and cut its body in half. He was first dead of the two . . .

The most dramatic of the fifty appearances was certainly that of the wasp that visited the British Museum about midday, dropping out of the blue serene upon one of the innumerable pigeons that feed in the courtyard of that building, and flying up to the cornice to devour its victim at leisure. After that it crawled for a time over the museum roof, entered the dome of the reading-room by a skylight, buzzed about inside it for some little time – there was a stampede among the readers – and at last found another window and vanished again with a sudden silence from human observation.

Most of the other reports were of mere passings or descents. A picnic party was dispersed at Aldington Knoll and all its sweets and jam consumed, and a puppy was killed and torn to pieces near Whitstable under the very eyes of its mistress . . .

The streets that evening resounded with the cry, the newspaper placards gave themselves up exclusively in the biggest of letters to the 'Gigantic Wasps in Kent'. Agitated editors and assistant editors ran up and down tortuous staircases bawling things about 'wasps'. And Professor Redwood, emerging from his college in Bond Street at five, flushed from a heated discussion with his committee about the price of bull calves, bought an evening paper, opened it, changed colour, forgot about bull calves and his committee forthwith, and took a hansom headlong for Bensington's flat.

5

The flat was occupied, it seemed to him – to the exclusion of all other sensible objects – by Mr Skinner and his voice, if indeed you can call either him or it a sensible object!

The voice was up very high slopping about among the notes of anguish. 'It'th impothible for uth to thtop, thir. We've thtopped on hoping thingth would get better and they've only got worth, thir. It ithn't on'y the waptheth, thir – there'th big earwigth, thir – big ath that, thir.' (He indicated all his hand and about three inches of fat dirty wrist.) 'They pretty near give Mithith Thkinner fitth, thir. And the thtinging nettleth by the runth, thir, *they're* growing, thir, and the canary creeper, thir, what we thowed near the think, thir– it put it'th tendril through the window in the night, thir, and very nearly caught Mithith Thkinner by the legth, thir. It'th that food of yourth, thir. Wherever we thplathed it about, thir, a bit, it'th thet everything growing ranker, thir, than I ever thought anything could grow. It'th impothible to thtop a month, thir. It'th more than our liveth are worth, thir. Even if the waptheth don't thting uth, we thall be thuffocated by the creeper, thir. You can't imagine, thir– unleth you come down to thee, thir– '

He turned his superior eye to the cornice above Redwood's head. ' 'Ow do we know the ratth 'aven't got it, thir! That 'th what I think of motht, thir. I 'aven't theen any big ratth, thir, but 'ow do I know, thir. We been frightened for dayth becauth of the earwigth we've theen – like lobthters they wath – two of 'em, thir– and the frightful way the canary creeper wath growing, and directly I heard the waptheth – directly I 'eard 'em, thir, I underthood. I didn't wait for nothing exthept to thow on a button I'd lortht, and then I came on up. Even now, thir, I'm arf wild with angthiety, thir. 'Ow do *I* know watth happenin' to Mithith Thkinner, thir! There'th the creeper growing all over the plathe like a thnake, thir – thwelp me but you 'ave to watch it, thir, and jump out of itth way! – and the earwigth gettin' bigger and bigger, and the waptheth – She 'athen't even got a Blue Bag, thir– if anything thould happen, thir!'

'But the hens,' said Mr Bensington; 'how are the hens?'

'We fed 'em up to yethterday, thwelp me,' said Mr Skinner, 'but thith morning we didn't *dare*, thir. The noithe of the waptheth wath – thome-thing awful, thir. They wath coming ont – dothenth. Ath big ath 'enth. I thayth, to 'er, I thayth you jutht thow me on a button or two, I thayth, for I can't go to London like thith, I thayth, and I'll go up to Mithter Benthington, I thayth, and ekthplain thingth to 'im. And you thtop in thith room till I come back to you, I thayth, and keep the windowth thut jutht ath tight ath ever you can, I thayth.'

'If you hadn't been so confoundedly untidy – ' began Redwood.

'Oh! don't thay *that*, thir,' said Skinner. 'Not now, thir. Not with me tho diththrethed, thir, about Mithith Thkinner, thir! Oh, *don't*, thir! I 'aven't the 'eart to argue with you. Thwelp me, thir, I 'aven't! It'th the ratth I keep a thinking of – 'Ow do I know they 'aven't got at Mithith Thkinner while I been up 'ere?'

'And you haven't got a solitary measurement of all these beautiful growth curves!' said Redwood.

'I been too upthet, thir,' said Mr Skinner. 'If you knew what we been through – me and the mithith! All thith latht month. We 'aven't known what to make of it, thir. What with the henth gettin' tho rank, and the earwigth, and the canary creeper. I dunno if I told you, thir – the canary creeper . . .'

'You've told us all that,' said Redwood. 'The thing is, Bensington, what are we to do?'

'What are *we* to do?' said Mr Skinner.

'You'll have to go back to Mrs Skinner,' said Redwood. 'You can't leave her there alone all night.'

'Not alone, thir, I won't. Not if there wath a dothen Mithith Thkinnerth. It'th Mither Benthington – '

'Nonsense,' said Redwood. 'The wasps will be all right at night. And the earwigs will get out of your way – '

'But about the ratth?'

'There aren't any rats,' said Redwood.

6

Mr Skinner might have forgone his chief anxiety. Mrs Skinner did not stop out her day.

About eleven the canary creeper, which had been quietly active all the morning, began to clamber over the window and darken it very greatly, and the darker it got the more and more clearly Mrs Skinner perceived that her position would speedily become untenable. And also that she had lived many ages since Skinner went. She peered out of the darkling window, through the stirring tendrils, for some time, and then went very cautiously and opened the bedroom door and listened . . .

Everything seemed quiet, and so, tucking her skirts high about her, Mrs Skinner made a bolt for the bedroom, and having first looked under the bed and locked herself in, proceeded with the methodical rapidity of an experienced woman to pack for departure. The bed had not been made, and the room was littered with pieces of the creeper that Skinner had hacked off in order to close the window overnight, but these disorders she did not heed. She packed in a decent sheet. She packed all her own wardrobe and a velveteen jacket that Skinner wore in his finer moments, and she packed a jar of pickles that had not been opened, and so far she was justified in her packing. But she also packed two of the hermetically closed tins containing Herakleophorbia IV that Mr Bensington had brought on his last visit. (She was honest, good woman – but she was a grandmother, and her heart had burned within her to see such good growth lavished on a lot of dratted chicks.)

And having packed all these things, she put on her bonnet, took off her apron, tied a new bootlace round her umbrella, and after listening for a long time at door and window, opened the door and sallied out into a perilous world. The umbrella was under her arm and she clutched the bundle with two gnarled and resolute hands. It was her best Sunday bonnet, and the two poppies that reared their heads amidst its splendours of band and bead seemed instinct with the same tremulous courage that possessed her.

The features about the roots of her nose wrinkled with determination. She had had enough of it! All alone there! Skinner might come back there if he liked.

She went out by the front door, going that way not because she wanted to go to Hickleybrow (her goal was Cheasing Eyebright,[30] where her married daughter resided), but because the back door was impassable on account of the canary creeper that had been growing so furiously ever since she upset the can of food near its roots. She listened for a space and closed the front door very carefully behind her.

At the corner of the house she paused and reconnoitred . . .

An extensive sandy scar upon the hillside beyond the pinewoods marked the nest of the giant wasps, and this she studied very earnestly. The coming and going of the morning was over, not a wasp chanced to be in sight then, and except for a sound scarcely more perceptible than a steam wood-saw at work amidst the pines would have been, everything was still. As for earwigs, she could see not one. Down among the cabbage indeed something was stirring, but it might just as probably be a cat stalking birds. She watched this for a time.

She went a few paces past the corner, came in sight of the run containing the giant chicks and stopped again. 'Ah!' she said, and shook her head slowly at the sight of them. They were at that time about the height of emus, but of course much thicker in the body – a larger thing altogether. They were all hens and five all told, now that the two cockerels had killed each other. She hesitated at their drooping attitudes. 'Poor dears!' she said, and put down her bundle; 'they've got no water. And they've 'ad no food these twenty-four hours! And such appetites, too, as they 'ave!' She put a lean finger to her lips and communed with herself.

Then this dirty old woman did what seems to me a quite heroic deed of mercy. She left her bundle and umbrella in the middle of the brick path and went to the well and drew no fewer than three pailfuls of water for the chickens' empty trough, and then while they were all crowding about that, she undid the door of the run very softly. After which she became extremely active, resumed her package, got over the hedge at the bottom of the garden, crossed the rank meadows (in order to avoid the wasps' nest) and toiled up the winding path towards Cheasing Eyebright.

She panted up the hill, and as she went she paused ever and again to rest her bundle and get her breath and stare back at the little cottage beside the pinewood below. And when at last, when she was near the crest of the hill, she saw afar off three several wasps dropping heavily westward, it helped her greatly on her way.

She soon got out of the open and into the high-banked lane beyond (which seemed a safer place to her), and so up by Hicklebrow Coombe to the downs. There at the foot of the downs where a big tree gave an air of shelter she rested for a space on a stile.

Then on again very resolutely . . .

You figure her, I hope, with her white bundle, a sort of erect black ant, hurrying along the little white path-thread athwart the downland slopes under the hot sun of the summer afternoon. On she struggled after her resolute indefatigable nose, and the poppies in her bonnet quivered perpetually and her spring-sided boots grew whiter and whiter with the downland dust. Flip-flap, flip-flap went her footfalls through the still heat of the day, and persistently, incurably, her umbrella sought to slip from under the elbow that retained it. The mouth wrinkle under her nose was pursed to an extreme resolution, and ever and again she told her umbrella to come up or gave her tightly clutched bundle a vindictive jerk. And at times her lips mumbled with fragments of some foreseen argument between herself and Skinner.

And far away, miles and miles away, a steeple and a hanger grew insensibly out of the vague blue to mark more and more distinctly the quiet corner where Cheasing Eyebright sheltered from the tumult of the world, recking little or nothing of the Herakleophorbia concealed in that white bundle that struggled so persistently towards its orderly retirement.

So far as I can gather, the pullets came into Hickleybrow about three o'clock in the afternoon. Their coming must have been a brisk affair, though nobody was out in the street to see it. The violent bellowing of little Skelmersdale seems to have been the first announcement of anything out of the way. Miss Durgan of the Post Office was at the window as usual, and saw the hen that had caught the unhappy child in violent flight up the street with its victim, closely pursued by two others. You know that swinging stride of the emancipated athletic latter-day pullet! You know the keen insistence of the hungry hen! There was Plymouth Rock in these birds, I am told, and even without Herakleophorbia that is a gaunt and striding strain.

Probably Miss Durgan was not altogether taken by surprise. In spite of Mr Bensington's insistence upon secrecy, rumours of the great chickens Mr Skinner was producing had been about the village for some weeks. 'Lor!' she cried, 'it's what I expected.'

She seems to have behaved with great presence of mind. She snatched up the sealed bag of letters that was waiting to go on to Urshot, and rushed out of the door at once. Almost simultaneously Mr Skelmersdale himself appeared down the village, gripping a watering-pot by the spout and very white in the face. And, of course, in a moment or so everyone in the village was rushing to the door or window. The spectacle of Miss Durgan all across the road, with the entire day's correspondence of Hickleybrow in her hand, gave pause to the pullet in possession of Master Skelmersdale. She halted through one instant's indecision and then turned for the open gates of Fulcher's yard. That instant was fatal. The second pullet ran in neatly, got possession of the child by a well-directed peck, and went over the wall into the vicarage garden.

'Charawk, chawk, chawk, chawk, chawk, chawk!' shrieked the hindmost hen, hit smartly by the watering-can Mr Skelmersdale had thrown, and fluttered wildly over Mrs Glue's cottage and so into the doctor's field, while the rest of those gargantuan birds pursued the pullet in possession of the child across the vicarage lawn.

'Good heavens!' cried the curate, or (as some say) something much more manly, and ran, whirling his croquet mallet and shouting, to head off the chase.

'Stop, you wretch!' cried the curate, as though giant hens were the commonest facts in life.

And then, finding he could not possibly intercept her, he hurled his mallet with all his might and main, and out it shot in a gracious curve within a foot or so of Master Skelmersdale's head and through the glass lantern of the conservatory. Smash! The new conservatory! The vicar's wife's beautiful new conservatory!

It frightened the hen. It might have frightened anyone. She dropped her victim into a Portugal laurel (from which he was presently extracted, disordered but, save for his less delicate garments, uninjured), made a flapping leap for the roof of Fulcher's stables, put her foot through a weak place in the tiles, and descended, so to speak, out of the infinite into the contemplative quiet of Mr Bumps the paralytic – who, it is now proved beyond all cavil, did, on this one occasion in his life, get down the entire length of his garden and indoors without any assistance whatever, bolt the door after him, and immediately relapse again into Christian resignation and helpless dependence upon his wife . . .

The rest of the pullets were headed off by the other croquet players, and went through the vicar's kitchen garden into the doctor's field, to which rendezvous the fifth also came at last, clucking disconsolately after an unsuccessful attempt to walk on the cucumber frames in Mr Witherspoon's place.

They seem to have stood about in a hen-like manner for a time, and scratched a little and chirrawked meditatively, and then one pecked at and pecked over a hive of the doctor's bees, and after that they set off in a gawky, jerky, feathery, fitful sort of way across the fields towards Urshot, and Hickleybrow Street saw them no more. Near Urshot they really came upon commensurate food in a field of swedes; and pecked for a space with gusto, until their fame overtook them.

The chief immediate reaction of this astonishing irruption of gigantic poultry upon the human mind was to arouse an extraordinary passion to whoop and run and throw things, and in quite a little time almost all the available manhood of Hickleybrow, and several ladies, were out with a remarkable assortment of flappish and whangable articles in hand – to commence the scooting of the giant hens. They drove them into Urshot, where there was a rural fête, and Urshot took them as the crowning glory of a happy day. They began to be shot at near Findon Beeches, but at first only with a rook rifle. Of course birds of that size could absorb an unlimited quantity of small shot without inconvenience. They scattered somewhere near Sevenoaks, and near Tonbridge one of them fled clucking for a time in excessive agitation, somewhat ahead of and parallel with the afternoon boat express – to the great astonishment of everyone therein.

And about half-past five two of them were caught very cleverly by a circus proprietor at Tunbridge Wells, who lured them into a cage, rendered vacant through the death of a widowed dromedary, by scattering cakes and bread ...

8

When the unfortunate Skinner got out of the South-Eastern train at Urshot that evening it was already nearly dusk. The train was late, but not inordinately late – and Mr Skinner remarked as much to the station-master. Perhaps he saw a certain pregnancy in the station-master's eye. After the briefest hesitation and with a confidential movement of his hand to the side of his mouth he asked if 'anything' had happened that day.

'How d'yer *mean*?' said the station-master, a man with a hard, emphatic voice.

'Thethe 'ere waptheth and thingth.'

'We 'aven't 'ad much time to think of *waptheth*,' said the station-master agreeably. 'We've been too busy with your brasted 'ens,' and he broke the news of the pullets to Mr Skinner as one might break the window of an adverse politician.

'You ain't 'eard anything of Mithith Thkinner?' asked Skinner, amidst that missile shower of pithy information and comment.

'No fear!' said the station-master – as though even he drew the line somewhere in the matter of knowledge.

'I mutht make enquireth bout thith,' said Mr Skinner, edging out of reach of the station-master's concluding generalisations about the responsibility attaching to the excessive nurture of hens ...

Going through Urshot Mr Skinner was hailed by a lime-burner from the pits over by Hankey and asked if he was looking for his hens.

'You ain't 'eard anything of Mithith Thkinner?' he asked.

The lime-burner – his exact phrases need not concern us – expressed his superior interest in hens ...

It was already dark – as dark at least as a clear night in the English June can be – when Skinner – or his head at any rate – came into the bar of the Jolly Drovers and said: ' 'Ello! You 'aven't 'eard anything of thith 'ere thtory bout my 'enth, 'ave you?'

'Oh, *'aven't* we!' said Mr Fulcher. 'Why, part of the story's been and bust into my stable roof and one chapter smashed a 'ole in Missis Vicar's green 'ouse – I beg 'er pardon – conservarratory.'

Skinner came in. 'I'd like thomething a little comforting,' he said, ' 'ot gin and water'th about my figure,' and everybody began to tell him things about the pullets.

'*Grathuth* me!' said Skinner.

'You 'aven't 'eard anything about Mithith Thkinner, 'ave you?' he asked in a pause.

'That we 'aven't!' said Mr Witherspoon. 'We 'aven't thought of 'er. We ain't thought nothing of either of you.'

'Ain't you been 'ome today?' asked Fulcher over a tankard.

'If one of those brasted birds 'ave pecked 'er,' began Mr Witherspoon, and left the full horror to their unaided imaginations . . .

It appeared to the meeting at the time that it would be an interesting end to an eventful day to go on with Skinner and see if anything *had* happened to Mrs Skinner. One never knows what luck one may have when accidents are at large. But Skinner, standing at the bar and drinking his hot gin and water, with one eye roving over the things at the back of the bar and the other fixed on the Absolute, missed the psychological moment.

'I thuppothe there 'athen't been any trouble with any of thethe big waptheth today anywhere?' he asked, with an elaborate detachment of manner.

'Been too busy with your 'ens,' said Fulcher.

'I thuppothe they've all gone in now anyhow,' said Skinner.

'What – the 'ens?'

'I wath thinking of the waptheth more particularly,' said Skinner.

And then, with an air of circumspection that would have awakened suspicion in a week-old baby, and laying the accent heavily on most of the words he chose, he asked, 'I *thuppothe nobody* 'athn't 'eard of any other *big* thingth about, 'ave they? Big *dogth* or *catth* or anything of *that* thort? Theemth to me if there'th big henth and big waptheth comin' on – '

He laughed with a fine pretence of talking idly.

But a brooding expression came upon the faces of the Hickleybrow men. Fulcher was the first to give their condensing thought the concrete shape of words.

'A cat to match them 'ens – ' said Fulcher.

'Ay!' said Witherspoon, 'a cat to match they 'ens.'

' 'Twould be a tiger,' said Fulcher.

'More'n a tiger,' said Witherspoon . . .

When at last Skinner followed the lonely footpath over the swelling field that separated Hickleybrow from the sombre pine-shaded hollow in whose black shadows the gigantic canary-creeper grappled silently with the Experimental Farm, he followed it alone.

He was distinctly seen to rise against the skyline, against the warm clear immensity of the northern sky – for so far public interest followed him – and to descend again into the night, into an obscurity from which it would seem he will nevermore emerge. He passed – into a mystery. No one knows to this day what happened to him after he crossed the brow. When later on the two Fulchers and Witherspoon, moved by their own imaginations, came up the hill and stared after him, the flight had swallowed him up altogether.

The three men stood close. There was not a sound out of the wooded blackness that hid the farm from their eyes.

'It's all right,' said young Fulcher, ending a silence.

'Don't see any lights,' said Witherspoon.

'You wouldn't from here.'

'It's misty,' said the elder Fulcher.

They meditated for a space.

' 'E'd 'ave come back if anything was wrong,' said young Fulcher, and this seemed so obvious and conclusive that presently old Fulcher said, 'Well,' and the three went home to bed – thoughtfully I will admit . . .

A shepherd out by Huckster's Farm heard a squealing in the night that he thought was foxes, and in the morning one of his lambs had been killed, dragged halfway towards Hickleybrow and partially devoured . . .

The inexplicable part of it all is the absence of any indisputable remains of Skinner!

Many weeks after, amidst the charred ruins of the Experimental Farm, there was found something which may or may not have been a human shoulder-blade and in another part of the ruins a long bone greatly gnawed and equally doubtful. Near the stile going up towards Eyebright there was found a glass eye, and many people discovered thereupon that Skinner owed much of his personal charm to such a possession. It stared out upon the world with that same inevitable effect of detachment, that same severe melancholy that had been the redemption of his else worldly countenance.

And about the ruins industrous research discovered the metal rings and charred coverings of two linen buttons, three shanked buttons entire, and one of that metallic sort which is used in the less conspicuous sutures of the human Oeconomy.[31] These remains have been accepted by persons in authority as conclusive of a destroyed and scattered Skinner, but for my own entire conviction, and in view of his distinctive idiosyncrasy, I must confess I should prefer fewer buttons and more bones.

The glass eye of course has an air of extreme conviction, but if it really *is* Skinner's – and even Mrs Skinner did not certainly know if that immobile eye of his was glass – something has changed it from a liquid brown to a serene and confident blue. That shoulder-blade is an extremely doubtful document, and I would like to put it side by side with the gnawed scapulae of a few of the commoner domestic animals before I admitted its humanity.

And where were Skinner's boots, for example? Perverted and strange as a rat's appetite must be, is it conceivable that the same creatures that could leave a lamb only half eaten, would finish up Skinner – hair, bones, teeth and boots?

I have closely questioned as many as I could of those who knew Skinner at all intimately, and they one and all agree that they cannot imagine *anything* eating him. He was the sort of man, as a retired seafaring person living in one of Mr W. W. Jacobs's[33] cottages at Dunton Green told me, with a guarded significance of manner not uncommon in those parts, who would 'get washed up anyhow', and as regards *the* devouring element was 'fit to put a fire out'. He considered that Skinner would be as safe on a raft as anywhere. The retired seafaring man added that he wished to say nothing whatever against Skinner; facts were facts. And rather than have his clothes made by Skinner, the retired seafaring man remarked he would take his chance of being locked up. These observations certainly do not present Skinner in the light of an appetising object.

To be perfectly frank with the reader, I do not believe he ever went back to the Experimental Farm. I believe he hovered through long hesitations about the fields of the Hickleybrow glebe, and finally, when that squealing began, took the line of least resistance out of his perplexities into the Incognito.

And in the Incognito, whether of this or of some other world unknown to us, he obstinately and quite indisputably has remained to this day . . .

CHAPTER 3

The Giant Rats

It was two nights after the disappearance of Mr Skinner that the Podbourne doctor was out late near Hankey, driving in his buggy. He had been up all night assisting another undistinguished citizen into this curious world of ours, and his task accomplished, he was driving homeward in a drowsy mood enough. It was about two o'clock in the morning, and the waning moon was rising. The summer night had gone cold, and there was a low-lying whitish mist that made things indistinct. He was quite alone – for his coachman was ill in bed – and there was nothing to be seen on either hand but a drifting mystery of hedge running athwart the yellow glare of his lamps, and nothing to hear but the clitter-clatter of his horse and the echo of his wheels. His horse was as trustworthy as himself, and one does not wonder that he dozed . . .

You know that intermittent drowsing as one sits, the drooping of the head, the nodding to the rhythm of the wheels then chin upon the breast, and at once the sudden start up again.

Pitter, litter, patter.

'What was that?'

It seemed to the doctor he had heard a thin shrill squeal close at hand. In a moment he was quite awake. He said a word or two of undeserved rebuke to his horse, and looked about him. He tried to persuade himself that he had heard the distant squeal of a fox – or perhaps a young rabbit gripped by a ferret.

Swish, swish, swish, pitter, patter, swish . . .

What was that?

He felt he was getting fanciful. He shook his shoulders and told his horse to get on. He listened, and heard nothing.

Or was it nothing?

He had the queerest impression that something had just peeped over the hedge at him, a queer big head. With round ears! He peered hard, but he could see nothing.

'Nonsense,' said he.

He sat up with an idea that he had dropped into a nightmare, gave his horse the slightest touch of the whip, spoke to it and peered again over the hedge. The glare of his lamp, however, together with the mist, rendered things indistinct, and he could distinguish nothing. It came into his head, he says, that there could be nothing there, because if there was his horse would have shied at it. Yet for all that his senses remained nervously awake.

Then he heard quite distinctly a soft pattering of feet in pursuit along the road.

He would not believe his ears about that. He could not look round, for the road had a sinuous curve just there. He whipped up his horse and glanced sideways again. And then he saw quite distinctly where a ray from his lamp leapt a low stretch of hedge, the curved back of – some big animal, he couldn't tell what, going along in quick convulsive leaps.

He says he thought of the old tales of witchcraft – the thing was so utterly unlike any animal he knew, and he tightened his hold on the reins for fear of the fear of his horse. Educated man as he was, he admits he asked himself if this could be something that his horse could not see.

Ahead, and drawing near in silhouette against the rising moon, was the outline of the little hamlet of Hankey, comforting, though it showed never a light, and he cracked his whip and spoke again, and then in a flash the rats were at him!

He had passed a gate, and as he did so, the foremost rat came leaping over into the road. The thing sprang upon him out of vagueness into the utmost clearness, the sharp, eager, round-eared face, the long body exaggerated by its movement; and what particularly struck him, the pink, webbed forefeet of the beast. What must have made it more horrible to him at the time was that he had no idea the thing was any created beast he knew. He did not recognise it as a rat, because of the size. His horse gave a bound as the thing dropped into the road beside it. The little lane woke into tumult at the report of the whip and the doctor's shout. The whole thing suddenly went fast.

Rattle-clatter, clash, clatter.

The doctor, one gathers, stood up, shouted to his horse, and slashed with all his strength. The rat winced and swerved most reassuringly at his blow – in the glare of his lamp he could see the fur furrow under the lash – and he slashed again and again, heedless and unaware of the second pursuer that gained upon his offside.

He let the reins go, and glanced back to discover the third rat in pursuit behind . . .

His horse bounded forward. The buggy leapt high at a rut. For a frantic minute perhaps everything seemed to be going in leaps and bounds . . .

It was sheer good luck the horse came down in Hankey, and not either before or after the houses had been passed.

No one knows how the horse came down, whether it stumbled or whether the rat on the offside really got home with one of those slashing down strokes of the teeth (given with the full weight of the body); and the doctor never discovered that he himself was bitten until he was inside the brickmaker's house, much less did he discover when the bite occurred, though bitten he was and badly – a long slash like the slash of a double tomahawk that had cut two parallel ribbons of flesh from his left shoulder.

He was standing up in his buggy at one moment, and in the next he had leapt to the ground, with his ankle, though he did not know it, badly sprained, and he was cutting furiously at a third rat that was flying directly at him. He scarcely remembers the leap he must have made over the top of the wheel as the buggy came over, so obliteratingly hot and swift did his impressions rush upon him. I think myself the horse reared up with the rat biting again at its throat, and fell sideways, and carried the whole affair over; and that the doctor sprang, as it were, instinctively. As the buggy came down, the receiver of the lamp smashed, and suddenly poured a flare of blazing oil, a thud of white flame, into the struggle.

That was the first thing the brickmaker saw.

He had heard the clatter of the doctor's approach and – though the doctor's memory has nothing of this – wild shouting. He had got out of bed hastily, and as he did so came the terrific smash, and up shot the glare outside the rising blind. 'It was brighter than day,' he says. He stood, blind cord in hand, and stared out of the window at a nightmare transformation of the familiar road before him. The black figure of the doctor with its whirling whip danced out against the flame. The horse kicked indistinctly, half hidden by the blaze, with a rat at its throat. In the obscurity against the churchyard wall, the eyes of a second monster shone wickedly. Another – a mere dreadful blackness with red-lit eyes and flesh-coloured hands – clutched unsteadily on the wall coping to which it had leapt at the flash of the exploding lamp.

You know the keen face of a rat, those two sharp teeth, those pitiless eyes. Seen magnified to near six times its linear dimensions, and still more magnified by darkness and amazement and the leaping fancies of a fitful blaze, it must have been an ill sight for the brickmaker – still more than half asleep.

Then the doctor had grasped the opportunity, that momentary respite the flare afforded, and was out of the brickmaker's sight below battering the door with the butt of his whip . . .

The brickmaker would not let him in until he had got a light.

There are those who have blamed the man for that, but until I know my own courage better, I hesitate to join their number.

The doctor yelled and hammered . . .

The brickmaker says he was weeping with terror when at last the door was opened.

'Bolt,' said the doctor, 'bolt' – he could not say 'bolt the door'. He tried to help, and was of no service. The brickmaker fastened the door, and the doctor had to sit on the chair beside the clock for a space before he could go upstairs . . .

'I don't know what they *are*!' he repeated several times. 'I don't know what they *are*' – with a high note on the 'are'.

The brickmaker would have got him whisky, but the doctor would not be left alone with nothing but a flickering light just then.

It was long before the brickmaker could get him to go upstairs . . .

And when the fire was out the giant rats came back, took the dead horse, dragged it across the churchyard into the brickfield and ate at it until it was dawn, none even then daring to disturb them . . .

2

Redwood went round to Bensington about eleven the next morning with the second editions of three evening papers in his hand.

Bensington looked up from a despondent meditation over the forgotten pages of the most distracting novel the Brompton Road librarian had been able to find him. 'Anything fresh?' he asked.

'Two men stung near Chartham.'

'They ought to let us smoke out that nest. They really did. It's their own fault.'

'It's their own fault, certainly,' said Redwood.

'Have you heard anything – about buying the farm?'

'The House Agent,' said Redwood, 'is a thing with a big mouth and made of dense wood. It pretends someone else is after the house – it always does, you know – and won't understand there's a hurry. "This is a matter of life and death," I said, "don't you understand?" It drooped its eyes half shut and said, "Then why don't you go the other two hundred pounds?" I'd rather live in a world of solid wasps than give in to the stonewalling stupidity of that offensive creature. I – '

He paused, feeling that a sentence like that might very easily be spoiled by its context.

'It's too much to hope,' said Bensington, 'that one of the wasps – '

'The wasp has no more idea of public utility than a – than a house agent,' said Redwood.

He talked for a little while about house agents and solicitors and people of that sort, in the unjust, unreasonable way that so many people do somehow get to talk of these business calculi ('Of all the cranky things in this cranky world, the most cranky of all to my mind is that while we expect honour, courage, efficiency from a doctor or a soldier as a matter of course, a solicitor or a house agent is not only permitted but expected to display nothing but a sort of greedy, greasy, obstructive, over-reaching imbecility – ' etc.) and then, greatly relieved, he went to the window and stared out at the Sloane Street traffic.

Bensington had put the most exciting novel conceivable on the little table that carried his electric standard. He joined the fingers of his opposed hands very carefully and regarded them. 'Redwood,' he said. 'Do they say much about *Us*?'

'Not so much as I should expect.'

'They don't denounce us at all?'

'Not a bit. But, on the other hand, they don't back up what I point out must be done. I've written to *The Times*, you know, explaining the whole thing – '

'We take the *Daily Chronicle*,' said Bensington.

'And *The Times* has a long leader on the subject – a very high-class, well-written leader, with three pieces of *Times* Latin – *status quo* is one – and it reads like the voice of Somebody Impersonal of the Greatest Importance suffering from Influenza Headache and talking through sheets and sheets of felt without getting any relief from it whatever. Reading between the lines, you know, it's pretty clear that *The Times* considers that it is useless to mince matters and that something (indefinite, of course) has to be done at once. Otherwise still more undesirable consequences – *Times* English, you know, for more wasps and stings. Thoroughly statesmanlike article!'

'And meanwhile this Bigness is spreading in all sorts of ugly ways.'

'Precisely.'

'I wonder if Skinner was right about those big rats – '

'Oh no! That would be too much,' said Redwood.

He came and stood by Bensington's chair.

'By the by,' he said, with a slightly lowered voice, 'how does *she* – ?' He indicated the closed door.

'Cousin Jane? She simply knows nothing about it. Doesn't connect us with it and won't read the articles. "Gigantic wasps!" she says, "I haven't patience to read the papers." '

'That's very fortunate,' said Redwood.

'I suppose – Mrs Redwood – ?'

'No,' said Redwood, 'just at present it happens – she's terribly worried about the child. You know, he keeps on.'

'Growing?'

'Yes. Put on forty-one ounces in ten days. Weighs nearly four stone. And only six months old! Naturally rather alarming.'

'Healthy?'

'Vigorous. His nurse is leaving because he kicks so forcibly. And everything, of course, shockingly outgrown. Everything, you know, has had to be made fresh, clothes and everything. Perambulator – light affair – broke one wheel, and the youngster had to be brought home on the milkman's hand-truck. Yes. Quite a crowd . . . And we've put Georgina Phyllis back into his cot and put him into the bed of Georgina Phyllis. His mother – naturally alarmed. Proud at first and inclined to praise Winkles. Not now. Feels the thing *can't* be wholesome. *You* know.'

'I imagined you were going to put him on diminishing doses.'

'I tried it.'

'Didn't it work?'

'Howls. In the ordinary way the cry of a child is loud and distressing; it is for the good of the species that this should be so – but since he has been on the Herakleophorbia treatment – '

'Mm,' said Bensington, regarding his fingers with more resignation than he had hitherto displayed.

'Practically the thing *must* come out. People will hear of this child, connect it up with our hens and things, and the whole thing will come round to my wife . . . How she will take it I haven't the remotest idea.'

'It *is* difficult,' said Mr Bensington, 'to form any plan – certainly.'

He removed his glasses and wiped them carefully.

'It is another instance,' he generalised, 'of the thing that is continually happening. We – if indeed I may presume to the adjective – *scientific* men – we work of course always for a theoretical result – a purely theoretical result. But, incidentally, we do set forces in operation – *new* forces. We mustn't control them – and nobody else *can*. Practically, Redwood, the thing is out of our hands. *We* supply the material – '

'And they,' said Redwood, turning to the window, 'get the experience.'

'So far as this trouble down in Kent goes I am not disposed to worry further.'

'Unless they worry us.'

'Exactly. And if they like to muddle about with solicitors and pettifoggers and legal obstructions and weighty considerations of the tomfool order, until they have got a number of new gigantic species of vermin well established . . . Things always *have* been in a muddle, Redwood.'

Redwood traced a twisted, tangled line in the air.

'And our real interest lies at present with your boy.'

Redwood turned about and came and stared at his collaborator.

'What do you think of him, Bensington? You can look at this business with a greater detachment than I can. What am I to do about him?'

'Go on feeding him.'

'On Herakleophorbia?'

'On Herakleophorbia.'

'And then he'll grow.'

'He'll grow, as far as I can calculate from the hens and the wasps, to the height of about five-and-thirty feet – with everything in proportion – '

'And then what'll he do?'

'That,' said Mr Bensington, 'is just what makes the whole thing so interesting.'

'Confound it, man! Think of his clothes.'

'And when he's grown up,' said Redwood, 'he'll only be one solitary Gulliver in a pigmy world.'

Mr Bensington's eye over his gold rim was pregnant.

'Why solitary?' he said, and repeated still more darkly, '*Why solitary?*'

'But you don't propose – ?'

'I said,' said Mr Bensington, with the self-complacency of a man who has produced a good significant saying, 'Why solitary?'

'Meaning that one might bring up other children – ?'

'Meaning nothing beyond my enquiry.'

Redwood began to walk about the room. 'Of course,' he said, 'one might – But still! What are we coming to?'

Bensington evidently enjoyed his line of high intellectual detachment. 'The thing that interests me most, Redwood, of all this, is to think that his brain at the top of him will also, so far as my reasoning goes, be five-and- thirty feet or so above our level . . . What's the matter?'

Redwood stood at the window and stared at a news placard on a paper-cart that rattled up the street.

'What's the matter?' repeated Bensington, rising.

Redwood exclaimed violently.

'What is it?' said Bensington.

'Get a paper,' said Redwood, moving doorwards.

'Why?'

'Get a paper. Something – I didn't quite catch – Gigantic rats – !'

'Rats?'

'Yes, rats. Skinner was right after all!'

'What do you mean?'

'How the deuce am *I* to know till I see a paper? Great rats! Good Lord! I wonder if he's been eaten!'

He glanced for his hat, and decided to go hatless.

As he rushed downstairs two steps at a time, he could hear along the street the mighty howlings to and fro of the hooligan paper-sellers making a Boom.

' 'Orrible affair in Kent – 'orrible affair in Kent. Doctor . . . eaten by rats. 'Orrible affair – 'orrible affair – rats – eaten by Stchewpendous rats. Full perticulars – 'orrible affair.'

3

Cossar, the well-known civil engineer, found them in the great doorway of the flat mansions, Redwood holding out the damp pink paper, and Bensington on tiptoe reading over his arm. Cossar was a large-bodied man with gaunt inelegant limbs casually placed at convenient corners of his body, and a face like a carving abandoned at an early stage as altogether too unpromising for completion. His nose had been left square, and his lower jaw projected beyond his upper. He breathed audibly. Few people considered him handsome. His hair was entirely tangential, and his voice, which he used sparingly, was pitched high, and had commonly a quality of bitter protest. He wore a grey-cloth jacket suit and a silk hat on all occasions. He plumbed an abysmal trouser pocket with a vast red hand, paid his cabman, and came panting resolutely up the steps, a copy of the pink paper clutched about the middle, like Jove's thunderbolt, in his hand.

'Skinner?' Bensington was saying, regardless of his approach.

'Nothing about him,' said Redwood. 'Bound to be eaten. Both of them. It's too terrible . . . Hello! Cossar!'

'This your stuff?' asked Cossar, waving the paper.

'*Yes!* Well, why don't you stop it?' he demanded.

' *Can't* be jiggered!' said Cossar.

'*Buy the place?*' he cried. 'What nonsense! Burn it! I knew you chaps would fumble this.

'*What are you to do?* Why – what I tell you.

'*You? Do?* Why! Go up the street to the gunsmith's, of course.

'*Why?* For guns. Yes – there's only one shop. Get eight guns! Rifles.

Not elephant guns – no! Too big. Not army rifles – too small. Say it's to kill – kill a bull. Say it's to shoot buffalo! See? Eh? Rats? No! How the deuce are they to understand that? Because we *want* eight. Get a lot of ammunition. Don't get guns without ammunition – No! Take the lot in a cab to – where's the place? *Urshot*? Charing Cross, then. There's a train – Well, the first train that starts after two. Think you can do it? All right. Licence? Get eight at a post-office, of course. Gun licences, you know. Not game. Why? It's rats, man.

'You – Bensington. Got a telephone? Yes. I'll ring up five of my chaps from Ealing. *Why* five? Because it's the right number!

'Where you going, Redwood? Get a hat! *Nonsense*. Have mine. You want guns, man – not hats. Got money? Enough? All right. So long.

'Where's the telephone, Bensington?'

Bensington wheeled about obediently and led the way.

Cossar used and replaced the instrument. 'Then there's the wasps,' he said. 'Sulphur and nitre'll do that. Obviously. Plaster of Paris. You're a chemist. Where can I get sulphur by the ton in portable sacks? *What for*? Why, Lord *bless* my heart and soul! – to smoke out the nest, of course! I suppose it must be sulphur, eh? You're a chemist. Sulphur best, eh?'

'Yes, I should *think* sulphur.'

'Nothing better? Right. That's your job. That's all right. Get as much sulphur as you can – saltpetre to make it burn. Sent? Charing Cross. Right away. See they do it. Follow it up. Anything?'

He thought a moment.

'Plaster of Paris – any sort of plaster – bung up nest – holes – you know. That *I'd* better get.'

'How much?'

'How much what?'

'Sulphur.'

'Ton. See?'

Bensington tightened his glasses with a hand tremulous with determination. 'Right,' he said, very curtly.

'Money in your pocket?' asked Cossar. 'Hang cheques. They may not know you. Pay cash. Obviously. Where's your bank? All right. Stop on the way and get forty pounds – notes and gold.'

Another meditation. 'If we leave this job for public officials we shall have all Kent in tatters,' said Cossar. 'Now is there – anything? *No! Hi!*'

He stretched a vast hand towards a cab that became convulsively eager to serve him ('Cab, sir?' said the cabman. 'Obviously,' said Cossar); and Bensington, still hatless, paddled down the steps and prepared to mount.

'I *think*,' he said, with his hand on the cab apron, and a sudden glance up at the windows of his flat, 'I *ought* to tell my cousin Jane – '

'More time to tell her when you come back,' said Cossar, thrusting him in with a vast hand expanded over his back . . .

'Clever chaps,' remarked Cossar, 'but no initiative whatever. Cousin Jane indeed! I know her. Rot, these Cousin Janes! Country infested with 'em. I suppose I shall have to spend the whole blessed night seeing they do what they know perfectly well they ought to have done all along. I wonder if it's Research makes 'em like that or Cousin Jane or what?'

He dismissed this obscure problem, meditated for a space upon his watch, and decided there would be just time to drop into a restaurant and get some lunch before he hunted up the plaster of Paris and took it to Charing Cross.

The train started at five minutes past three, and he arrived at Charing Cross at a quarter to three, to find Bensington in heated argument between two policemen and his van-driver outside, and Redwood in the luggage office involved in some technical obscurity about this ammunition. Everybody was pretending not to know anything or to have any authority, in the way dear to South-Eastern officials when they catch you in a hurry.

'Pity they can't shoot all these officials and get a new lot,' remarked Cossar with a sigh. But the time was too limited for anything funda-mental, and so he swept through these minor controversies, disinterred what may or may not have been the station-master from some obscure hiding-place, walked about the premises holding him and giving orders in his name, and was out of the station with everybody and everything aboard before that official was fully awake to the breaches in the most sacred routines and regulations that were being committed.

'Who *was* he?' said the high official, caressing the arm Cossar had gripped, and smiling with knit brows.

' 'E was a gentleman, sir,' said a porter, 'anyhow. 'Im and all 'is party travelled first class.'

'Well, we got him and his stuff off pretty sharp – whoever he was,' said the high official, rubbing his arm with something approaching satisfaction.

And as he walked slowly back, blinking in the unaccustomed daylight, towards that dignified retirement in which the higher officials at Charing Cross shelter from the importunity of the vulgar, he smiled still at his unaccustomed energy. It was a very gratifying revelation of his own possibilities, in spite of the stiffness of his arm. He wished some of those confounded armchair critics of railway management could have seen it.

By five o'clock that evening this amazing Cossar, with no appearance of hurry at all, had got all the stuff for his fight with insurgent Bigness out of Urshot and on the road to Hickleybrow. Two barrels of paraffin and a load of dry brushwood he had bought in Urshot; plentiful sacks of sulphur, eight big-game guns and ammunition, three light breech-loaders, with small-shot ammunition for the wasps, a hatchet, two bill-hooks, a pick and three spades, two coils of rope, some bottled beer, soda and whisky, one gross of packets of rat poison, and cold provisions for three days, had come down from London. All these things he had sent on in a coal trolley and a hay waggon in the most businesslike way, except the guns and ammunition, which were stuck under the seat of the Red Lion waggonette appointed to bring on Redwood and the five picked men who had come up from Ealing at Cossar's summons.

Cossar conducted all these transactions with an invincible air of commonplace, in spite of the fact that Urshot was in a panic about the rats, and all the drivers had to be specially paid. All the shops were shut in the place, and scarcely a soul abroad in the street, and when he banged at a door a window was apt to open. He seemed to consider that the conduct of business from open windows was an entirely legitimate and obvious method. Finally he and Bensington got the Red Lion dogcart and set off with the waggonette to overtake the baggage. They did this a little beyond the crossroads, and so reached Hickleybrow first.

Bensington, with a gun between his knees, sitting beside Cossar in the dogcart, developed a long germinated amazement. All they were doing was, no doubt, as Cossar insisted, quite the obvious thing to do, only – ! In England one so rarely does the obvious thing. He glanced from his neighbour's feet to the boldly sketched hands upon the reins. Cossar had apparently never driven before, and he was keeping the line of least resistance down the middle of the road by some no doubt quite obvious but certainly unusual light of his own.

'Why don't we all do the obvious?' thought Bensington. 'How the world would travel if one did! I wonder for instance why I don't do such a lot of things I know would be all right to do – things I *want* to do. Is everybody like that, or is it peculiar to me!' He plunged into obscure speculation about the Will. He thought of the complex organised futilities of the daily life, and in contrast with them the plain and manifest things to do, the sweet and splendid things to do, that some incredible influences will never permit us to do. Cousin Jane? Cousin Jane he perceived was important in the question, in some subtle and difficult way. Why should we after all eat, drink and sleep, remain unmarried, go here, abstain from going there, all out of deference to Cousin Jane? She became symbolical without ceasing to be incomprehensible!

A stile and a path across the fields caught his eye and reminded him of that other bright day, so recent in time, so remote in its emotions, when he had walked from Urshot to the Experimental Farm to see the giant chicks.

Fate plays with us.

'Tcheck, tcheck,' said Cossar. 'Get up.'

It was a hot midday afternoon, not a breath of wind, and the dust was thick on the roads. Few people were about, but the deer beyond the park palings browsed in profound tranquillity. They saw a couple of big wasps stripping a gooseberry bush just outside Hickleybrow, and another was crawling up and down the front of the little grocer's shop in the village street trying to find an entry. The grocer was dimly visible within, with an ancient fowling-piece in hand, watching its endeavours. The driver of the waggonette pulled up outside the Jolly Drovers and informed Redwood that his part of the bargain was done. In this contention he was presently joined by the drivers of the waggon and the trolley. Not only did they maintain this, but they refused to let the horses be taken farther.

'Them big rats is nuts on 'orses,' the trolley driver kept on repeating.

Cossar surveyed the controversy for a moment.

'Get the things out of that waggonette,' he said, and one of his men, a tall, fair, dirty engineer, obeyed.

'Gimme that shotgun,' said Cossar.

He placed himself between the drivers. 'We don't want *you* to drive,' he said. 'You can say what you like,' he conceded, 'but we want these horses.'

They began to argue, but he continued speaking.

'If you try and assault us I shall, in self-defence, let fly at your legs. The horses are going on.'

He treated the incident as closed. 'Get up on that waggon, Flack,' he said to a thickset, wiry little man. 'Boon, take the trolley.'

The two drivers blustered to Redwood.

'You've done your duty to your employers,' said Redwood. 'You stop in this village until we come back. No one will blame you, seeing we've got guns. We've no wish to do anything unjust or violent, but this occasion is pressing. I'll pay if anything happens to the horses, never fear.'

'*That's* all right,' said Cossar, who rarely promised.

They left the waggonette behind, and the men who were not driving went afoot. Over each shoulder sloped a gun. It was the oddest little expedition for an English country road, more like a Yankee party, trekking west in the good old Indian days.

They went up the road, until at the crest by the stile they came into sight of the Experimental Farm. They found a little group of men there with a gun or so – the two Fulchers were among them – and one man, a stranger from Maidstone, stood out before the others and watched the place through an opera-glass.

These men turned about and stared at Redwood's party.

'Anything fresh?' said Cossar.

'The waspses keeps a comin' and a goin',' said old Fulcher. 'Can't see as they bring anything.'

'The canary creeper's got in among the pine trees now,' said the man with the lorgnette. 'It wasn't there this morning. You can see it grow while you watch it.'

He took out a handkerchief and wiped his object-glasses with careful deliberation.

'I reckon you're going down there,' ventured Skelmersdale.

'Will you come?' said Cossar.

Skelmersdale seemed to hesitate.

'It's an all-night job.'

Skelmersdale decided that he wouldn't.

'Rats about?' asked Cossar.

'One was up in the pines this morning – rabbiting, we reckon.'

Cossar slouched on to overtake his party.

Bensington, regarding the Experimental Farm under his hand, was able to gauge now the vigour of the Food. His first impression was that the house was smaller than he had thought – very much smaller; his second was to perceive that all the vegetation between the house and the pinewood had become extremely large. The roof over the well peeped amidst tussocks of grass a good eight feet high, and the canary creeper wrapped about the chimney stack and gesticulated with stiff tendrils towards the heavens. Its flowers were vivid yellow splashes, distinctly visible as separate specks this mile away. A great green cable had writhed across the big wire enclosures of the giant hens' run, and flung twining leaf stems about two outstanding pines. Fully half as tall as these was the grove of nettles running round behind the cart-shed. The whole prospect, as they drew nearer, became more and more suggestive of a raid of pigmies upon a dolls' house that has been left in a neglected corner of some great garden.

There was a busy coming and going from the wasps' nest, they saw. A swarm of black shapes interlaced in the air above the rusty hill-front beyond the pine cluster, and ever and again one of these would dart up into the sky with incredible swiftness and soar off upon some distant quest. Their humming became audible at more than half a mile's distance from the Experimental Farm. Once a yellow-striped monster dropped towards them and hung for a space watching them with its great compound eyes, but at an ineffectual shot from Cossar it darted off again. Down in a corner of the field, away to the right, several were crawling about over some ragged bones that were probably the remains of the lamb the rats had brought from Huxter's Farm. The horses became very restless as they drew near these creatures. None of the party was an expert driver, and they had to put a man to lead each horse and encourage it with the voice.

They could see nothing of the rats as they came up to the house, and everything seemed perfectly still except for the rising and falling 'whoozzzzzzZZZ, whoooo-zoo-oo' of the wasps' nest.

They led the horses into the yard, and one of Cossar's men, seeing the door open – the whole of the middle portion of the door had been gnawed out – walked into the house. Nobody missed him for the time, the rest being occupied with the barrels of paraffin, and the first intimation they had of his separation from them was the report of his gun and the whizz of his bullet. 'Bang, bang,' both barrels, and his first bullet it seems went through the cask of sulphur, smashed out a stave from the farther side, and filled the air with yellow dust. Redwood had kept his gun in hand and let fly at something grey that leapt past him. He had a vision of the broad hindquarters, the long scaly tail and long soles of the hind-feet of a rat, and fired his second barrel. He saw Bensington drop as the beast vanished round the corner.

Then for a time everybody was busy with a gun. For three minutes lives were cheap at the Experimental Farm, and the banging of guns filled the air. Redwood, careless of Bensington in his excitement, rushed in pursuit, and was knocked headlong by a mass of brick fragments, mortar, plaster and rotten lath splinters that came flying out at him as a bullet whacked through the wall.

He found himself sitting on the ground with blood on his hands and lips, and a great stillness brooded over all about him.

Then a flattish voice from within the house remarked: 'Gee-whizz!'

'Hello!' said Redwood.

'Hello there!' answered the voice.

And then: 'Did you chaps get 'im?'

A sense of the duties of friendship returned to Redwood. 'Is Mr Bensington hurt?' he said.

The man inside heard imperfectly. 'No one ain't to blame if I ain't,' said the voice inside.

It became clearer to Redwood that he must have shot Bensington. He forgot the cuts upon his face, arose and came back to find Bensington seated on the ground and rubbing his shoulder. Bensington looked over his glasses. 'We peppered him, Redwood,' he said, and then: 'He tried to jump over me, and knocked me down. But I let him have it with both barrels, and my! how it has hurt my shoulder, to be sure.'

A man appeared in the doorway. 'I got him once in the chest and once in the side,' he said.

'Where's the waggons?' said Cossar, appearing amidst a thicket of gigantic canary-creeper leaves.

It became evident, to Redwood's amazement, first, that no one had been shot, and, secondly, that the trolley and waggon had shifted fifty yards, and were now standing with interlocked wheels amidst the tangled distortions of Skinner's kitchen garden. The horses had stopped their plunging. Halfway towards them, the burst barrel of sulphur lay in the path with a cloud of sulphur dust above it. He indicated this to Cossar and walked towards it. 'Has anyone seen that rat?' shouted Cossar, following. 'I got him in between the ribs once, and once in the face as he turned on me.'

They were joined by two men, as they worried at the locked wheels. 'I killed that rat,' said one of the men.

'Have they got him?' asked Cossar.

'Jim Bates has found him, beyond the hedge. I got him jest as he came round the corner . . . Whack behind the shoulder . . . '

When things were a little shipshape again Redwood went and stared at the huge misshapen corpse. The brute lay on its side, with its body slightly bent. Its rodent teeth overhanging its receding lower jaw gave its face a look of colossal feebleness, of weak avidity. It seemed not in the least ferocious or terrible. Its forepaws reminded him of lank emaciated hands. Except for one neat round hole with a scorched rim on either side of its neck, the creature was absolutely intact. He meditated over this fact for some time. 'There must have been two rats,' he said at last, turning away.

'Yes. And the one that everybody hit – got away.'

'I am certain that my own shot – '

A canary-creeper-leaf tendril, engaged in that mysterious search for a holdfast which constitutes a tendril's career, bent itself engagingly towards his neck and made him step aside hastily.

'Whoo–z–z z–z–z–z–Z–Z–Z,' from the distant wasps' nest, 'whoo-oo zoo-oo.'

5

This incident left the party alert but not unstrung.

They got their stores into the house, which had evidently been ransacked by the rats after the flight of Mrs Skinner, and four of the men took the two horses back to Hickleybrow. They dragged the dead rat through the hedge and into a position commanded by the windows of the house, and incidentally came upon a cluster of giant earwigs in the ditch. These creatures dispersed hastily, but Cossar reached out incalculable limbs and managed to kill several with his boots and gun-butt. Then two of the men hacked through several of the main stems of the canary creeper – huge cylinders they were, a couple of feet in diameter, that came out by the sink at the back; and while Cossar set the house in order for the night, Bensington, Redwood and one of the assistant electricians went cautiously round by the fowl runs in search of the rat-holes.

They skirted the giant nettles widely, for these huge weeds threatened them with poison-thorns a good inch long. Then round beyond the gnawed, dismantled stile they came abruptly on the huge cavernous throat of the most westerly of the giant rat-holes, an evil-smelling profundity that drew them up into a line together.

'I *hope* they'll come out,' said Redwood, with a glance at the penthouse of the well.

'If they don't – ' reflected Bensington.

'They will,' said Redwood.

They meditated.

'We shall have to rig up some sort of flare if we *do* go in,' said Redwood.

They went up a little path of white sand through the pinewood and halted presently within sight of the wasp-holes.

The sun was setting now, and the wasps were coming home for good; their wings in the golden light made twirling haloes about them.

The three men peered out from under the trees – they did not care to go right to the edge of the wood – and watched these tremendous insects drop and crawl for a little and enter and disappear. 'They will be still in a couple of hours from now,' said Redwood . . . 'This is like being a boy again.'

'We can't miss those holes,' said Bensington, 'even if the night is dark. By the by – about the light – '

'Full moon,' said the electrician. 'I looked it up.'

They went back and consulted with Cossar.

He said that 'obviously' they must get the sulphur, nitre and plaster of Paris through the wood before twilight, and for that they broke bulk and carried the sacks. After the necessary shouting of the preliminary directions, never a word was spoken, and as the buzzing of the wasps' nest died away there was scarcely a sound in the world but the noise of footsteps, the heavy breathing of burthened men and the thud of the sacks. They all took turns at that labour except Mr Bensington, who was manifestly unfit. He took post in the Skinners' bedroom with a rifle, to watch the carcass of the dead rat; and of the others, they took turns to rest from sack-carrying and to keep watch two at a time upon the rat-holes behind the nettle grove. The pollen sacs of the nettles were ripe, and every now and then the vigil would be enlivened by the dehiscence of these, the bursting of the sacs sounding exactly like the crack of a pistol, and the pollen grains as big as buckshot pattered all about them.

Mr Bensington sat at his window on a hard horse-hair-stuffed arm-chair, covered by a grubby antimacassar that had given a touch of social distinction to the Skinners' sitting-room for many years. His unaccustomed rifle rested on the sill, and his spectacles anon watched the dark bulk of the dead rat in the thickening twilight, anon wandered about him in curious meditation. There was a faint smell of paraffin without, for one of the casks leaked, and it mingled with a less un-pleasant odour arising from the hacked and crushed creeper.

Within, when he turned his head, a blend of faint domestic scents, beer, cheese, rotten apples and old boots as the leading *motifs*, was full of reminiscences of the vanished Skinners. He regarded the dim room for a space. The furniture had been greatly disordered – perhaps by some inquisitive rat – but a coat upon a clothes-peg on the door, a razor and some dirty scraps of paper, and a piece of soap that had hardened through years of disuse into a horny cube, were redolent of Skinner's distinctive personality. It came to Bensington's mind with a complete novelty of realisation that in all probability the man had been killed and eaten, at least in part, by the monster that now lay dead there in the darkling.

To think of all that a harmless-looking discovery in chemistry may lead to!

Here he was in homely England and yet in infinite danger, sitting out alone with a gun in a twilit, ruined house, remote from every comfort, his shoulder dreadfully bruised from a gun-kick, and – by Jove!

He grasped now how profoundly the order of the universe had changed for him. He had come right away to this amazing experience, *without even saying a word to his cousin Jane*!

What must she be thinking of him?

He tried to imagine it and he could not. He had an extraordinary feeling that she and he were parted for ever and would never meet again. He felt he had taken a step and come into a world of new immensities. What other monsters might not those deepening shadows hide? The tips of the giant nettles came out sharp and black against the pale green and amber of the western sky. Everything was very still – very still indeed. He wondered why he could not hear the others away there round the corner of the house. The shadow in the cart-shed was now an abysmal black.

Bang . . . Bang . . . Bang.

A sequence of echoes and a shout.

A long silence.

Bang and a *diminuendo* of echoes.

Stillness.

Then, thank goodness! Redwood and Cossar were coming out of the inaudible darkness, and Redwood was calling, 'Bensington! Bensington! We've bagged another of the rats! Cossar's bagged another of the rats!'

When the Expedition had finished refreshment, the night had fully come. The stars were at their brightest, and a growing pallor towards Hankey heralded the moon. The watch on the rat-holes had been maintained, but the watchers had shifted to the hill slope above the holes, feeling this a safer firing-point. They squatted there in a rather abundant dew, fighting the damp with whisky. The others rested in the house, and the three leaders discussed the night's work with the men. The moon rose towards midnight, and as soon as it was clear of the downs, everyone except the rat-hole sentinels started off in single file, led by Cossar, towards the wasps' nest.

So far as the wasps' nest went, they found their task exceptionally easy – astonishingly easy. Except that it was a longer labour, it was no graver affair than any common wasps' nest might have been. Danger there was, no doubt, danger to life, but it never so much as thrust its head out of that portentous hillside. They stuffed in the sulphur and nitre, they bunged the holes soundly and fired their trains. Then with a common impulse all the party but Cossar turned and ran athwart the long shadows of the pines, and, finding Cossar had stayed behind, came to a halt together in a knot, a hundred yards away, convenient to a ditch that offered cover. Just for a minute or two the moonlit night, all black and white, was heavy with a suffocated buzz that rose and mingled to a roar, a deep abundant note, and culminated and died, and then almost incredibly the night was still.

'By Jove!' said Bensington, almost in a whisper, '*it's done!*'

All stood intent. The hillside above the black point-lace of the pine shadows seemed as bright as day and as colourless as snow. The setting plaster in the holes positively shone. Cossar's loose framework moved towards them.

'So far – ' said Cossar.

Crack – *bang*!

A shot from near the house and then – stillness.

'What's *that*?' said Bensington.

'One of the rats put its head out,' suggested one of the men.

'By the by, we left our guns up there,' said Redwood. 'By the sacks.'

Everyone began to walk towards the hill again.

'That must be the rats,' said Bensington.

'Obviously,' said Cossar, gnawing his fingernails.

Bang!

'Hello?' said one of the men.

Then abruptly came a shout, two shots, a loud shout that was almost a scream, three shots in rapid succession and a splintering of wood. All these sounds were very clear and very small in the immense stillness of the night. Then for some moments nothing but a minute muffled confusion from the direction of the rat-holes, and then again a wild yell . . . Each man found himself running hard for the guns.

Two shots.

Bensington found himself, gun in hand, going hard through the pine trees after a number of receding backs. It is curious that the thought uppermost in his mind at that moment was the wish that his cousin Jane could see him. His bulbous slashed boots flew out in wild strides, and his face was distorted into a permanent grin, because that wrinkled his nose and kept his glasses in place. Also he held the muzzle of his gun projecting straight before him as he flew through the chequered moonlight. The man who had run away met them full tilt – he had dropped his gun.

'Hello,' said Cossar, and caught him in his arms. 'What's this?'

'They came out together,' said the man.

'The rats?'

'Yes, six of them.'

'Where's Flack?'

'Down.'

'What's he say?' panted Bensington, coming up, unheeded. 'Flack's down?'

'He fell down.'

'They came out one after the other.'

'What?'

'Made a rush. I fired both barrels first.'

'You left Flack?'

'They were on to us.'

'Come on,' said Cossar. 'You come with us. Where's Flack? Show us.'

The whole party moved forward. Further details of the engagement dropped from the man who had run away. The others clustered about him, except Cossar, who led.

'Where are they?'

'Back in their holes, perhaps. I cleared. They made a rush for their holes.'

'What do you mean? Did you get behind them?'

'We got down by their holes. Saw 'em come out, you know, and tried to cut 'em off. They lolloped out – like rabbits. We ran down and let fly. They ran about wild after our first shot and suddenly came at us. *Went* for us.'

'How many?'

'Six or seven.'

Cossar led the way to the edge of the pinewood and halted.

'D'yer mean they *got* Flack?' asked someone.

'One of 'em was on to him.'

'Didn't you shoot?'

'How *could* I?'

'Everyone loaded?' said Cossar over his shoulder.

There was a confirmatory movement.

'But Flack – ' said one.

'D'yer mean – Flack? – ' said another.

'There's no time to lose,' said Cossar, and shouted, 'Flack!' as he led the way. The whole force advanced towards the rat-holes, the man who had run away a little to the rear. They went forward through the rank exaggerated weeds and skirted the body of the second dead rat. They were extended in a bunchy line, each man with his gun pointing forward, and they peered about them in the clear moonlight for some crumpled, ominous shape, some crouching form. They found the gun of the man who had run away very speedily.

'Flack!' cried Cossar. 'Flack!'

'He ran past the nettles and fell down,' volunteered the man who ran away.

'Where?'

'Round about there.'

'Where did he fall?'

He hesitated and led them athwart the long black shadows for a space and turned judicially. 'About here, I think.'

'Well, he's not here now.'

'But his gun – ?'

'Confound it!' swore Cossar, 'where's everything got to?' He strode a step towards the black shadows on the hillside that masked the holes and stood staring. Then he swore again. 'If they *have* dragged him in! – '

So they hung for a space tossing each other the fragments of thoughts. Bensington's glasses flashed like diamonds as he looked from one to the other. The men's faces changed from cold clearness to mysterious obscurity as they turned them to or from the moon. Everyone spoke, no one completed a sentence. Then abruptly Cossar chose his line. He flapped limbs this way and that and expelled orders in pellets. It was obvious he wanted lamps. Everyone except Cossar was moving towards the house.

'You're going into the holes?' asked Redwood.

'Obviously,' said Cossar.

He made it clear once more that the lamps of the cart and trolley were to be got and brought to him.

Bensington, grasping this, started off along the path by the well. He glanced over his shoulder, and saw Cossar's gigantic figure standing out as if he were regarding the holes pensively. At the sight Bensington halted for a moment and half turned. They were all leaving Cossar – !

Cossar was able to take care of himself, of course!

Suddenly Bensington saw something that made him shout a windless 'HI!' In a second three rats had projected themselves from the dark tangle of the creeper towards Cossar. For three seconds Cossar stood unaware of them, and then he had become the most active thing in the world. He didn't fire his gun. Apparently he had no time to aim, or to think of aiming; he ducked a leaping rat, Bensington saw, and then smashed at the back of its head with the butt of his gun. The monster gave one leap and fell over itself.

Cossar's form went right down out of sight among the reedy grass, and then he rose again, running towards another of the rats and whirling his gun overhead. A faint shout came to Bensington's ears, and then he perceived the remaining two rats bolting divergently, and Cossar in pursuit towards the holes.

The whole thing was an affair of misty shadows; all three fighting monsters were exaggerated and made unreal by the delusive clearness of the light. At moments Cossar was colossal, at moments invisible. The rats flashed athwart the eye in sudden unexpected leaps, or ran with a movement of the feet so swift, they seemed to run on wheels. It was all over in half a minute. No one saw it but Bensington. He could hear the others behind him still receding towards the house. He shouted something inarticulate and then ran back towards Cossar, while the rats vanished. He came up to him outside the holes. In the moonlight the distribution of shadows that constituted Cossar's visage intimated calm. 'Hello,' said Cossar, 'back already? Where's the lamps? They're all back now in their holes. One I broke the neck of as it ran past me . . . See? There!' And he pointed a gaunt finger.

Bensington was too astonished for conversation.

The lamps seemed an interminable time in coming. At last they appeared, first one unwinking luminous eye, preceded by a swaying yellow glare, and then, winking now and then and then shining out again, two others. About them came little figures with little voices, and then enormous shadows. This group made as it were a spot of inflammation upon the gigantic dreamland of moonshine.

'Flack,' said the voices. 'Flack.'

An illuminating sentence floated up. 'Locked himself in the attic.'

Cossar was continually more wonderful. He produced great handfuls of cotton wool and stuffed them in his ears – Bensington wondered why. Then he loaded his gun with a quarter charge of powder. Who else could have thought of that? Wonderland culminated with the disappearance of Cossar's twin realms of boot sole up the central hole.

Cossar was on all fours with two guns, one trailing on each side from a string under his chin; and his most trusted assistant, a little dark man with a grave face, was to go in stooping behind him, holding a lantern over his head. Everything had been made as sane and obvious and proper as a lunatic's dream. The wool, it seems, was on account of the concussion of the rifle; the man had some too. Obviously! So long as the rats turned tail on Cossar no harm could come to him, and directly they headed for him he would see their eyes and fire between them. Since they would have to come down the cylinder of the hole, Cossar could hardly fail to hit them. It was, Cossar insisted, the obvious method, a little tedious perhaps, but absolutely certain. As the assistant stooped to enter, Bensington saw that the end of a ball of twine had been tied to the tail of his coat. By this he was to draw in the rope if it should be needed to drag out the bodies of the rats.

Bensington perceived that the object he held in his hand was Cossar's silk hat.

How had it got there?

It would be something to remember him by, anyhow.

At each of the adjacent holes stood a little group with a lantern on the ground shining up the hole, and with one man kneeling and aiming at the round void before him, waiting for anything that might emerge.

There was an interminable suspense.

Then they heard Cossar's first shot, like an explosion in a mine.

Everyone's nerves and muscles tightened at that, and bang! bang! bang! the rats had tried a bolt, and two more were dead. Then the man who held the ball of twine reported a twitching. 'He's killed one in there,' said Bensington, 'and he wants the rope.'

He watched the rope creep into the hole, and it seemed as though it had become animated by a serpentine intelligence – for the darkness made the twine invisible. At last it stopped crawling, and there was a long pause. Then what seemed to Bensington the queerest monster of all crept slowly from the hole, and resolved itself into the little engineer emerging backwards. After him, and ploughing deep furrows, Cossar's boots thrust out, and then came his lantern-illuminated back . . .

Only one rat was left alive now, and this poor, doomed wretch cowered in the inmost recesses until Cossar and the lantern went in again and slew it; and finally Cossar, that human ferret, went through all the runs to make sure.

'We got 'em,' he said to his nearly awestricken company at last. 'And if I hadn't been a mud-headed mucker I should have stripped to the waist. Obviously. Feel my sleeves, Bensington! I'm wet through with perspiration. Jolly hard to think of everything. Only a halfway-up of whisky can save me from a cold.'

7

There were moments during that wonderful night when it seemed to Bensington that he was planned by nature for a life of fantastic adventure. This was particularly the case for an hour or so after he had taken a stiff whisky. 'Shan't go back to Sloane Street,' he confided to the tall, fair, dirty engineer.

'You won't, eh?'

'No fear,' said Bensington, nodding darkly.

The exertion of dragging the seven dead rats to the funeral pyre by the nettle grove left him bathed in perspiration, and Cossar pointed out the obvious physical reaction of whisky to save him from the otherwise inevitable chill. There was a sort of brigands' supper in the old bricked kitchen, with the row of dead rats lying in the moonlight against the hen-runs outside, and after thirty minutes or so of rest, Cossar roused them all to the labours that were still to do. 'Obviously,' as he said, they had to 'wipe the place out. No litter – no scandal. See?' He stirred them up to the idea of making destruction complete. They smashed and splintered every fragment of wood in the house; they built trails of chopped wood wherever big vegetation was springing; they made a pyre for the rat bodies and soaked them in paraffin.

Bensington worked like a conscientious navvy. He had a sort of climax of exhilaration and energy towards two o'clock. When in the work of destruction he wielded an axe the bravest fled his neighbourhood. Afterwards he was a little sobered by the temporary loss of his spectacles, which were found for him at last in his side coat-pocket.

Men went to and fro about him – grimy, energetic men. Cossar moved amongst them like a god.

Bensington drank that delight of human fellowship that comes to happy armies, to sturdy expeditions – never to those who live the life of the sober citizen in cities. After Cossar had taken his axe away and set him to carry wood he went to and fro, saying they were all 'good fellows'. He kept on – long after he was aware of fatigue.

At last all was ready, and the broaching of the paraffin began. The moon, robbed now of all its meagre night retinue of stars, shone high above the dawn.

'Burn everything,' said Cossar, going to and fro – 'burn the ground and make a clean sweep of it. See?'

Bensington became aware of him, looking now very gaunt and horrible in the pale beginnings of the daylight, hurrying past with his lower jaw projected and a flaring torch of touchwood in his hand.

'Come away!' said someone, pulling Bensington's arm.

The still dawn – no birds were singing there – was suddenly full of a tumultuous crackling; a little dull red flame ran about the base of the pyre, changed to blue upon the ground, and set out to clamber, leaf by leaf, up the stem of a giant nettle. A singing sound mingled with the crackling.

They snatched their guns from the corner of the Skinners' living-room, and then everyone was running. Cossar came after them with heavy strides . . .

Then they were standing looking back at the Experimental Farm. It was boiling up; the smoke and flames poured out like a crowd in a panic, from doors and windows and from a thousand cracks and crevices in the roof. Trust Cossar to build a fire! A great column of smoke, shot with blood-red tongues and darting flashes, rushed up into the sky. It was like some huge giant suddenly standing up, straining upward and abruptly spreading his great arms out across the sky. It cast the night back upon them, utterly hiding and obliterating the incandescence of the sun that rose behind it. All Hickleybrow was soon aware of that stupendous pillar of smoke, and came out upon the crest, in various deshabille, to watch them coming.

Behind, like some fantastic fungus, this smoke pillar swayed and fluctuated, up, up, into the sky – making the downs seem low and all other objects petty, and in the foreground, led by Cossar, the makers of this mischief followed the path, eight little black figures coming wearily, guns shouldered, across the meadow.

As Bensington looked back there came into his jaded brain, and echoed there, a familiar formula. What was it? 'You have lit today – ? You have lit today – ?' Then he remembered Latimer's words: 'We have lit this day such a candle in England as no man may ever put out again – '

What a man Cossar was, to be sure! He admired his back view for a space, and was proud to have held that hat. Proud! Although he was an eminent investigator and Cossar only engaged in applied science.

Suddenly he fell to shivering and yawning enormously and wishing he was warmly tucked away in bed in his little flat that looked out upon Sloane Street. (It didn't do even to think of Cousin Jane.) His legs became cotton strands, his feet lead. He wondered if anyone would get them coffee in Hickleybrow. He had never been up all night for three-and-thirty years.

8

And while these eight adventurers fought with rats about the Experimental Farm, nine miles away, in the village of Cheasing Eyebright, an old lady with an excessive nose struggled with great difficulties by the light of a flickering candle. She gripped a sardine-tin opener in one gnarled hand, and in the other she held a tin of Herakleophorbia, which she had resolved to open or die. She struggled indefatigably, grunting at each fresh effort, while through the flimsy partition the voice of the Caddles infant wailed.

'Bless 'is poor 'art,' said Mrs Skinner; and then, with her solitary tooth biting her lip in an ecstasy of determination, 'Come *up*!'

And presently, '*Jab!*' a fresh supply of the Food of the Gods was let loose to wreak its powers of giantry upon the world.

CHAPTER 4

The Giant Children

For a time at least the spreading circle of residual consequences about the Experimental Farm must pass out of the focus of our narrative – how for a long time a power of bigness, in fungus and toadstool, in grass and weed, radiated from that charred but not absolutely obliterated centre. Nor can we tell here at any length how those mournful spinsters, the two surviving hens, made a wonder of and a show, spent their remaining years in eggless celebrity. The reader who is hungry for fuller details in these matters is referred to the newspapers of the period – to the voluminous, indiscriminate files of the modern Recording Angel. Our business lies with Mr Bensington at the focus of the disturbance.

He had come back to London to find himself a quite terribly famous man. In a night the whole world had changed with respect to him. Everybody understood. Cousin Jane, it seemed, knew all about it; the people in the streets knew all about it; the newspapers all and more. To meet Cousin Jane was terrible, of course, but when it was over not so terrible after all. The good woman had limits even to her power over facts; it was clear that she had communed with herself and accepted the Food as something in the nature of things.

She took the line of huffy dutifulness. She disapproved highly, it was evident, but she did not prohibit. The flight of Bensington, as she must have considered it, may have shaken her, and her worst was to treat him with bitter persistence for a cold he had not caught and fatigue he had long since forgotten, and to buy him a new sort of hygienic all-wool combination underwear that was apt to get involved and turned partially inside out and partially not and was as difficult to get into for an absent-minded man as – Society. And so for a space, and as far as this convenience left him leisure, he still continued to participate in the development of this new element in human history, the Food of the Gods.

The public mind, following its own mysterious laws of selection, had chosen him as the one and only responsible Inventor and Promoter of this new wonder; it would hear nothing of Redwood, and without a protest it allowed Cossar to follow his natural impulse into a terribly prolific obscurity. Before he was aware of the drift of these things, Mr Bensington was, so to speak, stark and dissected upon the hoardings. His baldness, his curious general pinkness and his golden spectacles had become a national possession. Resolute young men with large expensive-looking cameras and a general air of complete authorisation took possession of the flat for brief but fruitful periods, let off flashlights in it that filled it for days with dense, intolerable vapour, and retired to fill the pages of the syndicated magazines with their admirable photographs of Mr Bensington complete and at home in his second-best jacket and his slashed shoes. Other resolute-mannered persons of various ages and sexes dropped in and told him things about Boomfood – it was *Punch*[34] first called the stuff 'Boomfood' – and afterwards reproduced what they had said as his own original contribution to the interview. The thing became quite an obsession with Broadbeam, the Popular Humourist. He scented another confounded thing he could not understand, and he fretted dreadfully in his efforts to 'laugh the thing down'. One saw him in clubs, a great clumsy presence with the evidences of his midnight-oil burning manifest upon his large unwholesome face, explaining to everyone he could buttonhole: 'These Scientific chaps, you know, haven't a Sense of Humour, you know. That's what it is. This Science – kills it.' His jests at Bensington became malignant libels.

An enterprising press-cutting agency sent Bensington a long article about himself from a sixpenny weekly, entitled 'A New Terror', and offered to supply one hundred such disturbances for a guinea, and two extremely charming young ladies, totally unknown to him, called, and, to the speechless indignation of Cousin Jane, had tea with him and afterwards sent him their birthday books for his signature. He was speedily quite hardened to seeing his name associated with the most incongruous ideas in the public press, and to discover in the reviews articles written about Boomfood and himself in a tone of the utmost intimacy by people he had never heard of. And whatever delusions he may have cherished in the days of his obscurity about the pleasantness of Fame were dispelled utterly and for ever.

At first – except for Broadbeam – the tone of the public mind was quite free from any touch of hostility. It did not seem to occur to the public mind as anything but a mere playful supposition that any more Herakleophorbia was going to escape again. And it did not seem to occur to the public mind that the growing little band of babies now being fed on the food would presently be growing more 'up' than most of us ever grow. The sort of thing that pleased the public mind was caricatures of eminent politicians after a course of Boomfeeding, uses of the idea on hoardings, and such edifying exhibitions as the dead wasps that had escaped the fire and the remaining hens.

Beyond that the public did not care to look, until very strenuous efforts were made to turn its eyes to the remoter consequences, and even then for a while its enthusiasm for action was partial. 'There's always somethin' New,' said the public – a public so glutted with novelty that it would hear of the earth being split as one splits an apple without surprise, and, 'I wonder what they'll do next.'

But there were one or two people outside the public, as it were, who did already take that further glance, and some it seems were frightened by what they saw there. There was young Caterham, for example, cousin of the Earl of Pewterstone, and one of the most promising of English politicians, who, taking the risk of being thought a faddist, wrote a long article in *The Nineteenth Century and After*[35] to suggest its total suppression. And – in certain of his moods there was Bensington.

'They don't seem to realise – ' he said to Cossar.

'No, they don't.'

'And do we? Sometimes, when I think of what it means – This poor child of Redwood's – And, of course, your three . . . Forty feet high, perhaps! After all, *ought* we to go on with it?'

'Go on with it!' cried Cossar, convulsed with inelegant astonishment and pitching his note higher than ever. 'Of *course* you'll go on with it! What d'you think you were made for? Just to loaf about between meal-times?

'Serious consequences,' he screamed, 'of course! Enormous. Obviously. Ob-viously. Why, man, it's the only chance you'll ever get of a serious consequence! And you want to shirk it!' For a moment his indignation was speechless, 'It's downright Wicked!' he said at last, and repeated explosively, 'Wicked!'

But Bensington worked in his laboratory now with more emotion than zest. He couldn't tell whether he wanted serious consequences to his life or not; he was a man of quiet tastes. It was a marvellous discovery, of course, quite marvellous – but – He had already become the proprietor of several acres of scorched, discredited property near Hickleybrow, at a price of nearly £90 an acre, and at times he was disposed to think this as serious a consequence of speculative chemistry as any unambitious man could wish. Of course he was Famous – terribly Famous. More than satisfying, altogether more than satisfying, was the Fame he had attained.

But the habit of Research was strong in him . . .

And at moments, rare moments in the laboratory chiefly, he would find something else than habit and Cossar's arguments to urge him to his work. This little spectacled man, poised perhaps with his slashed shoes wrapped about the legs of his high stool and his hand upon the tweezer of his balance weights, would have again a flash of that adolescent vision, would have a momentary perception of the eternal unfolding of the seed that had been sown in his brain, would see as it were in the sky, behind the grotesque shapes and accidents of the present, the coming world of giants and all the mighty things the future has in store – vague and splendid, like some glittering palace seen suddenly in the passing of a sunbeam far away . . . And presently it would be with him as though that distant splendour had never shone upon his brain, and he would perceive nothing ahead but sinister shadows, vast declivities and darknesses, inhospitable immensities, cold, wild and terrible things.

2

Amidst the complex and confused happenings, the impacts from the great outer world that constituted Mr Bensington's fame, a shining and active figure presently became conspicuous – became almost, as it were, a leader and marshal of these externalities in Mr Bensington's eyes. This was Dr Winkles, that convincing young practitioner who has already appeared in this story as the means whereby Redwood was able to convey the Food to his son. Even before the great outbreak, it was evident that the mysterious powders Redwood had given him had awakened this gentleman's interest immensely, and so soon as the first wasps came he was putting two and two together.

He was the sort of doctor that is in manners, in morals, in methods and appearance, most succinctly and finally expressed by the word 'rising'. He was large and fair, with a hard, alert, superficial, aluminium-coloured eye and hair like chalk mud, even-featured and muscular about the clean-shaven mouth, erect in figure and energetic in movement, quick and spinning on the heel, and he wore long frock coats, black silk ties and plain gold studs and chains and his silk hats had a special shape and brim that made him look wiser and better than anybody. He looked as young or old as anybody grown up. And after that first wonderful outbreak he took to Bensington and Redwood and the Food of the Gods with such a convincing air of proprietorship, that at times, in spite of the testimony of the press to the contrary, Bensington was disposed to regard him as the original inventor of the whole affair.

'These accidents,' said Winkles, when Bensington hinted at the dangers of further escapes, 'are nothing. Nothing. The discovery is everything. Properly developed, suitably handled, sanely controlled, we have – we have something very portentous indeed in this food of ours . . . We must keep our eye on it . . . We mustn't let it out of control again, and – we mustn't let it rest.'

He certainly did not mean to do that. He was at Bensington's now almost every day. Bensington, glancing from the window, would see the faultless equipage come spanking up Sloane Street and after an incredibly brief interval Winkles would enter the room with a light, strong motion, and pervade it, and protrude some newspaper and supply information and make remarks.

'Well,' he would say, rubbing his hands, 'how are we getting on?' and so pass to the current discussion about it.

'Do you see,' he would say, for example, 'that Caterham has been talking about our stuff at the Church Association?'

'Dear me!' said Bensington, 'that's a cousin of the Prime Minister, isn't it?'

'Yes,' said Winkles, 'a very able young man – very able. Quite wrong-headed, you know, violently reactionary – but thoroughly able. And he's evidently disposed to make capital out of this stuff of ours. Takes a very emphatic line. Talks of our proposal to use it in the elementary schools – '

'Our proposal to use it in the elementary schools!'

'*I* said something about that the other day – quite in passing – little affair at a Polytechnic. Trying to make it clear the stuff was really highly beneficial. Not in the slightest degree dangerous, in spite of those first little accidents. Which cannot possibly occur again . . . You know it *would* be rather good stuff – But he's taken it up.'

'What did you say?'

'Mere obvious nothings. But as you see – ! Takes it up with perfect gravity. Treats the thing as an attack. Says there is already a sufficient waste of public money in elementary schools without this. Tells the old stories about piano lessons again – *you* know. No one, he says, wishes to prevent the children of the lower classes obtaining an education suited to their condition, but to give them a food of this sort will be to destroy their sense of proportion utterly. Expands the topic. What Good will it do, he asks, to make poor people six-and-thirty feet high? He really believes, you know, that they *will* be thirty-six feet high.'

'So they would be,' said Bensington, 'if you gave them our food at all regularly. But nobody said anything – '

'*I* said something.'

'But, my dear Winkles – !'

'They'll be bigger, of course,' interrupted Winkles, with an air of knowing all about it, and discouraging the crude ideas of Bensington. 'Bigger indisputably. But listen to what he says! Will it make them happier? That's his point. Curious, isn't it? Will it make them better? Will they be more respectful to properly constituted authority? Is it fair to the children themselves? Curious how anxious his sort are for justice – so far as any future arrangements go. Even nowadays, he says, the cost of feeding and clothing children is more than many of their parents can contrive, and if this sort of thing is to be permitted – ! Eh?

'You see he makes my mere passing suggestion into a positive proposal. And then he calculates how much a pair of breeches for a growing lad of twenty feet high or so will cost. Just as though he really believed ... Ten pounds, he reckons, for the merest decency. Curious this Caterham! So concrete! The honest and struggling ratepayer will have to contribute to that, he says. He says we have to consider the Rights of the Parent. It's all here. Two columns. Every parent has a right to have his children brought up in his own size ...

'Then comes the question of school accommodation, cost of enlarged desks and forms for our already too greatly burthened National Schools. And to get what? – a proletariat of hungry giants. Winds up with a very serious passage, says even if this wild suggestion – mere passing fancy of mine, you know, and misinterpreted at that – this wild suggestion about the schools comes to nothing, that doesn't end the matter. This is a strange food, so strange as to seem to him almost wicked. It has been scattered recklessly – so he says – and it may be scattered again. Once you've taken it, it's poison unless you go on with it. ['So it is,' said Bensington.] And in short he proposes the formation of a National Society for the Preservation of the Proper Proportions of Things. Odd? Eh? People are hanging on to the idea like anything.'

'But what do they propose to do?'

Winkles shrugged his shoulders and threw out his hands. 'Form a Society,' he said, 'and fuss. They want to make it illegal to manufacture this Herakleophorbia – or at any rate to circulate the knowledge of it. I've written about a bit to show that Caterham's idea of the stuff is very much exaggerated – very much exaggerated indeed, but that doesn't seem to check it. Curious how people are turning against it. And the National Temperance Association, by the by, has founded a branch for Temperance in Growth.'

'Mm,' said Bensington and stroked his nose.

'After all that has happened there's bound to be this uproar. On the face of it the thing's – *startling*.'

Winkles walked about the room for a time, hesitated, and departed.

It became evident there was something at the back of his mind, some aspect of crucial importance to him, that he waited to display. One day, when Redwood and Bensington were at the flat together, he gave them a glimpse of this something in reserve.

'How's it all going?' he said; rubbing his hands together.

'We're getting together a sort of report.'

'For the Royal Society?'

'Yes.'

'Hm,' said Winkles, very profoundly, and walked to the hearthrug. 'Hm. But – Here's the point. *Ought* you?'

'Ought we – what?'

'Ought you to publish?'

'We're not in the Middle Ages,' said Redwood.

'I know.'

'As Cossar says, swapping wisdom – that's the true scientific method.'

'In most cases, certainly. But – this is exceptional.'

'We shall put the whole thing before the Royal Society in the proper way,' said Redwood.

Winkles returned to that on a later occasion.

'It's in many ways an Exceptional Discovery.'

'That doesn't matter,' said Redwood.

'It's the sort of knowledge that could easily be subject to grave abuse – grave dangers, as Caterham puts it.'

Redwood said nothing.

'Even carelessness, you know – '

'If we were to form a committee of trustworthy people to control the manufacture of Boomfood – Herakleophorbia, I *should* say – we might – '

He paused, and Redwood, with a certain private discomfort, pretended that he did not see any sort of interrogation . . .

Outside the apartments of Redwood and Bensington, Winkles, in spite of the incompleteness of his instructions, became a leading authority upon Boomfood. He wrote letters defending its use; he made notes and articles explaining its possibilities; he jumped up irrelevantly at the meetings of the scientific and medical associations to talk about it; he identified himself with it. He published a pamphlet called 'The Truth about Boomfood', in which he minimised the whole of the Hickleybrow affair almost to nothing. He said that it was absurd to say Boomfood would make people thirty-seven feet high. That was 'obviously exaggerated'. It would make them bigger, of course, but that was all . . .

Within that intimate circle of two it was chiefly evident that Winkles was extremely anxious to help in the making of Herakleophorbia, help in correcting any proofs there might be of any paper there might be in preparation upon the subject – do anything indeed that might lead up to his participation in the details of the making of Herakleophorbia. He was continually telling them both that he felt it was a Big Thing, that it had big possibilities. If only they were – 'safeguarded in some way'. And at last one day he asked outright to be told just how it was made.

'I've been thinking over what you said,' said Redwood.

'Well?' said Winkles brightly.

'It's the sort of knowledge that could easily be subject to grave abuse,' said Redwood.

'But I don't see how that applies,' said Winkles.

'It does,' said Redwood.

Winkles thought it over for a day or so. Then he came to Redwood and said that he doubted if he ought to give powders about which he knew nothing to Redwood's little boy; it seemed to him it was uncommonly like taking responsibility in the dark. That made Redwood thoughtful.

'You've seen that the Society for the Total Suppression of Boomfood claims to have several thousand members,' said Winkles, changing the subject. 'They've drafted a Bill,' said Winkles. 'They've got young Caterham to take it up – readily enough. They're in earnest. They're forming local committees to influence candidates. They want to make it penal to prepare and store Herakleophorbia without special licence, and a felony – matter of imprisonment without option – to administer Boomfood – that's what they call it, you know – to any person under one-and-twenty. But there's collateral societies, you know. All sorts of people. The Society for the Preservation of Ancient Statures is going to have Mr Frederic Harrison[35] on the council, they say. You know he's written an essay about it; says it is vulgar, and entirely inharmonious with that Revelation of Humanity that is found in the teachings of Comte. It is the sort of thing the Eighteenth Century *couldn't* have produced even in its worst moments. The idea of the Food never entered the head of Comte – which shows how wicked it really is. No one, he says, who really understood Comte . . . '

'But you don't mean to say – ' said Redwood, alarmed out of his disdain for Winkles.

'They'll not do all that,' said Winkles. 'But public opinion is public opinion, and votes are votes. Everybody can see you are up to a disturbing thing. And the human instinct is all against disturbance, you know. Nobody seems to believe Caterham's idea of people thirty-seven feet high, who won't be able to get inside a church, or a meeting-house, or any social or human institution. But for all that they're not so easy in their minds about it. They see there's something – something more than a common discovery – '

'There is,' said Redwood, 'in every discovery.'

'Anyhow, they're getting – restive. Caterham keeps harping on what may happen if it gets loose again. I say over and over again, it won't, and it can't. But – there it is!'

And he bounced about the room for a little while as if he meant to reopen the topic of the secret, and then thought better of it and went.

The two scientific men looked at one another. For a space only their eyes spoke.

'If the worst comes to the worst,' said Redwood at last, in a strenuously calm voice, 'I shall give the Food to my little Teddy with my own hands.'

3

It was only a few days after this that Redwood opened his paper to find that the Prime Minister had promised a Royal Commission on Boomfood. This sent him, newspaper in hand, round to Bensington's flat.

'Winkles, I believe, is making mischief for the stuff. He plays into the hands of Caterham. He keeps on talking about it, and what it is going to do, and alarming people. If he goes on, I really believe he'll hamper our enquiries. Even as it is – with this trouble about my little boy – '

Bensington wished Winkles wouldn't.

'Do you notice how he has dropped into the way of calling it Boomfood?'

'I don't like that name,' said Bensington, with a glance over his glasses.

'It is just so exactly what it is – to Winkles.'

'Why does he keep on about it? It isn't his!'

'It's something called Booming,' said Redwood. '*I* don't understand. If it isn't his, everybody is getting to think it is. Not that *that* matters.'

'In the event of this ignorant, this ridiculous agitation becoming – serious – ' began Bensington.

'My little boy can't get on without the stuff,' said Redwood. 'I don't see how I can help myself now. If the worst comes to the worst – '

A slight bouncing noise proclaimed the presence of Winkles. He became visible in the middle of the room rubbing his hands together.

'I wish you'd knock,' said Bensington, looking vicious over the gold rims.

Winkles was apologetic. Then he turned to Redwood. 'I'm glad to find you here,' he began; 'the fact is – '

'Have you seen about this Royal Commission?' interrupted Redwood.

'Yes,' said Winkles, thrown out. 'Yes.'

'What do you think of it?'

'Excellent thing,' said Winkles. 'Bound to stop most of this clamour. Ventilate the whole affair. Shut up Caterham. But that's not what I came round for, Redwood. The fact is – '

'I don't like this Royal Commission,' said Bensington.

'I can assure you it will be all right. I may say – I don't think it's a breach of confidence – that very possibly *I* may have a place on the Commission – '

'Oom,' said Redwood, looking into the fire.

'I can put the whole thing right. I can make it perfectly clear, first, that the stuff is controllable, and, secondly, that nothing short of a miracle is needed before anything like that catastrophe at Hickleybrow can possibly happen again. That is just what is wanted, an authoritative assurance. Of course, I could speak with more confidence if I knew – But that's quite by the way. And just at present there's something else, another little matter, upon which I'm wanting to consult you. Ahem. The fact is – Well – I happen to be in a slight difficulty, and you can help me out.'

Redwood raised his eyebrows, and was secretly glad.

'The matter is – highly confidential.'

'Go on,' said Redwood. 'Don't worry about that.'

'I have recently been entrusted with a child – the child of – of an Exalted Personage.'

Winkles coughed.

'You're getting on,' said Redwood.

'I must confess it's largely your powders – and the reputation of my success with your little boy – There is, I cannot disguise, a strong feeling against its use. And yet I find that among the more intelligent – One must go quietly in these things, you know – little by little. Still, in the case of Her Serene High – I mean this new little patient of mine . . . As a matter of fact – the suggestion came from the parent. Or I should never – '

He struck Redwood as being embarrassed.

'I thought you had a doubt of the advisability of using these powders,' said Redwood.

'Merely a passing doubt.'

'You don't propose to discontinue – '

'In the case of your little boy? Certainly not!'

'So far as I can see, it would be murder.'

'I wouldn't do it for the world.'

'You shall have the powders,' said Redwood.

'I suppose you couldn't – '

'No fear,' said Redwood. 'There isn't a recipe. It's no good, Winkles, if you'll pardon my frankness. I'll make you the powders myself.'

'Just as well, perhaps,' said Winkles, after a momentary hard stare at Redwood – 'just as well.' And then: 'I can assure you I really don't mind in the least.'

4

When Winkles had gone Bensington came and stood on the hearthrug and looked down at Redwood.

'Her Serene Highness!' he remarked.

'Her Serene Highness!' said Redwood.

'It's the Princess of Weser Dreiburg!'

'No further than a third cousin.'

'Redwood,' said Bensington; 'it's a curious thing to say, I know, but – do you think Winkles understands?'

'What?'

'Just what it is we have made.'

'Does he really understand,' said Bensington, dropping his voice and keeping his eye doorwards, 'that in the Family – the Family of his new patient – '

'Go on,' said Redwood.

'Who have always been if anything a little *under* – '

'The Average?'

'Yes. And so *very* tactfully undistinguished in *any* way, he is going to produce a royal personage – an outsize royal personage – of *that* size. You know, Redwood, I'm not sure whether there is not something almost – *treasonable* . . . '

He transferred his eyes from the door to Redwood.

Redwood flung a momentary gesture – index finger erect – at the fire. 'By Jove!' he said, 'he *doesn't* know!'

'That man,' said Redwood, 'doesn't know anything. That was his most exasperating quality as a student. Nothing. He passed all his examinations, he had all his facts – and he had just as much knowledge – as a rotating bookshelf containing *The Times Encyclopedia*. And he doesn't know anything *now*. He's Winkles, and incapable of really assimilating anything not immediately and directly related to his superficial self. He is utterly void of imagination and, as a consequence, incapable of knowledge. No one could possibly pass so many examinations and be so well dressed, so well done, and so successful as a doctor without that precise incapacity. That's it. And in spite of all he's seen and heard and been told, there he is – he has no idea whatever of what he has set going. He has got a Boom on, he's working it well on Boomfood, and someone has let him in to this new Royal Baby – and that's Boomier than ever! And the fact that Weser Dreiburg will presently have to face the gigantic problem of a thirty-odd-foot princess not only hasn't entered his head, but couldn't – it couldn't!'

'There'll be a fearful row,' said Bensington.

'In a year or so.'

'So soon as they really see she is going on growing.'

'Unless after their fashion – they hush it up.'

'It's a lot to hush up.'

'Rather!'

'I wonder what they'll do?'

'They never do anything – Royal tact.'

'They're bound to do something.'

'Perhaps *she* will.'

'Oh Lord! Yes.'

'They'll suppress her. Such things have been known.'

Redwood burst into desperate laughter. 'The redundant royalty – the bouncing babe in the Iron Mask!' he said. 'They'll have to put her in the tallest tower of the old Weser Dreiburg castle and make holes in the ceilings as she grows from floor to floor! Well, I'm in the very same pickle. And Cossar and his three boys. And – Well, well.'

'There'll be a fearful row,' Bensington repeated, not joining in the laughter. 'A *fearful* row.'

'I suppose,' he argued, 'you've really thought it out thoroughly, Redwood. You're quite sure it wouldn't be wiser to warn Winkles, wean your little boy gradually, and – and rely upon the Theoretical Triumph?'

'I wish to goodness you'd spend half an hour in my nursery when the Food's a little late,' said Redwood, with a note of exasperation in his voice; 'then you wouldn't talk like that, Bensington. Besides – Fancy warning Winkles . . . No! The tide of this thing has caught us unawares, and whether we're frightened or whether we're not – *we've got to swim!*'

'I suppose we have,' said Bensington, staring at his toes. 'Yes. We've got to swim. And your boy will have to swim, and Cossar's boys – he's given it to all three of them. Nothing partial about Cossar – all or nothing! And Her Serene Highness. And everything. We are going on making the Food. Cossar also. We're only just in the dawn of the beginning, Redwood. It's evident all sorts of things are to follow. Monstrous great things. But I can't imagine them, Redwood. Except – '

He scanned his fingernails. He looked up at Redwood with eyes bland through his glasses.

'I've half a mind,' he adventured, 'that Caterham is right. At times. It's going to destroy the Proportion of Things. It's going to dislocate – What isn't it going to dislocate?'

'Whatever it dislocates,' said Redwood, 'my little boy must have the Food.'

They heard someone falling rapidly upstairs. Then Cossar put his head into the fiat. 'Hello!' he said at their expressions, and entering, 'Well?'

They told him about the princess.

'*Difficult question!*' he remarked. 'Not a bit of it. *She'll* grow. Your boy'll grow. All the others you give it to'll grow. Everything. Like anything. What's difficult about that? That's all right. A child could tell you that. Where's the bother?'

They tried to make it clear to him.

'*Not go on with it!*' he shrieked. 'But – ! You can't help yourselves now. It's what you're for. It's what Winkles is for. It's all right. Often wondered what Winkles was for. *Now* it's obvious. What's the trouble?

'*Disturbance*? Obviously. *Upset things*? Upset everything. Finally – upset every human concern. Plain as a pikestaff. They're going to try and stop it, but they're too late. It's their way to be too late. You go on and start as much of it as you can. Thank God He has a use for you!'

'But the conflict!' said Bensington, 'the stress! I don't know if you have imagined – '

'You ought to have been some sort of little vegetable, Bensington,' said Cossar – 'that's what you ought to have been. Something growing over a rockery. Here you are, fearfully and wonderfully made, and all you think you're made for is just to sit about and take your vittles. D'you think this world was made for old women to mope about in? Well, anyhow, you can't help yourselves now – you've *got* to go on.'

'I suppose we must,' said Redwood. 'Slowly – '

'No!' said Cossar, in a huge shout. 'No! Make as much as you can and as soon as you can. Spread it about!'

He was inspired to a stroke of wit. He parodied one of Redwood's curves with a vast upward sweep of his arm.

'Redwood!' he said, to point the allusion, 'make it SO!'

There is, it seems, an upward limit to the pride of maternity, and this in the case of Mrs Redwood was reached when her offspring completed his sixth month of terrestrial existence, broke down his high-class bassinet-perambulator and was brought home, bawling, in the milk-truck. Young Redwood at that time weighed fifty-nine and a half pounds, measured forty-eight inches in height, and gripped about sixty pounds. He was carried upstairs to the nursery by the cook and housemaid. After that, discovery was only a question of days. One afternoon Redwood came home from his laboratory to find his unfortunate wife deep in the fascinating pages of *The Mighty Atom*, and at the sight of him she put the book aside and ran violently forward and burst into tears on his shoulder.

'Tell me what you have *done* to him,' she wailed. 'Tell me what you have done.' Redwood took her hand and led her to the sofa, while he tried to think of a satisfactory line of defence.

'It's all right, my dear,' he said; 'it's all right. You're only a little overwrought. It's that cheap perambulator. I've arranged for a bath-chair man to come round with something stouter tomorrow – '

Mrs Redwood looked at him tearfully over the top of her hand-kerchief.

'A baby in a bath-chair?' she sobbed.

'Well, why not?'

'It's like a cripple.'

'It's like a young giant, my dear, and you've no cause to be ashamed of him.'

'You've done something to him, Dandy,' she said. 'I can see it in your face.'

'Well, it hasn't stopped his growth, anyhow,' said Redwood heartlessly.

'I *knew*,' said Mrs Redwood, and clenched her pocket-handkerchief ball fashion in one hand. She looked at him with a sudden change to severity. 'What have you done to our child, Dandy?'

'What's wrong with him?'

'He's so big. He's a monster.'

'Nonsense. He's as straight and clean a baby as ever a woman had. What's wrong with him?'

'Look at his size.'

'That's all right. Look at the puny little brutes about us! He's the finest baby – '

'He's *too* fine,' said Mrs Redwood.

'It won't go on,' said Redwood reassuringly; 'it's just a start he's taken.'

But he knew perfectly well it would go on. And it did. By the time this baby was twelve months old he tottered just one inch under five feet high and scaled eight stone three; he was as big in fact as a St Peter's *in Vaticano* cherub, and his affectionate clutch at the hair and features of visitors became the talk of West Kensington. They had an invalid's chair to carry him up and down to his nursery, and his special nurse, a muscular young person just out of training, used to take him for his airings in a Panhard 8 h.p. hill-climbing perambulator specially made to meet his requirements. It was lucky in every way that Redwood had his expert-witness connection in addition to his professorship.

When one got over the shock of little Redwood's enormous size, he was, I am told by people who used to see him almost daily *teufteufing*[36] slowly about Hyde Park, a singularly bright and pretty baby. He rarely cried or needed a dummy. Commonly he clutched a big rattle, and sometimes he went along hailing the bus-drivers and policemen along the road outside the railings as 'Dadda!' and 'Babba!' in a sociable, democratic way.

'There goes that there great Boomfood baby,' the bus-driver used to say.

'Looks 'ealthy,' the forward passenger would remark.

'Bottle fed,' the bus-driver would explain. 'They say it 'olds a gallon and 'ad to be specially made for 'im.'

'Very 'ealthy child any'ow,' the forward passenger would conclude.

When Mrs Redwood realised that his growth was indeed going on indefinitely and logically – and this she really did for the first time when the motor-perambulator arrived – she gave way to a passion of grief. She declared she never wished to enter her nursery again, wished she was dead, wished the child was dead, wished everybody was dead, wished she had never married Redwood, wished no one ever married anybody, Ajaxed a little, and retired to her own room, where she lived almost exclusively on chicken broth for three days. When Redwood came to remonstrate with her, she banged pillows about and wept and tangled her hair.

'*He's* all right,' said Redwood. 'He's all the better for being big. You wouldn't like him smaller than other people's children.'

'I want him to be *like* other children, neither smaller nor bigger. I wanted him to be a nice little boy, just as Georgina Phyllis is a nice little girl, and I wanted to bring him up nicely in a nice way, and here he is' – and the unfortunate woman's voice broke – 'wearing number four grown-up shoes and being wheeled about by – boohoo! – petroleum!

'I can never love him,' she wailed, 'never! He's too much for me! I can never be a mother to him, such as I meant to be!'

But at last they contrived to get her into the nursery, and there was Edward Monson Redwood ('Pantagruel'[39] was only a later nickname) swinging in a specially strengthened rocking-chair and smiling and talking 'goo' and 'wow'. And the heart of Mrs Redwood warmed again to her child, and she went and held him in her arms and wept.

'They've done something to you,' she sobbed, 'and you'll grow and grow, dear; but whatever I can do to bring you up nice I'll do for you, whatever your father may say.'

And Redwood, who had helped to bring her to the door, went down the passage much relieved.

(Eh! but it's a base job this being a man – with women as they are!)

6

Before the year was out there were, in addition to Redwood's pioneer vehicle, quite a number of motor-perambulators to be seen in the west of London. I am told there were as many as eleven; but the most careful enquiries yield trustworthy evidence of only six within the Metropolitan area at that time. It would seem the stuff acted differently upon different types of constitution. At first Herakleophorbia was not adapted to injection, and there can be no doubt that quite a considerable proportion of human beings are incapable of absorbing this substance in the normal course of digestion. It was given, for example, to Winkles's youngest boy; but he seems to have been as incapable of growth as, if Redwood was right, his father was incapable of knowledge. Others again, according to the Society for the Total Suppression of Boomfood, became in some inexplicable way corrupted by it, and perished at the onset of infantile disorders. The Cossar boys took to it with amazing avidity.

Of course a thing of this kind never comes with absolute simplicity of application into the life of man; growth in particular is a complex thing, and all generalisations must needs be a little inaccurate. But the general law of the Food would seem to be this, that when it could be taken into the system in any way it stimulated it in very nearly the same degree in all cases. It increased the amount of growth from six to seven times, and it did not go beyond that, whatever amount of the Food in excess was taken. Excess of Herakleophorbia indeed beyond the necessary minimum led, it was found, to morbid disturbances of nutrition, to cancer and tumours, ossifications and the like. And once growth upon the large scale had begun, it was soon evident that it could only continue upon that scale, and that the continuous administration of Herakleophorbia in small but sufficient doses was imperative.

If it was discontinued while growth was still going on, there was first a vague restlessness and distress, then a period of voracity – as in the case of the young rats at Hankey – and then the growing creature had a sort of exaggerated anaemia and sickened and died. Plants suffered in a similar way. This, however, applied only to the growth period. So soon as adolescence was attained – in plants this was represented by the formation of the first flower-buds – the need and appetite for Herakleophorbia diminished, and so soon as the plant or animal was fully adult, it became altogether independent of any further supply of the food. It was, as it were, completely established on the new scale. It was so completely established on the new scale that, as the thistles about Hickleybrow and the grass of the down side already demonstrated, its seed produced giant offspring after its kind.

And presently little Redwood, pioneer of the new race, first child of all who ate the food, was crawling about his nursery, smashing furniture, biting like a horse, pinching like a vice and bawling gigantic babytalk at his 'Nanny' and 'Mammy' – and the rather scared and awestricken 'Daddy' who had set this mischief going.

The child was born with good intentions. 'Padda be good, be good,' he used to say as the breakables flew before him. 'Padda' was his rendering of Pantagruel, the nickname Redwood imposed on him. And Cossar, disregarding certain Ancient Lights that presently led to trouble, did, after a conflict with the local building regulations, get building on a vacant piece of ground adjacent to Redwood's home a comfortable well-lit playroom, schoolroom and nursery for their four boys – sixty feet square about this room was, and forty feet high.

Redwood fell in love with that great nursery as he and Cossar built it, and his interest in curves faded, as he had never dreamt it could fade, before the pressing needs of his son. 'There is much,' he said, 'in fitting a nursery. Much.

'The walls, the things in it, they will all speak to this new mind of ours, a little more, a little less eloquently, and teach it or fail to teach it a thousand things.'

'Obviously,' said Cossar, reaching hastily for his hat.

They worked together harmoniously, but Redwood supplied most of the educational theory required.

They had the walls and woodwork painted with a cheerful vigour; for the most part a slightly warmed white prevailed, but there were bands of bright clean colour to enforce the simple lines of construction. 'Clean colours we *must* have,' said Redwood, and in one place had a neat horizontal band of squares, in which crimson and purple, orange and lemon, blues and greens, in many hues and many shades, did themselves honour. These squares the giant children should arrange and rearrange to their pleasure. 'Decorations must follow,' said Redwood; 'let them first get the range of all the tints, and then this may go away. There is no reason why one should bias them in favour of any particular colour or design.'

Then, 'The place must be full of interest,' said Redwood. 'Interest is food for a child, and blankness torture and starvation. He must have pictures galore.' There were no pictures hung about the room for any permanent service, however, but blank frames were provided into which new pictures would come and pass thence into a portfolio so soon as their fresh interest had passed. There was one window that looked down the length of a street, and in addition, for an added interest, Redwood had contrived above the roof of the nursery a camera obscura that watched the Kensington High Street and not a little of the Gardens.

In one corner that most worthy implement, an abacus, four feet square, a specially strengthened piece of ironmongery with rounded corners, awaited the young giants' incipient computations. There were few woolly lambs and suchlike idols, but instead Cossar, without explanation, had brought one day in three four-wheelers a great number of toys (all just too big for the coming children to swallow) that could be piled up, arranged in rows, rolled about, bitten, made to flap and rattle, smacked together, felt over, pulled out, opened, closed, and mauled and experimented with to an interminable extent. There were many bricks of wood in diverse colours, oblong and cuboid, bricks of polished china, bricks of transparent glass and bricks of india-rubber; there were slabs and slates; there were cones, truncated cones, and cylinders; there were oblate and prolate spheroids, balls of varied substances, solid and hollow, many boxes of diverse size and shape, with hinged lids and screw lids and fitting lids, and one or two to catch and lock; there were bands of elastic and leather, and a number of rough and sturdy little objects of a size together that could stand up steadily and suggest the shape of a man. 'Give 'em these,' said Cossar. 'One at a time.'

These things Redwood arranged in a locker in one corner. Along one side of the room, at a convenient height for a six- or eight-foot child, there was a blackboard, on which the youngsters might flourish in white and coloured chalk, and near by a sort of drawing block, from which sheet after sheet might be torn, and on which they could draw in charcoal; and a little desk there was, furnished with great carpenter's pencils of varying hardness and a copious supply of paper on which the boys might first scribble and then draw more neatly. And moreover Redwood gave orders, so far ahead did his imagination go, for specially large tubes of liquid paint and boxes of pastels against the time when they should be needed. He laid in a cask or so of plasticine and modelling clay. 'At first he and his tutor shall model together,' he said, 'and when he is more skilful he shall copy casts and perhaps animals. And that reminds me, I must also have made for him a box of tools!

'Then books. I shall have to look out a lot of books to put in his way, and they'll have to be big type. Now what sort of books will he need? There is his imagination to be fed. That, after all, is the crown of every education. The crown – as sound habits of mind and conduct are the throne. No imagination at all is brutality; a base imagination is lust and cowardice; but a noble imagination is God walking the earth again. He must dream too of a dainty fairyland and of all the quaint little things of life, in due time. But he must feed chiefly on the splendid real; he shall have stories of travel through all the world, travels and adventures and how the world was won; he shall have stories of beasts, great books splendidly and clearly done of animals and birds and plants and creeping things, great books about the deeps of the sky and the mystery of the sea; he shall have histories and maps of all the empires the world has seen, pictures and stories of all the tribes and habits and customs of men. And he must have books and pictures to quicken his sense of beauty, subtle Japanese pictures to make him love the subtler beauties of bird and tendril and falling flower, and Western pictures too, pictures of gracious men and women, sweet groupings and broad views of land and sea. He shall have books on the building of houses and palaces; he shall plan rooms and invent cities –

'I think I must give him a little theatre.

'Then there is music!'

Redwood thought that over and decided that his son might best begin with a very pure-sounding harmonicon of one octave, to which afterwards there could be an extension. 'He shall play with this first, sing to it and give names to the notes,' said Redwood, 'and afterwards? – '

He stared up at the window-sill overhead and measured the size of the room with his eye.

'They'll have to build his piano in here,' he said. 'Bring it in in pieces.'

He hovered about amidst his preparations, a pensive, dark, little figure. If you could have seen him there he would have looked to you like a ten-inch man amidst common nursery things. A great rug – indeed it was a Turkey carpet – four hundred square feet of it, upon which young Redwood was soon to crawl – stretched to the grill-guarded electric radiator that was to warm the whole place. A man from Cossar's hung amidst scaffolding overhead, fixing the great frame that was to hold the transitory pictures. A blotting-paper book for plant specimens as big as a house door leant against the wall, and from it projected a gigantic stalk, a leaf edge or so and one flower of chickweed, all of that gigantic size that was soon to make Urshot famous throughout the botanical world.

A sort of incredulity came to Redwood as he stood among these things.

'If it really *is* going on – ' said Redwood, staring up at the remote ceiling.

From far away came a sound like the bellowing of a Mafficking[38] bull, almost as if in answer.

'It's going on all right,' said Redwood. 'Evidently.'

There followed resounding blows upon a table, followed by a vast crowing shout, 'Gooloo! Boozoo! Bzz . . . '

'The best thing I can do,' said Redwood, following out some divergent line of thought, 'is to teach him myself.'

That beating became more insistent. For a moment it seemed to Redwood that it caught the rhythm of an engine's throbbing – the engine he could have imagined of some great train of events that bore down upon him. Then a descendant flight of sharper beats broke up that effect, and were repeated.

'Come in,' he cried, perceiving that someone rapped, and the door that was big enough for a cathedral opened slowly a little way. The new winch ceased to creak, and Bensington appeared in the crack, gleaming benevolently under his protruded baldness and over his glasses.

'I've ventured round to *see*,' he whispered in a confidentially furtive manner.

'Come in,' said Redwood, and he did, shutting the door behind him.

He walked forward, hands behind his back, advanced a few steps, and peered up with a birdlike movement at the dimensions about him. He rubbed his chin thoughtfully.

'Every time I come in,' he said, with a subdued note in his voice, 'it strikes me as – *Big*.'

'Yes,' said Redwood, surveying it all again also, as if in an endeavour to keep hold of the visible impression. 'Yes. They're going to be big, too, you know.'

'I know,' said Bensington, with a note that was nearly awe. '*Very* big.'

They looked at one another, almost, as it were, apprehensively.

'Very big indeed,' said Bensington, stroking the bridge of his nose, and with one eye that watched Redwood doubtfully for a confirmatory expression. 'All of them, you know – fearfully big. I don't seem able to imagine – even with this – just how big they're all going to be.'

CHAPTER 5

The Minimificence of Mr Bensington

It was while the Royal Commission on Boomfood was preparing its report that Herakleophorbia really began to demonstrate its capacity for leakage. And the earliness of this second outbreak was the more unfortunate, from the point of view of Cossar at any rate, since the draft report still in existence shows that the commission had, under the tutelage of that most able member, Dr Stephen Winkles (FRS, MD, FRCP, DSC, JP, DL, etc.), already quite made up its mind that accidental leakages were impossible, and was prepared to recommend that to entrust the preparation of Boomfood to a qualified committee (Winkles chiefly), with an entire control over its sale, was quite enough to satisfy all reasonable objections to its free diffusion. This committee was to have an absolute monopoly. And it is, no doubt, to be considered as a part of the irony of life that the first and most alarming of this second series of leakages occurred within fifty yards of a little cottage at Keston occupied during the summer months by Dr Winkles.

There can be little doubt now that Redwood's refusal to acquaint Winkles with the composition of Herakleophorbia IV had aroused in that gentleman a novel and intense desire towards analytical chemistry. He was not a very expert manipulator, and for that reason probably he saw fit to do his work not in the excellently equipped laboratories that were at his disposal in London, but, without consulting anyone, and almost with an air of secrecy, in a rough little garden laboratory at the Keston establishment. He does not seem to have shown either very great energy or very great ability in this quest; indeed one gathers he dropped the inquiry after working at it intermittently for about a month.

This garden laboratory, in which the work was done, was very roughly equipped, supplied by a standpipe tap with water and draining into a pipe that ran down into a swampy rush-bordered pool under an alder tree in a secluded corner of the common just outside the garden hedge. The pipe was cracked, and the residuum of the Food of the Gods escaped through the crack into a little puddle amidst clumps of rushes, just in time for the spring awakening.

Everything was astir with life in that scummy little corner. There was frog spawn adrift, tremulous with tadpoles just bursting their gelatinous envelopes; there were little pond snails creeping out into life; and under the green skin of the rush stems the larvae of a big water beetle were struggling out of their egg cases. I doubt if the reader knows the larva of the beetle called (I know not why) Dytiscus. It is a jointed, queer-looking thing, very muscular and sudden in its movements, and given to swimming head downward with its tail out of water; the length of a man's top thumb joint it is, and more – two inches, that is for those who have not eaten the Food – and it has two sharp jaws that meet in front of its head – tubular jaws with sharp points – through which its habit is to suck its victim's blood.

The first things to get at the drifting grains of the Food were the little tadpoles and the little water snails; the little wriggling tadpoles in particular, once they had the taste of it, took to it with zest. But scarcely did one of them begin to grow into a conspicuous position in that little tadpole world and try a smaller brother or so as an aid to a vegetarian dietary, when nip! one of the beetle larva had its curved bloodsucking prongs gripping into his heart, and with that red stream went Herakleophorbia IV, in a state of solution, into the being of a new client. The only thing that had a chance with these monsters to get any share of the Food were the rushes and slimy green scum in the water and the seedling weeds in the mud at the bottom. A clean up of the study presently washed a fresh spate of the Food into the puddle, and overflowed it, and carried all this sinister expansion of the struggle for life into the adjacent pool under the roots of the alder . . .

The first person to discover what was going on was a Mr Lukey Carrington, a special science teacher under the London Education Board, and, in his leisure, a specialist in freshwater algae, and he is certainly not to be envied his discovery. He had come down to Keston Common for the day to fill a number of specimen tubes for subsequent examination, and he came, with a dozen or so corked tubes clanking faintly in his pocket, over the sandy crest and down towards the pool, spiked walking stick in hand. A garden lad standing on the top of the kitchen steps clipping Dr Winkles's hedge saw him in this unfrequented corner, and found him and his occupation sufficiently inexplicable and interesting to watch him pretty closely.

He saw Mr Carrington stoop down by the side of the pool, with his hand against the old alder stem, and peer into the water, but of course he could not appreciate the surprise and pleasure with which Mr Carrington beheld the big unfamiliar-looking blobs and threads of the algal scum at the bottom. There were no tadpoles visible – they had all been killed by that time – and it would seem Mr Carrington saw nothing at all unusual except the excessive vegetation. He bared his arm to the elbow, leant forward, and dipped deep in pursuit of a specimen. His seeking hand went down. Instantly there flashed out of the cool shadow under the tree roots something –

Flash! It had buried its fangs deep into his arm – a bizarre shape it was, a foot long and more, brown and jointed like a scorpion.

Its ugly apparition and the sharp amazing painfulness of its bite were too much for Mr Carrington's equilibrium. He felt himself going, and yelled aloud. Over he toppled, face foremost, splash! into the pool.

The boy saw him vanish, and heard the splashing of his struggle in the water. The unfortunate man emerged again into the boy's field of vision, hatless and streaming with water, and screaming!

Never before had the boy heard screams from a man.

This astonishing stranger appeared to be tearing at something on the side of his face. There appeared streaks of blood there. He flung out his arms as if in despair, leapt in the air like a frantic creature, ran violently ten or twelve yards, and then fell and rolled on the ground and over and out of sight of the boy. The lad was down the steps and through the hedge in a trice – happily with the garden shears still in hand. As he came crashing through the gorse bushes, he says he was half minded to turn back, fearing he had to deal with a lunatic, but the possession of the shears reassured him. 'I could 'ave jabbed his eyes,' he explained, 'anyhow.' Directly Mr Carrington caught sight of him, his demeanour became at once that of a sane but desperate man. He struggled to his feet, stumbled, stood up, and came to meet the boy.

'Look!' he cried, 'I can't get 'em off!'

And with a qualm of horror the boy saw that, attached to Mr Carrington's cheek, to his bare arm and to his thigh, and lashing furiously with their lithe brown muscular bodies, were three of these horrible larvae, their great jaws buried deep in his flesh and sucking for dear life. They had the grip of bulldogs, and Mr Carrington's efforts to detach the monsters from his face had only served to lacerate the flesh to which it had attached itself, and streak face and neck and coat with living scarlet.

'I'll cut 'em,' cried the boy; ' 'old on, sir.'

And with the zest of his age in such proceedings, he severed one by one the heads from the bodies of Mr Carrington's assailants. 'Yup,' said the boy with a wincing face as each one fell before him. Even then, so tough and determined was their grip that the severed heads remained for a space, still fiercely biting home and still sucking, with the blood streaming out of their necks behind. But the boy stopped that with a few more slashes of his scissors – in one of which Mr Carrington was implicated.

'I couldn't get 'em off!' repeated Carrington, and stood for a space, swaying and bleeding profusely. He dabbed feeble hands at his injuries and examined the result upon his palms. Then he gave way at the knees and fell headlong in a dead faint at the boy's feet, between the still leaping bodies of his defeated foes. Very luckily it didn't occur to the boy to splash water on his face – for there were still more of these horrors under the alder roots – and instead he passed back by the pond and went into the garden with the intention of calling assistance. And there he met the gardener-coachman and told him of the whole affair.

When they got back to Mr Carrington he was sitting up, dazed and weak, but able to warn them against the danger in the pool.

2

Such were the circumstances by which the world had its first notification that the Food was loose again. In another week Keston Common was in full operation as what naturalists call a centre of distribution. This time there were no wasps or rats, no earwigs and no nettles, but there were at least three water-spiders, several dragonfly larvae which presently became dragonflies, dazzling all Kent with their hovering sapphire bodies, and a nasty gelatinous, scummy growth that swelled over the pond margin, and sent its slimy green masses surging halfway up the garden path to Dr Winkles's house. And there began a growth of rushes and equisetum and potamogeton[39] that ended only with the drying of the pond.

It speedily became evident to the public mind that this time there was not simply one centre of distribution, but quite a number of centres. There was one at Ealing – there can be no doubt now – and from that came the plague of flies and red spiders; there was one at Sunbury, productive of ferocious great eels that could come ashore and kill sheep; and there was one in Bloomsbury that gave the world a new strain of cockroaches of a quite terrible sort – an old house it was in Bloomsbury, and much inhabited by undesirable things. Abruptly the world found itself confronted with the Hickleybrow experiences all over again, with all sorts of queer exaggerations of familiar monsters in the place of the giant hens and rats and wasps. Each centre burst out with its own characteristic local fauna and flora.

We know now that every one of these centres corresponded to one of the patients of Dr Winkles, but that was by no means apparent at the time. Dr Winkles was the last person to incur any odium in the matter. There was a panic quite naturally, a passionate indignation, but it was indignation not against Dr Winkles but against the Food, and not so much against the Food as against the unfortunate Bensington, whom from the very first the popular imagination had insisted upon regarding as the sole and only person responsible for this new thing.

The attempt to lynch him that followed is just one of those explosive events that bulk largely in history and are in reality the least significant of occurrences.

The history of the outbreak is a mystery. The nucleus of the crowd certainly came from an Anti-Boomfood meeting in Hyde Park organised by extremists of the Caterham party, but there seems no one in the world who actually first proposed, no one who ever first hinted a suggestion of the outrage at which so many people assisted. It is a problem for M. Gustave le Bon – a mystery in the psychology of crowds. The fact emerges that about three o'clock on Sunday afternoon a remarkably big and ugly London crowd, entirely out of hand, came rolling down Thursday Street intent on Bensington's exemplary death as a warning to all scientific investigators, and that it came nearer accomplishing its object than any London crowd has ever come since the Hyde Park railings came down in remote middle-Victorian times. This crowd came so close to its object indeed, that for the space of an hour or more a word would have settled the unfortunate gentleman's fate.

The first intimation he had of the thing was the noise of the people outside. He went to the window and peered, realising nothing of what impended. For a minute perhaps he watched them seething about the entrance, disposing of an ineffectual dozen of policemen who barred their way, before he fully realised his own importance in the affair. It came upon him in a flash – that that roaring, swaying multitude was after him. He was all alone in the flat – fortunately perhaps – his cousin Jane having gone down to Ealing to have tea with a relation on her mother's side, and he had no more idea of how to behave under such circumstances than he had of the etiquette of the Day of Judgement. He was still dashing about the flat asking his furniture what he should do, turning keys in locks and then unlocking them again, making darts at door and window and bedroom – when the porter for his floor came to him.

'There isn't a moment, sir,' he said. 'They've got your number from the board in the hall! They're coming straight up!'

He ran Mr Bensington out into the passage, already echoing with the approaching tumult from the great staircase, locked the door behind them, and led the way into the opposite flat by means of his duplicate key.

'It's our only chance now,' he said.

He flung up a window which opened on a ventilating shaft, and showed that the wall was set with iron staples that made the rudest and most perilous of wall ladders to serve as a fire escape from the upper flats. He shoved Mr Bensington out of the window, showed him how to cling on, and pursued him up the ladder, goading and jabbing his legs with a bunch of keys whenever he desisted from climbing. It seemed to Bensington at times that he must climb that vertical ladder for evermore. Above, the parapet was inaccessibly remote, a mile perhaps; below – He did not care to think of things below.

'Steady on!' cried the porter, and gripped his ankle. It was quite horrible having his ankle gripped like that, and Mr Bensington tightened his hold on the iron staple above to a drowning clutch, and gave a faint squeal of terror.

It became evident the porter had broken a window, and then it seemed he had leapt a vast distance sideways, and there came the noise of a window-frame sliding in its sash. He was bawling things.

Mr Bensington moved his head round cautiously until he could see the porter. 'Come down six steps,' the porter commanded.

All this moving about seemed very foolish, but very, very cautiously Mr Bensington lowered a foot.

'Don't pull me!' he cried, as the porter made to help him from the open window.

It seemed to him that to reach the window from the ladder would be a very respectable feat for a flying fox, and it was rather with the idea of a decent suicide than in any hope of accomplishing it that he made the step at last, and quite ruthlessly the porter pulled him in. 'You'll have to stop here,' said the porter; 'my keys are no good here. It's an American lock. I'll get out and slam the door behind me and see if I can find the man of this floor. You'll be locked in. Don't go to the window, that's all. It's the ugliest crowd I've ever seen. If only they think you're out they'll probably content themselves by breaking up your stuff – '

'The indicator said In,' said Bensington.

'The devil it did! Well, anyhow, I'd better not be found – '

He vanished with a slam of the door.

Bensington was left to his own initiative again.

It took him under the bed.

There presently he was found by Cossar.

Bensington was almost comatose with terror when he was found, for Cossar had burst the door in with his shoulder by jumping at it across the breadth of the passage.

'Come out of it, Bensington,' he said. 'It's all right. It's me. We've got to get out of this. They're setting the place on fire. The porters are all clearing out. The servants are gone. It's lucky I caught the man who knew.

'Look here!'

Bensington, peering from under the bed, became aware of some unaccountable garments on Cossar's arm, and, of all things, a black bonnet in his hand!

'They're having a clear out,' said Cossar. 'If they don't set the place on fire they'll come here. Troops may not be here for an hour yet. Fifty per cent hooligans in the crowd, and the more furnished flats they go into the better they'll like it. Obviously . . . They mean a clear out. You put this skirt and bonnet on, Bensington, and clear out with me.'

'D'you *mean* – ?' began Bensington, protruding a head, tortoise fashion.

'I mean, put 'em on and come! Obviously,' And with a sudden vehemence he dragged Bensington from under the bed and began to dress him for his new impersonation of an elderly woman of the people.

He rolled up his trousers and made him kick off his slippers, took off his collar and tie and coat and waistcoat, slipped a black skirt over his head, and put on a red-flannel bodice and over it a blouse. He made him take off his all-too-characteristic spectacles and clapped the bonnet on his head. 'You might have been born an old woman,' he said as he tied the strings. Then came the spring-sided boots – a terrible wrench for corns – and the shawl, and the disguise was complete. 'Up and down,' said Cossar, and Bensington obeyed.

'You'll do,' said Cossar.

And in this guise it was, stumbling awkwardly over his unaccustomed skirts, shouting womanly imprecations upon his own head in a weird falsetto to sustain his part, assailed by the roaring note of a crowd bent upon lynching him, that the original discoverer of Herakleophorbia IV proceeded down the corridor of Chesterfield Mansions, mingled with that inflamed disorderly multitude and passed out altogether from the thread of events that constitutes our story.

Never once after that escape did he meddle again with the stupendous development of the Food of the Gods he of all men had done most to begin.

This little man who started the whole thing passes out of the story, and after a time he passed altogether out of the world of things, visible and tellable. But because he started the whole thing it is seemly to give his exit an intercalary page of attention. One may picture him in his later days as Tunbridge Wells came to know him. For it was at Tunbridge Wells he reappeared after a temporary obscurity, so soon as he fully realised how transitory, how quite exceptional and unmeaning that fury of rioting was. He reappeared under the wing of Cousin Jane, treating himself for nervous shock to the exclusion of all other interests, and totally indifferent, as it seemed, to the battles that were raging then about those new centres of distribution, and about the baby Children of the Food.

He took up his quarters at the Mount Glory Hydrotherapeutic Hotel, where there are quite extraordinary facilities for baths: Carbonated Baths, Creosote Baths, Galvanic and Faradic Treatment, Massage, Pine Baths, Starch and Hemlock Baths, Radium Baths, Light Baths, Heat Baths, Bran and Needle Baths, Tar and Birdsdown Baths – all sorts of baths; and he devoted his mind to the development of that system of curative treatment that was still imperfect when he died. And sometimes he would go out in a hired vehicle and a sealskin-trimmed coat, and sometimes, when his feet permitted, he would walk to the Pantiles, and there he would sip chalybeate water under the eye of his cousin Jane.

His stooping shoulders, his pink appearance, his beaming glasses, became a 'feature' of Tunbridge Wells. No one was the least bit unkind to him, and indeed the place and the hotel seemed very glad to have the distinction of his presence. Nothing could rob him of that distinction now. And though he preferred not to follow the development of his great invention in the daily papers, yet when he crossed the lounge of the hotel or walked down the Pantiles and heard the whisper, 'There he is! That's him!' it was not dissatisfaction that softened his mouth and gleamed for a moment in his eye.

This little figure, this minute little figure, launched the Food of the Gods upon the world! One does not know which is the most amazing, the greatness or the littleness of these scientific and philosophical men. You figure him there on the Pantiles, in the overcoat trimmed with fur. He stands under that chinaware window where the spring spouts, and holds and sips the glass of chalybeate water in his hand. One bright eye over the gilt rim is fixed, with an expression of inscrutable severity, on Cousin Jane, 'Mm,' he says, and sips.

So we make our souvenir, so we focus and photograph this discoverer of ours for the last time, and leave him, a mere dot in our foreground, and pass to the greater picture that has developed about him, to the story of his Food, how the scattered Giant Children grew up day by day into a world that was all too small for them, and how the net of Boomfood Laws and Boomfood Conventions, which the Boomfood Commission was weaving even then, drew closer and closer upon them with every year of their growth. Until –

BOOK TWO

The Food in the Village

CHAPTER 1

The Coming of the Food

Our theme, which began so compactly in Mr Bensington's study, has already spread and branched, until it points this way and that, and henceforth our whole story is one of dissemination. To follow the Food of the Gods farther is to trace the ramifications of a perpetually branching tree; in a little while, in the quarter of a lifetime, the Food had trickled and increased from its first spring in the little farm near Hickleybrow until it had spread – it and the report and shadow of its power – throughout the world. It spread beyond England very speedily. Soon in America, all over the continent of Europe, in Japan, in Australia, at last all over the world, the thing was working towards its appointed end. Always it worked slowly, by indirect courses and against resistance. It was bigness insurgent. In spite of prejudice, in spite of law and regulation, in spite of all that obstinate conservatism that lies at the base of the formal order of mankind, the Food of the Gods, once it had been set going, pursued its subtle and invincible progress.

The Children of the Food grew steadily through all these years; that was the cardinal fact of the time. But it is the leakages make history. The children who had eaten grew, and soon there were other children growing; and all the best intentions in the world could not stop further leakages and still further leakages. The Food insisted on escaping with the pertinacity of a thing alive. Flour treated with the stuff crumbled in dry weather almost as if by intention into an impalpable powder, and would lift and travel before the lightest breeze. Now it would be some fresh insect won its way to a temporary fatal new development, now some fresh outbreak from the sewers of rats and suchlike vermin. For some days the village of Pangbourne in Berkshire fought with giant ants. Three men were bitten and died. There would be a panic, there would be a struggle, and the salient evil would be fought down again, leaving always something behind, in the obscurer things of life, changed for ever. Then again another acute and startling outbreak, a swift upgrowth of monstrous weedy thickets, a drifting dissemination about the world of inhumanly growing thistles, of cockroaches men fought with shotguns, or a plague of mighty flies.

There were some strange and desperate struggles in obscure places. The Food begot heroes in the cause of littleness . . .

And men took such happenings into their lives, and met them by the expedients of the moment, and told one another there was 'no change in the essential order of things'. After the first great panic, Caterham, in spite of his power of eloquence, became a secondary figure in the political world, remained in men's minds as the exponent of an extreme view.

Only slowly did he win a way towards a central position in affairs. 'There was no change in the essential order of things' – that eminent leader of modern thought, Dr Winkles, was very clear upon this – and the exponents of what was called in those days Progressive Liberalism grew quite sentimental upon the essential insincerity of their progress. Their dreams, it would appear, ran wholly on little nations, little languages, little households, each self-supported on its little farm. A fashion for the small and neat set in. To be big was to be 'vulgar', and dainty, neat, mignon, miniature, 'minutely perfect', became the keywords of critical approval . . .

Meanwhile, quietly, taking their time as children must, the Children of the Food, growing into a world that changed to receive them, gathered strength and stature and knowledge, became individual and purposeful, rose slowly towards the dimensions of their destiny. Presently they seemed a natural part of the world; all these stirrings of bigness seemed a natural part of the world, and men wondered how things had been before their time. There came to men's ears stories of things the giant boys could do, and they said, 'Wonderful!' – without a spark of wonder. The popular papers would tell of the three sons of Cossar, and how these amazing children would lift great cannons, hurl masses of iron for hundreds of yards and leap two hundred feet. They were said to be digging a well, deeper than any well or mine that man had ever made, seeking, it was said, for treasures hidden in the earth since ever the earth began.

These Children, said the popular magazines, will level mountains, bridge seas, tunnel your earth to a honeycomb. 'Wonderful!' said the little folks, 'isn't it? What a lot of conveniences we shall have!' and went about their business as though there was no such thing as the Food of the Gods on earth. And indeed these things were no more than the first hints and promises of the powers of the Children of the Food. It was still no more than child's play with them, no more than the first use of a strength in which no purpose had arisen. They did not know themselves for what they were. They were children – slow-growing children of a new race. The giant strength grew day by day – the giant will had still to grow into purpose and an aim.

Looking at it in a shortened perspective of time, those years of transition have the quality of a single consecutive occurrence; but indeed no one saw the coming of Bigness in the world, as no one in all the world till centuries had passed saw, as one happening, the Decline and Fall of Rome. They who lived in those days were too much among these developments to see them together as a single thing. It seemed even to wise men that the Food was giving the world nothing but a crop of unmanageable, disconnected irrelevancies, that might shake and trouble indeed, but could do no more to the established order and fabric of mankind.

To one observer at least the most wonderful thing throughout that period of accumulating stress is the invincible inertia of the great mass of people, their quiet persistence in all that ignored the enormous presences, the promise of still more enormous things, that grew among them. Just as many a stream will be at its smoothest, will look most tranquil, running deep and strong, at the very verge of a cataract, so all that is most conservative in man seemed settling quietly into a serene ascendency during these latter days. Reaction became popular: there was talk of the bankruptcy of science, of the dying of Progress, of the advent of the Mandarins – talk of such things amidst the echoing footsteps of the Children of the Food. The fussy pointless revolutions of the old time, a vast crowd of silly little people chasing some silly little monarch and the like, had indeed died out and passed away; but Change had not died out. It was only Change that had changed. The New was coming in its own fashion and beyond the common understanding of the world.

To tell fully of its coming would be to write a great history, but everywhere there was a parallel chain of happenings. To tell therefore of the manner of its coming in one place is to tell something of the whole. It chanced one stray seed of Immensity fell into the pretty, petty village of Cheasing Eyebright in Kent, and from the story of its queer germination there and of the tragic futility that ensued one may attempt – following one thread, as it were – to show the direction in which the whole great interwoven fabric of the thing rolled off the loom of Time.

Cheasing Eyebright had of course a vicar. There are vicars and vicars, and of all sorts I love an innovating vicar, a piebald progressive professional reactionary, the least. But the vicar of Cheasing Eyebright was one of the least innovating of vicars, a most worthy, plump, ripe and conservative-minded little man. It is becoming to go back a little in our story to tell of him. He matched his village, and one may figure them best together as they used to be, on the sunset evening when Mrs Skinner – you will remember her flight! – brought the Food with her all unsuspected into these rustic serenities.

The village was looking its very best just then, under that western light. It lay down along the valley beneath the beechwoods of the hanger, a beading of thatched and red-tiled cottages – cottages with trellised porches and pyracanthus-lined faces, that clustered closer and closer as the road dropped from the yew trees by the church towards the bridge. The vicarage peeped not too ostentatiously between the trees beyond the inn, an early Georgian front ripened by time, and the spire of the church rose happily in the depression made by the valley in the outline of the hills. A winding stream, a thin intermittency of sky blue and foam, glittered amidst a thick margin of reeds and loosestrife and overhanging willows, along the centre of a sinuous pennant of meadow. The whole prospect had that curiously English quality of ripened cultivation – that look of still completeness – that apes perfection, under the sunset warmth.

And the vicar too looked mellow. He looked habitually and essentially mellow, as though he had been a mellow baby born into a mellow class, a ripe and juicy little boy. One could see, even before he mentioned it, that he had gone to an ivy-clad public school in its anecdotage, with magnificent traditions, aristocratic associations, and no chemical laboratories, and proceeded thence to a venerable college in the very ripest Gothic. Few books he had younger than a thousand years; of these, Yarrow and Ellis and good pre-Methodist sermons made the bulk. He was a man of moderate height, a little shortened in appearance by his equatorial dimensions, and a face that had been mellow from the first was now climacterically ripe. The beard of a David hid his redundancy of chin; he wore no watch-chain out of refinement, and his modest clerical garments were made by a West End tailor . . . And he sat with a hand on either shin, blinking at his village in beatific approval. He waved a plump palm towards it. His burthen sang out again. What more could anyone desire?

'We are fortunately situated,' he said, putting the thing tamely.

'We are in a fastness of the hills,' he expanded.

He explained himself at length. 'We are out of it all.'

For they had been talking, he and his friend, of the Horrors of the Age, of Democracy, and Secular Education, and Sky Scrapers, and Motor Cars, and the American Invasion, the Scrappy Reading of the Public, and the disappearance of any Taste at all.

'We are out of it all,' he repeated, and even as he spoke the footsteps of someone coming smote upon his ear, and he rolled over and regarded her.

You figure the old woman's steadfastly tremulous advance, the bundle clutched in her gnarled lank hand, her nose (which was her countenance) wrinkled with breathless resolution. You see the poppies nodding fatefully on her bonnet, and the dust-white spring-sided boots beneath her skimpy skirts, pointing with an irrevocable slow alternation east and west. Beneath her arm, a restive captive, waggled and slipped a scarcely valuable umbrella. What was there to tell the vicar that this grotesque old figure was – so far as his village was concerned at any rate – no less than Fruitful Chance and the Unforeseen, the Hag weak men call Fate. But for us, you understand, no more than Mrs Skinner.

As she was too much encumbered for a curtsey, she pretended not to see him and his friend at all, and so passed, flip-flop, within three yards of them, onward down towards the village. The vicar watched her slow transit in silence, and ripened a remark the while . . .

The incident seemed to him of no importance whatever. Old womankind, *aere perennius*,[40] has carried bundles since the world began. What difference has it made?

'We are out of it all,' said the vicar. 'We live in an atmosphere of simple and permanent things, Birth and Toil, simple seed-time and simple harvest. The Uproar passes us by.' He was always very great upon what he called the permanent things. 'Things change,' he would say, 'but Humanity – *aere perennius*.'

Thus the vicar. He loved a classical quotation subtly misapplied. Below, Mrs Skinner, inelegant but resolute, had involved herself curiously with Wilmerding's stile.

No one knows what the vicar made of the giant puff-balls.

No doubt he was among the first to discover them. They were scattered at intervals up and down the path between the near down and the village end – a path he frequented daily in his constitutional round. Altogether, of these abnormal fungi there were, from first to last, quite thirty. The vicar seems to have stared at each severally, and to have prodded most of them with his stick once or twice. One he attempted to measure with his arms, but it burst at his Ixion embrace.

He spoke to several people about them, and said they were 'marvellous!', and he related to at least seven different persons the well-known story of the flagstone that was lifted from the cellar floor by a growth of fungi beneath. He looked up his Sowerby to see if it was *Lycoperdon coelatum* or *giganteum* – like all his kind since Gilbert White became famous, he Gilbert-Whited. He cherished a theory that *giganteum* is unfairly named.

One does not know if he observed that those white spheres lay in the very track that old woman of yesterday had followed, or if he noted that the last of the series swelled not a score of yards from the gate of the Caddleses' cottage. If he observed these things, he made no attempt to place his observation on record. His observation in matters botanical was what the inferior sort of scientific people call a 'trained observation' – you look for certain definite things and neglect everything else. And he did nothing to link this phenomenon with the remarkable expansion of the Caddleses' baby that had been going on now for some weeks, indeed ever since Caddles walked over one Sunday afternoon a month or more ago to see his mother-in-law and hear Mr Skinner (since defunct) brag about his management of hens.

The growth of the puff-balls following on the expansion of the Caddleses' baby really ought to have opened the vicar's eyes. The latter fact had already come right into his arms at the christening – almost over-poweringly . . .

The youngster bawled with deafening violence when the cold water that sealed its divine inheritance and its right to the name of 'Albert

Edward Caddles' fell upon its brow. It was already beyond maternal porterage, and Caddles, staggering indeed, but grinning triumphantly at quantitatively inferior parents, bore it back to the free-sitting occupied by his party.

'I never saw such a child!' said the vicar. This was the first public intimation that the Caddleses' baby, which had begun its earthly career a little under seven pounds, did after all intend to be a credit to its parents. Very soon it was clear it meant to be not only a credit but a glory. And within a month their glory shone so brightly as to be, in connection with people in the Caddleses' position, improper.

The butcher weighed the infant eleven times. He was a man of few words, and he soon got through with them. The first time he said, ' 'E's a good un'; the next time he said, 'My word!'; the third time he said, '*Well*, mum,' and after that he simply blew enormously each time, scratched his head, and looked at his scales with an unprecedented mistrust. Everyone came to see the Big Baby – so it was called by universal consent – and most of them said, ' 'E's a Bouncer,' and almost all remarked to him, '*Did* they?' Miss Fletcher came and said she 'never *did*', which was perfectly true.

Lady Wondershoot, the village tyrant, arrived the day after the third weighing, and inspected the phenomenon narrowly through glasses that filled it with howling terror. 'It's an unusually Big child,' she told its mother, in a loud instructive voice. 'You ought to take unusual care of it, Caddles. Of course it won't go on like this, being bottle fed, but we must do what we can for it. I'll send you down some more flannel.'

The doctor came and measured the child with a tape, and put the figures in a notebook, and old Mr Drifthassock, who farmed by Up Marden, brought a manure traveller two miles out of their way to look at it. The traveller asked the child's age three times over, and said finally that he was blowed. He left it to be inferred how and why he was blowed; apparently it was the child's size blowed him. He also said it ought to be put into a baby show. And all day long, out of school hours, little children kept coming and saying, 'Please, Mrs Caddles, mum, may we have a look at your baby, please, mum?' until Mrs Caddles had to put a stop to it. And amidst all these scenes of amazement came Mrs Skinner, and stood and smiled, standing somewhat in the background, with each sharp elbow in a lank gnarled hand, and smiling, smiling under and about her nose, with a smile of infinite profundity.

'It makes even that old wretch of a grandmother look quite pleasant,' said Lady Wondershoot. 'Though I'm sorry she's come back to the village.'

Of course, as with almost all cottagers' babies, the eleemosynary[41] element had already come in, but the child soon made it clear by colossal bawling that so far as the filling of its bottle went, it hadn't come in yet nearly enough.

The baby was entitled to a nine days' wonder, and everyone wondered happily over its amazing growth for twice that time and more. And then you know, instead of its dropping into the background and giving place to other marvels, it went on growing more than ever!

Lady Wondershoot heard Mrs Greenfield, her housekeeper, with infinite amazement.

'Caddles downstairs again? No food for the child! My dear Greenfield, it's impossible. The creature eats like a hippopotamus! I'm sure it can't be true.'

'I'm sure I hope you're not being imposed upon, my lady,' said Mrs Greenfield.

'It's so difficult to tell with these people,' said Lady Wondershoot. 'Now I do wish, my good Greenfield, that you'd just go down there yourself this afternoon and *see* – see it have its bottle. Big as it is, I cannot imagine that it needs more than six pints a day.'

'It hasn't no business to, my lady,' said Mrs Greenfield.

The hand of Lady Wondershoot quivered, with that code-of-silence sort of emotion, that suspicious rage that stirs in all true aristocrats at the thought that possibly the meaner classes are after all as mean as their betters, and – where the sting lies – scoring points in the game.

But Mrs Greenfield could observe no evidence of peculation, and the order for an increasing daily supply to the Caddleses' nursery was issued. Scarcely had the first instalment gone, when Caddles was back again at the great house in a state abjectly apologetic.

'We took the greates' care of 'em, Mrs Greenfield, I do assure you, mum, but he's regular bust 'em! They flew with such vilence, mum, that one button broke a pane of the window, mum, and one hit me a regular stinger jest 'ere, mum.'

Lady Wondershoot, when she heard that this amazing child had positively burst out of its beautiful charity clothes, decided that she must speak to Caddles herself. He appeared in her presence with his hair hastily wetted and smoothed by hand, breathless, and clinging to his hat brim as though it was a life-belt, and he stumbled at the carpet edge out of sheer distress of mind.

Lady Wondershoot liked bullying Caddles. Caddles was her ideal lower-class person, dishonest, faithful, abject, industrious and inconceivably incapable of responsibility. She told him it was a serious matter, the way his child was going on. 'It's 'is appetite, my ladyship,' said Caddles, with a rising note.

'Check 'im, my ladyship, you can't,' said Caddles. 'There 'e lies, my ladyship, and kicks out 'e does, and 'owls – it's that distressin'. We 'aven't the 'eart, my ladyship. If we 'ad – the neighbours would interfere . . . '

Lady Wondershoot consulted the parish doctor.

'What I want to know,' said Lady Wondershoot, 'is it *right* this child should have such an extraordinary quantity of milk?'

'The proper allowance for a child of that age,' said the parish doctor, 'is a pint and a half to two pints in the twenty-four hours. I don't see that you are called upon to provide more. If you do, it is your own generosity. Of course we might try the legitimate quantity for a few days. But the child, I must admit, seems for some reason to be physiologically different. Possibly what is called a Sport. A case of General Hypertrophy.'

'It isn't fair to the other parish children,' said Lady Wondershoot. 'I am certain we shall have complaints if this goes on.'

'I don't see that anyone can be expected to give more than the recognised allowance. We might insist on its doing with that, or if it wouldn't, send it as a case into the Infirmary.'

'I suppose,' said Lady Wondershoot, reflecting, 'that apart from the size and the appetite, you don't find anything else abnormal – nothing monstrous?'

'No. No, I don't. But no doubt if this growth goes on, we shall find grave moral and intellectual deficiencies. One might almost prophesy that from Max Nordau's[42] law. A most gifted and celebrated philosopher, Lady Wondershoot. He discovered that the abnormal is – abnormal, a most valuable discovery, and well worth bearing in mind. I find it of the utmost help in practice. When I come upon anything abnormal, I say at once, "This is abnormal." ' His eyes became profound, his voice dropped, his manner verged upon the intimately confidential. He raised one hand stiffly. 'And I treat it in that spirit,' he said.

5

'Tut, tut!' said the vicar to his breakfast things – the day after the coming of Mrs Skinner. 'Tut, tut! what's this?' and poised his glasses at his paper with a general air of remonstrance. 'Giant wasps! What's the world coming to? American journalists, I suppose! Hang these Novelties! Giant gooseberries are good enough for me.

'Nonsense!' said the vicar, and drank off his coffee at a gulp, eyes steadfast on the paper, and smacked his lips incredulously.

'Bosh!' said the vicar, rejecting the hint altogether.

But the next day there was more of it, and the light came.

Not all at once, however. When he went for his constitutional that day he was still chuckling at the absurd story his paper would have had him believe. Wasps indeed – killing a dog! Incidentally as he passed by the site of that first crop of puff-balls he remarked that the grass was growing very rank there, but he did not connect that in any way with the matter of his amusement. 'We should certainly have heard something of it,' he said; 'Whitstable can't be twenty miles from here.'

Beyond he found another puff-ball, one of the second crop, rising like a roc's egg out of the abnormally coarsened turf.

The thing came upon him in a flash.

He did not take his usual round that morning. Instead he turned aside by the second stile and came round to the Caddleses' cottage. 'Where's that baby?' he demanded, and at the sight of it, 'Goodness me!'

He went up the village blessing his heart, and met the doctor full tilt coming down. He grasped his arm. 'What does this *mean*?' he said. 'Have you seen the paper these last few days?'

The doctor said he had.

'Well, what's the matter with that child? What's the matter with everything – wasps, puff-balls, babies, eh? What's making them grow so big? This is most unexpected. In Kent too! If it was America now – '

'It's a little difficult to say just what it is,' said the doctor. 'So far as I can grasp the symptoms – '

'Yes?'

'It's Hypertrophy – General Hypertrophy.'

'Hypertrophy?'

'Yes. General – affecting all the bodily structures – all the organism. I may say that in my own mind, between ourselves, I'm very nearly convinced it's that . . . But one has to be careful.'

'Ah,' said the vicar, a good deal relieved to find the doctor equal to the situation. 'But how is it it's breaking out in this fashion, all over the place?'

'That again,' said the doctor, 'is difficult to say.'

'Urshot. Here. It's a pretty clear case of spreading.'

'Yes,' said the doctor. 'Yes. I think so. It has a strong resemblance at any rate to some sort of epidemic. Probably Epidemic Hypertrophy will meet the case.'

'Epidemic!' said the vicar. 'You don't mean it's contagious?'

The doctor smiled gently and rubbed one hand against the other. 'That I couldn't say,' he said.

'But – !' cried the vicar, round-eyed. 'If it's *catching* – it – it affects *us*!' He made a stride up the road and turned about.

'I've just been there,' he cried. 'Hadn't I better – ? I'll go home at once and have a bath and fumigate my clothes.'

The doctor regarded his retreating back for a moment, and then turned about and went towards his own house . . .

But on the way he reflected that one case had been in the village a month without anyone catching the disease, and after a pause of hesitation decided to be as brave as a doctor should be and take the risks like a man.

And indeed he was well advised by his second thoughts. Growth was the last thing that could ever happen to him again. He could have eaten – and the vicar could have eaten – Herakleophorbia by the truckful. For growth had done with them. Growth had done with these two gentlemen for evermore.

6

It was a day or so after this conversation – a day or so, that is, after the burning of the Experimental Farm – that Winkles came to Redwood and showed him an insulting letter. It was an anonymous letter, and an author should respect his character's secrets. 'You are only taking credit for a natural phenomenon,' said the letter, 'and trying to advertise yourself by your letter to *The Times*. You and your Boomfood! Let me tell you, this absurdly named food of yours has only the most accidental connection with those big wasps and rats. The plain fact is there is an epidemic of Hypertrophy – Contagious Hypertrophy – which you have about as much claim to control as you have to control the solar system. The thing is as old as the hills. There was Hypertrophy in the family of Anak.[43] Quite outside your range, at Cheasing Eyebright, at the present time there is a baby – '

'Shaky up-and-down writing. Old gentleman apparently,' said Redwood. 'But it's odd a baby – '

He read a few lines further, and had an inspiration.

'By Jove!' said he. 'That's my missing Mrs Skinner!'

He descended upon her suddenly in the afternoon of the following day.

She was engaged in pulling onions in the little garden before her daughter's cottage when she saw him coming through the garden gate. She stood for a moment 'consternated', as the country folks say, and then folded her arms, and with the little bunch of onions held defensively under her left elbow, awaited his approach. Her mouth opened and shut several times; she mumbled her remaining tooth, and once quite suddenly she curtsied, like the blink of an arc-light.

'I thought I should find you,' said Redwood.

'I thought you might, sir,' she said, without joy.

'Where's Skinner?'

' 'E ain't never written to me, sir, not once, nor come nigh of me since I came here, sir.'

'Don't you know what's become of him?'

'Him not having written, no, sir,' and she edged a step towards the left with an imperfect idea of cutting off Redwood from the barn door.

'No one knows what has become of him,' said Redwood.

'I dessay 'e knows,' said Mrs Skinner.

'He doesn't tell.'

'He was always a great one for looking after 'imself and leaving them that was near and dear to 'im in trouble, was Skinner. Though clever as could be,' said Mrs Skinner.

'Where's this child?' asked Redwood abruptly.

She begged his pardon.

'This child I hear about, the child you've been giving our stuff to – the child that weighs two stone.'

Mrs Skinner's hands worked, and she dropped the onions. 'Reely, sir,' she protested, 'I don't hardly know, sir, what you mean. My daughter, sir, Mrs Caddles, 'as a baby, sir.' And she made an agitated curtsey and tried to look innocently enquiring by tilting her nose to one side.

'You'd better let me see that baby, Mrs Skinner,' said Redwood.

Mrs Skinner unmasked an eye at him as she led the way towards the barn. 'Of course, sir, there may 'ave been a *little*, in a little can of Nicey I give his father to bring over from the farm, or a little perhaps what I happened to bring about with me, so to speak. Me packing in a hurry and all . . .'

'Um!' said Redwood, after he had cluckered to the infant for a space. 'Oom!'

He told Mrs Caddles the baby was a very fine child indeed, a thing that was getting well home to her intelligence – and he ignored her altogether after that. Presently she left the barn – through sheer insignificance.

'Now you've started him, you'll have to keep on with him, you know,' he said to Mrs Skinner.

He turned on her abruptly. 'Don't splash it about *this* time,' he said.

'Splash it about, sir?'

'Oh! *you* know.'

She indicated knowledge by convulsive gestures.

'You haven't told these people here? The parents, the squire and so on at the big house, the doctor, no one?'

Mrs Skinner shook her head.

'I wouldn't,' said Redwood.

He went to the door of the barn and surveyed the world about him. The door of the barn looked between the end of the cottage and some disused piggeries through a five-barred gate upon the high road. Beyond was a high, red brick-wall rich with ivy and wallflower and pennywort, and set along the top with broken glass. Beyond the corner of the wall, a sunlit noticeboard amidst green and yellow branches reared itself above the rich tones of the first fallen leaves and announced that 'Trespassers in these Woods will be Prosecuted.' The dark shadow of a gap in the hedge threw a stretch of barbed wire into relief.

'Um,' said Redwood, then in a deeper note, 'Oom!'

There came a clatter of horses and the sound of wheels, and Lady Wondershoot's greys came into view. He marked the faces of coachman and footman as the equipage approached. The coachman was a very fine specimen, full and fruity, and he drove with a sort of sacramental dignity. Others might doubt their calling and position in the world, he at any rate was sure – he drove her ladyship. The footman sat beside him with folded arms and a face of inflexible certainties. Then the great lady herself became visible, in a hat and mantle disdainfully inelegant, peering through her glasses. Two young ladies protruded necks and peered also.

The vicar passing on the other side swept off the hat from his David's brow unheeded . . .

Redwood remained standing in the doorway for a long time after the carriage had passed, his hands folded behind him. His eyes went to the green-grey upland of down, and into the cloud-curdled sky, and came back to the glass-set wall. He turned upon the cool shadows within, and amidst spots and blurs of colour regarded the giant child amidst that Rembrandtesque gloom, naked except for a swathing of flannel, seated upon a huge truss of straw and playing with its toes.

'I begin to see what we have done,' he said.

He mused, and young Caddles and his own child and Cossar's brood mingled in his musing. He laughed abruptly. 'Good Lord!' he said at some passing thought.

He roused himself presently and addressed Mrs Skinner. 'Anyhow he mustn't be tortured by a break in his food. That at least we can prevent. I shall send you a can every six months. That ought to do for him all right.'

Mrs Skinner mumbled something about 'if you think so, sir,' and 'probably got packed by mistake . . . Thought no harm in giving him a little,' and so by the aid of various aspen gestures indicated that she understood.

So the child went on growing.

And growing.

'Practically,' said Lady Wondershoot, 'he's eaten up every calf in the place. If I have any more of this sort of thing from that man Caddles – '

7

But even so secluded a place as Cheasing Eyebright could not rest for long in the theory of Hypertrophy – Contagious or not – in view of the growing hubbub about the Food. In a little while there were painful explanations for Mrs Skinner – explanations that reduced her to speechless mumblings of her remaining tooth – explanations that probed her and ransacked her and exposed her – until at last she was driven to take refuge from a universal convergence of blame in the dignity of inconsolable widowhood. She turned her eye – which she constrained to be watery – upon the angry Lady of the Manor, and wiped suds from her hands.

'You forget, my lady, what I'm bearing up under.'

And she followed up this warning note with a slightly defiant: 'It's 'IM I think of, my lady, night *and* day.'

She compressed her lips, and her voice flattened and faltered: 'Bein' et, my lady.'

And having established herself on these grounds, she repeated the affirmation her ladyship had refused before. 'I 'ad no more idea what I was giving the child, my lady, than anyone *could* 'ave . . . '

Her ladyship turned her mind in more hopeful directions, wigging Caddles of course tremendously by the way. Emissaries, full of diplomatic threatenings, entered the whirling lives of Bensington and Redwood. They presented themselves as parish councillors, stolid and clinging phonographically to prearranged statements. 'We hold you responsible, Mr Bensington, for the injury inflicted upon our parish, sir. We hold you responsible.'

A firm of solicitors, with a snake of a style – Banghurst, Brown, Flapp, Codlin, Brown, Tedder and Snoxton, they called themselves, and appeared invariably in the form of a small rufous cunning-looking gentleman with a pointed nose – said vague things about damages, and there was a polished personage, her ladyship's agent, who came in suddenly upon Redwood one day and asked, 'Well, sir, and what do you propose to do?'

To which Redwood answered that he proposed to discontinue supplying the food for the child if he or Bensington were bothered any further about the matter. 'I give it for nothing as it is,' he said, 'and the child will yell your village to ruins before it dies if you don't let it have the stuff. The child's on your hands, and you have to keep it. Lady Wondershoot can't always be Lady Bountiful and Earthly Providence of her parish without sometimes meeting a responsibility, you know.'

'The mischief's done,' Lady Wondershoot decided when they told her – with expurgations – what Redwood had said.

'The mischief's done,' echoed the vicar.

Though indeed as a matter of fact the mischief was only beginning.

CHAPTER 2

The Brat Gigantic

The giant child was ugly – the vicar would insist. 'He always had been ugly – as all excessive things must be.' The vicar's views had carried him out of sight of just judgement in this matter. The child was much subjected to snapshots even in that rustic retirement, and their net testimony is against the vicar, testifying that the young monster was at first almost pretty, with a copious curl of hair reaching to his brow and a great readiness to smile. Usually Caddles, who was slightly built, stands smiling behind the baby, perspective emphasising his relative smallness.

After the second year the good looks of the child became more subtle and more contestable. He began to grow, as his unfortunate grandfather would no doubt have put it, 'rank'. He lost colour and developed an increasing effect of being somehow, albeit colossal, yet slight. He was vastly delicate. His eyes and something about his face grew finer – grew, as people say, 'interesting'. His hair, after one cutting, began to tangle into a mat. 'It's the degenerate strain coming out in him,' said the parish doctor, marking these things, but just how far he was right in that, and just how far the youngster's lapse from ideal healthfulness was the result of living entirely in a whitewashed barn upon Lady Wondershoot's sense of charity tempered by justice, is open to question.

The photographs of him that present him from three to six show him developing into a round-eyed, flaxen-haired youngster with a truncated nose and a friendly stare. There lurks about his lips that never very remote promise of a smile that all the photographs of the early giant children display. In summer he wears loose garments of ticking tacked together with string; there is usually one of those straw baskets upon his head that workmen use for their tools, and he is barefooted. In one picture he grins broadly and holds a bitten melon in his hand.

The winter pictures are less numerous and satisfactory. He wears huge sabots – no doubt of beechwood, and (as fragments of the inscription 'John Stickells, Iping', show) sacks for socks, and his trousers and jacket are unmistakably cut from the remains of a gaily patterned carpet. Underneath that there were rude swathings of flannel; five or six yards of flannel are tied comforter-fashion about his neck. The thing on his head is probably another sack. He stares, sometimes smiling, sometimes a little ruefully, at the camera. Even when he was only five years old, one sees that half-whimsical wrinkling over his soft brown eyes that characterised his face.

He was from the first, the vicar always declared, a terrible nuisance about the village. He seems to have had a proportionate impulse to play, much curiosity and sociability, and in addition there was a certain craving within him – I grieve to say – for more to eat. In spite of what Mrs Greenfield called an '*excessively* generous' allowance of food from Lady Wondershoot, he displayed what the doctor perceived at once was the 'Criminal Appetite'. It carries out only too completely Lady Wondershoot's worst experiences of the lower classes that, in spite of an allowance of nourishment inordinately beyond what is known to be the maximum necessity even of an adult human being, the creature was found to steal. And what he stole he ate with an inelegant voracity. His great hand would come over garden walls; he would covet the very bread in the bakers' carts. Cheeses went from Marlow's store loft, and never a pig trough was safe from him. Some farmer walking over his field of swedes would find the great spoor of his feet and the evidence of his nibbling hunger – a root picked here, a root picked there, and the holes, with childish cunning, heavily erased. He ate a swede as one devours a radish. He would stand and eat apples from a tree, if no one was about, as normal children eat blackberries from a bush. In one way at any rate this shortness of provisions was good for the peace of Cheasing Eyebright – for many years he ate up every grain very nearly of the Food of the Gods that was given him.

Indisputably the child was troublesome and out of place. 'He was always about,' the vicar used to say. He could not go to school; he could not go to church by virtue of the obvious limitations of its cubical content. There was some attempt to satisfy the spirit of that 'most foolish and destructive law' – I quote the vicar – the Elementary Education Act of 1870, by getting him to sit outside the open window while instruction was going on within. But his presence there destroyed the discipline of the other children. They were always popping up and peering at him, and every time he spoke they laughed together. His voice was so odd! So they let him stay away.

Nor did they persist in pressing him to come to church, for his vast proportions were of little help to devotion. Yet there they might have had an easier task; there are good reasons for guessing there were the germs of religious feeling somewhere in that big carcass. The music perhaps drew him. He was often in the churchyard on a Sunday morning, picking his way softly among the graves after the congregation had gone in, and he would sit the whole service out beside the porch, listening as one listens outside a hive of bees.

At first he showed a certain want of tact; the people inside would hear his great feet crunch restlessly round their place of worship, or become aware of his dim face peering in through the stained glass, half curious, half envious, and at times some simple hymn would catch him unawares, and he would howl lugubriously in a gigantic attempt at unison. Where-upon little Sloppet, who was organ-blower and verger and beadle and sexton and bell-ringer on Sundays, besides being postman and chimney-sweep all the week, would go out very briskly and valiantly and send him mournfully away. Sloppet, I am glad to say, felt it – in his more thoughtful moments at any rate. It was like sending a dog home when you start out for a walk, he told me.

But the intellectual and moral training of young Caddles, though fragmentary, was explicit. From the first, vicar, mother, and all the world, combined to make it clear to him that his giant strength was not for use. It was a misfortune that he had to make the best of. He had to mind what was told him, do what was set him, be careful never to break anything nor hurt anything. Particularly he must not go treading on things or jostling against things or jumping about. He had to salute the gentlefolks respectful and be grateful for the food and clothing they spared him out of their riches. And he learnt all these things sub-missively, being by nature and habit a teachable creature and only by food and accident gigantic.

For Lady Wondershoot, in these early days, he displayed the pro-foundest awe. She found she could talk to him best when she was in short skirts and had her dog-whip, and she gesticulated with that and was always a little contemptuous and shrill. But sometimes the vicar played master – a minute, middle-aged, rather breathless David pelting a childish Goliath with reproof and reproach and dictatorial command. The monster was now so big that it seems it was impossible for anyone to remember he was after all only a child of seven, with all a child's desire for notice and amusement and fresh experience, with all a child's craving for response, attention and affection, and all a child's capacity for dependence and unrestricted dullness and misery.

The vicar, walking down the village road some sunlit morning, would encounter an ungainly eighteen feet of the Inexplicable, as fantastic and unpleasant to him as some new form of Dissent, as it padded fitfully along with craning neck, seeking, always seeking the two primary needs of childhood – something to eat and something with which to play.

There would come a look of furtive respect into the creature's eyes and an attempt to touch the matted forelock.

In a limited way the vicar had an imagination – at any rate, the remains of one – and with young Caddles it took the line of developing the huge possibilities of personal injury such vast muscles must possess. Suppose a sudden madness – ! Suppose a mere lapse into disrespect – ! However, the truly brave man is not the man who does not feel fear but the man who overcomes it. Every time and always the vicar got his imagination under. And he used always to address young Caddles stoutly in a good clear service tenor.

'Being a good boy, Albert Edward?'

And the young giant, edging closer to the wall and blushing deeply, would answer, 'Yessir – trying.'

'Mind you do,' said the vicar, and would go past him with at most a slight acceleration of his breathing. And out of respect for his manhood he made it a rule, whatever he might fancy, never to look back at the danger when once it was passed.

In a fitful manner the vicar would give young Caddles private tuition. He never taught the monster to read – it was not needed; but he taught him the more important points of the Catechism – his duty to his neighbour for example, and of that Deity who would punish Caddles with extreme vindictiveness if ever he ventured to disobey the vicar and Lady Wondershoot. The lessons would go on in the vicar's yard, and passers-by would hear that great cranky childish voice droning out the essential teachings of the Established Church.

'To onner 'n 'bey the King and allooer put 'nthority under 'im. To s'bmit meself t'all my gov'ners, teachers, spir'shall pastors an' masters. To order myself lowly 'n rev'rently t'all my betters – '

Presently it became evident that the effect of the growing giant on unaccustomed horses was like that of a camel, and he was told to keep off the high road, not only near the shrubbery (where the oafish smile over the wall had exasperated her ladyship extremely), but altogether. That law he never completely obeyed, because of the vast interest the high road had for him. But it turned what had been his constant resort into a stolen pleasure. He was limited at last almost entirely to old pasture and the downs.

I do not know what he would have done if it had not been for the downs. There there were spaces where he might wander for miles, and over these spaces he wandered. He would pick branches from trees and make insane vast nosegays there until he was forbidden, take up sheep and put them in neat rows, from which they immediately wandered (at this he invariably laughed very heartily), until he was forbidden, dig away the turf, great wanton holes, until he was forbidden ...

He would wander over the downs as far as the hill above Wreckstone, but not farther, because there he came upon cultivated land, and the people, by reason of his depredations upon their root-crops, and inspired moreover by the sort of hostile timidity his big unkempt appearance frequently evoked, always came out against him with yapping dogs to drive him away. They would threaten him and lash at him with cart whips. I have heard that they would sometimes fire at him with shotguns. And in the other direction he ranged within sight of Hickleybrow. From above Thursley Hanger he could get a glimpse of the London, Chatham and Dover railway, but ploughed fields and a suspicious hamlet prevented his nearer access.

And after a time there came boards – great boards with red letters that barred him in every direction. He could not read what the letters said – 'Out of Bounds' – but in a little while he understood. He was often to be seen in those days, by the railway passengers, sitting, chin on knees, perched up on the down hard by the Thursley chalk pits, where afterwards he was set working. The train seemed to inspire a dim emotion of friendliness in him, and sometimes he would wave an enormous hand at it, and sometimes give it a rustic incoherent hail.

'Big,' the peering passenger would say. 'One of these Boom children. They say, sir, quite unable to do anything for itself – little better than an idiot in fact, and a great burden on the locality.'

'Parents quite poor, I'm told.'

'Lives on the charity of the local gentry.'

Every one would stare intelligently at that distant squatting monstrous figure for a space.

'Good thing that was put a stop to,' some spacious thinking mind would suggest. 'Nice to 'ave a few thousand of *them* on the rates, eh?'

And usually there was someone wise enough to tell this philosopher: 'You're about Right there, sir,' in hearty tones.

2

He had his bad days.

There was, for example, that trouble with the river.

He made little boats out of whole newspapers, an art he learnt by watching the Spender boy, and he set them sailing down the stream – great paper cocked-hats. When they vanished under the bridge which marks the boundary of the strictly private grounds about Eyebright House, he would give a great shout and run round and across Tormat's new field – Lord! how Tormat's pigs did scamper, to be sure, and turn their good fat into lean muscle! – and so meet his boats by the ford. Right across the nearer lawns these paper boats of his used to go, right in front of Eyebright House, right under Lady Wondershoot's eyes! Disorganising folded newspapers! A pretty thing!

Gathering enterprise from impunity, he began babyish hydraulic engineering. He delved a huge port for his paper fleets with an old shed door that served him as a spade, and, no one chancing to observe his operations just then, he devised an ingenious canal that incidentally flooded Lady Wondershoot's ice-house, and finally he dammed the river. He dammed it right across with a few vigorous doorfuls of earth – he must have worked like an avalanche – and down came a most amazing spate through the shrubbery and washed away Miss Spinks and her easel and the most promising watercolour sketch she had ever begun, or, at any rate, it washed away her easel and left her wet to the knees and dismally tucked up in flight to the house, and thence the waters rushed through the kitchen garden, and so by the green door into the lane and down into the river-bed again by Short's ditch.

Meanwhile, the vicar, interrupted in conversation with the blacksmith, was amazed to see distressful stranded fish leaping out of a few residual pools, and heaped green weed in the bed of the stream where ten minutes before there had been eight feet and more of clear cool water.

After that, horrified at his own consequences, young Caddles fled his home for two days and nights. He returned only at the insistent call of hunger, to bear with stoical calm an amount of violent scolding that was more in proportion to his size than anything else that had ever before fallen to his lot in the Happy Village.

3

Immediately after that affair Lady Wondershoot, casting about for exemplary additions to the abuse and fastings she had inflicted, issued a ukase.[44] She issued it first to her butler, and very suddenly, so that she made him jump. He was clearing away the breakfast things, and she was staring out of the tall window on the terrace where the fawns would come to be fed. 'Jobbet,' she said, in her most imperial voice – 'Jobbet, this Thing must work for its living.'

And she made it quite clear not only to Jobbet (which was easy), but to everyone else in the village, including young Caddles, that in this matter, as in all things, she meant what she said.

'Keep him employed,' said Lady Wondershoot. 'That's the tip for Master Caddles.'

'It's the Tip, I fancy, for all Humanity,' said the vicar. 'The simple duties, the modest round, seedtime and harvest – '

'Exactly,' said Lady Wondershoot. 'What *I* always say. Satan finds some mischief still for idle hands to do. At any rate among the labouring classes. We bring up our under-housemaids on that principle, always. What shall we set him to do?'

That was a little difficult. They thought of many things, and meanwhile they broke him in to labour a bit by using him instead of a horse messenger to carry telegrams and notes when extra speed was needed, and he also carried luggage and packing-cases and things of that sort very conveniently in a big net they found for him. He seemed to like employment, regarding it as a sort of game, and Kinkle, Lady Wondershoot's agent, seeing him shift a rockery for her one day, was struck by the brilliant idea of putting him into her chalk quarry at Thursley Hanger, hard by Hickleybrow. This idea was carried out, and it seemed they had settled his problem.

He worked in the chalk pit, at first with the zest of a playing child, and afterwards with an effect of habit – delving, loading, doing all the haulage of the trucks, running the full ones down the lines towards the siding, and hauling the empty ones up by the wire of a great windlass – working the entire quarry at last single-handed.

I am told that Kinkle made a very good thing indeed out of him for Lady Wondershoot, consuming as he did scarcely anything but his food, though that never restrained her denunciation of 'the Creature' as a gigantic parasite upon her charity.

At that time he used to wear a sort of smock of sacking, trousers of patched leather and iron-shod sabots. Over his head was sometimes a queer thing – a worn-out beehive straw chair it was, but usually he went bareheaded. He would be moving about the pit with a powerful deliberation, and the vicar on his constitutional round would get there about midday to find him shamefully eating his vast need of food with his back to all the world.

His food was brought to him every day, a mess of grain in the husk, in a truck – a small railway truck, like one of the trucks he was perpetually filling with chalk, and this load he used to char in an old limekiln and then devour. Sometimes he would mix with it a bag of sugar. Sometimes he would sit licking a lump of such salt as is given to cows, or eating a huge lump of dates, stones and all, such as one sees in London on barrows. For drink he walked to the rivulet beyond the burnt-out site of the Experimental Farm at Hickleybrow and put down his face to the stream. It was from his drinking in that way after eating that the Food of the Gods did at last get loose, spreading first of all in huge weeds from the riverside, then in big frogs, bigger trout and stranding carp, and at last in a fantastic exuberance of vegetation all over the little valley.

And after a year or so the queer monstrous grub things in the field before the blacksmith's grew so big and developed into such frightful skipjacks and cockchafers – motor cockchafers the boys called them – that they drove Lady Wondershoot abroad.

4

But soon the Food was to enter upon a new phase of its work in him. In spite of the simple instructions of the vicar – instructions intended to round off the modest natural life befitting a giant peasant, in the most complete and final manner – he began to ask questions, to enquire into things, to *think*. As he grew from boyhood to adolescence it became increasingly evident that his mind had processes of its own – out of the vicar's control. The vicar did his best to ignore this distressing phenomenon, but still – he could feel it there.

The young giant's material for thought lay about him. Quite involuntarily, with his spacious views, his constant overlooking of things, he must have seen a good deal of human life, and as it grew clearer to him that he too, save for this clumsy greatness of his, was also human, he must have come to realise more and more just how much was shut against him by his melancholy distinction. The sociable hum of the school, the mystery of religion that was partaken in such finery, and which exhaled so sweet a strain of melody, the jovial chorusing from the inn, the warmly glowing rooms, candlelit and fire-lit, into which he peered out of the darkness, or again the shouting excitement, the vigour of flannelled exercise upon some imperfectly understood issue that centred about the cricket-field – all these things must have cried aloud to his companionable heart. It would seem that as his adolescence crept upon him, he began to take a very considerable interest in the proceedings of lovers, in those preferences and pairings, those close intimacies that are so cardinal in life.

One Sunday, just about that hour when the stars and the bats and the passions of rural life come out, there chanced to be a young couple 'kissing each other a bit' in Love Lane, the deep hedged lane that runs out back towards the Upper Lodge. They were giving their little emotions play, as secure in the warm still twilight as any lovers could be. The only conceivable interruption they thought possible must come pacing visibly up the lane; the twelve-foot hedge towards the silent downs seemed to them an absolute guarantee.

Then suddenly – incredibly – they were lifted and drawn apart.

They discovered themselves held up, each with a finger and thumb under the armpits, and with the perplexed brown eyes of young Caddles scanning their warm flushed faces. They were naturally dumb with the emotions of their situation.

'*Why* do you like doing that?' asked young Caddles.

I gather the embarrassment continued until the swain, remembering his manhood, vehemently, with loud shouts, threats and virile blasphemies, such as became the occasion, bade young Caddles under penalties put them down. Whereupon young Caddles, remembering his manners, did put them down politely and very carefully, and conveniently near for a resumption of their embraces, and having hesitated above them for a while, vanished again into the twilight . . .

'But I felt precious silly,' the swain confided to me. 'We couldn't 'ardly look at one another – bein' caught like that.

'Kissing we was – *you* know.

'And the cur'ous thing is, she blamed it all on to me,' said the swain. 'Flew out something outrageous, and wouldn't 'ardly speak to me all the way 'ome . . . '

The giant was embarking upon investigations, there could be no doubt. His mind, it became manifest, was throwing up questions. He put them to few people as yet, but they troubled him. His mother, one gathers, sometimes came in for cross-examination.

He used to come into the yard behind his mother's cottage, and, after a careful inspection of the ground for hens and chicks, he would sit down slowly with his back against the barn. In a minute the chicks, who liked him, would be pecking all over him at the mossy chalk-mud in the seams of his clothing, and if it was blowing up for wet, Mrs Caddles's kitten, who never lost her confidence in him, would assume a sinuous form and start scampering into the cottage, up to the kitchen fender, round, out, up his leg, up his body, right up to his shoulder, meditative moment, and then scat! back again, and so on. Sometimes she would stick her claws in his face out of sheer gaiety of heart, but he never dared to touch her because of the uncertain weight of his hand upon a creature so frail. Besides, he rather liked to be tickled.

And after a time he would put some clumsy questions to his mother. 'Mother,' he would say, 'if it's good to work, why doesn't everyone work?'

His mother would look up at him and answer, 'It's good for the likes of us.'

He would meditate, '*Why*?'

And going unanswered, 'What's work *for*, mother? Why do I cut chalk and you wash clothes, day after day, while Lady Wondershoot goes about in her carriage, mother, and travels off to those beautiful foreign countries you and I mustn't see, mother?'

'She's a lady,' said Mrs Caddles.

'Oh,' said young Caddles, and meditated profoundly.

'If there wasn't gentlefolks to make work for us to do,' said Mrs Caddles, 'how should we poor people get a living?'

This had to be digested.

'Mother,' he tried again; 'if there wasn't any gentlefolks, wouldn't things belong to people like me and you, and if they did – '

'Lord sakes and *drat* the Boy!' Mrs Caddles would say – she had with the help of a good memory become quite a florid and vigorous individuality since Mrs Skinner died. 'Since your poor dear grandma was took, there's no abiding you. Don't you arst no questions and you won't be told no lies. If once I was to start out answerin' you *serious*, y'r father'd 'ave to go and arst someone else for 'is supper – let alone finishin' the washin'.'

'All right, mother,' he would say, after a wondering stare at her. 'I didn't mean to worry.'

And he would go on thinking.

5

He was thinking too four years after, when the vicar, now no longer ripe but overripe, saw him for the last time of all. You figure the old gentleman visibly a little older now, slacker in his girth, a little coarsened and a little weakened in his thought and speech, with a quivering shakiness in his hand and a quivering shakiness in his convictions, but his eye still bright and merry for all the trouble the Food had caused his village and himself. He had been frightened at times and disturbed, but was he not alive still and the same still? and fifteen long years – a fair sample of eternity – had turned the trouble into use and wont.

'It was a disturbance, I admit,' he would say, 'and things are different – different in many ways. There was a time when a boy could weed, but now a man must go out with axe and crowbar – in some places down by the thickets at least. And it's a little strange still to us old-fashioned people for all this valley, even what used to be the river bed before they irrigated, to be under wheat – as it is this year – twenty-five feet high. They used the old-fashioned scythe here twenty years ago, and they would bring home the harvest on a wain – rejoicing – in a simple honest fashion. A little simple drunkenness, a little innocent dalliance, perhaps, to conclude . . . poor dear Lady Wondershoot – she didn't like these Innovations. Very conservative, poor dear lady! A touch of the eighteenth century about her, I always said. Her language for example . . . Bluff vigour . . .

'She died comparatively poor. These big weeds got into her garden. She was not one of these gardening women, but she liked her garden in order – things growing where they were planted and as they were planted – under control . . . The way things grew was unexpected – upset her ideas . . . She didn't like the perpetual invasion of this young monster – at last she began to fancy he was always gaping at her over her wall . . . She didn't like his being nearly as high as her house . . . Jarred with her sense of proportion. Poor dear lady! I had hoped she would last my time. It was the big cockchafers we had for a year or so that decided her. They came from the giant larvae – nasty things as big as rats – in the valley turf . . .

'And the ants no doubt weighed with her also.

'Since everything was upset and there was no peace and quietness anywhere now, she said she thought she might just as well be at Monte Carlo as anywhere else. And she went.

'She played pretty boldly, I'm told. Died in a hotel there. Very sad end . . . Exile . . . Not – not what one considers meet . . . A natural leader of our English people . . . Uprooted. So I . . .

'Yet after all,' harped the vicar, 'it comes to very little. A nuisance, of course. Children cannot run about so freely as they used to do, what with ant bites and so forth. Perhaps it's as well . . . There used to be talk – as though this stuff would revolutionise everything . . . But there is something that defies all these forces of the new . . . I don't know of course. I'm not one of your modern philosophers – explain everything with ether and atoms. Evolution. Rubbish like that. What I mean is something the 'ologies don't include. Matter of reason – not under-standing. Ripe wisdom. Human nature. *Aere perennius.* . . . Call it what you will.'

And so at last it came to the last time.

The vicar had no intimation of what lay so close upon him. He did his customary walk, over by Farthing Down, as he had done it for more than a score of years, and so to the place whence he would watch young Caddles. He did the rise over by the chalk-pit crest a little puffily – he had long since lost the muscular Christian stride of early days; but Caddles was not at his work, and then, as he skirted the thicket of giant bracken that was beginning to obscure and overshadow the hanger, he came upon the monster's huge form seated on the hill – brooding as it were upon the world. Caddles's knees were drawn up, his cheek was on his hand, his head a little aslant. He sat with his shoulder towards the vicar, so that those perplexed eyes could not be seen. He must have been thinking very intently – at any rate he was sitting very still . . .

He never turned round. He never knew that the vicar, who had played so large a part in shaping his life, looked then at him for the very last of innumerable times – did not know even that he was there. (So it is so many partings happen.) The vicar was struck at the time by the fact that, after all, no one on earth had the slightest idea of what this great monster thought about when he saw fit to rest from his labours. But he was too indolent to follow up that new theme that day; he fell back from its suggestion into his older grooves of thought.

'*Aere perennius,*' he whispered, walking slowly homeward by a path that no longer ran straight athwart the turf after its former fashion, but wound circuitously to avoid new-sprung tussocks of giant grass. 'No! nothing is changed. Dimensions are nothing. The simple round, the common way –'

And that night, quite painlessly, and all unknowing, he himself went the common way – out of this Mystery of Change he had spent his life in denying.

They buried him in the churchyard of Cheasing Eyebright, near to the largest yew, and the modest tombstone bearing his epitaph – it ended with: *Ut in principio, nunc est et semper*[45] – was almost immediately hidden from the eye of man by a spread of giant grey tasselled grass too stout for scythe or sheep, that came sweeping like a fog over the village out of the germinating moisture of the valley meadows in which the Food of the Gods had been working.

BOOK THREE

The Harvest of the Food

CHAPTER 1

The Altered World

Change played in its new fashion with the world for twenty years. To most men the new things came little by little and day by day, remarkably enough, but not so abruptly as to overwhelm. But to one man at least the full accumulation of those two decades of the Food's work was to be revealed suddenly and amazingly in one day. For our purpose it is convenient to take him for that one day and to tell something of the things he saw. This man was a convict, a prisoner for life – his crime is no concern of ours – whom the law saw fit to pardon after twenty years. One summer morning this poor wretch, who had left the world a young man of three-and-twenty, found himself thrust out again from the grey simplicity of toil and discipline that had become his life into a dazzling freedom. They had put unaccustomed clothes upon him; his hair had been growing for some weeks, and he had parted it now for some days, and there he stood, in a sort of shabby and clumsy newness of body and mind, blinking with his eyes and blinking indeed with his soul, *outside* again, trying to realise one incredible thing, that after all he was again for a little while in the world of life, and for all other incredible things, totally unprepared. He was so fortunate as to have a brother who cared enough for their distant common memories to come and meet him and clasp his hand – a brother he had left a little lad, and who was now a bearded prosperous man – whose very eyes were unfamiliar. And together he and this stranger from his kindred came down into the town of Dover, saying little to one another and feeling many things.

They sat for a space in a public-house, the one answering the questions of the other about this person and that, reviving queer old points of view, brushing aside endless new aspects and new perspectives, and then it was time to go to the station and take the London train. Their names and the personal things they had to talk of do not matter to our story, but only the changes and all the strangeness that this poor returning soul found in the once familiar world.

In Dover itself he remarked little except the goodness of beer from pewter – never before had there been such a draught of beer, and it brought tears of gratitude to his eyes. 'Beer's as good as ever,' said he, believing it infinitely better . . .

It was only as the train rattled them past Folkestone that he could look out beyond his more immediate emotions, to see what had happened to the world. He peered out of the window. 'It's sunny,' he said for the twelfth time. 'I couldn't ha' had better weather.' And then for the first time it dawned upon him that there were novel disproportions in the world. 'Lord sakes,' he cried, sitting up and looking animated for the first time, 'but them's mortal great thissels growing out there on the bank by that broom. If so be they *be* thissels? Or 'ave I been forgetting?' But they were thistles, and what he took for tall bushes of broom was the new grass, and amidst these things a company of British soldiers – redcoated as ever – was skirmishing in accordance with the directions of the drill book that had been partially revised after the Boer War. Then whack! into a tunnel, and then into Sandling Junction, which was now embedded and dark – its lamps were all alight – in a great thicket of rhododendron that had crept out of some adjacent gardens and grown enormously up the valley. There was a train of trucks on the Sandgate siding piled high with rhododendron logs, and here it was the returning citizen heard first of Boomfood.

As they sped out into a country again that seemed absolutely unchanged, the two brothers were hard at their explanations. The one was full of eager, dull questions; the other had never thought, had never troubled to see the thing as a single fact, and he was allusive and difficult to follow. 'It's this here Boomfood stuff,' he said, touching his bottom rock of knowledge. 'Don't you know? 'Aven't they told you – any of 'em? Boomfood! You know – Boomfood. What all the election's about. Scientific sort of stuff. 'Asn't no one ever told you?'

He thought prison had made his brother a fearful duffer not to know that.

They made wide shots at each other by way of question and answer. Between these scraps of talk were intervals of window-gazing. At first the man's interest in things was vague and general. His imagination had been busy with what old so-and-so would say, how so-and-so would look, how he would say to all and sundry certain things that would present his 'putting away' in a mitigated light. This Boomfood came in at first as it were a thing in an odd paragraph of the newspapers, then as a source of intellectual difficulty with his brother. But it came to him presently that Boomfood was persistently coming in upon any topic he began.

In those days the world was a patchwork of transition, so that this great new fact came to him in a series of shocks of contrast. The process of change had not been uniform; it had spread from one centre of distribution here and another centre there. The country was in patches: great areas where the Food was still to come, and areas where it was already in the soil and in the air, sporadic and contagious. It was a bold new motif creeping in among ancient and venerable airs.

The contrast was very vivid indeed along the line from Dover to London at that time. For a space they traversed just such a countryside as he had known since his childhood, the small oblongs of field, hedge-lined, of a size for pigmy horses to plough, the little roads three cart-widths wide, the elms and oaks and poplars dotting these fields about, little thickets of willow beside the streams; ricks of hay no higher than a giant's knees, dolls' cottages with diamond panes, brickfields and straggling village streets, the larger houses of the petty great, flower-grown railway banks, garden-set stations, and all the little things of the vanished nineteenth century still holding out against Immensity. Here and there would be a patch of wind-sown, wind-tattered giant thistle defying the axe; here and there a ten-foot puff-ball or the ashen stems of some burnt-out patch of monster grass; but that was all there was to hint at the coming of the Food.

For a couple of score of miles there was nothing else to foreshadow in any way the strange bigness of the wheat and of the weeds that were hidden from him not a dozen miles from his route just over the hills in the Cheasing Eyebright valley. And then presently the traces of the Food would begin. The first striking thing was the great new viaduct at Tonbridge, where the swamp of the choked Medway (due to a giant variety of *Chara*[46]) began in those days. Then again the little country, and then, as the petty multitudinous immensity of London spread out under its haze, the traces of man's fight to keep out greatness became abundant and incessant.

In that south-eastern region of London at that time, and all about where Cossar and his children lived, the Food had become mysteriously insurgent at a hundred points; the little life went on amidst daily portents that only the deliberation of their increase, the slow parallel growth of usage to their presence, had robbed of their warning. But this returning citizen peered out to see for the first time the facts of the Food strange and predominant, scarred and blackened areas, big unsightly defences and preparations, barracks and arsenals that this subtle, persistent influence had forced into the life of men.

Here, on an ampler scale, the experience of the first Experimental Farm had been repeated time and again. It had been in the inferior and accidental things of life – under foot and in waste places, irregularly and irrelevantly – that the coming of a new force and new issues had first declared itself. There were great evil-smelling yards and enclosures where some invincible jungle of weed furnished fuel for gigantic machinery (little cockneys came to stare at its clangorous oiliness and tip the men a sixpence); there were roads and tracks for big motors and vehicles – roads made of the interwoven fibres of hypertrophied hemp; there were towers containing steam sirens that could yell at once and warn the world against any new insurgence of vermin, or, what was queerer, venerable church towers conspicuously fitted with a mechanical scream. There were little red-painted refuge huts and garrison shelters, each with its 300-yard rifle range, where the riflemen practised daily with soft-nosed ammunition at targets in the shape of monstrous rats.

Six times since the day of the Skinners there had been outbreaks of giant rats – each time from the south-west London sewers, and now they were as much an accepted fact there as tigers in the delta by Calcutta.

The man's brother had bought a paper in a heedless sort of way at Sandling, and at last this chanced to catch the eye of the released man. He opened the unfamiliar sheets – they seemed to him to be smaller, more numerous and different in type from the papers of the times before – and he found himself confronted with innumerable pictures about things so strange as to be uninteresting, and with tall columns of printed matter whose headings, for the most part, were as unmeaning as though they had been written in a foreign tongue – 'Great Speech by Mr Caterham'; 'The Boomfood Laws.'

'Who's this here Caterham?' he asked, in an attempt to make conversation.

'*He*'s all right,' said his brother.

'Ah! Sort of politician, eh?'

'Goin' to turn out the Government. Jolly well time he did.'

'Ah!' He reflected. 'I suppose all the lot *I* used to know – Chamberlain, Rosebery – all that lot – *What*?'

His brother had grasped his wrist and pointed out of the window.

'That's the Cossars!' The eyes of the released prisoner followed the finger's direction and saw –

'My Gawd!' he cried, for the first time really overcome with amazement. The paper dropped into final forgottenness between his feet. Through the trees he could see very distinctly, standing in an easy attitude, the legs wide apart and the hand grasping a ball as if about to throw it, a gigantic human figure a good forty feet high. The figure glittered in the sunlight, clad in a suit of woven white metal and belted with a broad belt of steel. For a moment it focused all attention, and then the eye was wrested to another more distant giant who stood prepared to catch, and it became apparent that the whole area of that great bay in the hills just north of Sevenoaks had been scarred to gigantic ends.

A hugely banked entrenchment overhung the chalk pit, in which stood the house, a monstrous squat Egyptian shape that Cossar had built for his sons when the Giant Nursery had served its turn, and behind was a great dark shed that might have covered a cathedral, in which a spluttering incandescence came and went, and from out of which came a titanic hammering to beat upon the ear. Then the attention leapt back to the giant as the great ball of iron-bound timber soared up out of his hand.

The two men stood up and stared. The ball seemed as big as a cask.

'Caught!' cried the man from prison, as a tree blotted out the thrower.

The train looked on these things only for the fraction of a minute and then passed behind trees into the Chislehurst tunnel. 'My Gawd!' said the man from prison again, as the darkness closed about them. 'Why! that chap was as 'igh as a 'ouse.'

'That's them young Cossars,' said his brother, jerking his head allusively – 'what all this trouble's about . . . '

They emerged again to discover more siren-surmounted towers, more red huts, and then the clustering villas of the outer suburbs. The art of bill-sticking had lost nothing in the interval, and from countless tall hoardings, from house ends, from palings and a hundred such points of vantage came the polychromatic appeals of the great Boomfood election. 'Caterham', 'Boomfood' and 'Jack the Giant-Killer' again and again and again, and monstrous caricatures and distortions – a hundred varieties of misrepresentations of those great and shining figures they had passed so nearly only a few minutes before.

2

It had been the purpose of the younger brother to do a very magnificent thing, to celebrate this return to life by a dinner at some restaurant of indisputable quality, a dinner that should be followed by all that glittering succession of impressions the Music Halls of those days were so capable of giving. It was a worthy plan to wipe off the more superficial stains of the prison house by this display of free indulgence; but so far as the second item went the plan was changed. The dinner stood, but there was a desire already more powerful than the appetite for shows, already more efficient in turning the man's mind away from his grim prepossession with his past than any theatre could be, and that was an enormous curiosity and perplexity about this Boomfood and these Boom children – this new portentous giantry that seemed to dominate the world. 'I 'aven't the 'ang of 'em,' he said. 'They disturve me.'

His brother had that fineness of mind that can even set aside a con-templated hospitality. 'It's *your* evening, dear old boy,' he said. 'We'll try to get into the mass meeting at the People's Palace.'

And at last the man from prison had the luck to find himself wedged into a packed multitude and staring from afar at a little brightly lit platform under an organ and a gallery. The organist had been playing something that had set boots tramping as the people swarmed in; but that was over now.

Hardly had the man from prison settled into place and done his quarrel with an importunate stranger who elbowed, before Caterham came. He walked out of a shadow towards the middle of the platform, the most insignificant little pigmy, away there in the distance, a little black figure with a pink dab for a face – in profile one saw his quite distinctive aquiline nose – a little figure that trailed after it most inexplicably – a cheer. A cheer it was that began away there and grew and spread. A little spluttering of voices about the platform at first that suddenly leapt up into a flame of sound and swept athwart the whole mass of humanity within the building and without. How they cheered! Hooray! Hooray!

No one in all those myriads cheered like the man from prison. The tears poured down his face, and he only stopped cheering at last because the thing had choked him. You must have been in prison as long as he before you can understand, or even begin to understand, what it means to a man to let his lungs go in a crowd. (But for all that he did not even pretend to himself that he knew what all this emotion was about.) Hooray! Oh God! – Hoo-ray!

And then a sort of silence. Caterham had subsided to a conspicuous patience, and subordinate and inaudible persons were saying and doing formal and insignificant things. It was like hearing voices through the noise of leaves in spring. 'Wawawawa – ' What did it matter? People in the audience talked to one another. 'Wawawawawa – ' the thing went on. Would that grey-headed duffer never have done? Interrupting? Of course they were interrupting. 'Wa, wa, wa, wa – ' But shall we hear Caterham any better?

Meanwhile at any rate there was Caterham to stare at, and one could stand and study the distant prospect of the great man's features. He was easy to draw was this man, and already the world had him to study at leisure on lamp chimneys and children's plates, on Anti-Boomfood medals and Anti-Boomfood flags, on the selvedges of Caterham silks and cottons and in the linings of Good Old English Caterham hats. He pervades all the caricature of that time. One sees him as a sailor standing to an old-fashioned gun, a port-fire labelled 'New Boomfood Laws' in his hand, while in the sea wallows that huge, ugly, threatening monster, 'Boomfood'; or he is cap-à-pie in armour, St George's cross on shield and helm, and a cowardly titanic Caliban sitting amidst desecrations at the mouth of a horrid cave declines his gauntlet of the 'New Boomfood Regulations'; or he comes flying down as Perseus and rescues a chained and beautiful Andromeda (labelled distinctly about her belt as 'Civilis-ation') from a wallowing waste of sea monster bearing upon its various necks and claws 'Irreligion', 'Trampling Egotism', 'Mechanism', 'Monstrosity', and the like. But it was as 'Jack the Giant-Killer' that the popular imagination considered Caterham most correctly cast, and it was in the vein of a Jack the Giant-Killer poster that the man from prison enlarged that distant miniature.

The 'Wawawawa' came abruptly to an end.

He's done. He's sitting down. Yes! No! Yes! It's Caterham! 'Cater-ham!' 'Caterham!' And then came the cheers.

It takes a multitude to make such a stillness as followed that disorder of cheering. A man alone in a wilderness – it's stillness of a sort no doubt, but he hears himself breathe, he hears himself move, he hears all sorts of things. Here the voice of Caterham was the one single thing heard, a thing very bright and clear, like a little light burning in a black velvet recess. Hear indeed! One heard him as though he spoke at one's elbow.

It was stupendously effective to the man from prison, that gesticulating little figure in a halo of light, in a halo of rich and swaying sounds; behind it, partially effaced as it were, sat its supporters on the platform, and in the foreground was a wide perspective of innumerable backs and profiles, a vast multitudinous attention. That little figure seemed to have absorbed the substance from them all.

Caterham spoke of our ancient institutions. 'Earearear,' roared the crowd. 'Ear! ear!' said the man from prison. He spoke of our ancient spirit of order and justice. 'Earearear!' roared the crowd. 'Ear! Ear!' cried the man from prison, deeply moved. He spoke of the wisdom of our forefathers, of the slow growth of venerable institutions, of moral and social traditions, that fitted our English national characteristics as the skin fits the hand. 'Ear! Ear!' groaned the man from prison, with tears of excitement on his cheeks. And now all these things were to go into the melting pot. Yes, into the melting pot! Because three men in

London twenty years ago had seen fit to mix something indescribable in a bottle, all the order and sanctity of things – Cries of 'No! No!' – Well, if it was not to be so, they must exert themselves, they must say goodbye to hesitation – Here there came a gust of cheering. They must say goodbye to hesitation and half measures.

'We have heard, gentlemen,' cried Caterham, 'of nettles that become giant nettles. At first they are no more than other nettles – little plants that a firm hand may grasp and wrench away; but if you leave them – if you leave them, they grow with such a power of poisonous expansion that at last you must needs have axe and rope, you must needs have danger to life and limb, you must needs have toil and distress – men may be killed in their felling, men may be killed in their felling – '

There came a stir and interruption, and then the man from prison heard Caterham's voice again, ringing clear and strong: 'Learn about Boomfood from Boomfood itself and – ' He paused – '*Grasp your nettle before it is too late!*'

He stopped and stood wiping his lips. 'A crystal,' cried someone, 'a crystal,' and then came that same strange swift growth to thunderous tumult, until the whole world seemed cheering . . .

The man from prison came out of the hall at last, marvellously stirred, and with that in his face that marks those who have seen a vision. He knew, everyone knew; his ideas were no longer vague. He had come back to a world in crisis, to the immediate decision of a stupendous issue. He must play his part in the great conflict like a man – like a free, responsible man. The antagonism presented itself as a picture. On the one hand those easy gigantic mail-clad figures of the morning – one saw them now in a different light – on the other this little black-clad gesticulating creature under the limelight, that pigmy thing with its ordered flow of melodious persuasion, its little, marvellously penetrating voice, John Caterham – 'Jack the Giant-Killer'. They must all unite to 'grasp the nettle' before it was 'too late'.

3

The tallest and strongest and most regarded of all the children of the Food were the three sons of Cossar. The mile or so of land near Sevenoaks in which their boyhood passed became so trenched, so dug out and twisted about, so covered with sheds and huge working models and all the play of their developing powers, it was like no other place on earth. And long since it had become too little for the things they sought to do. The eldest son was a mighty schemer of wheeled engines; he had made himself a sort of giant bicycle that no road in the world had room for, no bridge could bear. There it stood, a great thing of wheels and engines, capable of two hundred and fifty miles an hour, useless save that now and then he would mount it and fling himself backwards and forwards across that cumbered work-yard. He had meant to go around the little world with it; he had made it with that intention, while he was still no more than a dreaming boy. Now its spokes were rusted deep red like wounds, wherever the enamel had been chipped away.

'You must make a road for it first, Sonnie,' Cossar had said, 'before you can do that.'

So one morning about dawn the young giant and his brothers had set to work to make a road about the world. They seem to have had an inkling of opposition impending, and they had worked with remarkable vigour. The world had discovered them soon enough, driving that road as straight as the flight of a bullet towards the English Channel, already some miles of it levelled and made and stamped hard. They had been stopped before midday by a vast crowd of excited people, owners of land, land agents, local authorities, lawyers, policemen, soldiers even.

'We're making a road,' the biggest boy had explained.

'Make a road by all means,' said the leading lawyer on the ground, 'but please respect the rights of other people. You have already infringed the private rights of twenty-seven private proprietors; let alone the special privileges and property of an urban district board, nine parish councils, a county council, two gasworks and a railway company . . . '

'Goodney!' said the elder boy Cossar.

'You will have to stop it.'

'But don't you want a nice straight road in the place of all these rotten rutty little lanes?'

'I won't say it wouldn't be advantageous, but – '

'It isn't to be done,' said the eldest Cossar boy, picking up his tools.

'Not in this way,' said the lawyer, 'certainly.'

'How is it to be done?'

The leading lawyer's answer had been complicated and vague.

Cossar had come down to see the mischief his children had done, and reproved them severely and laughed enormously and seemed to be extremely happy over the affair. 'You boys must wait a bit,' he shouted up to them, 'before you can do things like that.'

'The lawyer told us we must begin by preparing a scheme, and getting special powers and all sorts of rot. Said it would take us years.'

'*We'll* have a scheme before long, little boy,' cried Cossar, hands to his mouth as he shouted, 'never fear. For a bit you'd better play about and make models of the things you want to do.'

They did as he told them like obedient sons.

But for all that the Cossar lads brooded a little.

'It's all very well,' said the second to the first, 'but I don't always want just to play about and plan, I want to do something *real*, you know. We didn't come into this world so strong as we are, just to play about in this messy little bit of ground, you know, and take little walks and keep out of the towns' – for by that time they were forbidden all boroughs and urban districts. 'Doing nothing's just wicked. Can't we find out something the little people *want* done and do it for them – just for the fun of doing it?

'Lots of them haven't houses fit to live in,' said the second boy, 'Let's go and build 'em a house close up to London that will hold heaps and heaps of them and be ever so comfortable and nice, and let's make 'em a nice little road to where they all go and do business – nice straight little road, and make it all as nice as nice. We'll make it all so clean and pretty that they won't any of them be able to live grubby and beastly like most of them do now. Water enough for them to wash with, we'll have – you know they're so dirty now that nine out of ten of their houses haven't even baths in them, the filthy little skunks! You know, the ones that have baths spit insults at the ones that haven't, instead of helping them to get them – and call 'em the Great Unwashed. *You* know. We'll alter all that. And we'll make electricity light and cook and clean up for them, and all. Fancy! They make their women – women who are going to be mothers – crawl about and scrub floors!

'We could make it all beautifully. We could bank up a valley in that range of hills over there and make a nice reservoir, and we could make a big place here to generate our electricity and have it all simply lovely. Couldn't we, brother? And then perhaps they'd let us do some other things.'

'Yes,' said the eldest brother, 'we could do it *very* nice for them.'

'Then *let's*,' said the second brother.

'*I* don't mind,' said the eldest brother, and looked about for a handy tool.

And that led to another dreadful bother.

Agitated multitudes were at them in no time, telling them for a thousand reasons to stop, telling them to stop for no reason at all – babbling, confused and varied multitudes. The place they were building was too high – it couldn't possibly be safe. It was ugly; it interfered with the letting of proper-sized houses in the neighbourhood; it ruined the tone of the neighbourhood; it was unneighbourly; it was contrary to the local Building Regulations; it infringed the right of the local authority to muddle about with a minute expensive electric supply of its own; it interfered with the concerns of the local water company.

Local Government Board clerks roused themselves to judicial obstruction. The little lawyer turned up again to represent about a dozen threatened interests; local landowners appeared in opposition; people with mysterious claims demanded to be bought off at exorbitant rates; the Trades Unions of all the building trades lifted up collective voices; and a ring of dealers in all sorts of building materials became a bar. Extraordinary associations of people with prophetic visions of aesthetic horrors rallied to protect the scenery of the place where they would build the great house, of the valley where they would bank up the water. These last people were absolutely the worst asses of the lot, the Cossar boys considered. That beautiful house of the Cossar boys was just like a walking-stick thrust into a wasps' nest, in no time.

'I never did!' said the eldest boy.

'We can't go on,' said the second brother.

'Rotten little beasts they are,' said the third of the brothers; 'we can't do *anything!*'

'Even when it's for their own comfort. Such a *nice* place we'd have made for them too.'

'They seem to spend their silly little lives getting in each other's way,' said the eldest boy. 'Rights and laws and regulations and rascalities; it's like a game of spellicans . . . Well, anyhow, they'll have to live in their grubby, dirty, silly little houses for a bit longer. It's very evident *we* can't go on with this.'

And the Cossar children left that great house unfinished, a mere hole for foundations and the beginnings of a wall, and sulked back to their big enclosure. After a time the hole was filled with water and with stagnation, and weeds and vermin, and the Food, either dropped there by the sons of Cossar or blowing thither as dust, set growth going in its usual fashion. Water voles came out over the country and did infinite havoc, and one day a farmer caught his pigs drinking there, and instantly and with great presence of mind – for he knew of the great hog of Oakham – slew them all. And from that deep pool it was the mosquitoes came, quite terrible mosquitoes, whose only virtue was that the sons of Cossar, after being bitten for a little, could stand the thing no longer, but chose a moonlight night when law and order were abed and drained the water clean away into the river by Brook.

But they left the big weeds and the big water voles and all sorts of big undesirable things still living and breeding on the site they had chosen – the site on which the fair great house of the little people might have towered to heaven . . .

4

That had been in the boyhood of the sons, but now they were nearly men. And the chains had been tightening upon them and tightening with every year of growth. Each year they grew, and the Food spread and great things multiplied, each year the stress and tension rose. The Food had been at first for the great mass of mankind a distant marvel, and now It was coming home to every threshold, and threatening, pressing against and distorting the whole order of life. It blocked this, it overturned that; it changed natural products, and by changing natural products it stopped employments and threw men out of work by the hundred thousands; it swept over boundaries and turned the world of trade into a world of cataclysms; no wonder mankind hated it.

And since it is easier to hate animate than inanimate things, animals more than plants, and one's fellow men more completely than any animals, the fear and trouble engendered by giant nettles and six-foot grass blades, awful insects and tiger-like vermin, grew all into one great power of detestation that aimed itself with a simple directness at that scattered band of great human beings, the Children of the Food. That hatred had become the central force in political affairs. The old party lines had been traversed and effaced altogether under the insistence of these newer issues, and the conflict lay now with the party of the temporisers, who were for putting little political men to control and regulate the Food, and the party of reaction for whom Caterham spoke, speaking always with a more sinister ambiguity, crystallising his intention first in one threatening phrase and then another, now that men must 'prune the bramble growths', now that they must find a 'cure for elephantiasis', and at last upon the eve of the election that they must 'grasp the nettle'.

One day the three sons of Cossar, who were now no longer boys but men, sat among the masses of their futile work and talked together after their fashion of all these things. They had been working all day at one of a series of great and complicated trenches their father had bid them make, and now it was sunset, and they sat in the little garden space before the great house and looked at the world and rested, until the little servants within should say their food was ready.

You must figure these mighty forms, forty feet high the least of them was, reclining on a patch of turf that would have seemed a stubble of reeds to a common man. One sat up and chipped earth from his huge boots with an iron girder he grasped in his hand; the second rested on his elbow; the third whittled a pine tree into shape and made a smell of resin in the air. They were clothed not in cloth but in undergarments of woven rope and outer clothes of felted aluminium wire; they were shod with timber and iron, and the links and buttons and belts of their clothing were all of plated steel. The great single-storeyed house they lived in, Egyptian in its massiveness, half built of monstrous blocks of chalk and half excavated from the living rock of the hill, had a front a full hundred feet in height, and beyond, the chimneys and wheels, the cranes and covers of their work sheds rose marvellously against the sky. Through a circular window in the house there was visible a spout from which some white-hot metal dripped and dripped in measured drops into a receptacle out of sight. The place was enclosed and rudely fortified by monstrous banks of earth, backed with steel both over the crests of the downs above and across the dip of the valley. It needed something of common size to mark the nature of the scale. The train that came rattling from Sevenoaks athwart their vision, and presently plunged into the tunnel out of their sight, looked by contrast with them like some small-sized automatic toy.

'They have made all the woods this side of Ightham out of bounds,' said one, 'and moved the board that was out by Knockholt two miles and more this way.'

'It is the least they could do,' said the youngest, after a pause. 'They are trying to take the wind out of Caterham's sails.'

'It's not enough for that, and – it is almost too much for us,' said the third.

'They are cutting us off from Brother Redwood. Last time I went to him the red notices had crept a mile in, either way. The road to him along the downs is no more than a narrow lane.'

The speaker thought. 'What has come to our brother Redwood?'

'Why?' said the eldest brother.

The speaker hacked a bough from his pine. 'He was like – as though he wasn't awake. He didn't seem to listen to what I had to say. And he said something of – love.'

The youngest tapped his girder on the edge of his iron sole and laughed. 'Brother Redwood,' he said, 'has dreams.'

Neither spoke for a space. Then the eldest brother said, 'This cooping up and cooping up grows more than I can bear. At last, I believe, they will draw a line round our boots and tell us to live on that.'

The middle brother swept aside a heap of pine boughs with one hand and shifted his attitude. 'What they do now is nothing to what they will do when Caterham has power.'

'If he gets power,' said the youngest brother, smiting the ground with his girder.

'As he will,' said the eldest, staring at his feet.

The middle brother ceased his lopping, and his eye went to the great banks that sheltered them about. 'Then, brothers,' he said, 'our youth will be over, and, as Father Redwood said to us long ago, we must quit ourselves like men.'

'Yes,' said the eldest brother; 'but what exactly does that mean? Just what does it mean – when that day of trouble comes?'

He too glanced at those rude vast suggestions of entrenchment about them, looking not so much at them as through them and over the hills to the innumerable multitudes beyond. Something of the same sort came into all their minds – a vision of little people coming out to war, in a flood, the little people, inexhaustible, incessant, malignant . . .

'They are little,' said the youngest brother; 'but they have numbers beyond counting, like the sands of the sea.'

'They have arms – they have weapons even, that our brothers in Sunderland have made.'

'Besides, brothers, except for vermin, except for little accidents with evil things, what have we seen of killing?'

'I know,' said the eldest brother. 'For all that – we are what we are. When the day of trouble comes we must do the thing we have to do.'

He closed his knife with a snap – the blade was the length of a man – and used his new pine staff to help himself rise. He stood up and turned towards the squat grey immensity of the house. The crimson of the sunset caught him as he rose, caught the mail and clasps about his neck and the woven metal of his arms, and to the eyes of his brothers it seemed as though he was suddenly suffused with blood.

As the young giant rose a little black figure became visible to him against that western incandescence on the top of the embankment that towered above the summit of the down. The black limbs waved in ungainly gestures. Something in the fling of the limbs suggested haste to the young giant's mind. He waved his pine mast in reply, filled the whole valley with his vast Hello! threw a 'Something's up!' to his brothers, and set off in twenty-foot strides to meet and help his father.

It chanced too that a young man who was not a giant was delivering his soul about these sons of Cossar just at that same time. He had come over the hills beyond Sevenoaks, he and his friend, and he it was did the talking. In the hedge as they came along they had heard a pitiful squealing, and had intervened to rescue three nestling tits from the attack of a couple of giant ants. That adventure it was had set him talking.

'Reactionary!' he was saying, as they came within sight of the Cossar encampment. 'Who wouldn't be reactionary? Look at that square of ground, that space of God's earth that was once sweet and fair, torn, desecrated, disembowelled! Those sheds! That great wind-wheel! That monstrous wheeled machine! Those dykes! Look at those three monsters squatting there, plotting some ugly devilment or other! Look – look at all the land!'

His friend glanced at his face. 'You have been listening to Caterham,' he said.

'Using my eyes. Looking a little into the peace and order of the past we leave behind. This foul Food is the last shape of the Devil, still set as ever upon the ruin of our world. Think what the world must have been before our days, what it was still when our mothers bore us, and see it now! Think how these slopes once smiled under the golden harvest, how the hedges, full of sweet little flowers, parted the modest portion of this man from that, how the ruddy farmhouses dotted the land, and the voice of the church bells from yonder tower stilled the whole world each Sabbath into Sabbath prayer. And now, every year, still more and more of monstrous weeds, of monstrous vermin, and these giants growing all about us, straddling over us, blundering against all that is subtle and sacred in our world. Why here – Look!'

He pointed, and his friend's eyes followed the line of his white finger.

'One of their footmarks. See! It has smashed itself three feet deep and more, a pitfall for horse and rider, a trap to the unwary. There is a briar rose smashed to death; there is grass uprooted and a teazle crushed aside, a farmer's drainpipe snapped and the edge of the pathway broken down. Destruction! So they are doing all over the world, all over the order and decency the world of men has made. Trampling on all things. Reaction! What else?'

'But – reaction. What do you hope to do?'

'Stop it!' cried the young man from Oxford. 'Before it is too late.'

'But – '

'It's *not* impossible,' cried the young man from Oxford, with a jump in his voice. 'We want the firm hand; we want the subtle plan, the resolute mind. We have been mealy-mouthed and weak-handed; we have trifled and temporised and the Food has grown and grown. Yet even now – '

He stopped for a moment. 'This is the echo of Caterham,' said his friend.

'Even now. Even now there is hope – abundant hope, if only we make sure of what we want and what we mean to destroy. The mass of people are with us, much more with us than they were a few years ago; the law is with us, the constitution and order of society, the spirit of the established religions, the customs and habits of mankind are with us – and against the Food. Why should we temporise? Why should we lie? We hate it, we don't want it; why then should we have it? Do you mean to just grizzle and obstruct passively and do nothing – till the sands are out?'

He stopped short and turned about. 'Look at that grove of nettles there. In the midst of them are homes – deserted – where once clean families of simple men played out their honest lives!

'And there!' he swung round to where the young Cossars muttered to one another of their wrongs.

'Look at them! And I know their father, a brute, a sort of brute beast with an intolerant loud voice, a creature who has ran amuck in our all-too-merciful world for the last thirty years and more. An engineer! To him all that we hold dear and sacred is nothing. Nothing! The splendid traditions of our race and land, the noble institutions, the venerable order, the broad slow march from precedent to precedent that has made our English people great and this sunny island free – it is all an idle tale, told and done with. Some claptrap about the Future is worth all these sacred things . . . The sort of man who would run a tramway over his mother's grave if he thought that was the cheapest line the tramway could take . . . And you think to temporise, to make some scheme of compromise, that will enable you to live in your way while that – that machinery – lives in its. I tell you it is hopeless – hopeless. As well make treaties with a tiger! They want things monstrous – we want them sane and sweet. It is one thing or the other.'

'But what can you do?'

'Much! All! Stop the Food! They are still scattered, these giants; still immature and disunited. Chain them, gag them, muzzle them. At any cost stop them. It is their world or ours! Stop the Food. Shut up these men who make it. Do anything to stop Cossar! You don't seem to remember – one generation – only one generation needs holding down, and then – Then we could level those mounds there, fill up their footsteps, take the ugly sirens from our church towers, smash all our elephant guns, and turn our faces again to the old order, the ripe old civilisation for which the soul of man is fitted.'

'It's a mighty effort.'

'For a mighty end. And if we don't? Don't you see the prospect before us clear as day? Everywhere the giants will increase and multiply; everywhere they will make and scatter the Food. The grass will grow gigantic in our fields, the weeds in our hedges, the vermin in the thickets, the rats in the drains. More and more and more. This is only a beginning. The insect world will rise on us, the plant world, the very fishes in the sea, will swamp and drown our ships. Tremendous growths will obscure and hide our houses, smother our churches, smash and destroy all the order of our cities, and we shall become no more than a feeble vermin under the heels of the new race. Mankind will be swamped and drowned in things of its own begetting! And all for nothing! Size! Mere size! Enlargement and *da capo*.[47] Already we go picking our way among the first beginnings of the coming time. And all we do is to say, "How inconvenient!" To grumble and do nothing. *No!*'

He raised his hand.

'Let them do the thing they have to do! So also will I. I am for Reaction – unstinted and fearless Reaction. Unless you mean to take this Food also, what else is there to do in all the world? We have trifled in the middle ways too long. You! Trifling in the middle ways is your habit, your circle of existence, your space and time. So, not I! I am against the Food, with all my strength and purpose against the Food.'

He turned on his companion's grunt of dissent. 'Where are you?'

'It's a complicated business – '

'Oh! – Driftwood!' said the young man from Oxford, very bitterly, with a fling of all his limbs. 'The middle way is nothingness. It is one thing or the other. Eat or destroy. Eat or destroy! What else is there to do?'

CHAPTER 2

The Giant Lovers

Now it chanced in the days when Caterham was campaigning against the Boom-children before the General Election that was – amidst the most tragic and terrible circumstances – to bring him into power, that the giant princess, that Serene Highness whose early nutrition had played so great a part in the brilliant career of Dr Winkles, had come from the kingdom of her father to England, on an occasion that was deemed important. She was affianced for reasons of state to a certain prince – and the wedding was to be made an event of international significance. There had arisen mysterious delays. Rumour and Imagination collaborated in the story and many things were said. There were suggestions of a recalcitrant prince who declared he would not be made to look like a fool – at least to this extent. People sympathised with him. That is the most significant aspect of the affair.

Now it may seem a strange thing, but it is a fact that the giant princess, when she came to England, knew of no other giants whatever. She had lived in a world where tact is almost a passion and reservations the air of one's life. They had kept the thing from her; they had hedged her about from sight or suspicion of any gigantic form, until her appointed coming to England was due. Until she met young Redwood she had no inkling that there was such a thing as another giant in the world.

In the kingdom of the father of the princess there were wild wastes of upland and mountains where she had been accustomed to roam freely. She loved the sunrise and the sunset and all the great drama of the open heavens more than anything else in the world, but among a people at once so democratic and so vehemently loyal as the English her freedom was much restricted. People came in brakes, in excursion trains, in organised multitudes to see her; they would cycle long distances to stare at her, and it was necessary to rise betimes if she would walk in peace. It was still near the dawn that morning when young Redwood came upon her.

The great park near the palace where she lodged stretched, for a score of miles and more, west and south of the western palace gates. The chestnut trees of its avenues reached high above her head. Each one as she passed it seemed to proffer a more abundant wealth of blossom. For a time she was content with sight and scent, but at last she was won over by these offers, and set herself so busily to choose and pick that she did not perceive young Redwood until he was close upon her.

She moved among the chestnut trees, with the destined lover drawing near to her, unanticipated, unsuspected. She thrust her hands in among the branches, breaking them and gathering them. She was alone in the world. Then –

She looked up, and in that moment she was mated.

We must needs put our imaginations to his stature to see the beauty he saw. That unapproachable greatness that prevents our immediate sympathy with her did not exist for him. There she stood, a gracious girl, the first created being that had ever seemed a mate for him, light and slender, lightly clad, the fresh breeze of the dawn moulding the subtly folding robe upon her against the soft strong lines of her form, and with a great mass of blossoming chestnut branches in her hands. The collar of her robe opened to show the whiteness of her neck and a soft shadowed roundness that passed out of sight towards her shoulders. The breeze had stolen a strand or so of her hair too, and strained its red-tipped brown across her cheek. Her eyes were open blue, and her lips rested always in the promise of a smile as she reached among the branches.

She turned upon him with a start, saw him, and for a space they regarded one another. For her, the sight of him was so amazing, so incredible, as to be, for some moments at least, terrible. He came to her with the shock of a supernatural apparition; he broke all the established law of her world. He was a youth of one-and-twenty then, slenderly built, with his father's darkness and his father's gravity. He was clad in close-fitting easy garments of a sober soft brown leather and in brown hose that shaped him bravely. His head went uncovered in all weathers. They stood regarding one another – she incredulously amazed, and he with his heart beating fast. It was a moment without a prelude, the cardinal meeting of their lives.

For him there was less surprise. He had been seeking her, and yet his heart beat fast. He came towards her, slowly, with his eyes upon her face.

'You are the princess,' he said. 'My father has told me. You are the princess who was given the Food of the Gods.'

'I am the princess – yes,' she said, with eyes of wonder. 'But – what are you?'

'I am the son of the man who made the Food of the Gods.'

'The Food of the Gods!'

'Yes, the Food of the Gods.'

'But – '

Her face expressed infinite perplexity.

'What? I don't understand. The Food of the Gods?'

'You have not heard?'

'The Food of the Gods! *No!*'

She found herself trembling violently. The colour left her face. 'I did not know,' she said. 'Do you mean – ?'

He waited for her.

'Do you mean there are other – giants?'

He repeated, 'Did you not know?'

And she answered, with the growing amazement of realisation, '*No!*'

The whole world and all the meaning of the world was changing for her. A branch of chestnut slipped from her hand. 'Do you mean to say,' she repeated stupidly, 'that there are other giants in the world? That some food – ?'

He caught her amazement.

'You know nothing?' he cried. 'You have never heard of us? You, whom the Food has made akin to us!'

There was terror still in the eyes that stared at him. Her hand rose towards her throat and fell again. She whispered, '*No.*'

It seemed to her that she must weep or faint. Then in a moment she had rule over herself and she was speaking and thinking clearly. 'All this has been kept from me,' she said. 'It is like a dream. I have dreamt – have dreamt such things. But waking – No. Tell me! Tell me! What are you? What is this Food of the Gods? Tell me slowly – and clearly. Why have they kept it from me, that I am not alone?'

2

'Tell me,' she said, and young Redwood, tremulous and excited, set himself to tell her – it was poor and broken telling for a time – of the Food of the Gods and the giant children who were scattered over the world.

You must figure them both, flushed and startled in their bearing; getting at one another's meaning through endless half-heard, half-spoken phrases, repeating, making perplexing breaks and new departures – a wonderful talk, in which she awakened from the ignorance of all her life. And very slowly it became clear to her that she was no exception to the order of mankind, but one of a scattered brotherhood, who had all eaten the Food and grown for ever out of the little limits of the folk beneath their feet. Young Redwood spoke of his father, of Cossar, of the Brothers scattered throughout the country, of the great dawn of wider meaning that had come at last into the history of the world. 'We are in the beginning of a beginning,' he said; 'this world of theirs is only the prelude to the world the Food will make.

'My father believes – and I also believe – that a time will come when littleness will have passed altogether out of the world of man – when giants shall go freely about this earth – their earth – doing continually greater and more splendid things. But that – that is to come. We are not even the first generation of that – we are the first experiments.'

'And of these things,' she said, 'I knew nothing!'

'There are times when it seems to me almost as if we had come too soon. Someone, I suppose, had to come first. But the world was all unprepared for our coming and for the coming of all the lesser great things that drew their greatness from the Food. There have been blunders; there have been conflicts. The little people hate our kind . . .

'They are hard towards us because they are so little . . . And because our feet are heavy on the things that make their lives. But at any rate they hate us now; they will have none of us – only if we could shrink back to the common size of them would they begin to forgive . . .

'They are happy in houses that are prison cells to us; their cities are too small for us; we go in misery along their narrow ways; we cannot worship in their churches . . .

'We see over their walls and over their protections; we look in-advertently into their upper windows; we look over their customs; their laws are no more than a net about our feet . . .

'Every time we stumble we hear them shouting; every time we blunder against their limits or stretch out to any spacious act . . .

'Our easy paces are wild flights to them, and all they deem great and wonderful no more than dolls' pyramids to us. Their pettiness of method and appliance and imagination hampers and defeats our powers. There are no machines to the power of our hands, no helps to fit our needs. They hold our greatness in servitude by a thousand invisible bands. We are stronger, man for man, a hundred times, but we are disarmed; our very greatness makes us debtors; they claim the land we stand upon; they tax our ampler need of food and shelter, and for all these things we must toil with the tools these dwarfs can make us – and to satisfy their dwarfish fancies . . .

'They pen us in, in every way. Even to live one must cross their boundaries. Even to meet you here today I have passed a limit. All that is reasonable and desirable in life they make out of bounds for us. We may not go into the towns; we may not cross the bridges; we may not step on their ploughed fields or into the harbours of the game they kill. I am cut off now from all our Brethren except the three sons of Cossar, and even that way the passage narrows day by day. One could think they sought occasion against us to do some more evil thing . . . '

'But we are strong,' she said.

'We should be strong – yes. We feel, all of us – you too I know must feel – that we have power, power to do great things, power insurgent in us. But before we can do anything – '

He flung out a hand that seemed to sweep away a world.

'Though I thought I was alone in the world,' she said, after a pause, 'I have thought of these things. They have taught me always that strength was almost a sin, that it was better to be little than great, that all true religion was to shelter the weak and little, encourage the weak and little, help them to multiply and multiply until at last they crawled over one another, to sacrifice all our strength in their cause. But . . . always I have doubted the thing they taught.'

'This life,' he said, 'these bodies of ours, are not for dying.'

'No.'

'Nor to live in futility. But if we would not do that, it is already plain to all our Brethren a conflict must come. I know not what bitterness of conflict must presently come, before the little folks will suffer us to live as we need to live. All the Brethren have thought of that. Cossar, of whom I told you: he too has thought of that.'

'They are very little and weak.'

'In their way. But you know all the means of death are in their hands, and made for their hands. For hundreds of thousands of years these little people, whose world we invade, have been learning how to kill one another. They are very able at that. They are able in many ways. And besides, they can deceive and change suddenly . . . I do not know . . . There comes a conflict. You – you perhaps are different from us. For us, assuredly, the conflict comes . . . The thing they call War. We know it. In a way we prepare for it. But you know – those little people! – we do not know how to kill, at least we do not want to kill – '

'Look,' she interrupted, and he heard a yelping horn.

He turned at the direction of her eyes, and found a bright yellow motor car, with dark goggled driver and fur-clad passengers, whooping, throbbing and buzzing resentfully at his heel. He moved his foot, and the mechanism, with three angry snorts, resumed its fussy way towards the town. 'Filling up the roadway!' floated up to him.

Then someone said, 'Look! Did you see? There is the monster princess over beyond the trees!' and all their goggled faces came round to stare.

'I say,' said another. '*That* won't do . . . '

'All this,' she said, 'is more amazing than I can tell.'

'That they should not have told you – ' he said, and left his sentence incomplete.

'Until you came upon me, I had lived in a world where I was great – alone. I had made myself a life – for that. I had thought I was the victim of some strange freak of nature. And now my world has crumbled down, in half an hour, and I see another world, other conditions, wider possibilities – fellowship – '

'Fellowship,' he answered.

'I want you to tell me more yet, and much more,' she said. 'You know this passes through my mind like a tale that is told. You even . . . In a day perhaps, or after several days, I shall believe in you. Now – Now I am dreaming . . . Listen!'

The first stroke of a clock above the palace offices far away had penetrated to them. Each counted mechanically, 'Seven.'

'This,' she said, 'should be the hour of my return. They will be taking the bowl of my coffee into the hall where I sleep. The little officials and servants – you cannot dream how grave they are – will be stirring about their little duties.'

'They will wonder . . . But I want to talk to you.'

She thought. 'But I want to think too. I want now to think alone, and think out this change in things, think away the old solitude, and think you and those others into my world . . . I shall go. I shall go back today to my place in the castle, and tomorrow, as the dawn comes, I shall come again – here.'

'I shall be here waiting for you.'

'All day I shall dream and dream of this new world you have given me. Even now, I can scarcely believe – '

She took a step back and surveyed him from the feet to the face. Their eyes met and locked for a moment.

'Yes,' she said, with a little laugh that was half a sob. 'You are real. But it is very wonderful! Do you think – indeed – ? Suppose tomorrow I come and find you – a pigmy like the others . . . Yes, I must think. And so for today – as the little people do – '

She held out her hand, and for the first time they touched one another. Their hands clasped firmly and their eyes met again.

'Goodbye,' she said, 'for today. Goodbye! Goodbye, Brother Giant!'

He hesitated with some unspoken thing, and at last he answered her simply, 'Goodbye.'

For a space they held each other's hands, studying each the other's face. And many times after they had parted, she looked back half doubtfully at him, standing still in the place where they had met.

She walked into her apartments across the great yard of the palace like one who walks in a dream, with a vast branch of chestnut trailing from her hand.

3

These two met altogether fourteen times before the beginning of the end. They met in the great park or on the heights and among the gorges of the rusty-roaded, heathery moorland, set with dusky pine-woods, that stretched to the south-west. Twice they met in the great avenue of chestnuts, and five times near the broad ornamental water the king, her great-grandfather, had made. There was a place where a great trim lawn, set with tall conifers, sloped graciously to the water's edge, and there she would sit, and he would lie at her knees and look up in her face and talk, telling of all the things that had been, and of the work his father had set before him, and of the great and spacious dream of what the giant people should one day be. Commonly they met in the early dawn, but once they met there in the afternoon, and found presently a multitude of peering eavesdroppers about them, cyclists, pedestrians, peeping from the bushes, rustling (as sparrows will rustle about one in the London parks) amidst the dead leaves in the woods behind, gliding down the lake in boats towards a point of view, trying to get nearer to them and hear.

It was the first hint that offered of the enormous interest the country-side was taking in their meetings. And once – it was the seventh time, and it precipitated the scandal – they met out upon the breezy moorland under a clear moonlight, and talked in whispers there, for the night was warm and still.

Very soon they had passed from the realisation that in them and through them a new world of giantry shaped itself in the earth, from the contemplation of the great struggle between big and little, in which they were clearly destined to participate, to interests at once more personal and more spacious. Each time they met and talked and looked on one another, it crept a little more out of their subconscious being towards recognition, that something more dear and wonderful than friendship was between them, and walked between them and drew their hands together. And in a little while they came to the word itself and found themselves lovers, the Adam and Eve of a new race in the world.

They set foot side by side into the wonderful valley of love, with its deep and quiet places. The world changed about them with their changing mood, until presently it had become, as it were, a tabernacular beauty about their meetings, and the stars were no more than flowers of light beneath the feet of their love, and the dawn and sunset the coloured hangings by the way. They ceased to be beings of flesh and blood to one another and themselves; they passed into a bodily texture of tenderness and desire. They gave it first whispers and then silence, and drew close and looked into one another's moonlit and shadowy faces under the infinite arch of the sky. And the still black pine trees stood about them like sentinels.

The beating steps of time were hushed into silence, and it seemed to them the universe hung still. Only their hearts were audible, beating. They seemed to be living together in a world where there is no death, and indeed so it was with them then. It seemed to them that they sounded, and indeed they sounded, such hidden splendours in the very heart of things as none have ever reached before. Even for mean and little souls, love is the revelation of splendours. And these were giant lovers who had eaten the Food of the Gods . . .

*   *   *

You may imagine the spreading consternation in this ordered world when it became known that the princess who was affianced to the prince, the princess, Her Serene Highness! with royal blood in her veins! met – frequently met – the hypertrophied offspring of a common professor of chemistry, a creature of no rank, no position, no wealth, and talked to him as though there were no kings and princes, no order, no reverence – nothing but giants and pigmies in the world, talked to him and, it was only too certain, held him as her lover.

'If those newspaper fellows get hold of it!' gasped Sir Arthur Poodle Bootlick . . .

'I am told – ' whispered the old Bishop of Frumps.

'New story upstairs,' said the first footman, as he nibbled among the dessert things. 'So far as I can make out this here giant princess – '

'They say – ' said the lady who kept the stationer's shop by the main entrance to the palace, where the little Americans get their tickets for the State Apartments . . .

And then: 'We are authorised to deny – ' said 'Picaroon' in *Gossip*.

And so the whole trouble came out.

'They say that we must part,' the princess said to her lover.

'But why?' he cried. 'What new folly have these people got into their heads?'

'Do you know,' she asked, 'that to love me – is high treason?'

'My dear,' he cried; 'but does it matter? What is their right – right without a shadow of reason – and their treason and their loyalty to us?'

'You shall hear,' she said, and told him of the things that had been told to her.

'It was the queerest little man who came to me with a soft, beautifully modulated voice, a softly moving little gentleman who sidled into the room like a cat and put his pretty white hand up so, whenever he had anything significant to say. He is bald, but not of course nakedly bald, and his nose and face are chubby rosy little things, and his beard is trimmed to a point in quite the loveliest way. He pretended to have emotions several times and made his eyes shine. You know he is quite a friend of the real royal family here, and he called me his dear young lady and was perfectly sympathetic even from the beginning. "My dear young lady," he said, "you know – *you mustn't*," several times, and then, "You owe a duty." '

'Where do they make such men?'

'He likes it,' she said.

'But I don't see – '

'He told me serious things.'

'You don't think,' he said, turning on her abruptly, 'that there's anything in the sort of thing he said?'

'There's something in it quite certainly,' said she.

'You mean – ?'

'I mean that without knowing it we have been trampling on the most sacred conceptions of the little folks. We who are royal are a class apart. We are worshipped prisoners, processional toys. We pay for worship by losing – our elementary freedom. And I was to have married that prince – You know nothing of him though. Well, a pigmy prince. He doesn't matter . . . It seems it would have strengthened the bonds between my country and another. And this country also was to profit. Imagine it! – strengthening the bonds!'

'And now?'

'They want me to go on with it – as though there was nothing between us two.'

'Nothing!'

'Yes. But that isn't all. He said – '

'Your specialist in Tact?'

'Yes. He said it would be better for you, better for all the giants, if we two – abstained from conversation. That was how he put it.'

'But what can they do if we don't?'

'He said you might have your freedom.'

'*I*!'

'He said, with a stress, "My dear young lady, it would be better, it would be more dignified, if you parted, willingly." That was all he said. With a stress on willingly.'

'But – ! What business is it of these little wretches where we love, how we love? What have they and their world to do with us?'

'They do not think that.'

'Of course,' he said, 'you disregard all this.'

'It seems utterly foolish to me.'

'That their laws should fetter us! That we, at the first spring of life, should be trapped by their old engagements, their aimless institutions! Oh – ! We disregard it.'

'I am yours. So far – yes.'

'So far? Isn't that all?'

'But they – If they want to part us – '

'What can they do?'

'I don't know. What *can* they do?'

'Who cares what they can do, or what they will do? I am yours and you are mine. What is there more than that? I am yours and you are mine – for ever. Do you think I will stop for their little rules, for their little prohibitions, their scarlet boards indeed! – and keep from *you*?'

'Yes. But still, what can they do?'

'You mean,' he said, 'what are we to do?'

'Yes.'

'We? We can go on.'

'But if they seek to prevent us?'

He clenched his hands. He looked round as if the little people were already coming to prevent them. Then turned away from her and looked about the world. 'Yes,' he said. 'Your question was the right one. What can they do?'

'Here in this little land – ' she said, and stopped.

He seemed to survey it all. 'They are everywhere.'

'But we might – '

'Whither?'

'We could go. We could swim the seas together. Beyond the seas – '

'I have never been beyond the seas.'

'There are great and desolate mountains amidst which we should seem no more than little people, there are remote and deserted valleys, there are hidden lakes and snow-girdled uplands untrodden by the feet of men. *There* – '

'But to get there we must fight our way day after day through millions and millions of mankind.'

'It is our only hope. In this crowded land there is no fastness, no shelter. What place is there for us among these multitudes? They who are little can hide from one another, but where are we to hide? There is no place where we could eat, no place where we could sleep. If we fled – night and day they would pursue our footsteps.'

A thought came to him.

'There is one place,' he said, 'even in this island.'

'Where?'

'The place our Brothers have made over beyond there. They have made great banks about their house, north and south and east and west; they have made deep pits and hidden places, and even now – one came over to me quite recently. He said – I did not altogether heed what he said then. But he spoke of arms. It may be – there – we should find shelter . . .

'For many days,' he said, after a pause, 'I have not seen our Brothers. Dear! I have been dreaming, I have been forgetting! The days have passed, and I have done nothing but look to see you again . . . I must go to them and talk to them, and tell them of you and of all the things that hang over us. If they will help us, they can help us. Then indeed we might hope. I do not know how strong their place is, but certainly Cossar will have made it strong. Before all this – before you came to me, I remember now – there was trouble brewing. There was an election – when all the little people settle things by counting heads. It must be over now. There were threats against all our race – against all our race, that is, but you. I must see our Brothers. I must tell them all that has happened between us, and all that threatens now.'

5

He did not come to their next meeting until she had waited some time. They were to meet that day about midday in a great space of park that fitted into a bend of the river, and as she waited, looking ever southward under her hand, it came to her that the world was very still, that indeed it was broodingly still. And then she perceived that, spite of the lateness of the hour, her customary retinue of voluntary spies had failed her. Left and right, when she came to look, there was no one in sight, and there was never a boat upon the silver curve of the Thames. She tried to find a reason for this strange stillness in the world . . .

Then, a grateful sight for her, she saw young Redwood far away over a gap in the tree masses that bounded her view.

Immediately the trees hid him, and presently he was thrusting through them and in sight again. She could see there was something different, and then she saw that he was hurrying unusually and then that he limped. He gestured to her, and she walked towards him. His face became clearer, and she saw with infinite concern that he winced at every stride.

She ran towards him, her mind full of questions and vague fear. He drew near to her and spoke without a greeting.

'Are we to part?' he panted.

'No,' she answered. 'Why? What is the matter?'

'But if we do not part – ! It is *now*.'

'What is the matter?'

'I do not want to part,' he said. 'Only – ' He broke off abruptly to ask, 'You will not part from me?'

She met his eyes with a steadfast look. 'What has happened?' she pressed.

'Not for a time?'

'What time?'

'Years perhaps.'

'Part! No!'

'You have thought?' he insisted.

'I will not part.' She took his hand. 'If this meant death, *now*, I would not let you go.'

'If it meant death,' he said, and she felt his grip upon her fingers.

He looked about him as if he feared to see the little people coming as he spoke. And then: 'It may mean death.'

'Now tell me,' she said.

'They tried to stop my coming.'

'How?'

'And as I came out of my workshop where I make the Food of the Gods for the Cossars to store in their camp, I found a little officer of police – a man in blue with white clean gloves – who beckoned me to stop. "This way is closed!" said he. I thought little of that; I went round my workshop to where another road runs west, and there was another officer. "This road is closed!" he said, and added: "All the roads are closed!" '

'And then?'

'I argued with him a little. "They are public roads!" I said.

' "That's it," said he. "You spoil them for the public."

' "Very well," said I, "I'll take the fields," and then, up leapt others from behind a hedge and said, "These fields are private."

' "Curse your public and private," I said, "I'm going to my princess," and I stooped down and picked him up very gently – kicking and shouting – and put him out of my way. In a minute all the fields about me seemed alive with running men. I saw one on horseback galloping beside me and reading something as he rode – shouting it. He finished and turned and galloped away from me – head down. I couldn't make it out. And then behind me I heard the crack of guns.'

'Guns!'

'Guns – just as they shoot at the rats. The bullets came through the air with a sound like things tearing: one stung me in the leg.'

'And you?'

'Came on to you here and left them shouting and running and shooting behind me. And now – '

'Now?'

'It is only the beginning. They mean that we shall part. Even now they are coming after me.'

'We will not.'

'No. But if we will not part – then you must come with me to our Brothers.'

'Which way?' she said.

'To the east. Yonder is the way my pursuers will be coming. This then is the way we must go. Along this avenue of trees. Let me go first, so that if they are waiting – '

He made a stride, but she had seized his arm.

'No,' cried she. 'I come close to you, holding you. Perhaps I am royal, perhaps I am sacred. If I hold you – Would God we could fly with my arms about you! – it may be, they will not shoot at you – '

She clasped his shoulder and seized his hand as she spoke; she pressed herself nearer to him. 'It may be they will not shoot you,' she repeated, and with a sudden passion of tenderness he took her into his arms and kissed her cheek. For a space he held her.

'Even if it is death,' she whispered.

She put her hands about his neck and lifted her face to his.

'Dearest, kiss me once more.'

He drew her to him. Silently they kissed one another on the lips, and for another moment clung to one another. Then hand in hand, and she striving always to keep her body near to his, they set forward if haply they might reach the camp of refuge the sons of Cossar had made, before the pursuit of the little people overtook them.

And as they crossed the great spaces of the park behind the castle there came horsemen galloping out from among the trees and vainly seeking to keep pace with their giant strides. And presently ahead of them were houses, and men with guns running out of the houses. At the sight of that, though he sought to go on and was even disposed to fight and push through, she made him turn aside towards the south.

As they fled a bullet whipped by them overhead.

CHAPTER 3

Young Caddles in London

All unaware of the trend of events, unaware of the laws that were closing in upon all the Brethren, unaware indeed that there lived a Brother for him on the earth, young Caddles chose this time to come out of his chalk pit and see the world. His brooding came at last to that. There was no answer to all his questions in Cheasing Eyebright; the new vicar was less luminous even than the old, and the riddle of his pointless labour grew at last to the dimensions of exasperation. 'Why should I work in this pit day after day?' he asked. 'Why should I walk within bounds and be refused all the wonders of the world beyond there? What have I done, to be condemned to this?'

And one day he stood up, straightened his back, and said in a loud voice, 'No!

'I won't,' he said, and then with great vigour cursed the pit.

Then, having few words, he sought to express his thought in acts. He took a truck half filled with chalk, lifted it and flung it, smash, against another. Then he grasped a whole row of empty trucks and spun them down a bank. He sent a huge boulder of chalk bursting among them, and then ripped up a dozen yards of rail with a mighty plunge of his foot. So he commenced the conscientious wrecking of the pit.

'Work all my days,' he said, 'at this!'

It was an astonishing five minutes for the little geologist he had, in his preoccupation, overlooked. This poor little creature having dodged two boulders by a hair's breadth, got out by the westward corner and fled athwart the hill, with flapping rucksack and twinkling knicker-bockered legs, leaving a trail of Cretaceous echinoderms[48] behind him; while young Caddles, satisfied with the destruction he had achieved, came striding out to fulfil his purpose in the world.

'Work in that old pit until I die and rot and stink! . . . What worm did they think was living in my giant body? Dig chalk for God knows what foolish purpose! Not *I*!'

The trend of road and railway perhaps, or mere chance it was, turned his face to London, and thither he came striding; over the downs and athwart the meadows through the hot afternoon, to the infinite amazement of the world. It signified nothing to him that torn posters in red and white bearing various names flapped from every wall and barn; he knew nothing of the electoral revolution that had flung Caterham, 'Jack the Giant-Killer', into power. It signified nothing to him that every police station along his route had what was known as Caterham's ukase upon its noticeboard that afternoon, proclaiming that no giant, no person whatever over eight feet in height, should go more than five miles from his 'place of location' without a special permission. It signified nothing to him that in his wake belated police officers, not a little relieved to find themselves belated, shook warning handbills at his retreating back. He was going to see what the world had to show him, poor incredulous blockhead, and he did not mean that occasional spirited persons shouting 'Hi!' at him should stay his course. He came on down by Rochester and Greenwich towards an ever-thickening aggregation of houses, walking rather slowly now, staring about him and swinging his huge chopper.

People in London had heard something of him before, how that he was idiotic but gentle, and wonderfully managed by Lady Wondershoot's agent and the vicar; how in his dull way he revered these authorities and was grateful to them for their care of him, and so forth. So that when they learnt from the newspaper placards that afternoon that he also was 'on strike', the thing appeared to many of them as a deliberate, concerted act.

'They mean to try our strength,' said the men in the trains going home from business.

'Lucky we have Caterham.'

'It's in answer to his proclamation.'

The men in the clubs were better informed. They clustered round the tape or talked in groups in their smoking-rooms.

'He has no weapons. He would have gone to Sevenoaks if he had been put up to it.'

'Caterham will handle him . . . '

The shopmen told their customers. The waiters in restaurants snatched a moment for an evening paper between the courses. The cabmen read it immediately after the betting news . . .

The placards of the chief government evening paper were conspicuous with 'Grasping the Nettle'. Others relied for effect on: 'Giant Redwood continues to meet the Princess'. The *Echo* struck a line of its own with: 'Rumoured Revolt of Giants in the North of England. The Sunderland Giants start for Scotland'. The *Westminster Gazette* sounded its usual warning note. 'Giants Beware', said the *Westminster Gazette*, and tried to make a point out of it that might perhaps serve towards uniting the Liberal party – at that time greatly torn between seven intensely egotistical leaders. The later newspapers dropped into uniformity. 'The Giant in the New Kent Road', they proclaimed.

'What I want to know,' said the pale young man in the tea shop, 'is why we aren't getting any news of the young Cossars. You'd think they'd be in it most of all . . . '

'They tell me there's another of them young giants got loose,' said the barmaid, wiping out a glass. 'I've always said they was dangerous things to 'ave about. Right away from the beginning . . . It ought to be put a stop to. Any 'ow, I 'ope 'e won't come along 'ere.'

'I'd like to 'ave a look at 'im,' said the young man at the bar recklessly, and added, 'I *seen* the princess.'

'D'you think they'll 'urt 'im?' said the barmaid.

'May 'ave to,' said the young man at the bar, finishing his glass.

Amidst a hum of ten million such sayings young Caddles came to London . . .

2

I think of young Caddles always as he was seen in the New Kent Road, the sunset warm upon his perplexed and staring face. The road was thick with its varied traffic, omnibuses, trams, vans, carts, trolleys, cyclists, motors, and a marvelling crowd – loafers, women, nursemaids, shopping women, children, venturesome hobbledehoys – gathered behind his gingerly moving feet. The hoardings were untidy everywhere with the tattered election paper. A babblement of voices surged about him. One sees the customers and shopmen crowding in the doorways of the shops, the faces that came and went at the windows, the little street boys running and shouting, the policemen taking it all quite stiffly and calmly, the workmen knocking off upon scaffoldings, the seething miscellany of the little folks. They shouted to him, vague encouragement, vague insults, the imbecile catchwords of the day, and he stared down at them, at such a multitude of living creatures as he had never before imagined in the world.

Now that he had fairly entered London he had had to slacken his pace more and more, the little folks crowded so mightily upon him. The crowd grew denser at every step, and at last, at a corner where two great ways converged, he came to a stop, and the multitude flowed about him and closed him in.

There he stood, with his feet a little apart, his back to a big corner gin palace that towered twice his height and ended in a sky sign, staring down at the pigmies and wondering – trying, I doubt not, to collate it all with the other things of his life, with the valley among the downlands, the nocturnal lovers, the singing in the church, the chalk he hammered daily, and with instinct and death and the sky, trying to see it all together coherent and significant. His brows were knit. He put up his huge paw to scratch his coarse hair, and groaned aloud.

'I don't see it,' he said.

His accent was unfamiliar. A great babblement went across the open space – a babblement amidst which the gongs of the trams, ploughing their obstinate way through the mass, rose like red poppies amidst corn. 'What did he say?' 'Said he didn't see.' 'Said, where is the sea?' 'Said, where is a seat?' 'He wants a seat.' 'Can't the brasted fool sit on a 'ouse or somethin'?'

'What are ye for, ye swarming little people? What are ye all doing, what are ye all for?

'What are ye doing up here, ye swarming little people, while I'm a-cuttin' chalk for ye, down in the chalk pits there?'

His queer voice, the voice that had been so bad for school discipline at Cheasing Eyebright, smote the multitude to silence while it sounded and splashed them all to tumult at the end. Some wit was audible screaming, 'Speech, speech!' 'What's he saying?' was the burthen of the public mind, and an opinion was abroad that he was drunk. 'Hi, hi, hi,' bawled the omnibus-drivers, threading a dangerous way. A drunken American sailor wandered about tearfully enquiring, 'What's he want anyhow?' A leathery-faced rag-dealer upon a little pony-drawn cart soared up over the tumult by virtue of his voice. 'Garn 'ome, you Brasted Giant!' he brawled. 'Garn 'ome! you Brasted Great Dangerous Thing! Can't you see you're a-frightening the 'orses? Go 'ome with you! 'Asn't anyone 'ad the sense to tell you the law?' And over all this uproar young Caddles stared, perplexed, expectant, saying no more.

Down a side road came a little string of solemn policemen, and threaded itself ingeniously into the traffic. 'Stand back,' said the little voices; 'keep moving, please.'

Young Caddles became aware of a little dark blue figure thumping at his shin. He looked down, and perceived two white hands gesticulating. '*What*?' he said, bending forward.

'Can't stand about here,' shouted the inspector. 'No! You can't stand about here,' he repeated.

'But where am I to go?'

'Back to your village. Place of location. Anyhow, now – you've got to move on. You're obstructing the traffic.'

'What traffic?'

'Along the road.'

'But where is it going? Where does it come from? What does it mean? They're all round me. What do they want? What are they doin'? I want to understand. I'm tired of cuttin' chalk and bein' all alone. What are they doin' for me while I'm a-cuttin' chalk? I may just as well understand here and now as anywhere.'

'Sorry. But we aren't here to explain things of that sort. I must arst you to move on.'

'Don't you know?'

'I must arst you to move on – *if* you please . . . I'd strongly advise you to get off 'ome. We've 'ad no special instructions yet – but it's against the law . . . Clear away there. Clear away.'

The pavement to his left became invitingly bare, and young Caddles went slowly on his way. But now his tongue was loosened.

'I don't understand,' he muttered. 'I don't understand.' He would appeal brokenly to the changing crowd that ever trailed beside him and behind. 'I didn't know there were such places as this. What are all you people doing with yourselves? What's it all for? What is it all for, and where do I come in?'

He had already begotten a new catchword. Young men of wit and spirit addressed each other in this manner, ' 'Ello, 'Arry, ol' cock. Wot's it all *for*? Eh? Wot's it all bloomin' well *for*?'

To which there sprang up a competing variety of repartees, for the most part impolite. The most popular and best adapted for general use appears to have been, '*Shut* it,' or, in a voice of scornful detachment, '*Garn!*'

There were others almost equally popular.

3

What was he seeking? He wanted something the pigmy world did not give, some end which the pigmy world prevented his attaining, prevented even his seeing clearly, which he was never to see clearly. It was the whole gigantic social side of this lonely dumb monster crying out for his race, for the things akin to him, for something he might love and something he might serve, for a purpose he might comprehend and a command he could obey. And, you know, all this was *dumb*, raged dumbly within him, could not even, had he met a fellow giant, have found outlet and expression in speech. All the life he knew was the dull round of the village, all the speech he knew was the talk of the cottage, that failed and collapsed at the bare outline of his least gigantic need. He knew nothing of money, this monstrous simpleton, nothing of trade, nothing of the complex pretences upon which the social fabric of the little folks was built. He needed, he needed – Whatever he needed, he never found his need.

All through the day and the summer night he wandered, growing hungry but as yet untired, marking the varied traffic of the different streets, the inexplicable businesses of all these infinitesimal beings. In the aggregate it had no other colour than confusion for him . . .

He is said to have plucked a lady from her carriage in Kensington, a lady in evening dress of the smartest sort, to have scrutinised her closely, train and shoulder blades, and to have replaced her – a little carelessly – with the profoundest sigh. For that I cannot vouch. For an hour or so he watched people fighting for places in the omnibuses at the end of Piccadilly. He was seen looming over Kennington Oval for some moments in the afternoon, but when he saw these dense thousands were engaged with the mystery of cricket and quite regardless of him he went his way with a groan.

He came back to Piccadilly Circus between eleven and twelve at nights and found a new sort of multitude. Clearly they were very intent: full of things they, for inconceivable reasons, might do, and of others they might not do. They stared at him and jeered at him and went their way. The cabmen, vulture-eyed, followed one another continually along the edge of the swarming pavement. People emerged from the restaurants or entered them, grave, intent, dignified, or gently and agreeably excited, or keen and vigilant – beyond the cheating of the sharpest waiter born. The great giant, standing at his corner, peered at them all. 'What is it all for?' he murmured in a mournful vast undertone, 'What is it all for? They are all so earnest. What is it I do not understand?'

And none of them seemed to see, as he could do, the drink-sodden wretchedness of the painted women at the corner, the ragged misery that sneaked along the gutters, the infinite futility of all this employment. The infinite futility! None of them seemed to feel the shadow of that giant's need, that shadow of the future, that lay athwart their paths . . .

Across the road high up mysterious letters flamed and went, that might, could he have read them, have measured for him the dimensions of human interest, have told him of the fundamental needs and features of life as the little folks conceived it. First would come a flaming

T;

Then U would follow,

T U;

Then P,

T U P;

Until at last there stood complete, across the sky, this cheerful message to all who felt the burthen of life's earnestness:

TUPPER'S TONIC WINE FOR VIGOUR

Snap! and it had vanished into night, to be followed in the same slow development by a second universal solicitude:

BEAUTY SOAP

Not, you remark, mere cleansing chemicals, but something, as they say, 'ideal'; and then, completing the tripod of the little life:

YANKER'S YELLOW PILLS

After that there was nothing for it but Tupper again, in flaming crimson letters, snap, snap, across the void. T U P P . . .

Early in the small hours it would seem that young Caddles came to the shadowy quiet of Regent's Park, stepped over the railings and lay down on a grassy slope near where the people skate in wintertime, and there he slept an hour or so. And about six o'clock in the morning, he was talking to a draggled woman he had found sleeping in a ditch near Hampstead Heath, asking her very earnestly what she thought she was for . . .

4

The wandering of Caddles about London came to a head on the second day in the morning. For then his hunger overcame him. He hesitated where the hot-smelling loaves were being tossed into a cart, and then very quietly knelt down and commenced robbery. He emptied the cart while the baker's man fled for the police, and then his great hand came into the shop and cleared counter and cases. Then with an armful, still eating, he went his way looking for another shop to go on with his meal. It happened to be one of those seasons when work is scarce and food dear, and the crowd in that quarter was sympathetic even with a giant who took the food they all desired. They applauded the second phase of his meal, and laughed at his stupid grimace at the policeman.

'I woff hungry,' he said, with his mouth full.

'Brayvo!' cried the crowd. 'Brayvo!'

Then, when he was beginning his third baker's shop, he was stopped by half a dozen policemen hammering with truncheons at his shins. 'Look here, my fine giant, you come along o' me,' said the officer in charge. 'You ain't allowed away from home like this. You come off home with me.' They did their best to arrest him. There was a trolley, I am told, chasing up and down streets at that time, bearing rolls of chain and ship's cable to play the part of handcuffs in that great arrest. There was no intention then of killing him. 'He is no party to the plot,' Caterham had said. 'I will not have innocent blood upon my hands.' And added: ' – until everything else has been tried.'

At first Caddles did not understand the import of these attentions. When he did, he told the policemen not to be fools, and set off in great strides that left them all behind. The bakers' shops had been in the Harrow Road, and he followed the canal to St John's Wood and sat down in a private garden there to pick his teeth and be speedily assailed by another posse of constables.

'You lea' me alone,' he growled, and slouched through the gardens – spoiling several lawns and kicking down a fence or so, while the energetic little policemen followed him up, some through the gardens, some along the road in front of the houses. Here there were one or two with guns, but they made no use of them. When he came out into the Edgware Road there was a new note and a new movement in the crowd, and a mounted policeman rode over his foot and got upset for his pains.

'You lea' me alone,' said Caddles, facing the breathless crowd. 'I ain't done anything to you.' At that time he was unarmed, for he had left his chalk chopper in Regent's Park. But now, poor wretch, he seems to have felt the need of some weapon. He turned back towards the goods yard of the Great Western Railway, wrenched up the standard of a tall arc light, a formidable mace for him, and flung it over his shoulder. And finding the police still turning up to pester him, he went back along the Edgware Road, towards Cricklewood, and struck off sullenly to the north.

He wandered as far as Waltham, and then turned back westward and then again towards London, and came by the cemeteries and over the crest of Highgate about midday into view of the greatness of the city again. He turned aside and sat down in a garden, with his back to a house that overlooked all London. He was breathless, and his face was lowering, and now the people no longer crowded upon him as they had done when first he came to London, but lurked in the adjacent garden, and peeped from cautious securities. They knew by now the thing was grimmer than they had thought. 'Why can't they lea' me alone?' growled young Caddles. 'I *mus'* eat. Why can't they lea' me alone?'

He sat with a darkling face, gnawing at his knuckles and looking down over London. All the fatigue, worry, perplexity and impotent wrath of his wanderings was coming to a head in him. 'They mean nothing,' he whispered. 'They mean nothing. And they *won't* let me alone, and they *will* get in my way.' And again, over and over to himself, 'Meanin' nothing.

'Ugh! the little people!'

He bit harder at his knuckles and his scowl deepened. 'Cuttin' chalk for 'em,' he whispered. 'And all the world is theirs! *I* don't come in – nowhere.'

Presently with a spasm of sick anger he saw the now familiar form of a policeman astride the garden wall.

'Lea' me alone,' grunted the giant. 'Lea' me alone.'

'I got to do my duty,' said the little policeman, with a face that was white and resolute.

'You lea' me alone. I got to live as well as you. I got to think. I got to eat. You lea' me alone.'

'It's the Law,' said the little policeman, coming no farther. 'We never made the Law.'

'Nor me,' said young Caddles. 'You little people made all that before I was born. You and your Law! What I must and what I mustn't! No food for me to eat unless I work a slave, no rest, no shelter, nothin', and you tell me – '

'I ain't got no business with that,' said the policeman. 'I'm not one to argue. All I got to do is to carry out the Law.' And he brought his second leg over the wall and seemed disposed to get down. Other policemen appeared behind him.

'I got no quarrel with *you* – mind,' said young Caddles, with his grip tight upon his huge mace of iron, his face pale, and a lank explanatory great finger to the policeman. 'I got no quarrel with you. But – *You lea' me alone.*'

The policeman tried to be calm and commonplace, with a monstrous tragedy clear before his eyes. 'Give me the proclamation,' he said to some unseen follower, and a little white paper was handed to him.

'Lea' me alone,' said Caddles, scowling, tense and drawn together.

'This means,' said the policeman before he read, 'go 'ome. Go 'ome to your chalk pit. If not, you'll be hurt.'

Caddles gave an inarticulate growl.

Then when the proclamation had been read, the officer made a sign. Four men with rifles came into view and took up positions of affected ease along the wall. They wore the uniform of the rat police. At the sight of the guns, young Caddles blazed into anger. He remembered the sting of the Wreckstone farmers' shotguns. 'You going to shoot off those at me?' he said, pointing, and it seemed to the officer he must be afraid.

'If you don't march back to your pit – '

Then in an instant the officer had slung himself back over the wall, and sixty feet above him the great electric standard whirled down to his death. Bang, bang, bang, went the heavy guns, and smash! the shattered wall, the soil and subsoil of the garden flew. Something flew with it, that left red drops on one of the shooter's hands. The riflemen dodged this way and that and turned valiantly to fire again. But young Caddles, already shot twice through the body, had spun about to find who it was had hit him so heavily in the back. Bang! Bang! He had a vision of houses and greenhouses and gardens, of people dodging at windows, the whole swaying fearfully and mysteriously. He seems to have made three stumbling strides, to have raised and dropped his huge mace, and to have clutched his chest. He was stung and wrenched by pain.

What was this, warm and wet, on his hand?

One man peering from a bedroom window saw his face, saw him staring, with a grimace of weeping dismay, at the blood upon his hand, and then his knees bent under him and he came crashing to the earth, the first of the giant nettles to fall to Caterham's resolute clutch, the very last that he had reckoned would come into his hand.

CHAPTER 4

Redwood's Two Days

So soon as Caterham knew the moment for grasping his nettle had come, he took the law into his own hands and sent to arrest Cossar and Redwood.

Redwood was there for the taking. He had been undergoing an operation in the side, and the doctors had kept all disturbing things from him until his convalescence was assured. Now they had released him. He was just out of bed, sitting in a fire-warmed room, with a heap of newspapers about him, reading for the first time of the agitation that had swept the country into the hands of Caterham, and of the trouble that was darkening over the princess and his son. It was in the morning of the day when young Caddles died, and when the policeman tried to stop young Redwood on his way to the princess. The latest newspapers Redwood had did but vaguely prefigure these imminent things. He was rereading these first adumbrations of disaster with a sinking heart, reading the shadow of death more and more perceptibly into them, reading to occupy his mind until further news should come. When the officers followed the servant into his room, he looked up eagerly.

'I thought it was an early evening paper,' he said. Then standing up, and with a swift change of manner: 'What's this?'

After that Redwood had no news of anything for two days.

They had come with a vehicle to take him away, but when it became evident that he was ill, it was decided to leave him for a day or so until he could be safely removed, and his house was taken over by the police and converted into a temporary prison. It was the same house in winch Giant Redwood had been born and in which Herakleophorbia had for the first time been given to a human being, and Redwood had now been a widower and had lived alone in it eight years.

He had become an iron-grey man, with a little pointed grey beard and still active brown eyes. He was slender and soft-voiced, as he had ever been, but his features had now that indefinable quality that comes of brooding over mighty things. To the arresting officer his appearance was in impressive contrast to the enormity of his offences. 'Here's this feller,' said the officer in command to his next subordinate, 'has done his level best to bust up everything, and 'e's got a face like a quiet

country gentleman; and here's Judge Hangbrow keepin' everything nice
and in order for everyone, and 'e's got a 'ead like a 'og. Then their
manners! One all consideration and the other snort and grunt. Which
just shows you, doesn't it, that appearances aren't to be gone upon,
whatever else you do.'

But his praise of Redwood's consideration was presently dashed. The
officers found him troublesome at first until they had made it clear that
it was useless for him to ask questions or beg for papers. They made a
sort of inspection of his study indeed, and cleared away even the papers
he had. Redwood's voice was high and expostulatory. 'But don't you
see,' he said over and over again, 'it's my son, my only son, that is in this
trouble. It isn't the Food I care for, but my son.'

'I wish indeed I could tell you, sir,' said the officer. 'But our orders are
strict.'

'Who gave the orders?' cried Redwood.

'Ah! *that*, sir – ' said the officer, and moved towards the door . . .

' 'E's going up and down 'is room,' said the second officer, when his
superior came down. 'That's all right. He'll walk it off a bit.'

'I hope 'e will,' said the chief officer. 'The fact is I didn't see it in that
light before, but this here Giant what's been going on with the princess,
you know, is this man's son.'

The two regarded one another and the third policeman for a space.

'Then it is a bit rough on him,' the third policeman said.

It became evident that Redwood had still imperfectly apprehended
the fact that an iron curtain had dropped between him and the outer
world. They heard him go to the door, try the handle and rattle the
lock, and then the voice of the officer who was stationed on the landing
telling him it was no good to do that. Then afterwards they heard him
at the windows and saw the men outside looking up. 'It's no good that
way,' said the second officer. Then Redwood began upon the bell. The
senior officer went up and explained very patiently that it could do no
good to ring the bell like that, and if it was rung for nothing now it
might have to be disregarded presently when he had need of something.
'Any reasonable attendance, sir,' the officer said. 'But if you ring it just
by way of protest we shall be obliged, sir, to disconnect.'

The last word the officer heard was Redwood's high-pitched, 'But at
least you might tell me if my son – '

After that Redwood spent most of his time at the windows.

But the windows offered him little of the march of events outside. It was a quiet street at all times, and that day it was unusually quiet: scarcely a cab, scarcely a tradesman's cart passed all that morning. Now and then men went by – without any distinctive air of events – now and then a little group of children, a nursemaid and a woman going shopping, and so forth. They came on to the stage right or left, up or down the street, with an exasperating suggestion of indifference to any concerns more spacious than their own; they would discover the police-guarded house with amazement and exit in the opposite direction, where the great trusses of a giant hydrangea hung across the pavement, staring back or pointing. Now and then a man would come and ask one of the policemen a question and get a curt reply.

Opposite the houses seemed dead. A housemaid appeared once at a bedroom window and stared for a space, and it occurred to Redwood to signal to her. For a time she watched his gestures as if with interest and made a vague response to them, then looked over her shoulder suddenly and turned and went away. An old man hobbled out of Number 37 and came down the steps and went off to the right, altogether without looking up. For ten minutes the only occupant of the road was a cat . . .

With such events that interminable momentous morning lengthened out.

About twelve there came a bawling of news-vendors from the adjacent road; but it passed. Contrary to their wont they left Redwood's street alone, and a suspicion dawned upon him that the police were guarding the end of the street. He tried to open the window, but this brought a policeman into the room forthwith.

The clock of the parish church struck twelve, and after an abyss of time – one.

They mocked him with lunch.

He ate a mouthful and tumbled the food about a little in order to get it taken away, drank freely of whisky, and then took a chair and went back to the window. The minutes expanded into grey immensities, and for a time perhaps he slept . . .

He woke with a vague impression of remote concussions. He perceived a rattling of the windows, like the quiver of an earthquake, that lasted for a minute or so and died away. Then after a silence it returned . . . Then it died away again. He fancied it might be merely the passage of some heavy vehicle along the main road. What else could it be?

After a time he began to doubt whether he had heard this sound.

He began to reason interminably with himself. Why, after all, was he seized? Caterham had been in office two days – just long enough – to grasp his nettle! Grasp his Nettle! Grasp his Giant Nettle! The refrain, once started, sang through his mind and would not be dismissed.

What, after all, could Caterham do? He was a religious man. He was bound in a sort of way by that not to do violence without a cause.

Grasp his Nettle! Perhaps, for example, the princess was to be seized and sent abroad. There might be trouble with his son. In which case – ! But why had he been arrested? Why was it necessary to keep him in ignorance of a thing like that? The thing suggested – something more extensive.

Perhaps, for example – they meant to lay all the giants by the heels! They were all to be arrested together. There had been hints of that in the election speeches. And then?

No doubt they had got Cossar also?

Caterham was a religious man. Redwood clung to that. The back of his mind was a black curtain, and on that curtain there came and went a word – a word written in letters of fire. He struggled perpetually against that word. It was always as it were beginning to get written on the curtain and never getting completed.

He faced it at last. 'Massacre!' There was the word in its full brutality.

No! No! No! It was impossible! Caterham was a religious man, a civilised man. And besides after all these years, after all these hopes!

Redwood sprang up; he paced the room. He spoke to himself; he shouted, '*No!*'

Mankind was surely not so mad as that – surely not! It was impossible, it was incredible, it could not be. What good would it do to kill the giant human when the gigantic in all the lower things had now inevitably come? They could not be so mad as that! 'I must dismiss such an idea,' he said aloud; 'dismiss such an idea! Absolutely!'

He pulled up short. What was that?

Certainly the windows had rattled. He went to look out into the street. Opposite he saw the instant confirmation of his ears. At a bedroom at Number 35 was a woman, towel in hand, and at the dining-room of Number 37 a man was visible behind a great vase of hypertrophied maidenhair fern, both staring out and up, both disquieted and curious. He could see now too, quite clearly, that the policeman on the pavement had heard it also. The thing was not his imagination.

He turned to the darkling room.

'Guns,' he said.

He brooded. 'Guns?'

They brought him in strong tea, such as he was accustomed to have. It was evident his housekeeper had been taken into consultation. After drinking it, he was too restless to sit any longer at the window, and he paced the room. His mind became more capable of consecutive thought.

The room had been his study for four-and-twenty years. It had been furnished at his marriage, and all the essential equipment dated from then, the large complex writing-desk, the rotating chair, the easy chair at the fire, the rotating bookcase, the fixture of indexed pigeonholes that filled the farther recess. The vivid Turkey carpet, the later Victorian rugs and curtains had mellowed now to a rich dignity of effect, and copper and brass shone warm about the open fire. Electric lights had replaced the lamp of former days; that was the chief alteration in the original equipment. But among these things his connection with the Food had left abundant traces. Along one wall, above the dado, ran a crowded array of black-framed photographs and photogravures, showing his son and Cossar's sons and others of the Boom-children at various ages and amidst various surroundings. Even young Caddles's vacant visage had its place in that collection. In the corner stood a sheaf of the tassels of gigantic meadow grass from Cheasing Eyebright, and on the desk there lay three empty poppy heads as big as hats. The curtain rods were grass stems. And the tremendous skull of the great hog of Oakham hung, a portentous ivory overmantel, with a Chinese jar in either eye socket, snout down above the fire.

It was to the photographs that Redwood went, and in particular to the photographs of his son.

They brought back countless memories of things that had passed out of his mind, of the early days of the Food, of Bensington's timid presence, of his cousin Jane, of Cossar and the night work at the Experimental Farm. These things came to him now very little and bright and distinct, like things seen through a telescope on a sunny day. And then there was the giant nursery, the giant childhood, the young giant's first efforts to speak, his first clear signs of affection.

Guns?

It flowed in on him, irresistibly, overwhelmingly, that outside there, outside this accursed silence and mystery, his son and Cossar's sons, and all these glorious first-fruits of a greater age were even now – fighting. Fighting for life! Even now his son might be in some dismal quandary, cornered, wounded, overcome . . .

He swung away from the pictures and went up and down the room gesticulating. 'It cannot be,' he cried, 'it cannot be. It cannot end like that!'

'What was that?'

He stopped, stricken rigid.

The trembling of the windows had begun again, and then had come a thud – a vast concussion that shook the house. The concussion seemed to last for an age. It must have been very near. For a moment it seemed that something had struck the house above him – an enormous impact that broke into a tinkle of falling glass, and then a stillness that ended at last with a minute clear sound of running feet in the street below.

Those feet released him from his rigor. He turned towards the window, and saw it starred and broken.

His heart beat high with a sense of crisis, of conclusive occurrence, of release. And then again, his realisation of impotent confinement fell about him like a curtain!

He could see nothing outside except that the small electric lamp opposite was not lighted; he could hear nothing after the first suggestion of a wide alarm. He could add nothing to interpret or enlarge that mystery except that presently there came a reddish fluctuating brightness in the sky towards the south-east.

This light waxed and waned. When it waned he doubted if it had ever waxed. It had crept upon him very gradually with the darkling. It became the predominant fact in his long night of suspense. Sometimes it seemed to him it had the quiver one associates with dancing flames, at others he fancied it was no more than the normal reflection of the evening lights. It waxed and waned through the long hours, and only vanished at last when it was submerged altogether under the rising tide of dawn. Did it mean – ? What could it mean? Almost certainly it was some sort of fire, near or remote, but he could not even tell whether it was smoke or cloud drift that streamed across the sky. But about one o'clock there began a flickering of searchlights athwart that ruddy tumult, a flickering that continued for the rest of the night. That too might mean many things? What could it mean? What did it mean? Just this stained unrestful sky he had and the suggestion of a huge explosion to occupy his mind. There came no further sounds, no further running, nothing but a shouting that might have been only the distant efforts of drunken men . . .

He did not turn up his lights; he stood at his draughty broken window, a distressful, slight black outline to the officer who looked ever and again into the room and exhorted him to rest.

All night Redwood remained at his window peering up at the

ambiguous drift of the sky, and only with the coming of the dawn did
he obey his fatigue and lie down upon the little bed they had prepared
for him between his writing-desk and the sinking fire in the fireplace
under the great hog's skull.

3

For thirty-six long hours did Redwood remain imprisoned, closed in
and shut off from the great drama of the Two Days, while the little
people in the dawn of greatness fought against the Children of the
Food. Then abruptly the iron curtain rose again, and he found himself
near the very centre of the struggle. That curtain rose as unexpectedly
as it fell. In the late afternoon he was called to the window by the clatter
of a cab, that stopped without. A young man descended, and in another
minute stood before him in the room, a slightly built young man of
thirty perhaps, clean shaven, well dressed, well mannered.

'Mr Redwood, sir,' he began, 'would you be willing to come to Mr
Caterham? He needs your presence very urgently.'

'Needs my presence!' There leapt a question into Redwood's mind
that for a moment he could not put. He hesitated. Then in a voice that
broke he asked: 'What has he done to my son?' and stood breathless for
the reply.

'Your son, sir? Your son is doing well. So at least we gather.'

'Doing well?'

'He was wounded, sir, yesterday. Have you not heard?'

Redwood smote these pretences aside. His voice was no longer
coloured by fear, but by anger. 'You know I have not heard. You know
I have heard nothing.'

'Mr Caterham feared, sir – It was a time of upheaval. Everyone –
taken by surprise. He arrested you to save you, sir, from any mis-
adventure – '

'He arrested me to prevent my giving any warning or advice to my
son. Go on. Tell me what has happened. Have you succeeded? Have
you killed them all?'

The young man made a pace or so towards the window, and turned.

'No, sir,' he said concisely.

'What have you to tell me?'

'It's our proof, sir, that this fighting was not planned by us. They
found us . . . totally unprepared.'

'You mean?'

'I mean, sir, the Giants have – to a certain extent – held their own.'

The world changed, for Redwood. For a moment something like hysteria had the muscles of his face and throat. Then he gave vent to a profound 'Ah!' His heart bounded towards exultation. 'The Giants have held their own!'

'There has been terrible fighting – terrible destruction. It is all a most hideous misunderstanding . . . In the north and midlands Giants have been killed . . . Everywhere.'

'They are fighting now?'

'No, sir. There was a flag of truce.'

'From them?'

'No, sir. Mr Caterham sent a flag of truce. The whole thing is a hideous misunderstanding. That is why he wants to talk to you, and put his case before you. They insist, sir, that you should intervene – '

Redwood interrupted. 'Do you know what happened to my son?' he asked.

'He was wounded.'

'Tell me! Tell me!'

'He and the princess came before the movement to surround the Cossar camp was complete – the Cossar pit at Chislehurst. They came suddenly, sir, crashing through a dense thicket of giant oats, near River, upon a column of infantry . . . Soldiers had been very nervous all day, and this produced a panic.'

'They shot him?'

'No, sir. They ran away. Some shot at him – wildly – against orders.'

Redwood gave a note of denial.

'It's true, sir. Not on account of your son, I won't pretend, but on account of the princess.'

'Yes. That's true.'

'The two Giants ran shouting towards the encampment. The soldiers ran this way and that, and then some began firing. They say they saw him stagger – '

'Ugh!'

'Yes, sir. But we know he is not badly hurt.'

'How?'

'He sent the message, sir, that he was doing well!'

'To me?'

'Who else, sir?'

Redwood stood for nearly a minute with his arms tightly folded, taking this in. Then his indignation found a voice.

'Because you were fools in doing the thing, because you miscalculated and blundered, you would like me to think you are not murderers in intention. And besides – The rest?'

The young man looked interrogation.

'The other Giants?'

The young man made no further pretence of misunderstanding. His tone fell. 'Thirteen, sir, are dead.'

'And others wounded?'

'Yes, sir.'

'And Caterham,' he gasped, 'wants to meet me! Where are the others?'

'Some got to the encampment during the fighting, sir . . . They seem to have known – '

'Well, of course they did. If it hadn't been for Cossar – Cossar is there?'

'Yes, sir. And all the surviving Giants are there – the ones who didn't get to the camp in the fighting have gone, or are going now under the flag of trace.'

'That means,' said Redwood, 'that you are beaten.'

'We are not beaten. No, sir. You cannot say we are beaten. But your sons have broken the rules of war. Once last night, and now again. After our attack had been withdrawn. This afternoon they began to bombard London – '

'That's legitimate!'

'They have been firing shells filled with – poison.'

'Poison?'

'Yes. Poison. The Food – '

'Herakleophorbia?'

'Yes, sir. Mr Caterham, sir – '

'You are beaten! Of course that beats you. It's Cossar! What can you hope to do now? What good is it to do anything now? You will breathe it in the dust of every street. What is there to fight for more? Rules of war, indeed! And now Caterham wants to humbug me to help him bargain. Good heavens, man! Why should I come to your exploded windbag? He has played his game . . . murdered and muddled. Why should I?'

The young man stood with an air of vigilant respect.

'It is a fact, sir,' he interrupted, 'that the Giants insist that they shall see you. They will have no ambassador but you. Unless you come to them, I am afraid, sir, there will be more bloodshed.'

'On *your* side, perhaps.'

'No, sir – on both sides. The world is resolved the thing must end.'

Redwood looked about the study. His eyes rested for a moment on the photograph of his boy. He turned and met the expectation of the young man. 'Yes,' he said at last, 'I will come.'

His encounter with Caterham was entirely different from his anticipation. He had seen the man only twice in his life, once at dinner and once in the lobby of the House, and his imagination had been active not with the man but with the creation of the newspapers and caricaturists, the legendary Caterham, Jack the Giant-Killer, Perseus, and all the rest of it. The element of a human personality came in to disorder all that.

Here was not the face of the caricatures and portraits, but the face of a worn and sleepless man, lined and drawn, yellow in the whites of the eyes, a little weakened about the mouth. Here, indeed, were the red-brown eyes, the black hair, the distinctive aquiline profile of the great demagogue, but here was also something else that smote any pre-meditated scorn and rhetoric aside. This man was suffering; he was suffering acutely; he was under enormous stress. From the beginning he had an air of impersonating himself. Presently, with a single gesture, the slightest movement, he revealed to Redwood that he was keeping himself up with drugs. He moved a thumb to his waistcoat pocket, and then, after a few sentences more, threw concealment aside and slipped the little tabloid to his lips.

Moreover, in spite of the stresses upon him, in spite of the fact that he was in the wrong, and Redwood's junior by a dozen years, that strange quality in him, the something – personal magnetism one may call it for want of a better name – that had won his way for him to this eminence of disaster was with him still. On that also Redwood had failed to reckon. From the first, so far as the course and conduct of their speech went, Caterham prevailed over Redwood. All the quality of the first phase of their meeting was determined by him, all the tone and procedure were his. That happened as if it was a matter of course. All Redwood's expectations vanished at his presence. He shook hands before Redwood remembered that he meant to parry that familiarity; he pitched the note of their conference from the outset, sure and clear, as a search for expedients under a common catastrophe.

If he made any mistake it was when ever and again his fatigue got the better of his immediate attention, and the habit of the public meeting carried him away. Then he drew himself up – through all their interview both men stood – and looked away from Redwood, and began to fence and justify. Once even he said, 'Gentlemen!'

Quietly, expandingly, he began to talk . . .

There were moments when Redwood ceased even to feel himself an interlocutor, when he became the mere auditor of a monologue. He became the privileged spectator of an extraordinary phenomenon. He perceived something almost like a specific difference between himself and this being whose beautiful voice enveloped him, who was talking, talking. This mind before him was so powerful and so limited. From its driving energy, its personal weight, its invincible oblivion to certain things, there sprang up in Redwood's mind the most grotesque and strange of images. Instead of an antagonist who was a fellow-creature, a man one could hold morally responsible, and to whom one could address reasonable appeals, he saw Caterham as something, something like a monstrous rhinoceros, as it were, a civilised rhinoceros begotten of the jungle of democratic affairs, a monster of irresistible onset and invincible resistance. In all the crashing conflicts of that tangle he was supreme. And beyond? This man was a being supremely adapted to make his way through multitudes of men. For him there was no fault so important as self-contradiction, no science so significant as the reconciliation of 'interests'. Economic realities, topographical necessities, the barely touched mines of scientific expedients, existed for him no more than railways or rifled guns or geographical literature exist for his animal prototype. What did exist were gatherings, and caucuses, and votes – above all, votes. He was votes incarnate – millions of votes.

And now in the great crisis, with the Giants broken but not beaten, this vote-monster talked.

It was so evident that even now he had everything to learn. He did not know there were physical laws and economic laws, quantities and reactions that all humanity voting *nemine contradicente* cannot vote away, and that are disobeyed only at the price of destruction. He did not know there are moral laws that cannot be bent by any force of glamour, or are bent only to fly back with vindictive violence. In the face of shrapnel or the Judgement Day, it was evident to Redwood that this man would have sheltered behind some curiously dodged vote of the House of Commons.

What most concerned his mind now was not the powers that held the fastness away there to the south, not defeat and death, but the effect of these things upon his Majority, the cardinal reality in his life. He had to defeat the Giants or go under. He was by no means absolutely despairful. In this hour of his utmost failure, with blood and disaster upon his hands, and the rich promise of still more horrible disaster, with the gigantic destinies of the world towering and toppling over him, he was capable of a belief that by sheer exertion of his voice, by explaining and qualifying and restating, he might yet reconstitute his power. He was puzzled and distressed no doubt, fatigued and suffering, but if only he could keep up, if only he could keep talking –

As he talked he seemed to Redwood to advance and recede, to dilate and contract. Redwood's share of the talk was of the most subsidiary sort, wedges as it were suddenly thrust in. 'That's all nonsense.' 'No.' 'It's no use suggesting that.' 'Then why did you begin?'

It is doubtful if Caterham really heard him at all. Round such interpolations Caterham's speech flowed indeed like some swift stream about a rock. There this incredible man stood, on his official hearthrug, talking, talking with enormous power and skill, talking as though a pause in his talk, his explanations, his presentation of standpoints and lights, of considerations and expedients, would permit some antagonistic influence to leap into being – into vocal being, the only being he could comprehend. There he stood amidst the slightly faded splendours of that official room in which one man after another had succumbed to the belief that a certain power of intervention was the creative control of an empire . . .

The more he talked the more certain Redwood's sense of stupendous futility grew. Did this man realise that while he stood and talked there, the whole great world was moving, that the invincible tide of growth flowed and flowed, that there were any hours but parliamentary hours, or any weapons in the hands of the Avengers of Blood? Outside, darkling the whole room, a single leaf of giant Virginian creeper tapped unheeded on the pane.

Redwood became anxious to end this amazing monologue, to escape to sanity and judgement, to that beleaguered camp, the fastness of the future, where, at the very nucleus of greatness, the Sons were gathered together. For that this talking was endured. He had a curious impression that unless this monologue ended he would presently find himself carried away by it, that he must fight against Caterham's voice as one fights against a drug. Facts had altered and were altering beneath that spell.

What was the man saying?

Since Redwood had to report it to the Children of the Food, in a sort of way he perceived it did matter. He would have to listen and guard his sense of realities as well as he could.

Much about blood guiltiness. That was eloquence. That didn't matter. Next?

He was suggesting a convention!

He was suggesting that the surviving Children of the Food should capitulate and go apart and form a community of their own. There were precedents, he said, for this. 'We would assign them territory – '

'Where?' interjected Redwood, stooping to argue.

Caterham snatched at that concession. He turned his face to Redwood's, and his voice fell to a persuasive reasonableness. That could be determined. That, he contended, was a quite subsidiary question. Then he went on to stipulate: 'And except for them and where they are we must have absolute control, the Food and all the Fruits of the Food must be stamped out – '

Redwood found himself bargaining: 'The princess?'

'She stands apart.'

'No,' said Redwood, struggling to get back to the old footing. 'That's absurd.'

'That afterwards. At any rate we are agreed that the making of the Food must stop – '

'I have agreed to nothing. I have said nothing – '

'But on one planet, to have two races of men, one great, one small! Consider what has happened! Consider that is but a little foretaste of what might presently happen if this Food has its way! Consider all you have already brought upon this world! If there is to be a race of Giants, increasing and multiplying – '

'It is not for me to argue,' said Redwood. 'I must go to our sons. I want to go to my son. That is why I have come to you. Tell me exactly what you offer.'

Caterham made a speech upon his terms.

The Children of the Food were to be given a great reservation – in North America perhaps or Africa – in which they might live out their lives in their own fashion.

'But it's nonsense,' said Redwood. 'There are other Giants now abroad. All over Europe – here and there!'

'There could be an international convention. It's *not* impossible. Something of the sort indeed has already been spoken of . . . But in this reservation they can live out their own lives in their own way. They may do what they like; they may make what they like. We shall be glad if they will make us things. They may be happy. Think!'

'Provided there are no more Children.'

'Precisely. The children are for us. And so, sir, we shall save the world, we shall save it absolutely from the fruits of your terrible discovery. It is not too late for us. Only we are eager to temper expediency with mercy. Even now we are burning and searing the places their shells hit yesterday. We can get it under. Trust me we shall get it under. But in that way, without cruelty, without injustice – '

'And suppose the Children do not agree?'

For the first time Caterham looked Redwood fully in the face.

'They must!'

'I don't think they will.'

'Why should they not agree?' he asked, in richly toned amazement.

'Suppose they don't?'

'What can it be but war? We cannot have the thing go on. We cannot. sir. Have you scientific men *no* imagination? Have you no mercy? We cannot have our world trampled under a growing herd of such monsters and monstrous growths as your Food has made. We cannot and we cannot! I ask you, sir, what can it be but war? And remember – this that has happened is only a beginning! *This* was a skirmish. A mere affair of police. Believe me, a mere affair of police. Do not be cheated by perspective, by the immediate bigness of these newer things. Behind us is the nation – is humanity. Behind the thousands who have died there are millions. Were it not for the fear of bloodshed, sir, behind our first attacks there would be forming other attacks, even now. Whether we can kill this Food or not, most assuredly we can kill your sons! You reckon too much on the things of yesterday, on the happenings of a mere score of years, on one battle. You have no sense of the slow course of history. I offer this convention for the sake of lives, not because it can change the inevitable end. If you think that your poor two dozen of Giants can resist all the forces of our people and of all the alien peoples who will come to our aid; if you think you can change Humanity at a blow, in a single generation, and alter the nature and stature of Man – '

He flung out an arm. 'Go to them now, sir. I see them, for all the evil they have done, crouching among their wounded – '

He stopped, as though he had glanced at Redwood's son by chance.

There came a pause.

'Go to them,' he said.

'That is what I want to do.'

'Then go now . . . '

He turned and pressed the button of a bell; without, in immediate response, came a sound of opening doors and hastening feet.

The talk was at an end. The display was over. Abruptly Caterham seemed to contract, to shrivel up into a yellow-faced, fagged-out, middle-sized, middle-aged man. He stepped forward, as if he were stepping out of a picture, and, with a complete assumption of that friendliness that lies behind all the public conflicts of our race, he held out his hand to Redwood. As if it were a matter of course, Redwood shook hands with him for the second time.

CHAPTER 5

The Giant Leaguer

Presently Redwood found himself in a train going south over the Thames. He had a brief vision of the river shining under its lights, and of the smoke still going up from the place where the shell had fallen on the north bank, and where a vast multitude of men had been organised to burn the Herakleophorbia out of the ground. The southern bank was dark, for some reason even the streets were not lit, all that was clearly visible were the outlines of the tall alarm-towers and the dark bulks of flats and schools, and after a minute of peering scrutiny he turned his back on the window and sank into thought. There was nothing more to see or do until he saw the Sons . . .

He was fatigued by the stresses of the last two days; it seemed to him that his emotions must needs be exhausted, but he had fortified himself with strong coffee before starting, and his thoughts ran thin and clear. His mind touched many things. He reviewed again, but now in the enlightenment of accomplished events, the manner in which the Food had entered and unfolded itself in the world.

'Bensington thought it might be an excellent food for infants,' he whispered to himself, with a faint smile. Then there came into his mind as vivid as if they were still unsettled his own horrible doubts after he had committed himself by giving it to his own son. From that, with a steady unfaltering expansion, in spite of every effort of men to help and hinder, the Food had spread through the whole world of man. And now?

'Even if they kill them all,' Redwood whispered, 'the thing is done.'

The secret of its making was known far and wide. That had been his own work. Plants, animals, a multitude of distressful growing children would conspire irresistibly to force the world to revert again to the Food, whatever happened in the present struggle. 'The thing is done,' he said, with his mind swinging round beyond all his controlling to rest upon the present fate of the Children and his son. Would he find them exhausted by the efforts of the battle, wounded, starving, on the verge of defeat, or would he find them still stout and hopeful, ready for the still grimmer conflict of the morrow? His son was wounded! But he had sent a message!

His mind came back to his interview with Caterham.

He was roused from his thoughts by the stopping of his train in

Chislehurst station. He recognised the place by the huge rat alarm-tower that crested Camden Hill, and the row of blossoming giant hemlocks that lined the road . . .

Caterham's private secretary came to him from the other carriage and told him that half a mile farther the line had been wrecked, and that the rest of the journey was to be made in a motor car. Redwood descended upon a platform lit only by a hand lantern and swept by the cool night breeze. The quiet of that derelict, wood-set, weed-embedded suburb – for all the inhabitants had taken refuge in London at the outbreak of yesterday's conflict – became instantly impressive. His conductor took him down the steps to where a motor car was waiting with blazing lights – the only lights to be seen, handed him over to the care of the driver and bade him farewell.

'You will do your best for us,' he said, with an imitation of his master's manner, as he held Redwood's hand.

So soon as Redwood could be wrapped about they started out into the night. At one moment they stood still, and then the motor car was rushing softly and swiftly down the station incline. They turned one corner and another, followed the windings of a lane of villas, and then before them stretched the road. The motor droned up to its topmost speed, and the black night swept past them. Everything was very dark under the starlight, and the whole world crouched mysteriously and was gone without a sound. Not a breath stirred the flying things by the wayside; the deserted, pallid white villas on either hand, with their black unlit windows, reminded him of a noiseless procession of skulls. The driver beside him was a silent man, or stricken into silence by the conditions of his journey. He answered Redwood's brief questions in monosyllables, and gruffly. Athwart the southern sky the beams of searchlights waved noiseless passes; the sole strange evidences of life they seemed in all that derelict world about the hurrying machine.

The road was presently bordered on either side by gigantic blackthorn shoots that made it very dark, and by tall grass and big campions, huge giant dead-nettles as high as trees, flickering past darkly in silhouette overhead. Beyond Keston they came to a rising hill, and the driver went slow. At the crest he stopped. The engine throbbed and became still. 'There,' he said, and his big gloved finger pointed, a black misshapen thing before Redwood's eyes.

Far away as it seemed, the great embankment, crested by the blaze from which the searchlights sprang, rose up against the sky. Those beams went and came among the clouds and the hilly land about them as if they traced mysterious incantations.

'I don't know,' said the driver at last, and it was clear he was afraid to go on.

Presently a searchlight swept down the sky to them, stopped as it were with a start, scrutinised them, a blinding stare confused rather than mitigated by an intervening monstrous weed stem or so. They sat with their gloves held over their eyes, trying to look under them and meet that light.

'Go on,' said Redwood after a while.

The driver still had his doubts; he tried to express them, and died down to 'I don't know' again.

At last he ventured on. 'Here goes,' he said, and roused his machinery to motion again, followed intently by that great white eye.

To Redwood it seemed for a long time they were no longer on earth but passing in a state of palpitating hurry through a luminous cloud. Teuf, teuf, teuf, teuf, went the machine, and ever and again – obeying I know not what nervous impulse – the driver sounded his horn.

They passed into the welcome darkness of a high-fenced lane, and down into a hollow and past some houses into that blinding stare again. Then for a space the road ran naked across a down, and they seemed to hang throbbing in immensity. Once more giant weeds rose about them and whirled past. Then quite abruptly close upon them loomed the figure of a giant, shining brightly where the searchlight caught him below, and black against the sky above. 'Hello there!' he cried, and, 'stop! There's no more road beyond . . . Is that Father Redwood?'

Redwood stood up and gave a vague shout by way of answer, and then Cossar was in the road beside him, gripping both hands with both of his and pulling him out of the car.

'What of my son?' asked Redwood.

'He's all right,' said Cossar. 'They've hurt nothing serious in *him*.'

'And your lads?'

'Well. All of them, well. But we've had to make a fight for it.'

The Giant was saying something to the motor driver. Redwood stood aside as the machine wheeled round, and then suddenly Cossar vanished, everything vanished, and he was in absolute darkness for a space. The glare was following the motor back to the crest of the Keston hill. He watched the little conveyance receding in that white halo. It had a curious effect, as though it was not moving at all and the halo was. A group of war-blasted giant trees flashed into gaunt scarred gesticulations and were swallowed again by the night . . . Redwood turned to Cossar's dim outline again and clasped his hand. 'I have been shut up and kept in ignorance,' he said, 'for two whole days.'

'We fired the Food at them,' said Cossar. 'Obviously! Thirty shots. Eh!'

'I come from Caterham.'

'I know you do.' He laughed with a note of bitterness. 'I suppose he's wiping it up.'

2

'Where is my son?' said Redwood.

'He is all right. The Giants are waiting for your message.'

'Yes, but my son – '

He passed with Cossar down a long slanting tunnel that was lit red for a moment and then became dark again, and came out presently into the great pit of shelter the Giants had made.

Redwood's first impression was of an enormous arena bounded by very high cliffs and with its floor greatly encumbered. It was in darkness save for the passing reflections of the watchman's searchlights that whirled perpetually high overhead, and for a red glow that came and went from a distant corner where two Giants worked together amidst a metallic clangour. Against the sky, as the glare came about, his eye caught the familiar outlines of the old worksheds and playsheds that were made for the Cossar boys. They were hanging now, as it were, at a cliff brow, and strangely twisted and distorted with the guns of Caterham's bombardment. There were suggestions of huge gun emplacements above there, and nearer were piles of mighty cylinders that were perhaps ammunition. All about the wide space below, the forms of great engines and incomprehensible bulks were scattered in vague disorder. The Giants appeared and vanished among these masses and in the uncertain light; great shapes they were, not disproportionate to the things amidst which they moved. Some were actively employed, some sitting and lying as if they courted sleep, and one near at hand, whose body was bandaged, lay on a rough litter of pine boughs and was certainly asleep. Redwood peered at these dim forms; his eyes went from one stirring outline to another.

'Where is my son, Cossar?'

Then he saw him.

His son was sitting under the shadow of a great wall of steel. He presented himself as a black shape recognisable only by his pose – his features were invisible. He sat chin upon hand, as though weary or lost in thought. Beside him Redwood discovered the figure of the princess, the dark suggestion of her merely, and then, as the glow from the distant iron returned, he saw for an instant, red-lit and tender, the infinite kindliness of her shadowed face. She stood looking down upon her lover with her hand resting against the steel. It seemed that she whispered to him.

Redwood would have gone towards them.

'Presently,' said Cossar. 'First there is your message.'

'Yes,' said Redwood, 'but – '

He stopped. His son was now looking up and speaking to the princess, but in too low a tone for them to hear. Young Redwood raised his face, and she bent down towards him, and glanced aside before she spoke.

'But if we are beaten,' they heard the whispered voice of young Redwood.

She paused, and the red blaze showed her eyes bright with unshed tears. She bent nearer him and spoke still lower. There was something so intimate and private in their bearing, in their soft tones, that Redwood – Redwood who had thought for two whole days of nothing but his son – felt himself intrusive there. Abruptly he was checked. For the first time in his life perhaps he realised how much more a son may be to his father than a father can ever be to a son; he realised the full predominance of the future over the past. Here between these two he had no part. His part was played. He turned to Cossar, in the instant realisation. Their eyes met. His voice was changed to the tone of a grey resolve.

'I will deliver my message now,' he said. 'Afterwards – . . . It will be soon enough then.'

The pit was so enormous and so encumbered that it was a long and tortuous route to the place from which Redwood could speak to them all.

He and Cossar followed a steeply descending way that passed beneath an arch of interlocking machinery, and so came into a vast deep gang-way that ran athwart the bottom of the pit. This gangway, wide and vacant, and yet relatively narrow, conspired with everything about it to enhance Redwood's sense of his own littleness. It became, as it were, an excavated gorge. High overhead, separated from him by cliffs of darkness, the searchlights wheeled and blazed, and the shining shapes went to and fro. Giant voices called to one another above there, calling the Giants together to the Council of War, to hear the terms that Caterham had sent. The gangway still inclined downward towards black vastnesses, towards shadows and mysteries and inconceivable things, into which Redwood went slowly with reluctant footsteps and Cossar with a confident stride.

Redwood's thoughts were busy. The two men passed into the completest darkness, and Cossar took his companion's wrist. They went now slowly perforce.

Redwood was moved to speak. 'All this,' he said, 'is strange.'

'Big,' said Cossar.

'Strange. And strange that it should be strange to me – I, who am, in a sense, the beginning of it all. It's – '

He stopped, wrestling with his elusive meaning, and threw an unseen gesture at the cliff.

'I have not thought of it before. I have been busy, and the years have passed. But here I see. It is a new generation, Cossar, and new emotions and new needs. All this, Cossar – ' Cossar saw now his dim gesture to the things about them. 'All this is Youth.'

Cossar made no answers and his irregular footfalls went striding on.

'It isn't *our* youth, Cossar. They are taking things over. They are beginning upon their own emotions, their own experiences, their own way. We have made a new world, and it isn't ours. It isn't even – sympathetic. This great place – '

'I planned it,' said Cossar, his face close.

'But now?'

'Ah! I have given it to my sons.'

Redwood could feel the loose wave of the arm that he could not see.

'That is it. We are over – or almost over.'

'Your message!'

'Yes. And then – '

'We're over.'

'Well – ?'

'Of course we are out of it, we two old men,' said Cossar, with his familiar note of sudden anger. 'Of course we are. Obviously. Each man for his own time. And now – it's *their* time beginning. That's all right. Excavator's gang. We do our job and go. See? That is what Death is for. We work out all our little brains and all our little emotions, and then this lot begins afresh. Fresh and fresh! Perfectly simple. What's the trouble?'

He paused to guide Redwood to some steps.

'Yes,' said Redwood, 'but one feels – '

He left his sentence incomplete.

'That is what Death is for.' He heard Cossar below him insisting, 'How else could the thing be done? That is what Death is for.'

After devious windings and ascents they came out upon a projecting ledge from which it was possible to see over the greater extent of the Giants' pit, and from which Redwood might make himself heard by the whole of their assembly. The Giants were already gathered below and about him at different levels, to hear the message he had to deliver. The eldest son of Cossar stood on the bank overhead watching the revelations of the searchlights, for they feared a breach of the truce. The workers at the great apparatus in the corner stood out clear in their own light; they were near stripped; they turned their faces towards Redwood, but with a watchful reference ever and again to the castings that they could not leave. He saw these nearer figures with a fluctuating indistinctness by lights that came and went, and the remoter ones still less distinctly. They came from and vanished again into the depths of great obscurities. For these Giants had no more light than they could help in the pit, that their eyes might be ready to see effectually any attacking force that might spring upon them out of the darknesses around.

Ever and again some chance glare would pick out and display this group or that of tall and powerful forms, the Giants from Sunderland clothed in overlapping metal plates, and the others clad in leather, in woven rope or in woven metal, as their conditions had determined. They sat amidst or rested their hands upon or stood erect among machines and weapons as mighty as themselves, and all their faces, as they came and went from visible to invisible, had steadfast eyes.

He made an effort to begin and did not do so. Then for a moment his son's face glowed out in a hot insurgence of the fire, his son's face looking up to him, tender as well as strong; and at that he found a voice to reach them all, speaking across a gulf, as it were, to his son.

'I come from Caterham,' he said. 'He sent me to you, to tell you the terms he offers.'

He paused. 'They are impossible terms, I know, now that I see you here all together; they are impossible terms, but I brought them to you, because I wanted to see you all – and my son. Once more . . . I wanted to see my son . . .'

'Tell them the terms,' said Cossar.

'This is what Caterham offers. He wants you to go apart and leave his world!'

'Where?'

'He does not know. Vaguely somewhere in the world a great region is to be set apart . . . And you are to make no more of the Food, to have no children of your own, to live in your own way for your own time, and then to end for ever.'

He stopped.

'And that is all?'

'That is all.'

There followed a great stillness. The darkness that veiled the Giants seemed to look thoughtfully at him.

He felt a touch at his elbow, and Cossar was holding a chair for him – a queer fragment of doll's furniture amidst these piled immensities. He sat down and crossed his legs, and then put one across the knee of the other, and clutched his boot nervously, and felt small and self-conscious and acutely visible and absurdly placed.

Then at the sound of a voice he forgot himself again.

'You have heard, Brothers,' said this voice out of the shadows.

And another answered, 'We have heard.'

'And the answer, Brothers?'

'To Caterham? Is No!'

'And then?'

There was a silence for the space of some seconds.

Then a voice said: 'These people are right. After their lights, that is. They have been right in killing all that grew larger than its kind – beast and plant and all manner of great things that arose. They were right in trying to massacre us. They are right now in saying we must not marry our kind. According to their lights they are right. They know – it is time that we also knew – that you cannot have pigmies and giants in one world together. Caterham has said that again and again – clearly – their world or ours.'

'We are not half a hundred now,' said another, 'and they are endless millions.'

'So it may be. But the thing is as I have said.'

Then another long silence.

'And are we to die then?'

'God forbid!'

'Are they?'

'No.'

'But that is what Caterham says! He would have us live out our lives, die one by one, till only one remains, and that one at last would die also, and they would cut down all the giant plants and weeds, kill all the giant underlife, burn out the traces of the Food – make an end to us and to the Food for ever. Then the little pigmy world would be safe. They would go on – safe for ever, living their little pigmy lives, doing pigmy kindnesses and pigmy cruelties each to the other; they might even perhaps attain a sort of pigmy millennium, make an end to war, make an end to over-population, sit down in a worldwide city to practise pigmy arts, worshipping one another till the world begins to freeze . . . '

In the corner a sheet of iron fell in thunder to the ground.

'Brothers, we know what we mean to do.'

In a spluttering of light from the searchlights, Redwood saw earnest youthful faces turning to his son.

'It is easy now to make the Food. It would be easy for us to make Food for all the world.'

'You mean, Brother Redwood,' said a voice out of the darkness, 'that it is for the little people to eat the Food.'

'What else is there to do?'

'We are not half a hundred and they are many millions.'

'But we held our own.'

'So far.'

'If it is God's will, we may still hold our own.'

'Yes. But think of the dead!'

Another voice took up the strain. 'The dead?' it said. 'Think of the unborn . . . '

'Brothers,' came the voice of young Redwood, 'what can we do but fight them, and if we beat them, make them take the Food? They cannot help but take the Food now. Suppose we were to resign our heritage and do this folly that Caterham suggests! Suppose we could! Suppose we give up this great thing that stirs within us, repudiate this thing our fathers did for us – that *you*, father, did for us – and pass, when our time has come, into decay and nothingness! What then? Will this little world of theirs be as it was before? They may fight against greatness in us who are the children of men, but can they conquer? Even if they should destroy us every one, what then? Would it save them? No! For greatness is abroad, not only in us, not only in the Food, but in the purpose of all things! It is in the nature of all things; it is part of space and time. To grow and still to grow: from first to last that is Being – that is the law of life. What other law can there be?'

'To help others?'

'To grow. It is still, to grow. Unless we help them to fail . . . '

'They will fight hard to overcome us,' said a voice.

And another, 'What of that?'

'They will fight,' said young Redwood. 'If we refuse these terms, I doubt not they will fight. Indeed I hope they will be open and fight. If after all they offer peace, it will be only the better to catch us unawares. Make no mistake, Brothers; in some way or other they will fight. The war has begun, and we must fight, to the end. Unless we are wise, we may find presently we have lived only to make them better weapons against our children and our kind. This, so far, has been only the dawn of battle. All our lives will be a battle. Some of us will be killed in battle, some of us will be waylaid. There is no easy victory – no victory whatever that is not more than half defeat for us. Be sure of that. What of that? If only we keep a foothold, if only we leave behind us a growing host to fight when we are gone!'

'And tomorrow?'

'We will scatter the Food; we will saturate the world with the Food.'

'Suppose they come to terms?'

'Our terms are the Food. It is not as though little and great could live together in any perfection of compromise. It is one thing or the other. What right have parents to say, My child shall have no light but the light I have had, shall grow no greater than the greatness to which I have grown? Do I speak for you, Brothers?'

Assenting murmurs answered him.

'And to the children who will be women as well as to the children who will be men . . . ' said a voice from the darkness.

'Even more so – to be mothers of a new race . . . '

'But for the next generation there must be great and little,' said Redwood, with his eyes on his son's face.

'For many generations. And the little will hamper the great and the great press upon the little. So it must needs be, father.'

'There will be conflict.'

'Endless conflict. Endless misunderstanding. All life is that. Great and little cannot understand one another. But in every child born of man, Father Redwood, lurks some seed of greatness – waiting for the Food.'

'Then I am to go to Caterham again and tell him – '

'You will stay with us, Father Redwood. Our answer goes to Caterham at dawn.'

'He says that he will fight . . . '

'So be it,' said young Redwood, and his brethren murmured assent.

'*The iron waits,*' cried a voice, and the two Giants who were working in the corner began a rhythmic hammering that made a mighty music to the scene. The metal glowed out far more brightly than it had done before, and gave Redwood a clearer view of the encampment than had yet come to him. He saw the oblong space to its full extent, with the great engines of warfare ranged ready to hand. Beyond, and at a higher level, the house of the Cossars stood. About him were the young Giants, huge and beautiful, glittering in their mail, amidst the preparations for the morrow. The sight of them lifted his heart. They were so easily powerful! They were so tall and gracious! They were so steadfast in their movements! There was his son among them, and the first of all giant women, the princess . . .

There leapt into his mind the oddest contrast, a memory of Bensington, very bright and little – Bensington with his hand amid the soft breast feathers of that first great chick, standing in that conventionally furnished room of his, peering over his spectacles dubiously as Cousin Jane banged the door . . .

It had all happened in a yesterday of one-and-twenty years.

Then suddenly a strange doubt took hold of him: that this place and present greatness were but the texture of a dream; that he was dreaming, and would in an instant wake to find himself in his study again, the Giants slaughtered, the Food suppressed, and himself a prisoner locked in. What else indeed was life but that – always to be a prisoner locked in! This was the culmination and end of his dream. He would wake, through bloodshed and battle, to find his Food the most foolish of fancies, and his hopes and faith of a greater world to come no more than the coloured film upon a pool of bottomless decay. Littleness invincible!

So strong and deep was this wave of despondency, this suggestion of impending disillusionment, that he started to his feet. He stood and pressed his clenched fists into his eyes, and so for a moment remained, fearing to open them again and see, lest the dream should already have passed away . . .

The voice of the giant children spoke to one another, an undertone to that clangorous melody of the smiths. His tide of doubt ebbed. He heard the giant voices; he heard their movements about him still. It was real, surely it was real – as real as spiteful acts! More real, for these great things, it may be, are the coming things, and the littleness, bestiality and infirmity of men are the things that go. He opened his eyes.

'Done,' cried one of the two ironworkers, and they flung their hammers down.

A voice sounded above. The son of Cossar, standing on the great embankment, had turned and was now speaking to them all.

'It is not that we would oust the little people from the world,' he said, 'in order that we, who are no more than one step upwards from their littleness, may hold their world for ever. It is the step we fight for and not ourselves . . . We are here, Brothers, to what end? To serve the spirit and the purpose that has been breathed into our lives. We fight not for ourselves – for we are but the momentary hands and eyes of the Life of the World. So you, Father Redwood, taught us. Through us and through the little folk the Spirit looks and learns. From us by word and birth and act it must pass – to still greater lives. This earth is no resting place; this earth is no playing place, else indeed we might put our throats to the little people's knife, having no greater right to live than they. And they in their turn might yield to the ants and vermin. We fight not for ourselves but for growth – growth that goes on for ever. Tomorrow, whether we live or die, growth will conquer through us. That is the law of the spirit for ever more. To grow according to the will of God! To grow out of these cracks and crannies, out of these shadows and darknesses, into greatness and the light! Greater,' he said, speaking with slow deliberation, 'greater, my Brothers! And then – still greater. To grow, and again – to grow. To grow at last into the fellowship and understanding of God. Growing . . . Till the earth is no more than a footstool . . . Till the spirit shall have driven fear into nothingness, and spread . . . ' he swung his arm heavenward – '*there!*'

His voice ceased. The white glare of one of the searchlights wheeled about, and for a moment fell upon him, standing out gigantic with hand upraised against the sky.

For one instant he shone, looking up fearlessly into the starry deeps, mail-clad, young and strong, resolute and still. Then the light had passed, and he was no more than a great black outline against the starry sky – a great black outline that threatened with one mighty gesture the firmament of heaven and all its multitude of stars.

NOTES TO *THE INVISIBLE MAN*

1 (p. 33) *Bramblehurst*   a town in West Sussex

2 (p. 33) *Iping*   a village in West Sussex

3 (p. 41) *portmanteau*   a large, usually leather, travelling bag

4 (p. 45) *crepitation*   a crackling or rattling sound

5 (p. 47) *National School*   in England, schools run by the Church of England for the children of the poor

6 (p. 53) *sarsaparilla*   a mixture made of plant rhizomes, particularly smilax, used as a drink flavouring

7 (p. 61) *Unitarian*   a Christian movement that allows for a wide spectrum of religious beliefs

8 (p. 63) *Adderdean*   a fictitious village in Sussex

9 (p. 78) *West Surrey Gazette*   a fictional newspaper

10 (p. 81) *Port Stowe*   Wells appears to have invented this town.

11 (p. 85) *Port Burdock*   another of Wells's fictional towns

12 (p. 99) *St James's Gazette*   a London evening newspaper published from 1880 to 1905

13 (p. 99) *cum grano*   'with a grain of salt'

14 (p. 101) *Chesilstowe*   Griffin appears to be referring to some college – of Wells's invention – where he studied physics.

15 (p. 107) *Roentgën vibrations*   refers to the discovery of the principle of X-rays by Wilhelm Roentgën in the 1890s

16 (p. 107) *tapetum*   a reflective tissue layer behind the retina in the eyes of certain mammals

17 (p. 115) *Mudie's*   a lending library near the British Museum

18 (p. 137) *Hintondean*   another fictional town or village

19 (p. 142) *contra mundum*   against the world

20 (p. 146) *Sidney Cooper*   (1803–1902) a landscape painter famous for his paintings of farm animals

21 (p. 153) *Cobbett William*   Cobbett was a journalist and agriculturalist who wrote a book, *Rural Rides* (1830), about his journeys around the south-east of England.

NOTES TO *THE FOOD OF THE GODS*

22 (p. 164) *sphygmograph* an instrument for measuring the pulse

23 (p. 167) *Philosophical Transactions* the world's first science journal, which first appeared in 1665

24 (p. 172) *Huxley* Thomas Henry Huxley (1825–95) was an English biologist known as 'Darwin's Bulldog'. He taught H. G. Wells, who was heavily influenced by his ideas.

25 (p. 173) *Vivarium* a place for displaying live animals in a facsimile of their natural environment

26 (p. 173) *Urshot* a fictional town

27 (p. 173) *Dunton Green* a small village in the Sevenoaks District of Kent

28 (p. 178) *gallipot* a small earthenware or metal pot for holding medicines

29 (p. 182) *Westerham* a town in Kent

30 (p. 186) *Cheasing Eyebright* a fictional village in Kent

31 (p. 192) *Oeconomy* an archaic spelling of economy

32 (p. 193) *W. W. Jacobs* (1863–1943) an English writer of humorous short stories and novels

33 (p. 221) *Punch* a satirical magazine in circulation between 1841 and 1992

34 (p. 222) *The Nineteenth Century and After* a British monthly magazine that began as *The Nineteenth Century* in 1877 and closed as *The Twentieth Century* in 1972

35 (p. 227) *Frederic Harrison* a British jurist and historian (1831–1923)

36 (p. 234) *teufteufing* apparently a word made up by Wells to imitate the sound of a Model T motor car

37 (p. 235) *Pantagruel* a fictional giant, the son of Gargantua in Rabelais's sixteenth-century series of novels

38 (p. 239) *Mafficking* rollicking, celebrating boisterously

39 (p. 244) *equisetum and potamogeton* types of pond plants

40 (p. 257) *aere perennius* more lasting than bronze

41 (p. 260) *eleemosynary*   from the Latin; *eleemosyna* relates to charity and alms-giving

42 (p. 261) *Max Nordau*   (1849–1923) was the author of *Degeneration* (1892), an attack on various movements in the late nineteenth century that Nordau and his followers believed were leading to a decline in civilisation

43 (p. 263) *Anak*   from the Hebrew Bible; forefather of the Anakim, a mixed race of giant people

44 (p. 273) *ukase*   from the Russian *ukaz*, an edict or decree

45 (p. 279) *Ut in principio, nunc est semper*   Is now, and ever shall be

46 (p. 285) *Chara*   a freshwater-lake plant

47 (p. 299) *da capo*   a musical term meaning from the beginning

48 (p. 314) *Cretaceous echinoderms*   prehistoric invertebrate sea creatures like starfish, sea urchins and sea cucumbers